Tome of Alchemy

AUTHORS:
Courtney Campbell
Matt Finch

DEVELOPERS:
Zach Glazar
Matt Finch
Michael Russell
John Ling

EDITOR:
Jeff Harkness

LAYOUT:
Suzy Moseby

INTERIOR ART:
Sid Quade
C. J. Marsh
Adrian Landeros
Terry Pavlet
Brett Barkley
Josh Stewart
Lloyd, Metcalf
Hector Rodriguez

COVER ART:
Artem Shukaev

ART DIRECTOR:
Casey Christofferson

NECROMACER Games

ISBN: 978-1-6656-0096-5
PF PoD

TABLE OF CONTENTS

Tables 4

Introduction 5
  Why Alchemy? 5
  How to Use This Book...................................5

Chapter One: Alchemy Basics..........................6
  Background and Skills..................................6
  Availability 6
  Crafting and Researching.............................7
  Addiction...10
  Fire and Gases 10

Chapter Two: Materials and Essences 13
  Materials..13
  Mineral Essences...13
  Vital Essences 14

Chapter Three: Alchemical Items..................22
  Alchemical Devices......................................22
  Grenades, Pellets, and Stones 32
  Incense 39
  Liquids and Tonics.......................................41
  Ointments and Pastes.................................44
  Powders...46
  Solvents...50
  Tinctures..52

Chapter Four: Magic Items 54

Chapter Five: Alchemical Magecraft..............108

Chapter Six: Alchemy in Structures 128

Chapter Seven: Spells, Spellcasting, and Alchemy............132

Appendix 142

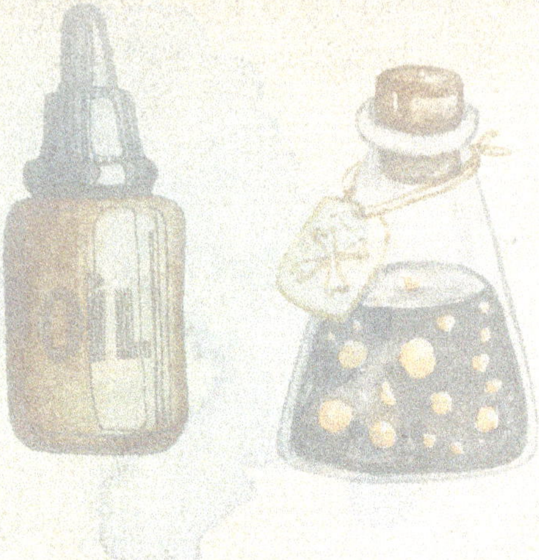

TABLES

For ease of use, a list of the various tables found throughout this book is presented below:

Table	Description
1–1	Alchemical Item Availability
1–2	Alchemist's Fire Damage Progression
1–3	Spell Research and Settlement Required
1–4	Research DCs
1–5	Potion Miscibility
1–6	Fire Progression
1–7	Gas Types
1–8	Gas Types Gas Ventilation Rates
2–1	Mineral Essences
2–2	Vital Essences
2–3	Vital Essence Types by Category
2–4	Sources of Vital Essences
2–5	Vital Essences by Monster
3–1	Alchemical Devices
3–2	Elemental Energy Gloves
3–3	Grenades, Pellets, and Stones
3–4	Incense
3–5	Liquids and Tonics
3–6	Ointments and Pastes
3–7	Powders
3–8	Incendiary Powder Amounts
3–9	Solvents
3–10	Tinctures
4–1	Brew Improved Potion Costs by Class and Level
4–2	Candles
4–3	Cusps, Eyes, and Spectacles
4–4	Dusts
4–5	Dust of Deprivation Effects
4–6	Elixir Price List
4–7	Elixir of Bestial Boon Physical Changes
4–8	Elixir of Animal Control
4–9	Elixir of Dragon Control Types
4–10	Elixir of Elemental Control Types
4–11	Elixir of Giant Control Types

Table	Description
4–12	Elixir of Human Control Types
4–13	Elixir of Undead Control Types
4–14	Elixir of Defense Bonuses
4–15	Elixir of Heroic Fighting Bonuses
4–16	Elixir of Super Heroic Fighting Bonuses
4–17	Elixir of Heroic Larceny Bonuses
4–18	Elixir of Giant Strength Type
4–19	Salves
4–20	Salve of Basic Blade Enhancement Formulas
4–21	Salve of Expert Blade Enhancement Formulas
4–22	Salve of Sharpness Strength Table
4–23	Wonderous Item Price List
4–24	Production of Alchemical Jug
4–25	Carafe of Steeds Random Mounts
4–26	Cloak of Eyestalk's Effects
4–27	Energy Bolt Glove Requirements
5–1	Mineral Alchemy Price List
5–2	Amber Fulminating Charge Power Increase
5–3	Carnelian Catagemma Power Increase
5–4	Chalcedony Fulminating Charge Power Increase
5–5	Diamond Fulminating Charge Power Increase
5–6	Fire Opal Fulminating Charge Power Increase
5–7	Onyx Fulminating Charge Power Increase
5–8	Ruby Catagemma Power Increase
5–9	Sigils
5–10	Dimensional Jaunt Essences
5–11	Sigil of Extrasenory Perception Effects
6–1	Alchemical Mortars
7–1	Alchemical Enhancements
7–2	Alchemist Spell List
7–3	Wizard/Sorcerer Spell List
A–1	Alchemical Mishaps
A–2	Potion Mishaps
A–3	Alchemical Quirks
A–4	Story Ideas

INTRODUCTION

The purpose of alchemy was similar to the purpose for the practice of all mystical arts: unity with the divine. It was not just a matter of concocting strange potions and reagents in dank laboratories.

The fact that it was some of the earliest proto-scientific study of chemistry and medicine was just a convenient byproduct.

Alchemists desired to change lead into gold or, more broadly, base metals into noble metals, because it was a physical manifestation of the spiritual purification of the soul. Their hope was to use the same or a similar process on themselves.

Alchemy is the study and process of change. Whether searching for the *universal solvent* to break things down, transmuting substances into other substances, or even seeking the means to extend life, it is the philosophical and practical search for knowledge.

Of course, once acquired, this knowledge was put to as many different uses as those who practiced it. For every spiritual seeker, there was one whose skills were put to practical use. For every alchemist who developed new medicines, others sold snake oil that did nothing or was even harmful.

WHY ALCHEMY?

Alchemy has always been something tangential to fantasy roleplaying. Something cool, but incomplete. It was something the wizard player asked about and the GM waved aside, because, where do you start? The items have to be balanced, meaning the GM would have to create a system of creation from whole cloth!

Today, a class exists in the *Pathfinder Roleplaying Game* devoted to the study of alchemy! Why not just say that it's complete? Because alchemy is more than just a spell in a bottle.

Where does the alchemist go when he's looking to craft something interesting? An item here and there scattered throughout half a dozen supplements? A PDF on the internet with 11, 25, or 40 items in it?

Let there be no question: This is an advanced tome filled with more than a thousand items for your enterprising alchemist. More importantly, this isn't a tool only for characters; this is a book of ideas for gaming. I wrote this because I wanted a tool and a reference for my own table. I hope you find alchemy an essential part of your gaming library, too.

HOW TO USE THIS BOOK

Looking at this book may be a bit overwhelming. I suggest two general guidelines:

First, assume that the book is filled with lost lore and not available to the players in total, and introduce sections, alchemical formulas, or items from the book a little at a time. A lot of items and options are in this book, and it is assumed that they are not all freely available and common knowledge. That's the best way to avoid a player using some strange corner case of items and class abilities to unbalance the game. Remember! The GM has the final word!

Second, it is strongly encouraged that you not just allow the characters to purchase or craft any item from this book unless you are interested in a campaign with a wildly varying power level. The *Pathfinder Roleplaying Game* characters can already push the boundaries of the upper limits of effectiveness with feats, class features, and existing magical items. Allowing them to acquire items cheaply that further leverage their abilities will put too much stress on this system. It is OK to use an item to bypass an encounter; after all, they spent the gold and used the resource. But creating a situation with an endless supply of an item can be a disaster. A number of the tools in this book are designed to allow you to control the frequency of such items may be used and how they may be created.

General rules cover situations and ideas the players might come up with and provide reasonable explanations for outcomes to help you with situations that might otherwise result in you saying, "You just can't" or "I don't know." Materials and essences cover an expansion to the crafting system. These provide ways to enhance spells and alchemical items and limit your characters crafting their way endlessly to being overpowered for their level.

The next section is the items. Hundreds of new (and a few classic) items are found here. Each contains rules for use and crafting.

Finally, we get into some of the more interesting and esoteric powers of wizards and alchemists. Here, you will find ideas that can drive anything from character concepts to campaigns. Material apotheosis provides either a powerful opponent or a long-term goal for alchemical and arcane characters!

CHAPTER ONE: ALCHEMY BASICS

BACKGROUND AND SKILLS

The study of alchemy is an individual pursuit. Most alchemists historically worked in a special code passed on from their mentors that was highly individualized. Alchemical formulas were gathered from experimentation. Their practice is much like that of the spellcasters: individualized, didactic, empirical, and arbitrary.

Alchemists are limited only by the nature and rules of alchemical processes and their equipment. A thorough examination of both follows.

WHAT IS AN ALCHEMIST?

For the purposes of this book, "alchemist" refers to any character with the Craft (alchemy) skills, not the alchemist class. However, the alchemist class is an exceptional alchemist, receiving a competency bonus to their Craft (alchemy) skill equal to their level. No other character can be their equal in the realm of alchemy.

AVAILABILITY

One of the advantages of alchemical items is that they provide useful, one-shot items that are available for purchase in cities and towns. However, this does not mean that you can purchase 50 *alchemist's fires* just because you have the gold. Unlike traditional magical items, alchemical items aren't permanent and this makes them unsuitable for use with the "Available Magic Items" table in Chapter 15 of the *Pathfinder Roleplaying Game Core Rulebook*. So how do you determine their availability?

To determine an item's availability for purchase, reference the item type and rarity on the following table. For each purchase attempt, roll percentiles. If they are less than the relevant number, the item is available for purchase. The number available for purchase is dependent on the size of the settlement and is listed next to the percentage.

If you instead go the other route and wish to stock a shop to simulate the distribution of goods, then use the following values to determine the number of different kinds and quantity of items. Roll on the relevant table in this book to determine the items (i.e. 75% of the items are available; roll to randomly determine which 25% are not). Minor items are grenades, liquids, and other craftable items; Major items are elixirs, potions, dusts, and other items that require a feat to craft.

TABLE 1–1: ALCHEMICAL ITEM AVAILABILITY

Item Type	Rarity	Thorp	Hamlet	Village	Small Town	Large Town	Small City	Large City	Metropolis
Minor Items	Common	25% / 1	50% / 1	75% / 1d3	80% / 1d4	90% / 1d6	95% / 2d6	99% / 2d10	100% / 5d10
Minor Items	Uncommon	10% / 1	25% / 1	50% / 1	75% / 1d3	80% / 1d4	90% / 1d6	95% / 2d6	99% / 2d10
Minor Items	Rare	5% / 1	10% / 1	25% / 1	50% / 1	65% / 1d3	80% / 1d4	90% / 1d6	90% / 2d6
Minor Items	Very Rare	1% / 1	5% / 1	10% / 1	25% / 1	30% / 1	55% / 1d3	70% / 1d4	80% / 1d6
Major Items	Common	5% / 1	10% / 1	25% / 1	50% / 1	75% / 1d3	80% / 1d4	90% / 1d6	95% / 2d6
Major Items	Uncommon	1% / 1	5% / 1	10% / 1	25% / 1	50% / 1	65% / 1d3	80% / 1d4	90% / 1d6
Major Items	Rare	*/*	1% / 1	5% / 1	10% / 1	15% / 1	40% / 1	65% / 1d3	80% / 1d4
Major Items	Very Rare	*/*	*/*	1% / 1	5% / 1	10% / 1	15% / 1	30% / 1	75% / 1d3

* Indicates appearances are only by GM decision.

Note that the above percentages are affected by the settlement's Economy modifier. Each point of the economy modifier adjusts the percentage chance that an item is available by 5%. A metropolis with a +4 economy has a 95% chance of having 1d3 very rare major items available for purchase (75% base, plus 20% for the economy modifier of +4). Note also that the purchase limit is not obviated by this table. If an item is too expensive to exist in the settlement, then it is not available; there is no need to roll.

It is also important to remember that if you are allowing people with the Craft (alchemy) skill to craft items once they learn the formula, then once they purchase an item in town, this effectively allows them to craft copies of it once they destroy it to learn the formula. This makes cities very desirable goals for players, as well as a method the GM can use to selectively introduce items.

SPECIAL CASES

"Because the rules say so" is never a very good response to a player's question. But there are very simple, very logical questions that go unaddressed in regard to alchemical items. Questions such as "We buy a keg of *alchemist's fire*. How much damage does that do?" or "I dilute the potion. What does it do now?" As the GM, responding "It's magic," or having your players say, "The GM doesn't like it when we ask that question," is unsatisfactory for player and GM alike.

So what to do in those cases?

LARGE VOLUME

When dealing with physical materials, you might face the situation of players attempting to get creative with some basic materials in this book such as *alchemist's fire*, solvents, and incendiary powder.

The first thing that quickly occurs is the question, "What if we all throw *alchemist's fire* at once?" Then comes the following question, stated with some excitement, "What if we create a trap that dumps 10 *alchemist's fire* at once on a target! What will happen then?"

The answer to this is fairly simple. Additional *alchemist's fires*, solvents, and quantities of incendiary powders increase the damage to a certain limit. It is not a straight one-to-one correlation of increased volume to damage. A good rule of thumb is that every doubling of material doubles the damage, up to a maximum of 10d6 points of damage. At this point, the target is completely doused or affected by the materials. This affect is countered by the cost and time required.

The following table shows the effects of alchemical fire as the damage increases.

TABLE 1–2: ALCHEMIST'S FIRE DAMAGE PROGRESSION

Number of Alchemist's Fires	Damage	Splash Damage	Cost	Weight
1	1d6	1	20 gp	1 lb.
2	2d6	2	40 gp	2 lbs.
4	3d6	3	80 gp	4 lbs.
8	4d6	4	160 gp	8 lbs.
16	5d6	5	320 gp	16 lbs.
32	6d6	6	640 gp	32 lbs.
64	7d6	7	1,280 gp	64 lbs.
128	8d6	8	2,560 gp	128 lbs.
256	9d6	9	5,120 gp	256 lbs.
512	10d6	10	10,240 gp	512 lbs.

Allowing a player to do 6d6 damage for the cost of 640 gp is reasonable, considering that a 6th-level wizard can do the same for free. An alchemist who wishes to craft 32 *alchemist's fires* can do so for 640 gp. How the oversized package is going to be delivered to the target must then be considered.

DILUTION

Sometimes you are faced with an alchemist who wants to divide a potion or dilute a potion. For some magical liquids and effects, this is simple. A *potion of cure serious wounds* crafted by a 6th-level cleric divides into three doses of 1d8 + 2 rather easily. However, it can be helpful to have guidelines if it comes up often.

When diluting a mixture the alchemist created himself, the character already knows the base. If diluting a mixture made by someone else, then the character must succeed at a DC 25 Craft (alchemy) skill check. This allows him or her to determine the solvent used. It may be anything from liquor to water to the blood of a giant. On a failure, this may not be reattempted.

Once the alchemist acquires a second ounce of the substance, the character may dilute the potion. The diluted mixture can divide dice effects evenly in terms of whole dice, such as the *potion of cure serious wounds*. If the potion or elixir has a single, non-variable effect, the duration can be split between the potions evenly. If the potion affects a target, the target's save is given a +2. For every additional dilution, the save bonus is doubled, i.e., +4, +8, etc.

Note that any attempt to dilute a potion, elixir, or oil past a certain point results in an inert concoction. These may last only seconds or have no effect at all. It is immediately obvious to the imbiber that the diluted concoction does not work at all. Any diluted concoction can be detected by a DC 11 Craft (alchemy) or Spellcraft check or by a DC 15 Appraise check. Con artists that attempt to pass off diluted product can get away with such things only in the smallest of thorps.

DRINKING MULTIPLE POTIONS

Some alchemists, not fearing miscibility or perhaps protected from it, may wish to drink more than one potion in the same round. However, much like extremely strong liquor, it is not possible to drink more than one potion a round — even if they are inside the same container. An attempt to drink more than one potion in a standard action is not possible due to the volume and the reaction of the drinker to the liquid.

Potions and elixirs do not mix unless using the miscibility rules, and in that case, they can be mixed only in an alchemist's lab or internally by drinking them one after the other. When combined into the same bottle, potions layer and can only be poured out in the order they are layered in. The first potion in is the last out.

ALTERNATE ITEM TYPES

Elixirs and potions do not necessarily need to be in liquid form. Many other forms are possible, including fruits, charms, and breads.

In order to craft an alternate item, the difficulty is raised by +5 to the DC needed to craft the item.

Certain settings may be more suited for certain types of items. A windblown desert planet may not have enough liquid for elixirs to be common, so elixirs may instead be fruits as standard. In the case of the specialized setting, make a different potion type as standard and have the difficulty raised for trying to create different forms of the potion.

Charms must be broken to release the effect. Fruits and breads must be eaten after their skin is broken or the magic dissipates in 10 minutes. The entire fruit or bread must be consumed. Elixirs or potions in fruit or bread form may stay fresh for a year and a day, for 99 years, or for another length of time the GM decides is appropriately mythic. After that time, the enchantment fades and the fruit rots or the bread molds.

ITEM VARIABILITY

Items are given in their most basic and direct forms and names for easy reference. Small changes create dozens of new item types, without the need for a whole new write-up. An *elixir of phasing*, *dust of ghost form*, *oil of spirit walking*, et. al., are essentially the same as a *salve of etherealness*. Feel free to make small mechanical changes to better fit the new form of the new item. Reference the appendix for ideas on names and other ways to uniquely identify your items. You totally have permission to make things more metal.

CRAFTING AND RESEARCHING

THE ALCHEMICAL LABORATORY

The tools of the alchemist are many and varied. The lab is not just for show. Creating alchemical items is a difficult and involved process requiring many different steps such as calcination, fermentation, exaltation, and more. Each of these processes takes time and requires certain specialized equipment to perform.

The type of equipment in a fully featured lab can be quite diverse. In addition to the standard chemistry accoutrements you might expect — vials, burners, cylinders, flasks, forceps, funnels, pipettes, stirring rods, droppers, glass and steel plates, evaporating dishes, spatulas, clamps, test tube racks and files — you might find musical instruments, mechanical oddities, forges and associated equipment, reed meditation mats, braziers, shrines, plaques and signs with alchemical references, brushes, brooms, and various cleaning apparatuses, chairs, seats, food, and even temporary quarters.

In order to craft items, an alchemist is assumed to have a simple, basic repertoire of tools if he or she is in a civilized area. However, you may rule that basic alchemical equipment is unavailable in certain situations and places. If this is the case, a classed alchemist can still attempt to create the item at a –5 penalty to his or her Craft (alchemy) checks. If an alchemist has a proper laboratory, he or she receives a +2 circumstance bonus to Craft (alchemy) checks. A portable lab provides only a +1 circumstance bonus to Craft (alchemy) checks.

An alchemy lab costs 200 gp and contains 40 pounds of equipment. It requires a building with at least 400 square feet. Portable alchemy labs are available, but are rarer and difficult to find. However, they do not require an entire building to construct or use. They cost 75 gp and weigh 20 pounds.

The specific items included in an alchemist's lab should generally be abstract, as part of the alchemist's supplies in a set of tools, with the more elaborate constructions just considered a sufficient laboratory supplied by paying the cost. Anything more detailed is likely to bog the game down in minutiae. However, a bit of flavor and terminology will be helpful to the player and to the GM, so a general list of items is described below.

Athanor: An athanor is an oven capable of reaching high temperatures. The athanor was often the signal component of an alchemist's lab, and it would be possible to have magical athanors that grant a bonus to crafting alchemical items.

Braziers: These are metal trays placed over a fire to heat large quantities of substances, usually solids. For liquids, one would ordinarily use a cauldron.

Burners: Small flames required for heating liquids are usually fired with bits of coal, and are relatively reliable.

Calipers: These are used for precise measurement of length. As a measuring tool, they are subject to inaccuracy unless they are made with tremendous care by an artisan whose own measuring tools are accurate in the first place.

Cauldron: A pot used for mixing liquids, since braziers are more prone to spillage and leaks.

Crucible: Crucibles are used to hold and mix molten metal, so they need to be able to handle very high heat.

Distilling Apparatus: A still is basically identical to the equipment used in producing alcoholic drinks.

Flasks and Beakers: Most of these are normal items of blown glass, but others had specific uses in distillation that required unusual shapes. These more specialized flasks could be quite expensive and require skilled glass blowers to produce them. Measuring flasks are also subject to markings too imprecise for the high level of accuracy required in alchemy.

Lenses: Lenses aren't needed for most alchemical work, but when an item requires etching or other related work, a good lab would include at least a magnification lens. Magical lenses might also allow an alchemist to gain knowledge about precise ratios of materials or other information that can be achieved in modern-day labs. Such items might, like magical athanors, grant bonuses to crafting rolls made in a lab.

Orrery and Astrolabe: Orreries are mechanical models of a solar system, while astrolabes are celestial measuring devices used before the development of the sextant. An astrolabe is a disk with measurements along the outside of the disk, and a pointer in the center. In a fantasy world, an astrolabe could comprise multiple disks related to aspects of the stars not comprehended within the ordinary world.

Scales and Balances: In addition to the obvious importance of measuring substances by weight, magical scales might exist that are capable of balancing and measuring non-material substances such as ethereal and astral presences.

Star Charts: Astrological charts depicting constellations at various times of the year are an important part of alchemy. Obtaining charts that are more accurate than others (or dealing with those that turned out to be less so) can be a good adventure hook.

Test Tubes: Racks of small, glass tubes are a mainstay of the well-prepared laboratory, especially when conducting research. If they aren't well-cleaned between uses they are a good explanation for an alchemical mishap (see **Table A–1: Alchemical Mishaps** in Appendix A).

RESEARCH

One of the assumptions of the *Pathfinder Roleplaying Game* is that characters immediately have access to all spells, alchemical formulas, crafting formulas, and other information. Research is never necessary.

This is very empowering for players but does create a situation as more material for the game becomes available where something with a very specific and limited use can be paired with something a certain class has, and the synergistic effects of such an interaction are much more powerful than either base item.

In addition, it prevents there being powers, magic, and items that the players don't know about. How can they have the joy of discovery if all they need to do to learn a spell is purchase a scroll?

Limiting the amount of material available to players has its own pitfalls. First, it's complicated and can frustrate the players since they won't know what their characters can and cannot use when reading the books. Second, the *Pathfinder Roleplaying Game* assumes that each character has a certain amount of wealth at every level in order to balance combat encounters. If you begin bleeding that wealth off to research base class abilities, then the characters will be underpowered for their level.

Neither problem is insurmountable, but before you make any decisions about limiting access to spells and gear, you should take a moment to consider the eventual effects. Requiring spell and alchemical research reduces the power level of "book" spellcasting classes and people using the alchemy skill, whereas characters not dependent on research become more powerful by comparison. Less money will be available for the whole party. The party usually will be underequipped for its level.

That said, spell and alchemical item research is a good idea. Spell research is already implicit in the rules, being that spellcasters can cast spells only of an appropriate level. This background research is also the driving force behind spellcasters gaining two new spells at each level.

If you'd like to have some simple restrictions on knowledge that the characters have, and don't want to disrupt your game too badly, here are some suggestions:

All items in the *Pathfinder Roleplaying Game Core Rulebook* should be available for all classes. For other items, use the following guidelines: For crafted items such as those made with Craft (alchemy) or Craft (armor), you do not know any formula with a base DC higher than your current skill ranks + 15. You must possess or find a copy of a magical item before you can discover how to craft a magical item.

This gives the GM more control over which items can be available in the game, prevents the players from using situational and circumstance bonuses from crafting something too powerful too soon, and does not significantly affect wealth by level.

DETAILED RESEARCH

What is actually involved in researching a new alchemical item, magical item, or spell? The process usually involves a mixed approach to discovering the secret or unknown method of production. Usually the spell or item is heard about first in conversation. The initial portion of research is spent gathering information and doing research in libraries. Many times, these libraries are owned by specific individuals who have their own requirements for research and lending. A process of experimentation and testing then takes place until eventually you succeed at making a discovery.

Another method of researching a new alchemical item, magical item, or spell is to take a copy of the item in the wild and destroy it to find out how it works. This is literally how a scroll functions. But for magical items and alchemical items, allowing a character to destroy the item to determine the formula is an excellent way to learn how to craft it.

However, assuming you do not have a copy of the magical item, alchemical item, or spell you are attempting to research, the following procedure can simulate the research of an item.

The player knows which item he wants to research. This represents his character hearing a rumor or story about the spell or item at some point in his past. He decides he wants to track down how to create such an item. His character begins attempting to gather information about the item or spell. This can include the history, when it was crafted or used, the creator, where it was created — any of these facts are useful when attempting to duplicate their work.

In order to track down this information, the character must succeed at a Diplomacy skill check to gather information. The base DC of this skill check is the Craft (alchemy) DC for alchemical items. For magical items, the DC of this Diplomacy skill check is DC 10 + the caster level of the item. For spells, the DC of the Diplomacy skill check is DC 10 + (2 x spell level). A success on this check means that the creator now knows the item exists and understands enough about it to begin researching how to make it. Unlike a normal attempt

to gather information, this Diplomacy skill check takes 1d4 days per attempt. If the character fails by 5 or more on this check, there is no information in this area to be had and he or she must try again in another city or settlement. This check is modified by the settlement's Lore value. A small hamlet is much less likely to have someone who knows about a rare item you are seeking to craft.

The next step is the research itself. This requires you to succeed at a Knowledge (arcana) check to discover the creation process. In order to make this check, you need access to an arcane library. An arcane library is a collection of nonmagical books on a variety of arcane topics. Cities and settlements are considered to have an arcane library equal in value to the size of their purchase limit modified by 1,000 gp times their Lore value. A large town (with a 10,000-gp purchase limit) and −3 Lore has an arcane library with a value of 7,000 gp (10,000-gp purchase limit − 3,000 gp [−3 Lore value x 1,000 gp]). A village (2,500-gp purchase limit) with a +5 Lore has an arcane library with a value of 7,500 gp (2,500 + 5,000 gp [+5 Lore value x 1,000 gp]). Many times these libraries are open only to citizens. In some cases, they are in the hands of private owners or merchants. Very rarely will a library — especially an arcane library — be open to the public.

Characters may build their own arcane library to avoid and defer costs of using public or private libraries in the settlements they visit. If they do not, they must use the available facilities in settlements to perform their research. Each item researched needs a certain size arcane library in order for any information on the item to be found. The characters may use their arcane library total and combine it with the arcane library in a settlement to do their research.

For spells, the library must be equal to 5 plus the level of the spell squared multiplied by 1,000 gold. A large town will have a large enough library to research a 1st-level spell (5 + [1 x 1] x 1,000), whereas you need to visit a small city to research 3rd-level spells (5 + [3 x 3] x 1,000). For alchemical items, the gold piece value of the arcane library must be equal to the Craft (alchemy) DC of the item times 1,000. For magical items, the gold piece value of the arcane library must be equal to four times the CL x 1,000.

TABLE 1–3: SPELL RESEARCH AND SETTLEMENT REQUIRED

Spell level	Arcane Library Required	Minimum Settlement Required (not adjusted for Lore)
1st	6,000 gp	Large Town
2nd	9,000 gp	Large Town
3rd	14,000 gp	Small City
4th	21,000 gp	Small City
5th	30,000 gp	Large City
6th	41,000 gp	Large City
7th	54,000 gp	Metropolis
8th	69,000 gp	Metropolis
9th	86,000 gp	Metropolis

You may then attempt to make the Knowledge (arcana) skill check. If you lack an appropriately sized arcane library, then the check is penalized by 1 for every 1,000 gold short your library is. The base DC of the Knowledge (arcana) check is equal to the Craft (alchemy) DC of alchemical items. The DC of this Knowledge (arcana) skill check is DC 10 + CL for magical items. For spells, the DC of the Knowledge (arcana) skill check is DC 10 + (2 x Spell Level).

If you fail, you may retry freely. Each time this check is made, you spend a number of days equal to the die roll researching. On a successful check, you discover the spell or item and may create it! For spells, this means going through the process of scribing a scroll. For alchemical and magical items, this means crafting the item normally.

Sera the 1st-level wizard decides she would like to research *magic missile*. She must first track down how to create such a spell. She makes a Diplomacy check with a difficulty of 12. She has a Diplomacy skill of +5. She is in a small town with no Lore modifier. Her first roll is a 4. This failure (4 + 5 Diplomacy is a 9) costs her 1d4 days. She rolls a 2. After two days pass, she tries again. This time she rolls a 14. This result (14 + 5) is enough to find some clue about the spell. She knows it exists and understands enough about the spell to begin making it.

She begins researching *magic missile*. The small town she is in has an arcane library equivalent to 5,000 gp. The spell *magic missile* is 1st level, requiring a library equal to 6,000 gp (5 + 1 x 1,000), which means it isn't big enough to perform the spell research. Instead of going to a larger city, she completes a quest to rescue a sage. He returns him to the small town. The addition of the sage increases the Lore value of the town by +1. The town now has an arcane library equal in value to 6,000 gp: 5,000 gp from its purchase limit and 1,000 gp from 1,000 times its lore value, provided by the sage. She could have continued the research with a −1 penalty for the small size of the arcane library, but the sage needed rescuing anyway.

Having the materials she needs at hand, she begins her research. Her Knowledge (arcana) skill is a +7. She needs to succeed at a DC 12 Knowledge (arcana) check. Her first die roll is a 6, resulting in a successful Knowledge (arcana) check of 13. She spends six days and has researched *magic missile*. She pays for the cost of the scroll and now has a scroll of *magic missile*.

To research a *headband of vast intelligence*, you must succeed at a DC 18 Diplomacy check, have access to an arcane library of 32,000 gp, and you must succeed at a DC 18 Knowledge (arcana) check.

TABLE 1–4: RESEARCH DCS

Research Type	Base DC
Spell	DC 10 + (2 x Spell Level)
Alchemical Item	Craft (alchemy) DC of item
Magical Item	DC 10 + CL

Sometimes your players may want to research a spell or craft an item that isn't in any book. If this is the case, then the procedure should be similar to the above. Because the item doesn't exist, skip the gathering information section, and the character instead proceeds with the research. Design the final item with the player giving you the information you need. It is suggested that you make sure this item is balanced for its cost. Once you have that, perform research as normal, requiring an arcane library 10,000 gp more valuable than normal. Also, increase the research DC by +5. On a successful result, the character successfully researches a new, never-before-seen item and may begin crafting it.

ALCHEMICAL ITEM IDENTIFICATION

Normally you can identify potions and magical items by using *detect magic* and succeeding at a Spellcraft check with a DC equal to 15 plus the caster level of the item. You can alternately identify potions and other consumables with a Perception check with a DC equal to 15 plus the spell level of the potion by using your normal senses.

This process is quick, easy, and trivially available for even the most low-level adventurers. If you'd like a process that is a little more interesting and dangerous, consider the following options. Using these options makes your job as the GM more complicated and challenging, though it increases the mystery and wonder associated with alchemical and magical items. Note that risk-adverse players may decide to refuse to perform any of this experimentation themselves. It is best if this alternative system is the only way to identify magic items. If they can just cart the item back to town and pay someone to do it, then that is what they will do, and it will turn identification of magic items into an exercise in bookkeeping and taxing player resources.

For interesting magical items such as unique items, miscellaneous magical items, potions, and elixirs — not unremarkable +1 magical items — you may consider the following alternative system. Instead of the standard identification system, assume that a Spellcraft check isn't enough to identify the item. It instead provides the results of your experimentation with the item.

The new process assumes that you handle or attempt to use the item in some way. A success on the identification roll gives you a reduced example of the effect. A *potion of fly* might make you feel less weighed down. A *potion of jump* might make your legs feel strong. This also works for special magic items, where only a description of what the player is doing to test the item providing a circumstance bonus of +1 to +4 to the identification check.

Other suggestions for having the identification of alchemical and magical items take a larger role in your game include:
- Give a percentage chance that if going through the identification process by magic, alchemical items are destroyed.
- Have potions be more effective if not identified magically; for example, reroll 1's, increase duration, etc.
- Have potions or items once disturbed have a 1-in-6 chance per hour of going bad unless identified.

POTION MISCIBILITY

Potions take a standard action to drink. This prevents drinking more than one potion at once, but each potion is only an ounce of liquid. What is to prevent someone from mixing potions or tying the bottles together and drinking more than one at once? What happens if you mix two potions? What happens if you mix them inside your stomach?!?

Magical potions, elixirs, and other strange alchemical items enact certain changes on the body, much like medicine. And like medicine, it's certainly possible for them to have unseen interactions.

The official rules state that imbibing a potion acts like a spell cast upon the wielder, having no unusual interactions or side effects. But what if like medicine, drinking one potion after another has unusual reactions? Below is a table for handing potion miscibility. This table could also easily apply to players who apply more than one spell to their characters at a time.

No two potions are created quite the same way. Because of this, this table is checked every time you mix two potions or when you drink a potion while under the effect of another. Your GM may optionally wish to make an exception for curing potions.

Normally, potions do not mix. When placed in the same container, potions and elixirs layer and remain separate. Note that potions layered in this way must be consumed in the reverse order they are layered in the container. The first potion in is on the bottom and is the last one consumed.

As an optional rule, you may forcefully mix the potions by agitation or the potions may be mixed within the body of the imbiber. When potions or elixirs are mixed, check the following table. For obvious reasons, effects may be more severe if mixed internally.

TABLE 1–5: POTION MISCIBILITY

d%	Result	Description
01	EXPLOSION	External mixture does 10d6 points of damage; DC 16 Reflex save for half damage in a 10-foot radius. Internal detonation does 4d6 x 10 points of damage with no saving throw, and those within five feet take 2d6 points of damage.
02–03	Lethal Poison	External 10-foot-square cloud of poison gas causing Constitution drain; DC 16 Fortitude save to avoid taking 2d6 Constitution drain. Internal mixture requires a DC 18 Fortitude save to avoid taking 4d6 Constitution drain.
04–08	Mild Toxin	External 10-foot-square cloud of poison gas; make a DC 16 Fortitude save to avoid taking 2d6 points of Constitution damage. Internal mixture requires a DC 18 Fortitude save to avoid taking 4d6 points of Constitution damage.
09–12	Curse	Once consumed, the new potion bestows a curse as the spell *bestow curse*. You may alternately devise an interesting curse related to the potion's effect.
13–19	Immiscible	Both potions destroyed.
20–30	Immiscible	One potion ruined. The other functions normally.
31–40	Immiscible	Both potions function, but with half duration and half effect.
41–89	Miscible	Both potions work normally, unless they contradict each other, in which case they are canceled.
90–92	DISCOVERY	Potions create a completely new potion. Determine this potion randomly. This potion or elixir is considered to be affected by the feats Empower Spell and Extend Spell.
93–95	DISCOVERY	The first potion is considered to be affected by the feats Empower Spell and Extend Spell. The second potion functions normally.
96–98	DISCOVERY	The second potion is considered to be affected by the feats Empower Spell and Extend Spell. The first potion functions normally.
99	DISCOVERY	Both potions are considered to be affected by the feats Empower Spell, Extend Spell, and Maximize Spell.
00+	DISCOVERY	One potion imbibed becomes permanent.

Roll secretly whenever miscibility occurs! Give no clues!

Certain potions always have the same effect if mixed, no matter which potion they are mixed with. Each of the following potions has a consistent effect if mixed.

- An *elixir of delusion* mixes with anything.
- *Elixir of treasure finding* always produces a lethal poison per the table.
- *Elixir of control* is always the elixir that fails to be altered.
- *Salve of slipperiness* mixed with *salve of etherealness* always mixes normally, but gives a 50% chance to become lost on the Ethereal Plane.

CRAFTING AN ITEM

Once the research phase is done and you have identified the materials and vital essences (see **Chapter Two: Materials and Essences**) required to create the item, you are ready to make the Craft (alchemy) check to turn your research into reality. The DC to craft the item is the standard DC. Items are crafted at one-third price, as per the traditional crafting rules.

ADDICTION

Addiction is another way to control alchemical and magical item use. Addiction rules are contained in the Drugs and Addiction chapter in the *Pathfinder Roleplaying Game: GameMastery Guide*. Making alchemical items and magical items such as elixirs and salves addictive creates a desire to avoid the use of alchemical and magical items. It can be used to control the use and abuse of substances and can also create interesting dynamics for the players as they make choices to avoid the consequences of addiction.

Whatever your decision on addiction, it should be consistent and communicated to the players, even if their characters are not aware of the consequences. When deciding what to make addictive, any substance that is common and likely to be abused may be useful selections.

ADDING ADDICTIVE QUALITIES TO ALCHEMICAL AND MAGICAL ITEMS

A good guideline for applying the degrees of severity of addiction is to note the rarity of the item. Uncommon items produce a minor addiction with a base DC 12 Fortitude save to avoid addiction; rare items produce a moderate addiction with a base DC of 16 to avoid addiction; and very rare items produce a severe addiction with a base DC of 20 to avoid addiction. For alchemical items, increase the addiction DC by 1 for every 10 points of the Craft (alchemy) DC, rounding down as normal. For potions or magical spells, low-level spells might produce a minor or moderate addiction, whereas potions of spells of 4th level or higher produce a severe addiction. Increase the DC of the addiction by 1 per spell level.

Another method for determining the addictive properties of alchemical items is to use the craft DC. Anything under 20 is a minor addiction, 20–25 is a moderate addiction, and anything higher produces a severe addiction. In this case, the Craft (alchemy) DC –2 can serve as the addiction value.

FIRE AND GASES

FIRE

Fire is pretty straightforward in the rules but it's not very fire-like. Here's a way to make fire a bit more interesting.

Any time fire is on something flammable — clothing, human skin, horses —the size of the fire may increase. Fire growth follows the progression found in **Table 1–6**.

TABLE 1–6: FIRE PROGRESSION

Type	Damage	Result	Spread
Flame	1d3	Extremity on fire. This is ignored when the fire burns out	Moves to next category on a 3, burns out entirely on a 1
Burning	1d6	Torso on fire	Moves to next category on a 6, burns down to a flame on a 1
On Fire	2d6	Person on fire	Moves to next category if either die rolls a 6, down a category if the roll is a 2
Conflagration	3d6	Area on fire (everything nearby takes 1d3 damage)	Becomes an Inferno if any die rolls a 6, down a category if the roll is a 3
Inferno	3d8	Area on fire (everything nearby takes 1d3 damage)	Fire spreads on a roll of 6+, and burns down a category if the roll is a 3

SOME CAVEATS

If everything in the area is destroyed, the fire dies down one step at a time.

If something highly flammable is burning, you may add a bonus for things to catch fire.

So, if a character throws *alchemist's fire* at a target and rolls a 6 for her damage roll, the next round she rolls 2d6 to determine how many points of damage she does. For a player who rolls a 1, the next round the fire does 1d3 points of damage to the target.

As long as there is still something for the fire to burn, growth results always supersede burnout results. If someone is on fire and the dice come up with a 6 and 1, then the fire becomes a conflagration the next round, and the character takes 3d6 points of damage. Also note on the table that as fire grows, it also becomes more likely to spread.

This makes fire an effective and deadly weapon.

GAS CLOUDS

All gas is not the same. Since it is unlikely that you game with experts in gas thermodynamics, refer to the following guidelines for handling issues involving gaseous substances and their dispersion rates.

TYPES OF CLOUDS

There are four kinds of vapors of interest: smoke, poison gas, alchemical gas, and magical clouds.

SMOKE

Smoke is produced by fire and is lethal. It is important to note that smoke is not produced by spells such as *burning hands* or *fireball*. These channel inner dimensional energy from the Plane of Fire; the resulting explosion produces heat and flame, but no object experiences combustion so there is no smoke.

Smoke and exposure to it is unpleasant, and anyone who can escape will flee long before they are injured by exposure to the smoke. If you are trapped in a smoky area, lung damage from irritants begins almost immediately, and asphyxiation begins immediately after. This quickly leads to difficulty breathing, headache, and confusion, followed by fainting, seizures, coma, and death.

A character exposed to smoke must make a DC 5 Fortitude save every round. For every consecutive round spent within the smoke, the DC increases by +2. On a failed check, the character falls prone and is staggered. The character must succeed at a DC 14 Will save or become *confused* as the spell. He or she continues to make the Will save every round spent in the smoke until the character becomes confused. The characters also continue making Fortitude saves every round. On a second failed Fortitude save, they fall unconscious. On the third failed fortitude save, they suffocate.

Smoke is opaque and provides total concealment.

POISON GAS

Deadly and fast-acting, and often transparent or invisible, poison gases affect and kill their targets extremely rapidly. These can be any gaseous substance — even oxygen can be deadly!

Poisonous gas is highly reactive and will not remain inside a sealed chamber indefinitely. This extreme reactivity is also why it is so deadly. Lesser concentrations of smoke or poison gas disperse proportionally faster.

Various nonmagical, non-alchemical substances are considered and treated as poisonous gases. They are listed below:

Asphyxiant: An asphyxiant gas has little to no negative effect chemically on the body. They are often inert. They asphyxiate by displacing oxygen. You're breathing, but there is no oxygen in the air, so you start to suffocate. The first symptoms include drowsiness and difficulty hearing. Your heart rate increases in an attempt to transfer more oxygen. Then you get a headache, become dizzy and short of breath, and then become confused. Finally, your sight dims, and you begin to experience tremors and sweat. Unconsciousness follows soon after.

While exposed to asphyxiant gases, the character begins to suffocate. Characters can hold their breath for two rounds per point of Constitution. If a character takes a standard or full-round action, the remaining duration that the character can hold his or her breath is reduced by one round. After this period of time, the character must make a DC 10 Constitution check in order to continue holding their breath. The check must be repeated each round, with the DC increasing by +1 for each previous success. If the character fails one of these Constitution checks, he or she begins to suffocate. In the first round, the character falls unconscious (0 hit points). In the following round, they drop to −1 hit points and are dying. In the third round, they suffocate.

Blister: This gas is nefarious because exposure to it has no immediate effects. Only hours later do symptoms appear. It is also important to note that this gas does not occur naturally. It is detectable by the scent of garlic, mustard, or horseradish. Initial symptoms include mucus membrane irritation, large fluid blisters, tearing and eye damage, and difficulty breathing.

Once exposed to blister gas, there is no immediate effect, but hideous blisters and sores cover the body 2d6 hours later. These blisters are painful and debilitating, dealing 2 damage to all physical stats per round of exposure. A successful DC 16 Fortitude save halves the damage.

Blood: When inhaled, this chemical is absorbed into the blood. The gas often prevents the body from processing oxygen, which causes victims to suffer from suffocation. After inhalation, the victim experiences dizziness, weakness, and nausea. Headaches begin shortly before seizures and coma. Exceptionally strong exposure can cause death within seconds.

If exposed to this gas, victims must make a DC 16 Fortitude save or suffer 2d6 Constitution drain. Victims must make a save each round with a cumulative +1 increase to the DC for each consecutive round spent within the gas.

Choking: This gas works primarily by inflaming the mucus membranes and the lungs. The mouth and lungs burn, and the victim experiences shortness of breath, dizziness, headache, and unsurprisingly, coughing. These symptoms are caused by gases that turn to acid in the lungs. Damage is immediate and deadly.

When exposed to this gas, victims must make a DC 16 Fortitude save or suffer 2d6 Constitution drain. Victims must save each round with a cumulative +1 increase to the DC for each consecutive round spent within the gas.

Nerve: This normally water-soluble liquid acts as a central nervous system toxin. It can be turned into a gaseous spray very easily and hangs around in the air much like a normal gas. The first symptoms are a runny nose and extremely dilated pupils. Then, there is a rapid onset of sweating, nausea, and vomiting. Finally, before death, involuntary urination and defecation occur, followed by seizures, coma, and death.

Exposure to nerve gas requires a character to make a DC 16 Fortitude save or suffer 2d6 Constitution drain. If the target does survive, he must make a second DC 16 Will save or suffer a degenerative nervous condition causing 4 points of Intelligence, Wisdom, and Charisma drain.

Tear: This gas irritates the mucus membranes, causing uncontrollable crying, sneezing, coughing, difficulty breathing, eye pain, and blindness. It is not often lethal unless exposure to a massive quantity occurs.

Exposure to tear gas requires a DC 16 Fortitude save. Victims must save each round with a cumulative +1 increase to the DC for each consecutive round spent within the gas. On a failure, the target is blinded and is sickened. After a rest period of six minutes of flushing the eyes with water, these conditions dissipate.

Vomiting: These gases are rarely toxic, but cause uncontrollable vomiting. These gases are usually thick and can often bypass protective measures. The subsequent vomiting usually forces the target to remove his or her personal protection, allowing a second gas to be more effective.

Exposure to vomiting gases on a failed DC 16 Fortitude save causes the victims to gain the nauseated condition for 1d4 + 1 rounds. Check every round that the victim is exposed to the gas.

TABLE 1–7: GAS TYPES

Lethal

Gas	Type	Onset	Weight Relative to Air	Color / Odor	Notes
Arsine	Blood	Days	Heavier	Colorless/Odorless	Bloody urine
Carbon Monoxide	Blood	10 minutes	Lighter	Colorless / Odorless	Cherry-red skin
Chlorine Gas	Choking	10 minutes	Heavier	Yellow-Green / Bleach	Flammable; byproduct of bleach and ammonia (chloramine gas)
Hydrogen Cyanide	Blood	10 minutes	Heavier	Colorless/Bitter almonds	
Hydrogen Fluoride	Choking	10 Minutes	Lighter	Colorless / "Offensive"	Flammable
Hydrogen Sulfide	Blood	10 minutes	Heavier	Colorless / Rotten eggs	Nullifies sense of smell; flammable
Nitrogen Mustard	Blister	12 hours	Heavier	Yellow-Brown / Garlic, Horseradish, Mustard	Liquid; Soluble in Water
Oxides of Nitrogen	Choking	120 minutes	Lighter	Red-brown / Fishy	
Phosgene	Choking	5 rounds	Heavier	Colorless / Fresh Mown Hay	
Sarin, Soman, Tabun	Nerve	1 round	Heavier	Colorless / Odorless	
Sulfur Dioxide	Choking	10 minutes	Heavier	Colorless / Brimstone	Non-flammable
Sulfur Mustards	Blister	12–360 minutes	Lighter	Yellow-Brown / Garlic, Horseradish, Mustard	

Non-Lethal

Gas	Type	Onset	Weight Relative to Air	Color / Odor	Notes
Adamsite	Vomit	1 round	Lighter	Canary-Yellow / Odorless	
Ammonia	Tear	1 round	Lighter	Colorless / Ammonia	
Carbon Dioxide	Asphyxiant	10 minutes	Lighter	Colorless / Odorless	
Chloropicrin	Vomit	1 round	Heavier	Colorless / Pungent Stinging	
Bromine	Tear	20 minutes	Heavier	Dark-rust Red / Bleach	
Propane	Asphyxiant	10 minutes	Lighter	Colorless / Odorless	Flammable
Methane	Asphyxiant	10 minutes	Lighter	Colorless / Odorless	Flammable

ALCHEMICAL GAS

Alchemical gases can be created from grenades, powders, and dusts. They expose anyone entering the cloud to the effects of the grenades, powders, and dusts. The specifics of the effects are identical to the listed grenade from which they are crafted, excepting the area of effect and duration, and the effect lasts until dispersed. Grenade types are listed in **Table 3–3: Grenades, Pellets, and Stones**.

MAGICAL GAS

Magical gases are created by spells and come in many different forms. The gas cloud lasts for the spell's duration and resists dispersion unless noted otherwise in the spell description. This means that wind and breezes can move them, but they maintain cohesion. They fill the volume as directed by the spell. They don't grow to a larger size or spread out; they don't become thinner or more diffuse; and if pushed or blown into a different shape, they resist. Exposure to a smaller space than their volume reshapes the cloud, but it desires to fill its volume in the easiest possible way, meaning it seeks to expand into the area of lowest pressure.

GAS DISPERSION

Over time, fresh air entering a room disperses nonmagical smoke and gas. However, as the fresh air mixes with the gas before forcing it out, it is this mixture that is leaving the room.

For safe entry, a smoky room has to be 90% fresh air, and an area with poisonous gas must be 99% fresh air. Characters entering a room once it starts to clear may receive circumstance bonuses on saving throws: +2 for 50% clear, and +4 for 80% clear or greater.

Five different categories of ventilation exist. Each reaches these thresholds at different rates:

TABLE 1–8: GAS TYPES GAS VENTILATION RATES

Ventilation	Smoke	Poison Gas	Alchemical Gas	Example
No Ventilation	Perpetual*	1 month	20 minutes	Sealed Crypt
Poor Ventilation	100 minutes	280 minutes	10 minutes	Dungeon
Standard Ventilation	50 minutes	140 minutes	5 minutes	Standard Room
Good Ventilation	10 minutes	30 minutes	3 minutes	Alchemist's Lab
Superb Ventilation	1 round	10 minutes	1 round	Outside on a Windy Day

* This smoke eventually settles and covers the surfaces in the sealed area with ash.

In order to craft an alchemical item (including potions, salves, and so forth), the alchemist needs to have the required materials and significant ingredients, which will have been identified during the research phase of crafting (see **Chapter One: Alchemy Basics**). There are two fundamental types of significant ingredients: mineral essences and vital essences.

Every alchemical formula contains a mix of mineral essences (rare earths, metals, and gemstones) and vital essences (which are ordinarily prepared elements from living creatures). Quantities are given in drams of distilled essence, or carats of powdered gemstone.

MATERIALS

You can't make something out of nothing. Every item you create has a cost in gold pieces to cover the raw materials necessary during item creation. This cost includes basic supplies such as talc, fuel for burners, purified platinum tongs, gem dust, purified liquids, and other one-use rarefied items. These are the normal costs necessary and are not listed in the item description.

MINERAL ESSENCES

RARE EARTH

Anyone with alchemical training can collect rare earths (wizards able to practice item creation, alchemists, etc.). It simply requires 1 rank in Craft (alchemy). Rare earths consist of elemental substances such as antimony, cinnabar, pitchblende, and various salts and metal oxides. They also contain trace amounts of all the elements and can be found in small quantities in all types of soil and sand. Collecting rare earths takes a day of labor. For every eight man-hours spent, with a successful DC 10 Craft (Alchemy) check a character can generate one dram of rare earth, with an additional dram for every 5 by which you exceed the DC. Rare earths appear as a bit of rich earth suffused with small crystals that reflect different colors of light. They have a rich, fresh, ethereal smell and require no special storage containers or requirements. They do not expire. On the open market, they can be purchased for 10 gp, but there is no cost (beyond time) to collecting them yourself. The cost of rare earths is included in the crafting price.

GEMSTONES

Twelve essential alchemical gemstones have specific spiritual resonances that people have known about for ages. The gemstones are agate, amethyst, diamond, emerald, jade, malachite, moonstone, onyx, pearl, ruby, sapphire, and turquoise. These alchemical gemstones can be ground into a fine powder for use in many alchemical formulas. The process of creation requires a certain amount of gemstone dust per item. Each powdered carat costs 10 gp. An alchemist can generate this by powdering these gemstones or purchase gemstones or gemstone powder from town. An alchemist who finds a ruby worth 253 gp can dust that gemstone, turning it into 25 carats of ruby gemstone powder suitable for crafting. The extra dust from the value of the gem is lost to the dusting process. Note that a gemstone cannot be partially ground down without completely destroying its value.

When reading the alchemical formulas for items, a gem showing in the formula is assumed to be 50 carats worth (500 gp). An entry reading "Diamond (x100)" would mean 5,000 carats of powdered diamond with a value of 50,000 gp.

In certain rare cases or in the case of crafting alchemical gemstone talismans, uncut or unpowdered gemstone is required. This is noted in the materials section.

RARE METALS

Sometimes you need certain rare metals such as silver, gold, or platinum to craft items. These metals are very powerful magical activators. Rarely, you can purchase pure samples of these metals, sometimes from dwarves or other creatures of the earth, but most commonly the source for these metals are coins. Coins, however, are very impure. To produce one pure dram of this metal from common coins, you need 10 coins. For example, if you needed to extract five

drams of platinum, you would need 50 platinum coins. The coins are melted down, and the impurities are removed. If the crafter has no in-game source for pure metals, he must make do with transmuting coinage into pure metals. The cost of these coins is included in the crafting price.

Note that in the above cases, if the crafter collects the necessary materials, he can use it to reduce the crafting price. Also note that if the crafter doesn't have access to a hamlet or greater, then it's possible that he can't purchase the above rare materials and must possess them to craft the item.

TABLE 2–1: MINERAL ESSENCES

Material	Purchase Price	Sale Price
Gemstones	10 gp	as gemstone
Vital essence	See **Table 2–2**	See **Table 2–2**
One dram of gold	10 gp	10 gp
One dram of iron	1 gp	1 gp
One dram of silver	1 gp	1 gp
One dram of platinum	100 gp	100 gp
Rare earths	10 gp	5 gp

VITAL ESSENCES

Vital essences are necessary mystical components from living (or unliving) creatures that are required to make powerful alchemical items function. The various types are discussed below.

The entire creature is not needed to collect and distill the essence, just the applicable part such as the ears, heart, or teeth. For the alchemist, all of the creature's essence can be distilled from this single part. No essence remains in the rest of the creature, as the collected portion now holds the essential energy. Distilling the rest of the hell hound produces nothing!

Vital essences have additional uses beyond their use in crafting. Having more of the appropriate essences can lower the cost of crafting even beyond what is listed. In addition, essences can be used to empower spells as they are cast. This is discussed in **Chapter Six: Alchemy in Structures**.

If you are using alchemy at a very abstract level and want your alchemist to be able to purchase relevant ingredients, you may use **Table 2–2** below to ascertain prices for necessary vital essences.

TABLE 2–2: VITAL ESSENCES

Vital Essence	Purchase Price	Sale Price
Aberration	10 gp	5 gp
Animal	1 gp	5 sp
Celestial	10 gp	5 gp
Construct	10 gp	5 gp
Dragon	10 gp	5 gp
Elemental	5 gp	2 gp 5 sp
Fey	5 gp	2 gp 5 sp
Fiend	10 gp	5 gp
Humanoid	1 gp	5 sp
Magical Beast	5 gp	2 gp 5 sp
Monstrous Humanoid	5 gp	2 gp 5 sp
Ooze	5 gp	2 gp 5 sp
Plant	1 gp	4 sp
Undead, Intelligent	5 gp	2 gp 5 sp
Undead, Mindless	1 gp	5 sp
Vermin	1 gp	5 sp

If vital essences are not generally available for sale, the characters will have to hunt monsters in order to obtain them.

Harvesting a monster's components must be done within one hour of death and takes 10 minutes per hit die and a successful DC 15 Survival or Profession (butcher) check, harvesting an extra hit die worth of components for every 5 by which you exceed the DC.

DISTILLING VITAL ESSENCES

When you distill down a harvested monster's components, you choose one of its available vital essences per hit die. Distilling this essence takes one hour per hit die and a DC 10 Craft (alchemy) check, distilling an extra dram of essence for every 5 by which you exceed the DC. It is up to the GM how long the raw material will keep for.

When distilling an essence from harvested components, a generic essence (such as Fire) yields 2 drams of the essence per hit die, and a specific essence (such as Agility) yields only 1 dram per hit die.

As an example, let's assume that the characters killed a red dragon with 15 hit dice. A red dragon, as you will see later, can produce the following vital essences: Azoth, Fire/Armor, Fear, Flight, Perception, Prowess. Azoth and Fire are categories, and the other essences are specific. Armor, for example, is an essence in the Earth category. The characters might be able to harvest as many as 15 different components from the dragon (assuming total success on die rolls). Once the components are in the alchemist's lab, they can be stored for use until they are needed. At that time, the alchemist can distill them down for whatever particular project for which they are needed, and can choose what essences — out of the available choices — to distill the components into.

One possibility, using the first of the 15 hit dice, would be to distill a generic Fire essence. The dragon's hit die will yield 2 drams of generic Fire essence since Fire is a generic category. The same is true of Azoth since it is also a general category (even though Azoth has no sub-essences). On the other hand, the alchemist might decide to distill the one hit die worth of components into an essence of Armor. Since Armor is a specific essence, doing so yields only 1 dram of Armor essence instead of the 2 Fire essence. However, the dram of Armor essence has more potential uses than a dram of generic Fire essence, since it can also substitute in formulas as a generic Earth essence (Armor is a subcategory of Earth). Most alchemical formulas require the use of a generic essence such as "Earth (any)," and the Armor essence can be used to fill that requirement since Armor is a subcategory of Earth.

Vital essences have additional uses beyond their use in crafting. In addition, essences can be used to empower spells as they are cast. This is discussed in **Chapter Six: Alchemy in Structures**.

VITAL ESSENCE TYPES

Many living (or undead) creatures contains essences that are used in alchemical formulas. There are 38 of these vital essences. All of these vital essences fall into one of eight categories: the four elemental essences (fire, water, earth, and air), the three alchemical essences (sulfur, salt, and mercury) and the category of azoth, which is primarily related to magical influences.

Table 2–3 shows which essences fall into which of the eight categories.

Every alchemical formula comprises a combination of vital essences (in addition to mineral essences). Many of these formulas specify one of the *categories* of vital essences as an ingredient rather than a specific vital essence. In this case, any vital essence from that category can be used to satisfy that part of the formula. If a particular vital essence, as opposed to just a category, is included in the formula then that specific essence is required.

TABLE 2–3: VITAL ESSENCE TYPES BY CATEGORY

Category	Vital Essences
Elemental Essences	
Air	Electricity
	Flight
	Illusion
	Speed
	Stealth
Earth	Acid
	Armor
	Disease
	Plant
	Strength
Fire	Agility
	Decay
	Light
	Pain
	Purity
Water	Cold
	Emotion
	Fear
	Memory
	Toxin
Alchemical Essences	
Mercury	Control
	Dream
	Mind
	Telesthetic
	Transmutation
	Transportation
Salt	Body
	Death
	Prophecy
	Protection
	Prowess
	Stasis
Sulfur	Healing
	Life
	Love
	Luck
	Perception
	Planar
Unique	
Azoth	Azoth

ALTERNATE VITAL ESSENCES

The examples of essences given are just that, examples. As lord of your milieu, some monsters will be included and others may not. Allow characters to extract any reasonable essence from creatures while keeping the verisimilitude of your campaign world in mind. If goblins are as common as dirt and their hearts work as healing essences, then your characters will be awash in healing potions.

You might restrict or keep this list secret, forcing the players to discover in play what essences are recoverable from which creature. However, this can put the alchemist in a position where they waste essences experimenting.

It is recommended that you remain somewhat flexible with essence availability. After all, the character picked the alchemist class to be able to create items. Without essences available, they cannot. A suggested list of reasonable essences for common creatures follows. These are only suggestions.

NOT USING ESSENCES

Removing this system makes it easier for characters to just craft the items they need in town. Keeping the essence system in the game drives the characters to collect the essences they need, giving them an in-game reason to track down and kill certain creatures.

SOURCES OF VITAL ESSENCES

The following table lists monsters that can be used to distill each vital essence.

TABLE 2–4: SOURCES OF VITAL ESSENCES

Acid	Ankheg, Black Dragon, Black Pudding, Copper Dragon, Earth Elemental, Gibbering Mouther, Gray Ooze, Green Dragon, Ochre Jelly, Purple Worm, Roper
Agility	Fire Elemental, Aarakocra, Balor, Giant Eagle, Giant Wolf Spider, Goblin, Kobold, Pteranodon, Saber-toothed Tiger
Air	Air Elemental, Cloaker, Cloud Giant, Cockatrice, Darkmantle, Djinni, Gold Dragon, Griffon, Harpy, Hippogriff, Invisible Stalker, Pegasus, Pteranodon, Roc, Sprite, Storm Giant, Wyvern
Armor	Ankheg, Ankylosaurus, Behir, Bulette, Chuul, Dragons (all), Dragon Turtle, Earth Elemental, Giant Crab, Giant Crocodile, Gorgon, Iron Golem, Triceratops
Azoth	Balor, Deva, Dragons (all), Drow, Ghast, Ghost, Ghoul, Guardian Naga, Homunculus, Lich, Mummy, Owlbear, Planetar, Pseudodragon, Shadow, Skeleton, Solar, Spectre, Spirit Naga, Tarrasque, Unicorn, Vampire, Wight, Will-o'-Wisp, Wraith, Zombie
Body	Chuul, Clay Golem, Ettin, Flesh Golem, Gnoll, Hill Giant, Giant Elk, Giant Lizard, Hobgoblin, Mammoth, Manticore, Minotaur, Ogre, Plesiosaurus, Tarrasque
Cold	Frost Giant, Ice Devil, Ice Mephit, Remorhaz, Silver Dragon, Water Elemental, White Dragon, Winter Wolf,
Control	Aboleth, Harpy, Lamia, Lycanthropes (all), Wraith
Death	Death Dog, Ghost, Sea Hag, Tarrasque, Shadow, Skeleton, Spectre, White Dragon, Wight, Will-o'-Wisp, Wraith, Zombie,
Decay	Balor, Bone Devil, Fire Elemental, Ghast, Ghoul, Giant Hyena, Giant Vulture, Gnoll, Mummy, Roper, Rust Monster, Skeleton, Violet Fungus, Wight, Zombie
Disease	Earth Elemental, Giant Rat, Horned Devil, Mummy, Otyugh
Dream	Djinni, Efreeti, Night Hag, Nightmare, Spectre, Treant
Earth	Allosaurus, Ankheg, Ankylosaurus, Basilisk, Black Pudding, Bulette, Clay Golem, Dryad, Dust Mephit, Earth Elemental, Gargoyle, Giant Badger, Giant Goat, Gibbering Mouther, Gorgon, Grick, Iron Golem, Otyugh, Purple Worm, Roper, Rust Monster, Satyr, Shambling Mound, Shrieker, Stone Giant, Stone Golem, Triceratops, Xorn, Treant, Violet Fungus
Electricity	Air Elemental, Behir, Blue Dragon, Bronze Dragon, Kraken, Oni, Shambling Mound, Storm Giant, Will-o'-Wisp
Emotion	Androsphinx, Djinni, Efreeti, Lycanthropes (all), Night Hag, Satyr, Sprite, Succubus/Incubus, Water Elemental
Fear	Allosaurus, Dragons (all), Hippogriff, Lich, Nalfeshnee, Pit Fiend, Saber-toothed Tiger Vampire, Water Elemental
Fire	Azer, Balor, Barbed Devil, Bearded Devil, Bone Devil, Brass Dragon, Chain Devil, Chimera, Dretch, Efreeti, Erinyes, Fire Elemental, Fire Giant, Glabrezu, Gold Dragon, Hell Hound, Hezrou, Horned Devil, Ice Devil, Imp, Lemure, Marilith, Nalfeshnee, Nightmare, Pit Fiend, Quasit, Red Dragon, Remorhaz, Salamander, Steam Mephit, Succubus/Incubus, Vrock
Flight	Aarakocra, Air Elemental, Cloaker, Dragons (all), Flying Snake, Griffon, Hippogriff, Manticore, Roc, Sprite, Stirge, Wyvern
Healing	Couatl, Deva, Guardian Naga, Hydra, Lemure, Solar, Tarrasque, Troll, Unicorn
Illusion	Aboleth, Air Elemental, Chain Devil, Green Hag, Grey Ooze, Lamia, Sea Hag
Life	Couatl, Deva, Ghost, Giant Boar, Guardian Naga, Kraken, Lich, Solar, Spectre, Spirit Naga, Tarrasque, Troll
Light	Azer, Balor, Darkmantle, Duergar, Fire Elemental, Giant Fire Beetle, Planetar, Shadow
Love	Couatl, Dryad, Satyr, Solar, Tarrasque

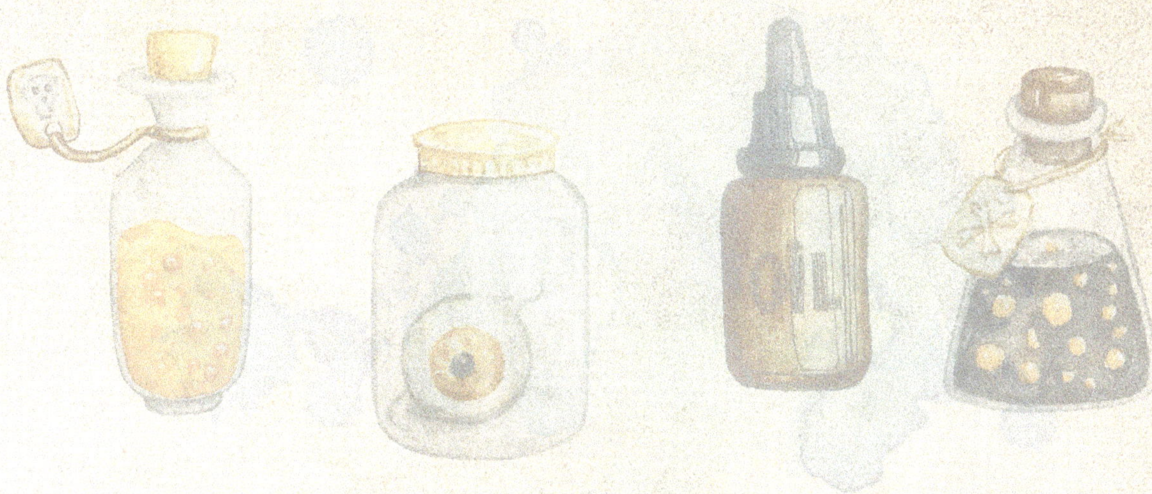

Luck	Centaur, Couatl, Satyr, Sprite, Merfolk, Tarrasque
Memory	Erinyes, Invisible Stalker, Mummy, Spectre, Water Elemental
Mercury	Aboleth, Androsphinx, Blink Dog, Chimera, Doppelganger, Drider, Gynosphinx, Lamia, Medusa, Mimic, Minotaur, Night Hag, Oni, Owlbear, Rakshasa
Mind	Drow, Giant Owl, Gynosphinx, Harpy, Kraken, Lich, Rakshasa, Treant
Pain	Balor, Barbed Devil, Dragon Turtle, Drow, Duergar, Fire Elemental, Giant Wasp, Goblin, Green Hag, Hell Hound, Merrow, Stirge
Perception	Androsphinx, Bugbear, Centaur, Couatl, Giant Bat, Giant Frog, Giant Octopus, Giant Toad, Giant Weasel, Gibbering Mouther, Gynosphinx, Red Dragon, Shrieker, Solar, Tarrasque
Planar	Azer, Barbed Devil, Bearded Devil, Bone Devil, Chain Devil, Couatl, Deva, Djinni, Dretch, Dust Mephit, Efreeti, Erinyes, Glabrezu, Hell Hound, Hezrou, Horned Devil, Ice Devil, Ice Mephit, Lemure, Magma Mephit, Marilith, Merrow, Nalfeshnee, Planetar, Pit Fiend, Quasit, Salamander, Steam Mephit, Succubus/Incubus, Tarrasque, Vrock, Xorn
Plant	Dryad, Earth Elemental, Shambling Mound, Shrieker, Treant, Violet Fungus
Prophecy	Centaur, Gynosphinx, Marilith, Storm Giant, Tarrasque
Protection	Black Pudding, Clay Golem, Gelatinous Cube, Gibbering Mouther, Solar, Tarrasque, Triceratops
Prowess	Bulette, Cloud Giant, Dragons (all), Fire Giant, Frost Giant, Giant Shark, Glabrezu, Griffon, Hill Giant, Iron Golem, Killer Whale, Kraken, Lion, Roc, Stone Giant, Stone Golem, Storm Giant, Tarrasque
Purity	Balor, Deva, Dryad, Fire Elemental, Pegasus, Planetar, Unicorn
Salt	Clay Golem, Ettin, Flesh Golem, Hill Giant, Manticore, Ogre, Otyugh, Stirge, Tarrasque
Speed	Air Elemental, Allosaurus, Behir, Pteranodon, Sprite
Stasis	Basilisk, Brass Dragon, Cockatrice, Gargoyle, Gelatinous Cube, Ghast, Ghoul, Giant Spider Gorgon, Medusa, Silver Dragon, Stirge, Tarrasque
Stealth	Air Elemental, Bugbear, Cloaker, Darkmantle, Doppelganger, Gargoyle, Gray Ooze, Grick, Invisible Stalker, Mimic
Strength	Ankylosaurus, Behir, Cloud Giant, Earth Elemental, Ettin, Fire Giant, Flesh Golem, Frost Giant, Giant Ape, Giant Constrictor Snake, Hydra, Mammoth, Minotaur, Ogre, Orc, Owlbear, Salamander, Shambling Mound, Stone Giant, Stone Golem, Xorn
Sulfur	Couatl, Griffon, Guardian Naga, Magma Mephit, Spirit Naga, Storm Giant, Tarrasque, Troll
Telesthetic	Drider, Otyugh, Pseudodragon
Toxin	Bearded Devil, Dretch, Drider, Ettercap, Giant Centipede, Giant Poisonous Snake, Giant Scorpion, Giant Spider, Hezrou, Imp, Medusa, Pseudodragon, Purple Worm, Spirit Naga, Vrock, Water Elemental, Wyvern
Transmutation	Bronze Dragon, Cockatrice, Copper Dragon, Doppelganger, Gold Dragon, Imp, Lycanthropes (all), Mimic, Ochre Jelly, Oni, Quasit, Rakshasa, Vampire
Transportation	Blink Dog, Nightmare, Phase Spider, Roc, Vampire, Wraith
Water	Chuul, Dragon Turtle, Frost Giant, Gelatinous Cube, Gray Ooze, Green Hag, Giant Sea Horse, Hydra, Ice Mephit, Kraken, Lizardfolk, Merfolk, Merrow, Ochre Jelly, Plesiosaurus, Sahuagin, Sea Hag, Steam Mephit, Water Elemental

In many situations it will be useful to cross-reference which vital essences are yielded by a particular monster, for which you will want to use **Table 2–5**.

ALLOSAURUS

ANKLYOSAURUS

EFREETI

TABLE 2–5: VITAL ESSENCES BY MONSTER

Monster	Vital Essences Yielded
Aarakocra	Agility, Flight
Aboleth	Mercury/ Control, Illusion
Air Elemental	Air/ Electricity, Flight, Illusion, Speed, Stealth
Allosaurus	Earth/ Fear, Speed
Androsphinx	Mercury/ Emotion, Perception
Ankheg	Earth/ Acid, Armor
Ankylosaurus	Earth/ Armor, Strength
Azer	Fire/ Light, Planar
Balor	Azoth, Fire/ Agility, Decay, Light, Pain, Purity
Barbed Devil	Fire/ Pain, Planar
Basilisk	Earth/ Stasis
Bearded Devil	Fire/ Planar, Toxin
Behir	Armor, Electric, Speed, Strength
Black Dragon	Azoth/ Acid, Armor, Fear, Flight, Prowess
Black Pudding	Earth/ Acid, Protection
Blink Dog	Mercury/ Transportation
Blue Dragon	Azoth/ Armor, Electricity, Fear, Flight, Prowess
Bone Devil	Fire/ Decay, Planar
Brass Dragon	Azoth/ Armor, Fear, Fire, Flight, Prowess, Stasis
Bronze Dragon	Azoth/ Armor, Electricity, Fear, Flight, Prowess, Transmutation
Bugbear	Perception, Stealth
Bulette	Earth/ Armor, Prowess
Centaur	Luck, Percipience, Prophecy
Chain Devil	Fire/ Illusion, Planar
Chimera	Fire, Mercury
Chuul	Water, Armor, Body
Clay Golem	Earth, Salt/ Body, Protection
Cloaker	Air, Flight, Stealth
Cloud Giant	Air/ Prowess, Strength
Cockatrice	Air/ Stasis, Transmutation
Copper Dragon	Azoth/ Acid, Armor, Fear, Flight, Prowess, Transmutation
Couatl	Sulfur/ Healing, Life, Love, Luck, Perception, Planar
Darkmantle	Air/ Light, Stealth
Death Dog	Death
Deva	Azoth/ Healing, Light, Planar, Purity
Djinni	Air/ Dream, Emotion, Planar
Doppelganger	Mercury/ Stealth, Transmutation
Dragon Turtle	Water/ Armor, Pain
Dretch	Fire/ Planar, Toxin
Drider	Mercury/ Telesthetic, Toxin
Dryad	Earth/ Love, Plant, Purity
Duergar	Light, Pain
Dust Mephit	Earth/ Planar
Earth Elemental	Earth/ Acid, Armor, Disease, Plant, Strength
Efreeti	Fire/ Dream, Emotion, Planar
Elf, Drow	Azoth/ Mind, Pain
Erinyes	Fire/ Planar, Memory
Ettercap	Toxin
Ettin	Salt/ Body, Strength

Monster	Vital Essences Yielded
Fire Elemental	Fire/ Agility, Decay, Light, Pain, Purity
Fire Giant	Fire/ Prowess, Strength
Flesh Golem	Salt/ Body, Strength
Flying Snake	Flight
Frost Giant	Water/ Cold, Prowess, Strength
Gargoyle	Earth/ Stasis, Stealth
Gelatinous Cube	Water/ Protection, Stasis
Ghast	Azoth/ Decay, Stasis
Ghost	Azoth, Death, Life
Ghoul	Azoth/ Decay, Stasis
Giant Ape	Strength
Giant Badger	Earth
Giant Bat	Perception
Giant Boar	Life
Giant Centipede	Toxin
Giant Constrictor Snake	Strength
Giant Crab	Armor
Giant Crocodile	Armor
Giant Eagle	Agility
Giant Elk	Body
Giant Fire Beetle	Light
Giant Frog	Perception
Giant Goat	Earth
Giant Hyena	Decay
Giant Lizard	Body
Giant Octopus	Perception
Giant Owl	Mind
Giant Poisonous Snake	Toxin
Giant Rat	Disease
Giant Scorpion	Toxin
Giant Sea Horse	Water
Giant Shark	Prowess
Giant Spider	Toxin, Stasis
Giant Toad	Perception
Giant Vulture	Decay
Giant Wasp	Pain
Giant Weasel	Perception
Giant Wolf Spider	Agility
Gibbering Mouther	Earth/ Acid, Perception, Protection
Glabrezu	Fire/ Planar, Prowess
Gnoll	Body/ Decay
Goblin	Agility, Pain
Gold Dragon	Azoth, Air, Fire/ Armor, Fear, Flight, Prowess, Transmutation
Gorgon	Earth/ Armor, Stasis
Gray Ooze	Water/ Acid, Illusion, Stealth
Green Dragon	Azoth/ Acid, Armor, Fear, Flight, Prowess
Green Hag	Water/ Illusion, Pain
Grick	Earth/ Strength
Griffon	Air, Sulfur/ Flight, Prowess
Guardian Naga	Azoth, Sulfur/ Healing, Life
Gynosphinx	Mercury/ Mind, Percipience, Prophecy

GIANT CRAB

GIANT SCORPION

GIANT SEAHORSE

HELLHOUND

MUMMY

Monster	Vital Essences Yielded
Harpy	Air/ Control, Mind
Hell Hound	Fire/ Pain, Planar
Hezrou	Fire/ Planar, Toxin
Hill Giant	Salt/ Body, Prowess
Hippogriff	Air/ Fear, Flight
Hobgoblin	Body
Homunculus	Azoth
Horned Devil	Fire/ Disease, Planar
Hydra	Water/ Healing, Strength
Ice Devil	Fire/ Cold, Planar
Ice Mephit	Water/ Cold, Planar
Imp	Fire/ Toxin, Transmutation
Invisible Stalker	Air/ Memory, Stealth
Iron Golem	Earth/ Armor, Prowess
Killer Whale	Prowess
Kobold	Agility
Kraken	Water/ Electricity, Life, Mind, Prowess
Lamia	Mercury/ Control, Illusion
Lemure	Fire/ Healing, Planar
Lich	Azoth/ Fear, Life, Mind
Lion	Prowess
Lizardfolk	Water
Lycanthropes (all)	Emotion, Transmutation
Magma Mephit	Sulfur/ Planar
Mammoth	Body, Strength
Manticore	Salt/ Body, Flight
Marilith	Fire/ Planar, Prophecy
Medusa	Mercury/ Stasis, Toxin
Merfolk	Water
Merrow	Water/ Pain, Planar
Mimic	Mercury/ Stealth, Transmutation
Minotaur	Mercury/ Body, Strength
Mummy	Azoth/ Decay, Disease, Memory
Nalfeshnee	Fire/ Fear, Planar
Night Hag	Mercury/ Dream, Emotion
Nightmare	Fire/ Dream, Transportation
Ochre Jelly	Water/ Acid, Transmutation
Ogre	Salt/ Body, Strength
Oni (Ogre Mage)	Mercury/ Electricity, Transmutation
Orc	Strength
Otyugh	Earth, Salt/ Disease, Telesthetic
Owlbear	Azoth, Mercury/ Strength
Pegasus	Air/ Purity, Transportation
Phase Spider	Transportation
Pit Fiend	Fire/ Fear, Planar
Planetar	Azoth/ Light, Planar, Purity
Plesiosaurus	Water/ Body
Pseudodragon	Azoth/ Telesthetic, Toxin
Pteranodon	Air/ Agility, Speed
Purple Worm	Earth/ Acid, Toxin
Quasit	Fire/ Planar, Transmutation

Monster	Vital Essences Yielded
Rakshasa	Mercury/ Mind, Transmutation
Red Dragon	Azoth, Fire/ Armor, Fear, Flight, Perception, Prowess
Remorhaz	Fire/ Cold
Roc	Air/ Flight, Prowess, Transportation
Roper	Earth/ Acid, Decay
Rust Monster	Earth/ Decay
Saber-toothed Tiger	Agility, Fear
Sahuagin	Water
Salamander	Fire/ Planar, Strength
Satyr	Earth/ Emotion, Love, Luck
Sea Hag	Water/ Death, Illusion
Shadow	Azoth/ Death, Light
Shambling Mound	Earth/ Electricity, Plant, Strength
Shrieker	Earth/ Perception, Plant
Silver Dragon	Azoth/ Armor, Cold, Fear, Flight, Prowess, Stasis
Skeleton	Azoth/ Death, Decay
Solar	Azoth/ Healing, Life, Love, Perception, Planar, Protection
Specter	Azoth/ Death, Dream, Life, Memory
Spirit Naga	Azoth, Sulfur/ Life, Toxin
Sprite	Air/ Emotion, Flight, Luck, Speed
Steam Mephit	Fire. Water/ Planar
Stirge	Salt/ Flight, Pain, Stasis
Stone Giant	Earth/ Prowess, Strength
Stone Golem	Earth/ Prowess, Strength
Storm Giant	Air, Sulfur/ Electricity, Prophecy, Prowess
Succubus/Incubus	Fire/ Emotion, Planar
Tarrasque	Azoth, Sulfur/ Body, Death, Prophecy, Protection, Prowess, Stasis
Treant	Earth/ Dream, Mind, Plant
Triceratops	Earth/ Armor, Protection
Troll	Sulfur/ Healing, Life
Tyrannosaurus Rex	Earth/ Fear, Prowess
Unicorn	Azoth/ Healing, Purity
Vampire	Azoth/ Fear, Transmutation, Transportation
Violet Fungus	Earth/ Decay, Plant
Vrock	Fire/ Planar, Toxin
Water Elemental	Water/ Cold, Emotion, Fear, Memory, Toxin
Werebear	Emotion, Transmutation
Wereboar	Emotion, Transmutation
Wererat	Emotion, Transmutation
Weretiger	Emotion, Transmutation
Werewolf	Emotion, Transmutation
White Dragon	Azoth/ Armor, Cold, Death, Fear, Flight, Prowess
Wight	Azoth/ Death, Decay
Will-o'-Wisp	Azoth/ Death, Electricity
Winter Wolf	Cold
Worg	Azoth
Wraith	Azoth/ Control, Death, Transportation
Wyvern	Air/ Flight, Toxin
Xorn	Earth/ Planar, Strength
Zombie	Azoth/ Death, Decay

SHADOW

SPIRIT NAGA

ZOMBIE

CHAPTER THREE: ALCHEMICAL ITEMS

Alchemical items are items and pieces of gear that can be produced only by someone with the Craft (alchemy) skill or other specialized skills. They perform specialized functions, greater than normal pieces of equipment, but less than that of magical gear. They do not require a feat to create. Alchemical items include Alchemical Devices, Grenades, Incense, Liquids and Tonics, Ointments and Pastes, Powders, Solvents, and Tinctures.

The listings in this chapter are laid out much like magic item creation guidelines. Each item is given its common name, then a description. Immediately following the description is the Rarity of the item, Craft DC to create the item, the price of the item, the cost, and any non-standard requirements to craft the item. The rarity simply communicates how frequently such items are available for purchase. The Craft DC is standard, and crafting works as the standard skill description. The cost is precalculated in gold pieces for you. Non-standard requirements are included in the price and include rare gem dusts and essences.

The price and cost include the price of all the reagents, special requirements, and ingredients. Normal ingredients are presumed to be available and constitute what is being spent as part of the base cost to craft the item. Special ingredients such as other Alchemical Concoctions, Gemstones, Rare Earths, and Essences do cost money, and might be restricted or difficult to find. Collecting these and using them can lower the crafting cost of many of these items. For each one you have, simply reduce the crafting cost by the appropriate value.

The components for alchemical items are listed in order by mineral essences, vital essences that comprise an entire category of possible components, and then specific alchemical essences that do not have substitutes. The Azoth category is listed as having "any" possible subcomponents even though it does not have actual subcomponents. This is done in case you decide to add subcategories to Azoth, which has some characteristics that could be subdivided (including animation, undeath, sound, and magic in general).

READING THE FORMULAS

An entry such as Air (any) (x2) indicates that any Air essence may be used, but two are required. Therefore, the alchemist might use two general Air essences, a general Air essence coupled with, for example, Speed, two of the same specific essence (such as two Speed essences), or two different specific Air essences (such as Speed and Stealth).

An entry such as Air (any 2 different) requires two different sources of the essence. Thus, a general Air essence might be coupled with a specific Air essence such as Speed, or two different specific essences might be used such as Speed and Stealth.

YOUR OWN FORMULAS

When you choose to make your own alchemical formulas or determine essences that might be derived from monsters not on the list, there are a few general guidelines for using the general categories. Air is generally associated with motion; Earth is less thematic but tends toward bodily features; Fire is intuitively associated with qualities attributed to fire; Mercury has to do with mental qualities and change; Salt is similar to Earth but has more of an emphasis on skill rather than innate properties of matter; and Sulfur generally has to do with external forces. There are absolutely a number of specific vital essences that contradict these general guidelines for understanding the overall categories, which gives you considerable flexibility to make associations that "feel" right.

Many of the specific vital essences may appear counterintuitive as they are used in the items. This is because a category such as Light also includes its own opposite: There is no essence of "Blindness" or "Darkness" because these may be counteracted alchemically by manipulating the essence of Light. In other words, essences are often used to contradictory effect.

ALCHEMICAL DEVICES

Alchemists often combine their substances with particular devices such as inks, arrows, and ropes. They are often more powerful and useful than standard equipment. Many alchemists make their living selling such goods to local merchants.

Anyone with the alchemy skill can produce the following devices. They are considered nonmagical items and tools. They are treated as standard equipment.

TABLE 3–1: ALCHEMICAL DEVICES

Name	Craft (alchemy) DC	Price	Weight
Alchemist's Bandage	20	40 gp	0.5 lb.
Alchemist's Fire Skewer	20	40 gp	1 lb.
Arcane Focus	30	2,500 gp	3 lbs.
Armorbreacher	20	15 gp	1 lb.
Armor Padding	15	50 gp	1 lb.
Arrow, Alchemical	15	5 gp	0.15 lb.
Arrow, Armor Piercing (20)	15	6 gp	3 lbs.
Arrow, Bleeding	25	160 gp	0.15 lb.
Arrow, Durable (20)	25	20 gp	3 lbs.
Arrow, Dye (20)	25	20 gp	3 lbs.
Arrow, Flare (20)	25	20 gp	3 lbs.
Arrow, Lodestone (20)	25	200 gp	3 lbs.
Arrow, Marking	28	20 gp	0.15 lb.
Arrow, Pheromone	25	15 gp	0.15 lb.
Arrow, Shrieking (20)	15	10 gp	3 lbs.
Arrow, Slowburn	25	100 gp	0.15 lb.
Arrow, Splintercloud	25	25 gp	0.15 lb.
Arrow, Stinker	15	2 gp	0.15 lb.
Arrow, Tangleshot	25	20 gp	0.15 lb.
Arrow, Thunder	25	5 gp	0.15 lb.
Arrow, Venipuncture	25	1 gp	0.15 lb.
Bag, Blinding	20	15 gp	2 lbs.
Blade, Alchemical	25	500 gp	0.1 lb.
Bladeball	20	15 gp	1 lb.
Bolt Cutters, Heavy Duty	15	15 gp	5 lbs.
Bolt Cutters, Small	15	6 gp	1 lb.
Bomb Launcher	8	10 gp	0.5 lb.
Boots, Alchemical	25	450 gp	4 lbs.
Boots, Sonic	25	450 gp	4 lbs.
Boots, Springing	25	450 gp	4 lbs.
Bullet, Alchemical	15	35 gp	0.5 lb.
Bullet, Concussive	26	150 gp	0.05 lb.
Buoyant Balloon	10	10 gp	1 lb.
Calculus	25	50 gp	4 lbs.
Chalk, Dark Flame	18	5 gp	0.05 lb.
Chalk, Enduring	18	5 gp	0.05 lb.
Chalk, Glow	15	5 gp	0.05 lb.
Chalk, Ice	15	5 gp	0.05 lb.
Cloak, Deception	24	350 gp	1 lb.
Cloak, Fragrant	25	350 gp	1 lb.
Cloak, Slowfall	30	450 gp	1 lb.
Cold Fire	18	10 gp	2 lbs.
Empyrean Stone	25	100 gp	3 lbs.
Fabric, Noncombustible	25	100 gp	7 lbs.
Fabric, Shadow	28	150 gp	4 lbs.
False Tooth	25	30 gp	—
Falsifier's Parchment	18	10 gp	0.05 lb.
Flame Blade	25	50 gp	0.1 lb.
Flamethrower, Large	30	1,500 gp	500 lbs.
Flamethrower, Personal	35	1,000 gp	200 lbs.
Gloves, Alchemical	25	650 gp	1 lb.
Glow Globe	10	3 gp	1 lb.
Glow Orb	18	200 gp	1 lb.
Heat Stone	15	300 gp	0.1 lb.
Helm of Lenses	30	500 gp	3 lbs.
Homing Rods	25	250 gp	2 lbs.
Hose, Personal Waterblast	35	1,000 gp	200 lbs.
Hose, Waterblast	30	1,500 gp	500 lbs.
Ink, Cloud Chaser	25	250 gp	0.1 lb.
Ink, Disappearing	20	50 gp	0.2 lb.
Ink, Firelight	22	15 gp	0.2 lb.
Ink, Glowing	20	50 gp	0.1 lb.
Ink, Incendiary	20	50 gp	0.1 lb.
Ink, Magelight	24	30 gp	0.2 lb.
Ink, Moonlight	22	25 gp	0.2 lb.
Ink, Underscript	20	75 gp	0.1 lb.
Ink, Waterproof	15	25 gp	0.1 lb.
Lantern, Solar	25	250 gp	2 lbs.
Lockrender	25	250 gp	2 lbs.
Marbles, Detonating	25	30 gp	2 lbs.
Mask, Gas	25	100 gp	8 lbs.
Mask, Superior Gas	30	125 gp	3 lbs.
Oil, Long-Burning	15	50 gp	1 lb.
Oil, Quick-Freeze	25	50 gp	1 lb.
Oil, Shadow	25	5 gp	1 lb.
Oil, Stink	20	15 gp	1 lb.
Oil, Thieves'	25	55 gp	1 lb.
Paper, Acidproof	15	12 gp	0.2 lb.
Paper, Fireproof	15	10 gp	0.2 lb.
Paper, Waterproof	15	8 gp	0.2 lb.
Pox Burster	20	50 gp	1 lb.
Ring, Poison Needle	25	150 gp	0.1 lb.
Ring, Secret Compartment	20	10 gp	0.1 lb.
Robe, Alchemical	20	65 gp	4 lbs.
Ring, Rogue's	20	300 gp	0.1 lb.
Rope, Cave Fisher Reel	22	250 gp	0.1 lb.
Rope, Liquid	25	75 gp	5 lbs.
Rope, Stoneweave	25	12 gp	7 lbs.
Rope, Terrafugia	28	100 gp	5 lbs.
Rope Ladder, Flittermouse	25	175 gp	15 lbs.
Shard, Various	15	45 gp	0.5 lb.
Shield, Alchemical	25	500 gp	15 lbs.
Shield, Hypnosis	25	+800 gp	15 lbs.
Smokestick (5)	20	100 gp	2.5 lb.
Smokestick, Noxious	25	80 gp	0.5 lb.
Sparkthrower, Large	30	1,500 gp	500 lbs.
Sparkthrower, Personal	35	1,000 gp	200 lbs.
Spike, Locking	25	800 gp	15 lbs.
Spike, Self-Driving	25	150 gp	5 lbs.
Spike, Silent	22	80 gp	0.5 lb.
Spray Bellows, Alchemical	22	80 gp	6 lbs.
Sunrod (40)	25	80 gp	40 lb.
Swiftlight	20	15 gp	2 lbs.
Tanglewire	20	25 gp	5 lbs.
Thermos	15	80 gp	0.5 lb.
Tindertwig (10)	15	10 gp	0.5 lb.
Towel, Alchemical	18	15 gp	3 lbs.
Trapblaster	25	150 gp	3 lbs.
Trapspringer	20	100 gp	Various
Vacuum Rod	25	500 gp	3 lbs.
Wall, Portable	25	400 gp	40 lbs.
Water Purification Sponge	15	25 gp	1 lb.
Weather Rune	15	20 gp	0.5 lb.

Alchemist's Bandage: This bandage is slathered in a blood-clotting paste. When applied to a bleeding or dying creature, these bandages stop the bleeding and stabilize the dying creature automatically and heal 1d4 points of damage.

DC 20 Craft (alchemy); *Rarity:* Uncommon; *Price:* 40 gp; *Weight:* 0.5 lb.; *Alchemical Formula:* Earth (any), Salt (any), Sulfur (any), Healing

Alchemist's Fire Skewer: These two-foot iron spikes can be wielded like daggers. When a target is struck, they automatically activate and begin burning.
They do 1d4 points of damage when striking and then burn, doing 1d6 points of damage the following two rounds. They can be removed with a standard action and a successful DC 12 Fortitude save.
They are used up on a successful strike. They can be thrown like daggers, but if they strike a target, they do not begin to burn.

DC 20 Craft (alchemy); *Rarity:* Uncommon; *Price:* 40 gp; *Weight:* 1 lb.; *Alchemical Formula:* Fire (any), Fire (any), Rare Earth

Arcane Focus: This item is a magical focus, made for a spellcaster. The alchemist may make one for themselves. Any spell cast using the focus treats the caster as 1 level higher for a specific arcane school of magic; i.e., the illusion school or the necromancy school. The item takes up a ring slot on the user.

DC 30 Craft (alchemy); *Rarity:* Very Rare; *Price:* 2,500 gp; *Weight:* 3 lbs.; *Alchemical Formula:* Azoth (any 5), Gold, Rare Earth

Armorbreacher: This device tears apart and weakens heavy armor. A successful melee touch attack against a target in heavy armor temporarily damages the armor, giving a −2 alchemical penalty to the armor bonus. This is considered an unarmed attack and has no effect on magic armor with a +2 enhancement bonus or better. If it is used on a creature not wearing armor with an armor bonus of +4 or better, in addition to the penalty, it causes 2d4 points of damage to the armor, ignoring hardness.
After combat, the armor can be removed and the armor repaired with a DC 10 Craft (armor) check that takes one hour. The *armorbreacher* is used up in the attempt.

DC 20 Craft (alchemy); *Rarity:* Uncommon; *Price:* 15 gp; *Weight:* 1 lb.; *Alchemical Formula:* Iron (x10), Rare Earth

Armor Padding: This is not an item, but instead a technique the alchemist can learn to modify armor. It reduces the armor check penalty by 2 for Stealth checks, but the armor penalty is increased by +1 for all other checks, and the maximum Dexterity bonus allowed is reduced by 1. A chain shirt modified by armor padding wouldn't penalize Stealth checks at all, but would have an armor check penalty of −3 for all other purposes. The maximum Dexterity bonus allowed would be reduced to +3.

DC 15 Craft (alchemy); *Rarity:* Rare; *Price:* 50 gp; *Weight:* +1 lb.; *Alchemical Formula:* Not applicable

Arrow, Alchemical: This arrow has a hollow tip. Upon striking a target, the tip shatters and the target is affected by the alchemical grenade used. The alchemist must select which grenade is going to be used at the time the item is created. The entire grenade is used up in the construction of the arrow. The cost of the grenade is not included in the crafting cost of the arrow.
The arrow does 1d4 points of damage (1d3 for small) and is limited to three-quarters maximum range. The alchemical mixture does half damage, or if no damage is applied, the target receives a +4 circumstance bonus to their save. Since the arrow may take any alchemical mixture, those must be purchased separately and applied. Note that this allows a tremendous variety of effects to be produced with the arrow.

DC 15 Craft (alchemy); *Rarity:* Uncommon; *Price:* 5 gp; *Weight:* —; *Alchemical Formula:* Not applicable

Arrow, Armor Piercing (20): This alchemically hardened arrow receives a +2 alchemical bonus to hit versus any target with an armor or natural armor bonus of +4 or greater.

DC 15 Craft (alchemy); *Rarity:* Uncommon; *Price:* 6 gp; *Weight:* —; *Alchemical Formula:* Iron (10), Rare Earth, Armor

Arrow, Bleeding: This sharpened hollow tube looks like the narrow proboscis of some giant insect, but it actually comes from a carnivorous plant. A *bleeding arrow* deals normal damage when it hits a creature and deals 1 point of bleed damage. A critical hit does not multiply the bleed damage.

DC 25 Craft (alchemy); *Rarity:* Rare; *Price:* 160 gp; *Weight:* —; *Alchemical Formula:* Air (any), Pain, Healing, Silver

Arrow, Durable (20): These arrows are tightly wrapped in strands of alchemical glue. *Durable arrows* don't break with normal use, whether or not they hit their target; unless a *durable arrow* goes missing, an archer can retrieve and reuse it again and again. *Durable arrows* can be broken in other ways (such as deliberate snapping, hitting a fire elemental, and so on). A magical *durable arrow* with an enhancement bonus or magic weapon special ability applies these magical effects only the first time it is used — afterward, the *durable arrow* becomes nonmagical, and it can be reused or imbued with magic again.

DC 25 Craft (alchemy); *Rarity:* Uncommon; *Price:* 20 gp; *Weight:* —; *Alchemical Formula:* Air (any), Earth (any), Body, Turquoise

Arrow, Dye (20): This arrow ends in a crystalline bubble filled with a viscous alchemical dyeing agent. Firing a dye arrow is a ranged touch attack; a creature struck by a dye arrow takes no damage but is splashed with enough black, blue, green, or red marker dye to coat about one square foot. The stain caused by marker dye cannot be washed off except with magic for the first 72 hours but fades completely after two weeks.

DC 25 Craft (alchemy); *Rarity:* Uncommon; *Price:* 20 gp; *Weight:* —; *Alchemical Formula:* Azoth (any), Earth (any)

Arrow, Flare (20): This arrow leaves a bright streak of light behind it in the air. All ranged attacks get a +1 circumstance bonus to hit against a creature hit by a flare arrow in the last minute.

DC 25 Craft (alchemy); *Rarity:* Rare; *Price:* 20 gp; *Weight:* —; *Alchemical Formula:* Fire (any), Fire (any)

Arrow, Lodestone (20): This heavy iron arrowhead is sealed with an alchemical resin. Pulling a small string (a move action) breaks the seal and triggers a reaction in the arrowhead, greatly increasing its magnetic properties. You gain a +4 circumstance bonus on attack rolls when firing a *lodestone arrow* at a target wearing metal armor or a target made of metal, but the magnetized arrow deals only half damage on a successful hit. The increased magnetism fades one round after you activate a *lodestone arrow*, after which it becomes a normal arrow.

DC 25 Craft (alchemy); *Rarity:* Rare; *Price:* 200 gp; *Weight:* —; *Alchemical Formula:* Rare Earth, Iron, Earth (any)

Arrow, Marking: These are not arrows for a bow, but triangular pointing arrows. When put on a surface, they sink down flush with the surface. They may be configured to glow in the visible or infrared spectrum. They may be removed with a keyword. A *dispel magic* destroys them, and they have a hardness of 8 and 15 hit points.

DC 28 Craft (alchemy); *Rarity:* Rare; *Price:* 10 gp; *Weight:* —; *Alchemical Formula:* Azoth (any), Mercury (any)

Arrow, Pheromone: The arrowhead of this arrow is coated with potent substances that react to blood and sweat, releasing a strong aroma that most predators recognize as the scent of tasty injured prey and that other creatures perceive as merely unpleasant. Any creature with the scent ability gains a +2 circumstance bonus on attack and damage rolls against a target marked with a pheromone arrow. This effect lasts for one hour or until the target spends one minute washing it off.

DC 25 Craft (alchemy); *Rarity:* Rare; *Price:* 15 gp; *Weight:* —; *Alchemical Formula:* Mercury (any), Love

Arrow, Shrieking (20): When fired, this arrow causes a terrible keening noise as if people were shrieking in pain as it flies through the air. All opponents must make a DC 12 Will save or become shaken. If already shaken, they become frightened; if frightened, they become panicked. This save is DC 16 if the opponents are primitive or superstitious. This arrow also attracts nearby wandering monsters.

DC 15 Craft (alchemy); *Rarity:* Rare; *Price:* 10 gp; *Weight:* —; *Alchemical Formula:* Rare Earth, Air (any), Fear

Arrow, Slowburn: A small receptacle of alchemical material behind the head of this arrow heats up when exposed to air and eventually combusts; barbs on the arrowhead pierce the pouch when it hits a target. If you hit a target with a *slowburn arrow*, it deals damage as normal, but at the beginning of your next turn, the arrow bursts into flames and deals 1d6 points of fire damage to the target.

DC 25 Craft (alchemy); *Rarity:* Rare; *Price:* 100 gp; *Weight:* —; *Alchemical Formula:* Rare Earth, Fire (any), Fire (any), Mercury (any)

Arrow, Splintercloud: The shaft of this arrow is formed from numerous small bone fragments painstakingly glued together. On a successful hit, a *splintercloud arrow* deals normal damage as it tears itself apart, creating a burst of razor-sharp bone shards centered on the target. These shards deal 1d3 points of piercing damage to the target and any creatures adjacent to the target (Reflex DC 18 negates).

DC 25 Craft (alchemy); *Rarity:* Rare; *Price:* 25 gp; *Weight:* —; *Alchemical Formula:* Air (any), Decay *or* Death

Arrow, Stinker: When this arrow strikes a target, it is splashed with a strong scent of rotting eggs. This provides a +2 alchemical bonus to tracking, doubled if the tracker has the scent special quality.

DC 15 Craft (alchemy); *Rarity:* Uncommon; *Price:* 2 gp; *Weight:* —; *Alchemical Formula:* Sulfur (any), Decay

Arrow, Tangleshot: This arrow is tipped with a tiny vial of tanglefoot goo. Firing a *tangleshot arrow* is a ranged touch attack; the arrow deals no damage when it hits, but the target is splashed with the alchemical adhesive. This effect is similar to that of a *tanglefoot bag*, but with the following adjustments: Reflex DC 10, Strength DC 12 to break, 10 points of slashing damage to cut through, Concentration DC 10 to cast spells. A *tangleshot arrow* imposes a –1 penalty on attack rolls because of its weight.

DC 25 Craft (alchemy); *Rarity:* Rare; *Price:* 20 gp; *Weight:* —; *Alchemical Formula:* Earth (any), Mercury (any), Stasis

Arrow, Thunder: This arrow emits a deafening bang when it strikes its target. Anyone within 10 feet must succeed at a DC 14 Fortitude save or be deafened for one minute. The range increment of the missile is cut in half.

DC 25 Craft (alchemy); *Rarity:* Uncommon; *Price:* 5 gp; *Weight:* —; *Alchemical Formula:* Air (any), Salt (any), Strength

Arrow, Venipuncture: When this arrow strikes a target, it drains and collects a single ounce of the target's blood.

DC 25 Craft (alchemy); *Rarity:* Rare; *Price:* 1 gp; *Weight:* —; *Alchemical Formula:* Not applicable

Bag, Blinding: If this bag is thrown over someone's head, it clamps itself shut! A ranged or melee touch attack must be made. The bag has a maximum range of 10 feet. The target can make a DC 16 Reflex save to avoid the attempt if the bag is thrown. If the save fails or the attack is a melee attack, the bag snaps shut and blinds your opponent. It can be ripped apart with a DC 14 Strength check. The bag has a hardness of 2 and 10 hit points.

DC 20 Craft (alchemy); *Rarity:* Uncommon; *Price:* 15 gp; *Weight:* 2 lbs.; *Alchemical Formula:* Iron, Mercury (any)

Blade, Alchemical: This modification to a masterwork blade allows the weapon to store an alchemical grenade. When striking a target, the wielder may choose to affect the target and only the target with the effects of the grenade. (Note: Any melee weapon can be modified in this manner, not just blades.) The cost of the alchemical grenade is not included in the crafting cost — it must be added to the weapon after it is made and after the grenade is used.

DC 25 Craft (alchemy); *Rarity:* Uncommon; *Price:* +500 gp; *Weight:* +2 lb.; *Alchemical Formula:* Not applicable

Bladeball: This small iron ball is about two inches in diameter. It can be thrown as a thrown weapon with a range increment of 20 feet. Because it is just a ball, it is a simple weapon. On a successful hit, it does 1d6 points of bludgeoning and piercing damage as spikes and blades explode out of the ball.

DC 20 Craft (alchemy); *Rarity:* Rare; *Price:* 15 gp; *Weight:* 1 lb.; *Alchemical Formula:* Iron, Air (any), Fire (any), Sulfur (any)

Bolt Cutters: This tool damages metal bars. It comes in two sizes: small and heavy duty. The small bolt cutters ignore 10 points of hardness and do 15 points of damage to bars up to one-half inch thick; the heavy-duty ones ignore 10 points of hardness and do 30 points of damage on bars up to one inch thick.

DC 15 Craft (alchemy); *Rarity:* Uncommon; *Price:* 6 gp / 15 gp; *Weight:* 1 lb. / 5 lbs.; *Alchemical Formula:* Not applicable

Bomb Launcher: Like the gnomish *calculus*, this is a one-use item "shell" that extends the range of a thrown alchemical device or bomb. These odd-looking, egg-shaped contraptions have cleverly placed fins that improve a bomb's accuracy. Goblin alchemists use these special containers to make their bombs more accurate when thrown over long distances. Using a *bomb launcher* when throwing a bomb increases the bomb's range increment to 30 feet (or increases the range increment of a bomb with the rocket bomb discovery to 70 feet). *Bomb launchers* are destroyed when used.

DC 8 Craft (alchemy); *Rarity:* Uncommon; *Price:* 10 gp; *Weight:* 0.5 lbs.; *Alchemical Formula:* Not applicable

Boots, Alchemical: These boots are exceptionally well-made and stable. They provide the alchemist with protection against his own tricks. First, they grant a +6 alchemical bonus to all saving throws to avoid being knocked prone or to fall down. The *alchemical boots* also provide a +2 alchemical bonus versus bull rushes and overrun attacks. Finally, these boots treat difficult terrain that is caused by alchemical items as normal terrain.

DC 25 Craft (alchemy), *Rarity:* Rare; *Price:* 450 gp; *Weight:* 4 lbs.; *Alchemical Formula:* Iron, Rare Earth, Earth (any), Agility, Strength

Boots, Sonic: While wearing these boots, the wearer can adjust the sound that they make. They can lower the noise produced to almost nothing, granting a +4 alchemical bonus on Stealth checks or they can be increased in volume until every footfall sounds like a storm giant walking around. It takes one round to adjust the volume.

DC 25 Craft (alchemy); *Rarity:* Rare; *Price:* 450 gp; *Weight:* 4 lbs.; *Alchemical Formula:* Rare Earth, Air (any), Mercury (any), Stealth

Boots, Springing: When triggered, these boots cause powerful springs to shoot the wearer high into the air. The wearer gains a +10 alchemical bonus to Acrobatics checks made to jump. In either case, they must make a DC 16 Reflex saving throw. This determines if they are able to land in such a way to reset the boots. If not, they are held three inches off the ground by springs and their movement is halved until they spend two rounds removing the boots or a full minute to reset them. On a success, the boots are reset and may be used again.

DC 25 Craft (alchemy); *Rarity:* Rare; *Price:* 450 gp; *Weight:* 4 lbs.; *Alchemical Formula:* Iron, Air (any), Flight

Bullet, Alchemical: This hollow glass sphere is designed to be fired from a sling. The alchemist must select which grenade type (see **Table 3–3: Grenades, Pellets, and Stones**) will be used at the time the item is created. The entire grenade is used up in the construction of the bullet. The cost of the grenade is not included in the cost of the item.

The bullet does 1d4 points of damage (1d3 if small). The alchemical mixture does half damage, or if no damage is applied, the target receives a +4 circumstance bonus to their save.

DC 15 Craft (alchemy); *Rarity:* Uncommon; *Price:* 35 gp; *Weight:* —; *Alchemical Formula:* Not applicable

Bullet, Concussive: If this bullet strikes a target, it detonates and knocks a target prone. On a successful hit, the target is subject to the damage from the bullet, as well as a trip attempt, using the value of the attack roll as the CMB. The bullet's range increment of this weapon is cut in half.

DC 26 Craft (alchemy); *Rarity:* Rare; *Price:* 150 gp; *Weight:* —; *Alchemical Formula:* Rare Earth, Air (any), Salt (any), Strength

Buoyant Balloon: This fist-sized alchemically treated animal bladder is tightly sealed around a small wooden grip. By giving the handle a sharp twist, you break a tiny glass ampoule just inside the bladder to fill the bag with buoyant gas and cause it to swell into a three-foot-diameter sphere. Inflating the balloon is a move action. Once filled, the balloon floats upward at a speed of 60 feet per round. The balloon can lift up to 20 pounds of weight as it rises, though carrying more than 10 pounds reduces its speed to 30 feet per round. Multiple balloons attached to a single object add their carrying capacities together when determining how much weight they can lift. If a balloon is not held or bound in place in some manner, it continues to rise until it reaches a height of 600 feet, or until 10 minutes pass, after which it pops or deflates and is destroyed.

DC 10 Craft (alchemy); *Rarity:* Uncommon; *Price:* 10 gp; *Weight:* 1 lb.; *Alchemical Formula:* Air (any), Air (any)

Calculus: This is an oversized mechanical sling designed to fire grenades and liquid flasks. It can fire *alchemist's fire*, powders, solvents, and other alchemical items. This has whatever effect the item has, but is fired with a range increment of 40 feet. This is an exotic gnomish weapon, and gnomes are considered to have natural proficiency with it.

DC 25 Craft (alchemy); *Rarity:* Rare; *Price:* 50 gp; *Weight:* 4 lbs.; *Alchemical Formula:* Not applicable

Chalk, Dark Flame: This chalk appears to write invisibly, but is clearly visible to darkvision.

DC 18 Craft (alchemy); *Rarity:* Uncommon; *Price:* 5 gp; *Weight:* —; *Alchemical Formula:* Rare Earth, Mercury (any), Sulfur (any)

Chalk, Enduring: This chalk makes indelible marks. Exposure to solvents, cleaners, motion, or other types of removal methods will not work. The marks can be erased with an *erase* spell or better.

DC 18 Craft (alchemy); *Rarity:* Rare; *Price:* 5 gp; *Weight:* —; *Alchemical Formula:* Rare Earth, Azoth (any)

Chalk, Glow: This chalk and writing made with it glow in the dark.

DC 15 Craft (alchemy); *Rarity:* Uncommon; *Price:* 5 gp; *Weight:* —; *Alchemical Formula:* Rare Earth, Light

Chalk, Ice: This chalk is able to write on ice.

DC 15 Craft (alchemy); *Rarity:* Uncommon; *Price:* 5 gp; *Weight:* —; *Alchemical Formula:* Rare Earth, Water (any)

Cloak, Deception: This cloak can be taken off and with one round of preparation appear to move on its own. The cloak stays standing where set and appears to be a cloaked creature from a distance. The cloak can also be set to move in a somewhat realistic way no more than five feet in any direction and then back. To determine that the cloak is not a person requires a DC 15 Perception check, with a doubled penalty for distance. This DC can be increased if the person setting up the cloak takes two full rounds to do so. The user can then make a Stealth check and add half the result to the Perception DC to notice that the cloak is not a person.
If struck by any weapon blow or attack, the cloak immediately collapses.

DC 24 Craft (alchemy); *Rarity:* Uncommon; *Price:* 350 gp; *Weight:* 3 lbs.; *Alchemical Formula:* Iron, Azoth, Illusion, Mind

Cloak, Fragrant: This is a cloak with a long-term scent neutralizer. It eliminates natural orders and leaves an odorless freshness behind. Attempts to track a person wearing a fragrant cloak have their DC increased by 8. Animals dependent on scent to locate prey, such as when blinded, treat such a cloaked creature as invisible.

DC 25 Craft (alchemy); *Rarity:* Uncommon; *Price:* 350 gp; *Weight:* 1 lb.; *Alchemical Formula:* Air (any), Fire (any), Salt (any), Stealth

Cloak, Slowfall: This cloak blooms out like a pair of wings behind the wearer when they fall. This allows them to slow their speed and drift. If an unexpected fall happens, it negates the first 10 feet of falling damage. If you intentionally jump, it allows you to fall (1d6 + 1) x 10 feet safely and allows you to move five feet horizontally for every 10 feet you fall.

DC 30 Craft (alchemy); *Rarity:* Rare; *Price:* 450 gp; *Weight:* 3 lbs.; *Alchemical Formula:* Iron, Rare Earth, Air (any), Flight

Cold Fire: These are small cubes or sticks. They begin to glow when doused in water. They shed light out to a 20-foot radius and dim light another 20 feet past that for two hours. This light produces no heat. They can be dried off before the duration expires.

DC 18 Craft (alchemy); *Rarity:* Uncommon; *Price:* 30 gp; *Weight:* 2 lbs.; *Alchemical Formula:* Rare Earth, Fire (any), Light

Empyrean Stone: This stone is attuned with a heavenly body when it is created. The stone glows when this body is in the sky, no matter how far underground the stone is taken. It is often attuned to the sun or the moon to allow for determining the passage of time.

DC 25 Craft (alchemy); *Rarity:* Rare; *Price:* 100 gp; *Weight:* 3 lbs.; *Alchemical Formula:* Diamond, Moonstone, Rare Earth, Light

Fabric, Noncombustible: This produces a rough cloth that is textured like stiff burlap. This cloth is resistant to fire and will not burn. It melts if exposed to extremely high temperatures, but it will not catch on fire. A single piece of clothing, such as a cloak, adds 2 to the check to put out a fire, and a full suit made of this cloth protects people from the continuing damage caused by *alchemist's fire* and other sources of burning damage.

DC 25 Craft (alchemy); *Rarity:* Rare; *Price:* 100 gp; *Weight:* 2 lbs.; *Alchemical Formula:* Fire (any), Salt (any), Water (any), Body

Fabric, Shadow: This matte fabric absorbs light and assists the user in hiding and stealthy movement. A cloak or single piece of clothing like a cloak provides a +1 alchemical bonus to Stealth, whereas a whole suit provides a +2 alchemical bonus to Stealth.

DC 28 Craft (alchemy); *Rarity:* Very Rare; *Price:* 150 gp; *Weight:* 4 lbs.; *Alchemical Formula:* Air (any), Azoth (any), Light, Stealth

False Tooth: This hollow tooth is implanted in the mouth and may contain anything that can fit in the space of a tooth.
Most often it is used to contain a single dose of an alchemical dust, liquid, powder, or poison. When cracked open, users may blow a breath to affect themselves and one adjacent target with the contents of the tooth. The price does not include the contents of the tooth.

DC 25 Craft (alchemy); *Rarity:* Uncommon; *Price:* 30 gp; *Weight:* —; *Alchemical Formula:* Pearl

Falsifier's Parchment: When this paper is exposed to mild heat, it turns nearly transparent. This is of particular use to forgers. At the end of an hour, the paper becomes opaque again and is indistinguishable from normal paper. Having this paper available doubles the bonus any original documents grant to the linguistics skill of the forger.

DC 18 Craft (alchemy); *Rarity:* Uncommon; *Price:* 10 gp; *Weight:* —; *Alchemical Formula:* Air (any), Fire (any)

Flame Blade: This small metal tube has a tab. When the tab is pulled, the reaction inside the tube causes a gout of flame to shoot from the end for a full minute. Make a touch attack against the target, doing 1d6 fire damage on a successful hit. If you construct this with fire essences from an evil outsider, then the blade does 2d4 + 2 damage.

DC 25 Craft (alchemy); *Rarity:* Uncommon; *Price:* 50 gp; *Weight:* —; *Alchemical Formula:* Rare Earth, Fire (any), Mercury (any), Flight

Flamethrower, Large: This 10-foot-by-10-foot immobile device can throw flame. It has a nozzle attached to a 10-foot-long hose. This hose allows the alchemist or any trained operator to stand adjacent to the projector and fire a 60-foot line or 30-foot cone of fire that does 4d6 points of damage and objects hit the burning condition. A DC 16 Reflex save halves the damage and prevents burning.

It takes a full round action to change from a line to a cone. The weapon cannot be fired during this time. When full, this item can be used six times. It takes a full round action to refill two uses. A refill weighs eight pounds and costs 160 gp.

This 500-pound projector can be mounted on wheels for an additional 500 gp. This allows it to be pushed or pulled forward or backward. It may turn in place.

Obviously, such a large volume of flammable liquid is very combustible. When taking any fire or electrical damage, it must make a Reflex save with a DC of 10 + points of damage taken; treat as if the object had a Reflex save of +5. If it fails this save, it explodes, doing 2d6 fire damage for every round of ammunition contained within to all targets within 30 feet. A DC 16 Reflex save allows a target to take half damage.

For an additional 500 gp and 200 pounds of weight, you can build a *large flamethrower* that has eight rounds of ammunition. For an additional 1,000 gp and 500 pounds of weight, you can build one that holds 10 rounds of ammunition. It has a hardness of 8 and 50 hit points.

DC 30 Craft (alchemy); *Rarity:* Rare; *Price:* 1,500 gp; *Weight:* 500 lbs.; *Alchemical Formula:* Rare Earth (x20), Earth (any) (x20), Fire (any) (x20), Sulfur (any), Mercury (any)

Flamethrower, Personal: This man-sized flame-throwing device is mounted on a five-foot-by-five-foot cart. It has a nozzle attached to a 10-foot-long hose. This hose allows the alchemist or any trained operator to stand adjacent to the projector and fire a 40-foot line or 20-foot cone of fire that does 2d6 points of damage and gives creatures and objects hit the burning condition. A DC 16 Reflex save halves the damage and prevents burning.

It takes a full round action to change from a line to a cone. The weapon cannot be fired during this time. When full, the flamethrower can be used four times. It takes a full round action to refill two uses. A refill weighs eight pounds and costs 160 gp.

Obviously, such a large volume of flammable liquid is very combustible. When taking any fire or electrical damage, it must make a Reflex save with a DC of 10 + points of damage taken; treat as if the object had a Reflex save of +5. If it fails this save, it explodes, doing 2d6 points of damage for every round of ammunition contained within to all targets within 20 feet. A DC 16 Reflex save allows a target to take half damage. It has a hardness of 6 and 25 hit points.

DC 35 Craft (alchemy); *Rarity:* Very Rare; *Price:* 1,000 gp; *Weight:* 200 lbs.; *Alchemical Formula:* Rare Earth (x10), Earth (any) (x10), Fire (any) (x10), Sulfur (any), Mercury (any)

Gloves, Alchemical: These gloves burst into elemental energy when triggered by the alchemist.

These gloves are protected by an internal lining. The wearer may activate these gloves as a standard action. Once activated, these gloves are covered in elemental energy for three rounds. This energy does an additional 1d6 points of damage on any melee attack, along with relevant secondary effects as noted below.

The wearer takes 1 point of elemental damage each round. Materials and effects are listed below. These gloves may be activated again after a minute passes.

Element	Essence	Effect
Acid	Acid	Ignores hardness
Cold	Cold	Reduces Break DC by 2
Electricity	Electricity	Deals 1 electrical damage to adjacent creatures
Fire	Fire (any 2 different fire essences)	Burns objects

DC 25 Craft (alchemy); *Rarity:* Rare; *Price:* 650 gp; *Weight:* 1 lb.; *Alchemical Formula:* Rare Earth (20), applicable essence (see **Table 3–2**)

Glow Globe: The light a *glow globe* casts is equivalent to a dim torch. It sheds normal light in a 15-foot radius and increases the light level by one step for an additional 15 feet beyond that area (darkness becomes dim light, and dim light becomes normal light). A glow globe does not increase the light level in normal light or bright light.

DC 10 Craft (alchemy); *Rarity:* Common; *Price:* 3 gp; *Weight:* 1 lb.; *Alchemical Formula:* Fire (any)

Glow Orb: This is similar to the *glow globe*, but substantively more useful. This sphere is adjustable between a dim glow all the way to a blinding flash, which causes a character to make a DC 16 Reflex save or be dazzled for 1d4 rounds. It also floats and supports up to 20 pounds. It sheds normal light in a 60-foot radius and increases the light level by one step for an additional 60 feet beyond that area (darkness becomes dim light, and dim light becomes normal light). It floats anywhere the user wishes within 10 feet. It is tiny (AC 12) with a hardness of 0 and 5 hit points.

DC 18 Craft (alchemy); *Rarity:* Rare; *Price:* 200 gp; *Weight:* 1 lb.; *Alchemical Formula:* Gold, Rare Earth, Air (any), Fire (any), Light

Heat Stone: When placed firmly on the ground and given a slight sprinkle of water, this small stone heats up. The area that heats up is the section painted with water. It boils water or heats food but does not catch flammables on fire or burn living creatures.

DC 15 Craft (alchemy); *Rarity:* Uncommon; *Price:* 300 gp; *Weight:* —; *Alchemical Formula:* Rare Earth, Ruby, Fire (any)

Helm of Lenses: A variety of lenses are attached to this helm. This allows the alchemist to receive a +1 or +2 alchemical bonus (character's choice) on Appraise, Perception, Disable Device, or relevant profession skills depending on vision. The user receives an equal penalty to attack rolls and other skills, and the character always act last in the round.

This helm also has a variety of slots where other normal and magical cusps and lenses can be inserted and used hands free.

It takes a full-round action to change a lens.

DC 30 Craft (alchemy); *Rarity:* Rare; *Price:* 500 gp; *Weight:* 3 lbs.; *Alchemical Formula:* Diamond, Rare Earth, Mercury (any), Perception, Prowess

Homing Rods: These two rods vibrate in harmony, allowing one to always locate the other. They can be set to either vibrate or ring as they get closer to each other.

DC 25 Craft (alchemy); *Rarity:* Uncommon; *Price:* 550 gp; *Weight:* 2 lbs. each; *Alchemical Formula:* Diamond, Iron, Rare Earth, Water (any 2 different water essences)

Hose, Personal Waterblast: This man-sized water sprayer sits on a five-foot-square cart. It has a nozzle attached to a 10-foot-long hose. This hose allows the alchemist or any trained operator to stand adjacent to the projector and fire a 40-foot line or 20-foot cone of water. Anyone in the way of the line takes 1d8 points of damage and must make a DC 16 Reflex save to avoid being knocked prone. If a target doesn't fall prone, everyone behind the character in the line takes only 1d4 points of damage and gets a +2 on their saving throw. The cone spray causes all creatures within 30 feet to move at half-speed, treating the terrain it covers as difficult, and anyone within 10 feet takes a point of damage and must make a DC 16 Reflex save to avoid being pushed back five feet.

It takes a full round action to change from a line to a cone. The weapon cannot be fired during this time. When full, this item can be used four times. It takes a full-round action to refill a use. A refill weighs 40 pounds and is free.

If the item takes any damage, it is disabled, being that it requires pressure (generated by steam) in order to fire. The materials used are too fragile to consider using any other substance in the *personal waterblast hose* other than water. It has a hardness of 8 and 25 hit points.

DC 35 Craft (alchemy); *Rarity:* Very Rare; *Price:* 1,000 gp; *Weight:* 200 lbs.; *Alchemical Formula:* Rare Earth, Fire (any 2 different fire essences), Sulfur (any) (x5), Water (any) (x10), Strength

Hose, Waterblast: This large immobile device can spray a powerful gout of water. It takes up 10 square feet. The device has a nozzle attached to a 10-foot-long hose. This hose allows the alchemist or any trained operator to stand adjacent to the projector and fire a 60-foot line or 30-foot cone of water. Anyone in the way of the line takes 2d6 points of damage and on a failed DC 16 Reflex save is knocked prone. If a target doesn't fall prone, everyone behind them in the line takes only 1d6 points of damage and gets a +2 on their saving throw. The cone spray causes all creatures within 30 feet to move at half-speed, treating the terrain it covers as difficult, and anyone within 10 feet takes a point of damage and must make a DC 16 Reflex Save to avoid being pushed back five feet.

It takes a full round action to change from a line to a cone. The weapon cannot be fired during this time. When full, this item can be used six times. It takes a full-round action to refill a use. A refill weighs 40 pounds and is free.

This 500-pound projector can be mounted on wheels for an additional 500 gp. This allows it to be pushed or pulled forward or backward. It may turn in place.

If the item takes any damage, it is disabled, being that it requires pressure (generated by steam) in order to fire. The interior may be acid coated for an additional 3,000 gp, but then each use takes 40 pounds of solvent. For the weakest solvent, that's a crafting cost of 400 gp. Solvent cannot be pressurized to the same degree as water, so the damage from the spray is halved (1d6 for the line) and a bonus of 4 is added to the save, though targets are covered in the solvent. The solvent damage is considered tripled, but still lasts for the same duration as the normal solvent. Also, the hose must be replaced after two uses and doing so takes a full minute.

For an additional 500 gp and 200 pounds of weight, you can build one that has eight rounds of ammunition. For an additional 1,000 gp and 500 pounds of weight you can build one that holds 10 rounds of ammunition. It has a hardness of 10 and 50 hit points.

DC 30 Craft (alchemy); *Rarity:* Rare; *Price:* 1,500 gp; *Weight:* 500 lbs.; *Alchemical Formula:* Rare Earth, Fire (any 3 different fire essences), Sulfur (any) (x10), Water (any) (x20), Strength

Ink, Cloud Chaser: When added to water, this ink spreads through the water like a darting fish toward the place where the water is closest to the sky.

DC 25 Craft (alchemy); *Rarity:* Very Rare; *Price:* 250 gp; *Weight:* —; *Alchemical Formula:* Pearl, Rare Earth, Water (any), Perception

Ink, Disappearing: This ink leaves a normal looking mark after it dries. One minute later, the ink disappears. The ink can be made to reappear with the application of Salt essence.

DC 20 Craft (alchemy); *Rarity:* Uncommon; *Price:* 50 gp; *Weight:* —; *Alchemical Formula:* Rare Earth, Mercury (any), Water (any)

Ink, Firelight: This ink leaves no mark after it dries. The marks reappear only when exposed to flame.

DC 22 Craft (alchemy); *Rarity:* Uncommon; *Price:* 30 gp; *Weight:* —; *Alchemical Formula:* Air (any), Mercury (any), Salt (any), Water (any)

Ink, Glowing: This ink glows a light green or orange when put to paper. It allows whatever is written to be read in the dark.

DC 20 Craft (alchemy); *Rarity:* Uncommon; *Price:* 50 gp; *Weight:* —; *Alchemical Formula:* Rare Earth, Light

Ink, Incendiary: This ink appears completely normal at first glance. However, once dusted with simple talc powder, the ink flares up and burns the sheet of paper and any attached papers to cinders.

DC 20 Craft (alchemy); *Rarity:* Rare; *Price:* 50 gp; *Weight:* —; *Alchemical Formula:* Rare Earth, Fire (any), Sulfur (any)

Ink, Magelight: This ink leaves no mark after it dries. The marks reappear only when exposed to magical light such as *continual flame* or a *light* spell.

DC 24 Craft (alchemy); *Rarity:* Rare; *Price:* 30 gp; *Weight:* —; *Alchemical Formula:* Rare Earth, Azoth (any), Fire (any)

Ink, Moonlight: This ink leaves no mark after it dries. The marks reappear only when exposed to moonlight.

DC 22 Craft (alchemy); *Rarity:* Rare; *Price:* 30 gp; *Weight:* —; *Alchemical Formula:* Moonstone, Azoth (any)

Ink, Underscript: This ink appears invisible when anyone attempts to write with it. However, it is highly visible to anyone who has darkvision.

DC 20 Craft (alchemy); *Rarity:* Uncommon; *Price:* 75 gp; *Weight:* —; *Alchemical Formula:* Rare Earth, Mercury (any), Water (any), Stealth

Ink, Waterproof: This ink is waterproof and will not run if exposed to water.

DC 15 Craft (alchemy); *Rarity:* Uncommon; *Price:* 25 gp; *Weight:* —; *Alchemical Formula:* Earth (any), Mercury (any), Salt (any), Water (any)

Lantern, Solar: This lantern requires no fuel source except the sun. Exposure to eight hours of sunlight allows it to cast light for a 12-hour period. The core must be replaced monthly at the cost of 10 gp, but otherwise it requires no fuel to function beyond exposure to the sun.

DC 25 Craft (alchemy); *Rarity:* Rare; *Price:* 250 gp; *Weight:* 2 lbs.; *Alchemical Formula:* Gold, Rare Earth, Fire (any), Light

Lockrender: This is an explosive shaped charge used to bypass doors. When set against a lock and lit, it burns for 1d4 + 1 rounds before igniting. At the end of this time, it creates a blast that blows out the lock.

The door and lock both take 4d6 points of damage, ignoring 10 points of hardness, and a check to break the door is made with a +10 bonus

Those standing within 10 feet of the blast must make a DC 12 Fortitude save to avoid taking 2d6 points of fire damage and being knocked prone.

DC 25 Craft (alchemy); *Rarity:* Uncommon; *Price:* 250 gp; *Weight:* 2 lbs.; *Alchemical Formula:* Iron, Rare Earth, Fire (any), Strength

Marbles, Detonating: These marbles may be used in different ways. They may be thrown, doing 1d4 points of fire damage on a hit, and 1 point of damage to everyone within five feet. Or they may be used like normal marbles. A creature entering a square with marbles scattered on it must succeed at a DC 10 Reflex save or fall prone (the creature's stability bonus to trip applies to this save). The marbles then all detonate, doing 1d6 points of fire damage to the first target to fall prone where they were. In either case, they continue to burn and smolder for one full minute, causing that five-foot area to be difficult terrain and illuminating the area within 10 feet brightly and double that distance dimly.

DC 25 Craft (alchemy); *Rarity:* Rare; *Price:* 30 gp; *Weight:* 2 lbs.; *Alchemical Formula:* Earth (any), Fire (any), Sulfur (any), Transmutation

Mask, Gas: This *gas mask* provides protection from inhaled toxins. All saves versus gas attacks, noxious fumes, or stenches are made with a +5 alchemical bonus. This mask functions while worn for 24 hours before needing to be replaced.

DC 25 Craft (alchemy); *Rarity:* Uncommon; *Price:* 100 gp; *Weight:* 8 lbs.; *Alchemical Formula:* Air (any 2 different Air essences), Earth (any), Water (any), Protection

Mask, Superior Gas: This mask is lighter and more effective than a standard *gas mask*, but provides the same +5 alchemical bonus at a lighter weight. It also allows the wearer to breathe underwater for two minutes. This mask functions while worn for 24 hours before needing to be replaced. Each minute used of water breathing reduces this length by eight hours.

DC 30 Craft (alchemy); *Rarity:* Rare; *Price:* 125 gp; *Weight:* 3 lbs.; *Alchemical Formula:* Air (any 3 different Air essences), Earth (any), Water (any 2 different Water essences), Protection

Oil, Long-Burning: When added to a torch or lamp, this oil fuels the burning reaction and causes it to burn for a greatly extended duration.
One dose can cause a campfire to burn for 24 hours, six torches to burn for 12 hours each, or it can keep an oil lamp burning for 72 hours.
It is not at all volatile and does not explode (and is even harder to light). It does not affect magical flames and has no effect on fires larger than a campfire.

DC 15 Craft (alchemy); *Rarity:* Uncommon; *Price:* 50 gp; *Weight:* 1 lb.;
Alchemical Formula: Rare Earth, Fire (any), Salt (any), Water (any), Light

Oil, Quick-Freeze: This bottle of viscous blue oil sublimates slightly when exposed to air. When poured over water, the oil pools on the surface and takes one round to spread out from the point of origin in a 20-foot radius. At the end of this round, the oil flash-freezes the surface of the water, creating an ice sheet over the affected area. Any five-foot square of this ice can support up to 200 pounds of weight. Weight in excess of this amount causes the entire sheet to crack and quickly break up. This ice sheet becomes unstable and breaks up on its own after one hour, or after 20 minutes in a hot climate. Any creature whose bare skin comes in contact with this oil takes 1d6 points of nonlethal damage each round because of the chemical's volatile nature, but the oil is ineffective as a splash weapon.

DC 25 Craft (alchemy); *Rarity:* Rare; *Price:* 50 gp; *Weight:* 1 lb.; *Alchemical Formula:* Rare Earth, Salt (any), Water (any), Cold

Oil, Shadow: When burned in a lantern, this works like normal oil in all ways such as burning time, but instead of producing a bright yellow light, it produces a dim, blue-green light.

DC 25 Craft (alchemy); *Rarity:* Uncommon; *Price:* 25 gp; *Weight:* 1 lb.;
Alchemical Formula: Earth (any), Fire (any), Water (any), Stealth

Oil, Stink: This glass container of foul-smelling oil shatters easily upon impact. You can throw a vial of *stink oil* as a splash weapon with a range increment of 10 feet. If a creature with the scent ability is standing in the square of impact, it must succeed at a DC 14 Fortitude save or be nauseated for 1d4 + 1 rounds. Any creature with scent in an adjacent square must succeed at a DC 12 Fortitude save or be sickened for one round. Creatures without the scent ability are not affected by *stink oil.*

DC 20 Craft (alchemy); *Rarity:* Uncommon; *Price:* 15 gp; *Weight:* 1 lb.;
Alchemical Formula: Rare Earth, Salt (any), Water (any), Decay

Oil, Thieves': When burned in a lantern, this works like normal oil in all ways such as burning time, but the light produced is visible only to the wielder.

DC 25 Craft (alchemy); *Rarity:* Very Rare; *Price:* 55 gp; *Weight:* 1 lb.; *Alchemical Formula:* Rare Earth, Azoth (any), Salt (any), Water (any), Stealth

Paper, Acidproof: This paper is acidproof. When exposed momentarily to mild acid, the pages are not ruined. When submerged in acid, it receives a +10 bonus to hardness vs. acid. The price is for a single sheet.

DC 15 Craft (alchemy); *Rarity:* Uncommon; *Price:* 12 gp; *Weight:* —; *Alchemical Formula:* Earth (any), Salt (any), Acid

Paper, Fireproof: This paper is fireproof. When exposed momentarily to fire and smoke, the pages are not ruined. When exposed to open heat and flame, it receives a +15 bonus to hardness vs. fire. The price is for a single sheet.

DC 15 Craft (alchemy); *Rarity:* Uncommon; *Price:* 10 gp; *Weight:* —; *Alchemical Formula:* Earth (any), Fire (any), Salt (any), Protection

Paper, Waterproof: This paper is waterproof. When exposed momentarily to rain, water splashes, ice, or snow, the ink will not run, and the pages are not ruined. When submerged in water, it repels the water for up to one minute. The price above is for a single sheet.

DC 15 Craft (alchemy); *Rarity:* Uncommon; *Price:* 8 gp; *Weight:* —; *Alchemical Formula:* Earth (any), Water (any), Salt (any), Protection

Applications of multiple proofing treatments are possible. Simply take the most expensive treatment and double the quantity for two applications, triple it for three, etc. These same treatments may also be applied to scroll cases made of leather.

Pox Burster: A *pox burster* is an alchemically preserved animal bladder or gourd filled with toxic, rotting materials. You can throw a *pox burster* as a splash weapon. Treat this attack as a ranged touch attack with a range increment of 10 feet. A direct hit forces a target to immediately make a DC 13 Fortitude save or contract filth fever. Every space adjacent to the target square of the *pox burster* is covered in disease-causing filth. For the next minute, any creature that is injured while in one of these spaces must also make a DC 9 Fortitude save or contract filth fever.

DC 20 Craft (alchemy); *Rarity:* Rare; *Price:* 50 gp; *Weight:* 1 lb.; *Alchemical Formula:* Salt (any), Decay, Disease, Toxin

Ring, Poison Needle: Any nonmagical ring and any poison may be used. The poison is not what is being created here and the ring, once crafted, is empty: It is the price and the difficulty involved in adding the needle mechanism that is reflected in the crafting price. Loading poison into the ring takes an action. Loading the poison into the ring takes the same time as normal.
Twisting the stone as a free action exudes a needle with one dose of poison. The needle may spring from the inside, outside, or both. The alchemist must succeed with an unarmed attack to poison the target.

DC 25 Craft (alchemy); *Rarity:* Uncommon; *Price:* 150 gp; *Weight:* —;
Alchemical Formula: Not applicable

Ring, Rogue's: This slightly oversized ring conceals a few lockpicks and other tools coiled inside its band. These discreet tools — made of a metal alloy that springs straight once the tool is removed from the band — are sufficient to attempt Disable Device checks without penalty and long enough to pick locks on manacles fastened around the wearer's hands (once he or she slips off the ring). The wearer gains a +2 circumstance bonus on Sleight of Hand checks made to conceal the ring's nature from anyone searching the character.

DC 20 Craft (alchemy); *Rarity:* Uncommon; *Price:* 300 gp; *Weight:* —;
Alchemical Formula: Rare Earth, Platinum, Earth (any), Stealth

Ring, Secret Compartment: Any nonmagical ring may be used or created. The price and difficulty to add the compartment are listed in **Table 3–1**.
This ring can store one dose of any potion, elixir, philter, liquid, tonic, tincture, dust, powder, or any other substance the GM deems feasible. It keeps it fresh and protected from harm for seven days. The compartment is waterproof.

DC 20 Craft (alchemy); *Rarity:* Uncommon; *Price:* 10 gp; *Weight:* —; *Alchemical Formula:* Not applicable

Robe, Alchemical: This robe is especially designed to hold up to 10 alchemical items weighing one pound or less in protected pockets. These items receive a +1 circumstance bonus on any saving throws they must make versus destruction if the robe is destroyed. Any item contained in the robe can be retrieved as a swift action.
The robe also has several harnesses to hold larger objects. It allows the alchemist to carry items as if her strength was one higher.

DC 20 Craft (alchemy); *Rarity:* Uncommon; *Price:* 65 gp; *Weight:* 4 lbs.;
Alchemical Formula: Protection, Strength

Rope, Cave Fisher Reel: This needle-thin, strong transparent rope supports 1,000 pounds. When paired with gloves and boots coated in a mixture of alchemical glue and solvent, *cave fisher reel rope* provides a +20 alchemical bonus to Climb checks.

DC 22 Craft (alchemy); *Rarity:* Very Rare; *Price:* 250 gp; *Weight:* —; *Alchemical Formula:* Rare Earth, Earth (any), Transmutation

Rope, Liquid: This liquid is in a squeezable pouch, most often a waterskin. When uncapped and squeezed out, it produces a length of green paste that firms up into a rope-like substance in one round. The tube can produce up to 500 feet of rope.
The rope lasts for 24 minutes when exposed to air before it begins to flake and fall apart into dust.

DC 25 Craft (alchemy); *Rarity:* Uncommon; *Price:* 75 gp; *Weight:* 5 lbs.;
Alchemical Formula: Rare Earth, Mercury (any), Water (any), Transmutation

Rope, Stoneweave: The dwarves make this rope with discarded metals. This rope has fine craftsmanship and has 12 hit points. It can be burst with a DC 30 Strength check.

DC 25 Craft (alchemy); *Rarity:* Rare; *Price:* 12 gp; *Weight:* 7 lbs.; *Alchemical Formula:* Iron, Earth (any), Strength

Rope, Terrafugia: This rope appears normal while coiled. However, once an end is freed, it falls upward. The rope always falls away from the earth. If unraveled out of doors, the rope falls away into the sky, though the slightest weight or pressure holds it down. This is primarily useful for underground exploration and travel.

DC 28 Craft (alchemy); *Rarity:* Very Rare; *Price:* 200 gp; *Weight:* 5 lbs.; *Alchemical Formula:* Rare Earth, Air (any), Flight

Rope Ladder, Flittermouse: This is a rope sculpture knotted in the form of a bat. When tossed in the air, it flies unerringly to any target within 60 feet and attempts to attach itself. It can attach to stone, rock, or hook to ledges or other surfaces easily. Once attached, a 60-foot rope ladder unfurls and falls down. It takes one minute to reknot the *flittermouse rope ladder* for use.

DC 25 Craft (alchemy); *Rarity:* Rare; *Price:* 175 gp; *Weight:* 15 lbs.; *Alchemical Formula:* Rare Earth, Air (any), Azoth (any), Prowess

Shard, Various: These useful items can be used for various purposes when immersed in water. Upon immersion, you may choose to boil the water, chill the water, or flavor it as stock. A *various shard* is useful for about 30 days before its potency starts to fade.

DC 15 Craft (alchemy); *Rarity:* Uncommon; *Price:* 45 gp; *Weight:* —; *Alchemical Formula:* Diamond, Earth (any), Fire (any), Water (any)

Shield, Alchemical: This modification to a masterwork shield allows the shield to store an alchemical grenade. When the shield is struck by a melee attack, the attacker and anyone within five feet of the outside of the shield is affected as if struck by the grenade (i.e., not the wielder, but the target and anyone to either side of the target). The shield is struck when the die roll indicates a hit on the shield (i.e., would hit the target, but does not due to the shield bonus) or if the wielder of the shield makes an CMB roll that beats his opponent's CMD for the round. The alchemical grenade must be purchased separately and is not contained in the cost.

DC 25 Craft (alchemy); *Rarity:* Uncommon; *Price:* +500 gp; *Weight:* +5 lbs.; *Alchemical Formula:* Not applicable

Shield, Hypnosis: This modification to a masterwork shield allows the shield to hypnotize opponents. As an action, the shield bearer can activate the shield, turning the black-and-white spiral on the front. All who view the shield that fail a DC 16 Will save gain the fascinated condition as they are captivated by the shield. Any attack against the targets, obvious danger presented to the targets, or a successful attack against or by the shield-holder snaps them out of their reverie.

DC 25 Craft (alchemy); *Rarity:* Very Rare; *Price:* +800 gp; *Weight:* +1 lb.; *Alchemical Formula:* Rare Earth, Control, Mind

Smokestick (5): This alchemically treated wooden stick instantly creates thick, opaque smoke when burned. The smoke fills a 10-foot cube (treat the effect as a *fog cloud* spell, except that a moderate or stronger wind dissipates the smoke in one round). The stick is consumed after one round, and the smoke dissipates naturally after one minute. See **Chapter One: Alchemy Basics** for alternate dispersion rates of smoke.

DC 20 Craft (alchemy); *Rarity:* Common; *Price:* 100 gp; *Weight:* —; *Alchemical Formula:* Rare Earth, Fire (any), Salt (any)

Smokestick, Noxious: This alchemically treated wooden stick instantly creates thick, opaque smoke when burned. The smoke fills a 10-foot cube (treat the effect as a *fog cloud* spell, except that a moderate or stronger wind dissipates the smoke in one round). The stick is consumed after one round, and the smoke dissipates naturally after one minute. Anyone exposed to this smoke must make a DC 14 Fortitude save or gain the nauseated condition. See **Chapter One: Alchemy Basics** for alternate dispersion rates of smoke.

DC 25 Craft (alchemy); *Rarity:* Uncommon; *Price:* 80 gp; *Weight:* —; *Alchemical Formula:* Rare Earth, Fire (any), Salt (any), Toxin

Sparkthrower, Large: This 10-foot-by-10-foot immobile device can throw bolts of electricity. It has a nozzle attached to a rubber-coated copper wire that is 10 feet long. This allows the alchemist or any trained operator to stand adjacent to the projector and fire a 60-foot line of electricity that does 4d6 points of damage to all targets in the line. A creature that makes a DC 16 Reflex save takes half damage. This weapon has no limit on the number of uses; however, it must be charged. It is charged manually by working the cycler and the pump. With a crew of three, the weapon can be charged and fired every other round. With a crew of two, the weapon can be fired and charged every third round. A single operator can charge and fire the weapon every fourth round. A charge is held for a single minute. This 500-pound projector can be mounted on wheels for an additional 500 gp. This allows it to be pushed or pulled forward or backward. It may turn in place.

After being damaged, the user and anyone adjacent must make a DC 16 Reflex save each round or be shocked for 1d6 points of damage. It no longer functions when broken. It has a hardness of 8 and 25 hit points.

DC 30 Craft (alchemy); *Rarity:* Rare; *Price:* 1,500 gp; *Weight:* 500 lbs.; *Alchemical Formula:* Rare Earth, Air (any) (x20), Earth (any) (x20), Sulfur (any) (x20), Electricity (any) (x2)

Sparkthrower, Personal: This man-sized immobile device mounted on a five-foot-by-five-foot cart can throw bolts of electricity. It has a nozzle attached to a rubber-coated copper wire that is 10 feet long. This allows the alchemist or any trained operator to stand adjacent to the projector and fire a 60-foot line of electricity that does 2d6 points of damage to all targets in the line. A creature that makes a DC 16 Reflex save takes half damage. This weapon has no limit on the number of uses; however, it must be charged. It is charged manually by working the cycler and the pump. With a crew of two, the weapon can be charged and fired every other round. A single operator can charge and fire the weapon every third round. A charge is held for a single minute. After being damaged, the user and anyone adjacent must make a DC 16 Reflex save each round or be shocked for 1d6 points of damage. It no longer functions when broken. It has a hardness of 6 and 15 hit points.

DC 35 Craft (alchemy); *Rarity:* Rare; *Price:* 1,000 gp; *Weight:* 200 lbs.; *Alchemical Formula:* Rare Earth, Air (any) (x10), Earth (any) (x10), Sulfur (any) (x10), Electricity (any)

Spike, Locking: These spikes are quite useful. They are enchanted so that when they spike a door closed, the door is affected by the spell *arcane lock*. Each spike can be used only once, and its enchantment vanishes after it is used to magically hold a door closed. The effect ends if the spike is removed but persists otherwise without end.

DC 25 Craft (alchemy); *Rarity:* Rare; *Price:* 800 gp; *Weight:* —; *Alchemical Formula:* Iron, Azoth (any), Stasis

Spike, Self-Driving: These spikes require no hammer to drive themselves in. They are placed in the appropriate position and triggered. One round later, a bright flame shoots out the back and the spike drives itself into the ground, drilling as it goes. This is somewhat quiet, producing little sound, but it does create a very bright light. These spikes can be used as a dagger to attack. They do 1d3 points of damage on a hit, and the next round the spike begins to drill into an opponent, doing 1d4 damage from drilling and 1d6 damage from flame. The target also must make a DC 12 Will save or be dazzled by the bright light for one round, having a –1 on attack rolls. It must be activated after being stuck into an opponent. Activating it after hitting an opponent with it requires a successful CMB attack versus the target's CMD. The target may remove a self-driving spike with a move action. A five-pound package of 10 is made for the price.

DC 25 Craft (alchemy); *Rarity:* Rare; *Price:* 150 gp; *Weight:* —; *Alchemical Formula:* Gold, Iron, Fire (any 2 different Fire Essences), Strength

Spike, Silent: An alchemist can create specially treated spikes. When used, climbed on, hammered into a surface, or interacted with in any way, they produce no sound. They also completely absorb any sound made from them being driven into a surface. A five-pound package of 10 is made for the price.

DC 22 Craft (alchemy); *Rarity:* Uncommon; *Price:* 80 gp; *Weight:* —; *Alchemical Formula:* Iron, Stealth

Spray Bellows, Alchemical: This device consists of one watertight central ammunition bladder and several air bladders linked by specialized nozzles. When the wielder compresses the air bladders (a standard action that doesn't provoke attacks of opportunity), the *alchemical spray bellows* sprays its ammunition in a 10-foot cone. Most adventurers use an *alchemical spray bellows* to spray powder over invisible foes or holy water over incorporeal undead, but it can also spray oil, *itching powder*, *sneezing powder*, or other mundane dusts and liquids.

Loading the ammunition bladder is a full-round action that provokes attacks of opportunity and requires either a four-pint jug of liquid (weighing up to four pounds) or a four-pound sack of powder; insufficient ammunition causes it to misfire harmlessly. Refilling the air bladders is a move action that doesn't provoke attacks of opportunity. Readying and firing an *alchemical spray bellows* requires two hands.

If an *alchemical spray bellows* fires ordinary powder or oil, each square in the cone is coated in that substance. If an *alchemical spray bellows* fires holy water, *itching powder*, or *sneezing powder*, treat each square in the cone as a square of impact and each square adjacent to the cone (including the wielder's) as an adjacent square for the purpose of determining effects and DCs. Loading an *alchemical spray bellows* with unstable compounds such as acid or *alchemist's fire* destroys the device.

DC 22 Craft (alchemy); *Rarity:* Uncommon; *Price:* 80 gp; *Weight:* 6 lbs. (empty); *Alchemical Formula:* Not applicable

Sunrod (40): This one-foot-long, gold-tipped iron rod glows brightly when struck (a standard action). It sheds normal light in a 30-foot radius and increases the light level by one step for an additional 30 feet beyond that area (darkness becomes dim light, and dim light becomes normal light). A *sunrod* does not increase the light level in normal light or bright light. It glows for six hours, after which the gold tip burns out and is worthless.

DC 25 Craft (alchemy); *Rarity:* Common; *Price:* 80 gp; *Weight:* 40 lb.; *Alchemical Formula:* Gold, Rare Earth, Light

Swiftlight: This is a fast-lighting torch that sheds light for 20 minutes. It can be lit as a free action when drawn, one time only.

DC 20 Craft (alchemy); *Rarity:* Uncommon; *Price:* 15 gp; *Weight:* 2 lbs.; *Alchemical Formula:* Fire (any), Speed

Tanglewire: This makes 10 feet of *tanglewire*. It takes one minute to string up as a barrier, but it can be put across a five-foot doorway in one round. If anyone traverses the area, they take 1d4 – 1 points of slashing damage.

Once damaged by the *tanglewire*, movement is inhibited. They must remain immobile or take 1d4 – 1 points of slashing damage when they move. A successful DC 20 Escape Artist or DC 15 Strength check allows you to escape. If you have a blade or slashing weapon, you can cut yourself free with a full-round action. It is not necessary to free yourself if you are willing to take the damage when you act.

DC 20 Craft (alchemy); *Rarity:* Uncommon; *Price:* 25 gp; *Weight:* 5 lbs.; *Alchemical Formula:* Iron, Rare Earth

Thermotic Container: This metal container maintains the temperature of liquids added to the bottle.

DC 15 Craft (alchemy); *Rarity:* Uncommon; *Price:* 80 gp; *Weight:* —; *Alchemical Formula:* Rare Earth, Earth (any), Fire (any), Water (any), Stasis

Tindertwig (10): The alchemical substance on the end of this small, wooden stick ignites when struck against a rough surface (a move action). Creating a flame with a *tindertwig* is much faster than creating a flame with tinder and a flint and steel or magnifying glass. Lighting a torch with a *tindertwig* is a standard action rather than a full-round action, and lighting any other fire with one is at least a standard action. A *tindertwig* burns for 1d2 rounds and sheds light as a candle. *Tindertwigs* are waterproof but must be dried before you can strike them.

DC 15 Craft (alchemy); *Rarity:* Uncommon; *Price:* 10 gp; *Weight:* —; *Alchemical Formula:* Rare Earth, Fire (any)

Towel, Alchemical: This amazing towel is comfortable and serves as a normal towel, except it has amazing absorbent properties. It can hold up to 60 times its weight in water and liquids. This means it can absorb approximately three cubic feet of water or more than 22 gallons. It's easily washable, won't scratch any surface, and you'll say wow every time you use it!

DC 18 Craft (alchemy); *Rarity:* Uncommon; *Price:* 15 gp; *Weight:* 3 lbs.; *Alchemical Formula:* Air (any), Water (any), Transmutation

Trapblaster: These two jagged, two-foot-long poles are attached to powerful springs. When thrown into a 10-foot square, they begin bouncing and ricocheting against any surface. Anyone in the square must make a DC 16 Reflex save or take 2d6 points of bludgeoning damage. It cuts any tripwires, damages trap mechanisms, and hits surfaces with 150 pounds of pressure. Using these generally results in their destruction.

If this is used in a room instead of a corridor, the *trapblaster* walks to a nearby square at the end of every round. Roll 1d10 on the grenade scatter table; a 9–10 means it stays in the same square. It traverses nine squares (45 feet) before breaking. If it moves into a wall, move it five feet in the opposite direction. It has a hardness of 4 and 15 hit points. It is very mobile and has an armor class of 15. Rewinding the *trapblaster* takes a full round action.

DC 25 Craft (alchemy); *Rarity:* Rare; *Price:* 150 gp; *Weight:* 3 lbs.; *Cost:* 50 gp; *Alchemical Formula:* Iron, Flight

Trapspringer: These rubberized globes can be thrown at surfaces. They come in a variety of weights. Each pound of the *trapspringer* trigger traps as a 25-pound object plus the strength of the thrower squared.

If a 16 strength human throws a one-pound *trapspringer*, it impacts the trap as if 281 pounds (25 + 256) had triggered it. That same person throwing a five-pound *trapspringer* would impact an area as a 381-pound (125 + 256) man. If thrown at a target, they do 1 damage, plus 1 additional for every 50 pounds of force. A 16 strength human throwing a one-pound *trapspringer* would do 6 damage. This is not a thrown weapon, so it takes a –4 penalty to the attack, and due to the way it functions, strength bonuses don't apply. *Trapspringers* weighing five pounds or more are considered two-handed weapons for the purposes of throwing.

DC 20 Craft (alchemy); *Rarity:* Uncommon; *Price:* 100 gp per lb.; *Weight:* 1–10 lbs.; *Alchemical Formula:* Rare Earth, Strength

Vacuum Rod: This rod has the ability to produce a powerful vacuum. When triggered, the wielder gains DR 5/— against all missile attacks. Everyone in a 30-foot cone in front of the user, friend and foe alike, moves at half speed and has a –2 circumstance penalty to attacks. Objects less than a pound are sucked up and into the rod where they are vaporized. The wielder may forgo these benefits and attempt to make an attack with the rod, doing 1d8 points of force damage versus an unarmored target. The attack does not affect targets with an armor bonus. After every round of use, there is a non-cumulative 1% chance that the rod ceases functioning and is broken and worthless; this chance increases by 5% in a round that the rod was used to strike someone.

DC 25 Craft (alchemy); *Rarity:* Rare; *Price:* 500 gp; *Weight:* 3 lbs.; *Alchemical Formula:* Rare Earth, Azoth (any) (x2), Salt (any), Sulfur (any), Transportation

Wall, Portable: This is a large brick weighing 40 pounds and taking up two cubic feet of space (12 inches by 18 inches by 16 inches). When set on the ground and activated as a full-round action, it turns into a barrier two feet thick, 10 feet wide, and four feet high. Standing behind this barrier provides partial cover, while ducking behind it provides full cover. The barrier is solid and treated as stone for hardness and hit points. It takes one minute to restore the wall back down to its portable form.

DC 25 Craft (alchemy); *Rarity:* Rare; *Price:* 400 gp; *Weight:* 40 lbs.; *Alchemical Formula:* Rare Earth, Earth (any 2 different Earth essences), Strength, Transmutation

Water Purification Sponge: This fist-sized blue sponge absorbs up to one pint of water; squeezing the water out of the sponge filters and purifies it, making it safe for drinking, washing, and similar activities. Filling and emptying the sponge is a full-round action. The filtration is enough to remove mundane impurities and common diseases, but does nothing to protect against poisons, magic, and other exotic threats. Each sponge can cleanse 25 pints of water before deteriorating and becoming useless.

DC 15 Craft (alchemy); *Rarity:* Uncommon; *Price:* 25 gp; *Weight:* 1 lb.; *Alchemical Formula:* Rare Earth, Water (any), Purity

Weather Rune: By reading the color changes in this stone, the alchemist is able to predict the weather with 90% accuracy. Note that no roll must be made to determine the current weather.

DC 15 Craft (alchemy); *Rarity:* Uncommon; *Price:* 20 gp; *Weight:* —; *Alchemical Formula:* Air (any), Earth (any), Salt (any), Water (any)

GRENADES, PELLETS, AND STONES

These are thrown weapons that often cause splash damage to nearby targets. Because they are alchemical items, a character's Strength bonus never affects the damage. Grenades, pellets, and stones may cause a splash effect. If they do, it will be noted in their description. Splash effects affect every target within five feet of the primary target. If the primary target is large or larger, calculate adjacent targets from the impact point. You may choose to target a surface at a particular grid intersection; hit AC 5 and all targets within five feet take the splash effect. If targeting a surface, no target takes direct damage.

Thrown grenades, pellets, and stones do not need a weapon proficiency and use Dexterity to modify their chance to hit. If attempting to throw an oversized volume of material, the attack has a –4 penalty to attack and takes a full-round action to throw. You cannot throw an object your size or larger. Oversized volumes include any item weighing more than one pound. Grenades, pellets, and stones cannot deal precision-based damage.

Selecting and drawing a grenade, pellet, or stone to throw is identical to drawing a weapon. It is a move action or can be drawn as part of a move action.

Grenades are specially scored to break on impact; any use of the grenade activates it. It cannot be recovered after battle, as it is used up. Remember that on any failed saving throw of a 1 by the character against a sonic attack, fire, or other area damage, the grenades themselves may be destroyed. They take damage from the attack. Most grenades are in glass or clay vials, with a hardness of 1 and 3 hit points. If exposed in a bandolier or carried on a belt, they are considered of a similar priority of a stowed or sheathed weapon; if carried in a pack or backpack, they are considered to be a similar priority of anything else, affected last. (See the Items Affected by Magical Attacks table in Chapter 9 of the *Pathfinder Roleplaying Game*.)

If you miss the target, roll a 1d8 for the direction of the miss. A 1 indicates that the throw is short, read the other numbers clockwise around a cardinal grid (i.e., 3 is to the thrower's left of the target, a 5 is a long throw, etc.). It lands five feet away in that direction for every range increment thrown.

Grenades and thrown weapons have a range increment of 10 feet. Stones have a range increment of 20 feet. Pellets have a range increment of five feet. You are considered armed when making attacks with these weapons. Every range increment beyond the first provides a –2 penalty to hit. A weapon can be thrown a maximum of five range increments.

You may fire a grenade from a sling to gain the range increment of the sling, but it does not fly well, receiving a –8 to hit.

Any item marked as a grenade can be converted into a mine that detonates if approached within five feet. A mine is placed as a full-round action on a grid intersection. Anyone within five feet is affected by direct damage. Anyone between five feet and 10 feet is affected by splash damage. It adds 300 gp to the crafting cost. You can avoid setting it off with a successful DC 20 Stealth check, and it can be disabled with a successful DC 25 Disable Device skill check. On a failure of more than 5, the mine is triggered.

Any item marked as a grenade can be converted into a gas, which persists and applies the grenade effect to all those within range of the grenade. This process is difficult and dangerous. On a failure by 5 or more during its creation, the alchemist is affected by a double strength version of the grenade instead of rolling on **Table A–1: Alchemical Mishaps** in **Appendix A**. Converting grenades into gases costs an additional 1,000 gp. This creates a gas cloud with a radius of 30 feet that is 10 feet high. The cloud persists for 30 rounds or until it is dispersed; this varies based on the local ventilation level (q.v. Gas Clouds). Anyone within the cloud receives the effect of the grenade each round while within the cloud. Grenades that are already gases cannot be modified in this way. Creating gaseous grenades increases the Craft (alchemy) check by 10.

TABLE 3–3: GRENADES, PELLETS, AND STONES

Name	Craft (alchemy) DC	Price	Weight
Aboleth Gel	25	400 gp	1 lb.
Alchemist's Alarm	25	200 gp	1 lb.
Alchemist's Barricade	25	180 gp	1 lb.
Alchemist's Befuddlement	26	200 gp	1 lb.
Alchemist's Censorship	25	200 gp	1 lb.
Alchemist's Fire	20	20 gp	1 lb.
Alchemist's Firewater	20	25 gp	1 lb.
Alchemist's Fist	25	50 gp	1 lb.
Alchemist's Inferno	25	600 gp	1 lb.
Alchemist's Knife	25	40 gp	1 lb.
Alchemist's Mortar	30	80 gp	1 lb.
Alchemist's Stupor	25	100 gp	1 lb.
Alchemist's Sunburst	20	250 gp	1 lb.
Alchemist's Surprise	25	150 gp	1 lb.
Alchemist's Terror	25	150 gp	1 lb.
Armor Stripper	25	200 gp	0.05 lb.
Black-Light	26	300 gp	1 lb.
Blanch Bomb (Adamantine)	30	250 gp	0.5 lb.
Blanch Bomb (Cold Iron)	25	150 gp	0.5 lb.
Blanch Bomb (Silver)	25	100 gp	0.5 lb.
Blessed Sphere	25	200 gp	1 lb.
Blister Broth	25	50 gp	1 lb.
Bottled Lightning	25	40 gp	1 lb.
Chronobreak	35	600 gp	1 lb.
Demi-Bomb	32	500 gp	1 lb.
Dye Bomb	21	25 gp	1 lb.
Earth Sphere	24	150 gp	1 lb.
Fireburst Pellet	20	10 gp	1 lb.
Fire Interruption Gas	25	25 gp	1 lb.
Firestone (5)	25	100 gp	5 lbs.
Firewater	20	25 gp	1 lb.

Name	Craft (alchemy) DC	Price	Weight
Flame Globe	30	500 gp	1 lb.
Flaming Morass	30	500 gp	1 lb.
Flash Pellet	25	50 gp	1 lb.
Frost Sap	25	40 gp	1 lb.
Frozen Fire	26	75 gp	1 lb.
Frozen Prison	26	500 gp	1 lb.
Glow Glue	20	35 gp	1 lb.
Gravity Globe	30	500 gp	1 lb.
Knockout Globe	28	200 gp	1 lb.
Lethargy Globe	30	1,000 gp	1 lb.
Levitation Grenade	35	200 gp	1 lb.
Liquid Ice	25	40 gp	1 lb.
Long-Burning Oil	15	50 gp	1 lb.
Mephitic Smoke	35	150 gp	1 lb.
Misery Vial	25	450 gp	1 lb.
Mitelight	25	80 gp	1 lb.
Nightblinder	25	100 gp	1 lb.
Noisemaker	20	20 gp	1 lb.
Puppet Blood	30	150 gp	1 lb.
Putrid Sphere	28	600 gp	1 lb.
Pyrotechnic Dazzler	25	50 gp	1 lb.
Sabotage Pulse	28	600 gp	1 lb.
Shadow Shell	28	200 gp	1 lb.
Shrieking Betty	20	30 gp	1 lb.
Sleepsmoke	25	50 gp	1 lb.
Slickshell	20	10 gp	1 lb.
Slime Bane	25	15 gp	1 lb.
Smoke Pellet	20	25 gp	1 lb.
Snarlweave	25	200 gp	1 lb.
Spore Stone	25	50 gp	1 lb.
Sticky Mist	28	400 gp	1 lb.
Stink Bomb	23	50 gp	1 lb.
Stun Gas	25	600 gp	1 lb.
Tanglefoot Bag	25	50 gp	1 lb.
Tanglefoot Bag, Acidic	28	200 gp	4 lbs.
Teleportation Grenade	35	500 gp	1 lb.
Thunder Globe	30	100 gp	1 lb.
Thunderstone (5)	25	150 gp	5 lb.
Void Bomb	35	1,000 gp	1 lb.
Voltaic Orb	32	600 gp	1 lb.
Wind Sphere	24	200 gp	1 lb.

Aboleth Gel: This grenade is made from the corpse of an aboleth and the eldritch gel it produces to allow its slaves to breathe water. One grenade can be produced per two hit dice of the aboleth used.

The gel affects just the target hit with no splash effect. The target must succeed on a DC 20 Fortitude save or lose the ability to breathe air for six minutes while gaining the ability to breathe water for these same six minutes. Breathing water in this way is not easy; while trying to breathe water this way, they are staggered. On a successful save, they do not lose the ability to breathe air.

DC 25 Craft (alchemy); *Type:* Grenade; *Rarity:* Rare; *Price:* 400 gp; *Weight:* 1 lb.; *Alchemical Formula:* An Aboleth, Agate, Rare Earth, Transmutation

Alchemist's Alarm: When this globe is shattered, all creatures sleeping within 60 feet are silently and immediately awakened from sleep. They are temporarily cleansed of any fatigue or exhaustion for one minute. This grenade has no effect on creatures that are awake.

DC 25 Craft (alchemy); *Type:* Grenade; *Rarity:* Rare; *Price:* 200 gp; *Weight:* 1 lb.; *Alchemical Formula:* Azoth, Mercury, Rare Earth (x5), Sulfur (any)

Alchemist's Barricade: When thrown, this green gel hardens into jagged spikes and creates a partial barricade about four feet high. It takes up one five-foot square. It is possible to move through the spikes, but they do 3d6 points of piercing damage to anyone who does so, and the barricade is destroyed. The barricade has hardness 8 and 30 hit points. The spikes do not provide complete protection, but the barricade does provide partial cover.

DC 26 Craft (alchemy); *Type:* Grenade; *Rarity:* Rare; *Price:* 180 gp; *Weight:* 1 lb.; *Alchemical Formula:* Rare Earth (x5), Sulfur (any), Plant, Transmutation

Alchemist's Befuddlement: A black bubbling sphere of aqueous oily liquid that fumes and smokes upon striking a target. The next round, the target must succeed at a DC 16 Will save or be confused as the spell for 1d4 + 4 rounds. There is no splash damage.

DC 26 Craft (alchemy); *Type:* Grenade; *Rarity:* Rare; *Price:* 200 gp; *Weight:* 1 lb.; *Alchemical Formula:* Mercury (any), Sulfur (any), Mind

Alchemist's Censorship: When this grenade strikes a target, they lose their voice for 1d4 + 1 rounds. They can still communicate but no louder than a whisper. If they attempt to cast a spell, there is a 20% chance of spell failure and they are unable to shout or yell commands in battle. During a chaotic situation, it may be more difficult to hear them if you are more than 10 feet away.

DC 25 Craft (alchemy); *Type:* Grenade; *Rarity:* Uncommon; *Price:* 200 gp; *Weight:* 1 lb.; *Alchemical Formula:* Salt (any 2 different Salt essences), Sulfur (any), Stasis

Alchemist's Fire: A direct hit deals 1d6 points of fire damage. Every creature within five feet of the point where the flask hits takes 1 point of fire damage from the splash. On the round following a direct hit, the target takes an additional 1d6 points of damage. If desired, the target can use a full-round action to attempt to extinguish the flames before taking this additional damage. Extinguishing the flames requires a DC 15 Reflex save. Rolling on the ground provides the target a +2 bonus on the save. Leaping into a lake or magically extinguishing the flames automatically smothers the fire.

DC 20 Craft (alchemy); *Type:* Grenade; *Rarity:* Common; *Price:* 20 gp; *Weight:* 1 lb.; *Alchemical Formula:* Rare Earth, Fire (any 2 different Fire Essences), Sulfur (any)

Alchemist's Firewater: This works as *alchemist's fire* but is nonreactive with air. When exposed to water, this substance catches on fire. Grenades made from this substance are filled with water that ignites the firewater when thrown. A direct hit deals 1d6 points of fire damage. Every creature within five feet of the point where the flask hits takes 1 point of fire damage from the splash. On the round following a direct hit, the target takes an additional 1d6 points of damage.

The target may attempt to extinguish the flames to prevent the second round of damage. A successful DC 15 Reflex save accomplishes this. Immersion in water does not extinguish the flame. Attempting to extinguish the fire using water causes the second round to do 1d6 + 2 points of damage.

DC 20 Craft (alchemy); *Type:* Grenade; *Rarity:* Uncommon; *Price:* 25 gp; *Weight:* 1 lb.; *Alchemical Formula:* Fire (any), Sulfur (any), Water (any), Transmutation

Alchemist's Fist: When this grenade strikes a target, they take 1d4 points of force damage and must succeed on a DC 18 Fortitude save or be knocked prone. Those in the splash damage radius take no damage but must succeed on a DC 10 Fortitude save or fall prone.

DC 25 Craft (alchemy); *Type:* Grenade; *Rarity:* Rare; *Price:* 50 gp; *Weight:* 1 lb.; *Alchemical Formula:* Air (any), Earth (any), Sulfur (any), Strength

Alchemist's Inferno: This flask of hot, long-burning flame does 3d6 points of fire damage to the target, and 1d6 points of splash fire damage to every adjacent creature. The next round, the target takes another 3d6 points of fire damage.

The target may attempt to extinguish the flames and prevent the second round of damage by succeeding at a DC 17 Reflex save. Dropping to the ground and rolling about provides a +2 circumstance bonus to the roll. Leaping into a lake or magically extinguishing the flames automatically smothers the fire.

DC 25 Craft (alchemy); *Type:* Grenade; *Rarity:* Very Rare; *Price:* 600 gp; *Weight:* 1 lb.; *Alchemical Formula:* Fire (any), Sulfur (any), Pain, Strength

Alchemist's Knife: When this strikes a target, shrapnel flies everywhere. They take 1d4 points of piercing and slashing damage and bleed 1 hit point per round. Every creature within five feet of the point where the flask hits takes 1 point of bleed damage from the splash. All those within the radius with an armor or natural armor bonus of +4 or greater are not affected.

DC 25 Craft (alchemy); *Type:* Grenade; *Rarity:* Uncommon; *Price:* 40 gp; *Weight:* 1 lb.; *Alchemical Formula:* Iron, Salt (any), Sulfur (any), Decay

Alchemist's Mortar: This is a round bomb with an adjustable fuse. It can be set to detonate instantly or at the start of your next turn or the turn after that. It does 2d6 fire damage to any target within five feet of the detonation, with 1d6 piercing damage in a 10-foot radius around the detonation.

DC 30 Craft (alchemy); *Type:* Grenade; *Rarity:* Rare; *Price:* 80 gp; *Weight:* 1 lb.; *Alchemical Formula:* Iron, Fire (any), Sulfur (any), Body, Strength

Alchemist's Stupor: This is a concussive explosive that works only if it hits the target. On a successful hit, the target must succeed at a DC 12 Fortitude save or be stunned for one round. On a failed save, the target is dazed.

DC 25 Craft (alchemy); *Type:* Grenade; *Rarity:* Rare; *Price:* 100 gp; *Weight:* 1 lb.; *Alchemical Formula:* Mercury (any), Salt (any), Sulfur (any), Stasis

Alchemist's Sunburst: This grenade contains the concentrated power of sunlight. It glows as sunlight with a range of 10 feet. When this grenade is thrown, it bursts in a brilliant shining explosion, showering a 15-foot radius with bright sunlight.

DC 20 Craft (alchemy); *Type:* Grenade; *Rarity:* Rare; *Price:* 250 gp; *Weight:* 1 lb.; *Alchemical Formula:* Gold, Air (any), Fire (any), Sulfur (any), Light

Alchemist's Surprise: This is a special admixture of *alchemist's fire* and acid. When a creature is hit with this substance, it takes 1d4 points of fire damage and 1d4 points of acid damage immediately. Every adjacent creature takes 1 point of fire splash damage and 1 point of acid splash damage. The following round, the target takes another 1d4 points of fire damage.

The target may attempt to extinguish the flames to prevent the second round of damage by succeeding at a DC 15 Reflex save. Dropping to the ground and rolling about provides a +2 circumstance bonus to the roll. Leaping into a lake or magically extinguishing the flames automatically smothers the fire.

DC 25 Craft (alchemy); *Type:* Grenade; *Rarity:* Uncommon; *Price:* 150 gp; *Weight:* 2 lbs.; *Alchemical Formula:* Rare Earth, Earth (any), Fire (any), Sulfur (any), Acid

Alchemist's Terror: This grenade is filled with a terrifying hallucinogenic oil. On a direct hit, the target must succeed at a DC 16 Will save or gain the frightened condition. Creatures splashed must succeed at a DC 12 Will save or become frightened.

DC 25 Craft (alchemy); *Type:* Grenade; *Rarity:* Uncommon; *Price:* 150 gp; *Weight:* 1 lb.; *Alchemical Formula:* Mercury (any), Sulfur (any), Water (any), Fear

Armor Stripper: When *armor stripper* strikes a target wearing armor or having natural protection such as scales or a tough hide, they take a −2 alchemical penalty to their Armor or Natural Armor score. This effect lasts for 1d4 + 1 rounds. Splash damage lowers the armor value by 1 point. Huge or bigger creatures may require two doses for the same effect.

DC 25 Craft (alchemy); *Type:* Grenade; *Rarity:* Very Rare; *Price:* 200 gp; *Weight:* 1 lb.; *Alchemical Formula:* Earth (any), Mercury (any), Acid, Plant

Black-Light: When thrown, this grenade creates a 20-foot radius of darkness where it shatters. The alchemist who prepared this grenade can see in this darkness as if it were daylight. All others within the radius gain the blinded condition. This effect is dispelled by *light* or superseded by any darkness spells.

DC 26 Craft (alchemy); *Type:* Grenade; *Rarity:* Rare; *Price:* 300 gp; *Weight:* 1 lb.; *Alchemical Formula:* Rare Earth, Mercury (any), Sulfur (any), Light

Blanch Bomb (Adamantine): The nearly invisible gas contained in this fragile glass sphere temporarily but drastically deteriorates the defenses — manufactured and natural — of those affected. A blanch bomb is effective only against a target that is vulnerable to the type of blanch bomb employed against it. A blanch bomb is thrown as a splash weapon with a range increment of 10 feet. Upon contact with a hard surface, the blanch bomb releases a hazy cloud of gas within a 10-foot-radius burst centered on the point of impact. This cloud lasts for 1d4 + 1 rounds and can be dispersed as *fog cloud*. If a creature whose damage reduction is overcome by the specified substance begins its turn in the affected area, the subject's DR/adamantine degrades at a rate of 5 points per round for as long as the creature remains in the area (to a minimum of DR 0). If the subject ends its turn outside the affected area, the creature's damage reduction returns to its original amount at a rate of 5 points per minute. The creature can also take a full-round action to recover 5 points.

DC 30 Craft (alchemy); *Type:* Grenade; *Rarity:* Rare; *Price:* 250 gp; *Weight:* 0.5 lb.; *Alchemical Formula:* Rare Earth, Adamantine, Azoth (any), Salt (any), Sulfur (any)

Blanch Bomb (Cold Iron): The nearly invisible gas contained in this fragile glass sphere temporarily but drastically deteriorates the defenses — both manufactured and natural — of those affected. A blanch bomb is effective only against a target that is vulnerable to the type of blanch bomb employed against it. A blanch bomb is thrown as a splash weapon with a range increment of 10 feet. Upon contact with a hard surface, the blanch bomb releases a hazy cloud of gas within a 10-foot-radius burst centered on the point of impact. This cloud lasts for 1d4 + 1 rounds and can be dispersed as *fog cloud*. If a creature whose damage reduction is overcome by the specified substance begins its turn in the affected area, the subject's DR/cold iron degrades at a rate of 5 points per round for as long as the creature remains in the area (to a minimum of DR 0). If the subject ends its turn outside the affected area, the creature's damage reduction returns to its original amount at a rate of 5 points per minute. The creature can also take a full-round action to recover 5 points.

DC 25 Craft (alchemy); *Type:* Grenade; *Rarity:* Rare; *Price:* 150 gp; *Weight:* 0.5 lb.; *Alchemical Formula:* Rare Earth, Iron, Azoth (any), Salt (any), Sulfur (any)

Blanch Bomb (Silver): The nearly invisible gas contained in this fragile glass sphere temporarily but drastically deteriorates the defenses — both manufactured and natural — of those affected. A blanch bomb is effective only against a target that is vulnerable to the type of blanch bomb employed against it. A blanch bomb is thrown as a splash weapon with a range increment of 10 feet. Upon contact with a hard surface, the blanch bomb releases a hazy cloud of gas within a 10-foot-radius burst centered on the point of impact. This cloud lasts for 1d4 + 1 rounds and can be dispersed as *fog cloud*. If a creature whose damage reduction is overcome by the specified substance begins its turn in the affected area, the subject's DR/silver degrades at a rate of 5 points per round for as long as the creature remains in the area (to a minimum of DR 0). If the subject ends its turn outside the affected area, the creature's damage reduction returns to its original amount at a rate of 5 points per minute. The creature can also take a full-round action to recover 5 points.

DC 25 Craft (alchemy); *Type:* Grenade; *Rarity:* Rare; *Price:* 100 gp; *Weight:* 0.5 lb.; *Alchemical Formula:* Rare Earth, Silver, Azoth (any), Salt (any), Sulfur (any)

Blessed Sphere: This divine mixture is very delicate, often carried in small glass spheres covered in golden wire. It is harmful to all those who carry evil in their hearts. Upon striking a target of evil alignment, it does 2d6 points holy damage to the target and 1d6 points of splash damage to every other adjacent evil target.

DC 25 Craft (alchemy); *Type:* Grenade; *Rarity:* Rare; *Price:* 200 gp; *Weight:* 1 lb.; *Alchemical Formula:* Fire (any), Sulfur (any), Light, Life

Blister Broth: When this strikes a target, they break out into blisters. They immediately take 2d4 points of acid damage, though a successful DC 16 Fortitude save halves this damage and prevents blisters from forming. This grenade does 1 point of acid splash damage.
Two minutes after exposure, the blisters become painful and burst, giving the target the sickened condition for one hour.

DC 25 Craft (alchemy); *Type:* Grenade; *Rarity:* Uncommon; *Price:* 50 gp; *Weight:* 1 lb.; *Alchemical Formula:* Rare Earth, Earth (any), Salt (any), Water (any), Acid

Bottled Lightning: Electricity crackles along a metal filament inside this small glass bottle. You can open the bottle as a standard action to unleash a small bolt of lightning toward an enemy within 20 feet of you. This is a ranged touch attack that deals 1d8 points of electrical damage. Any creature in a line between you and the target (including the target) takes 1 point of sonic damage from the terrific clap of thunder the bolt generates (Reflex DC 15 negates).

DC 25 Craft (alchemy); *Type:* Grenade; *Rarity:* Common; *Price:* 40 gp; *Weight:* 1 lb.; *Alchemical Formula:* Silver, Air (any), Sulfur (any), Electricity

Chronobreak: This grenade causes the target struck to be frozen in the timestream. The target must make a DC 24 Fortitude save. On a failed save, they are frozen in time, aware of their surroundings, but unable to move or affect them. They are also unable to be affected by them, although their frozen form can be picked up and moved. On a successful save, they are sluggish, giving the target a –4 penalty to Strength and Dexterity. The duration of all effects lasts for 1d4 + 1 rounds.

DC 35 Craft (alchemy); *Type:* Grenade; *Rarity:* Very Rare; *Price:* 600 gp; *Weight:* 1 lb.; *Alchemical Formula:* Agate, Emerald, Jade, Onyx, Azoth (any), Stasis

Demi-Bomb: This grenade creates a black spherical explosion that sucks in creatures in the area. It does 1d8 points of sonic damage and stuns any creature with less than 5 Hit Dice and deafens any creature with less than 10 hit dice. It does 3d8 points of sonic damage against undead that are sucked in. It occupies a grid intersection for 1d4 + 1 rounds, and anyone in or passing through the squares adjacent to this intersection must succeed at a DC 12 Fortitude to avoid getting sucked into the intersection. It is a DC 17 Strength check to break free.

DC 32 Craft (alchemy); *Type:* Grenade; *Rarity:* Rare; *Price:* 500 gp; *Weight:* 1 lb.; *Alchemical Formula:* Onyx, Rare Earth, Azoth (any), Death

Dye Bomb: These pellets explode when jostled or upon striking a target. Each contains a powerful indelible dye. Anything such as clothing, skin, or porous material covered in this dye is stained. Any nonporous surface covered in the dye must be cleaned off using an alcohol base.
The dye cannot be washed out through normal means and is usually of a conspicuous color selected by the alchemist. The color fades from the skin in 1d4 + 6 days. These are useful for drawing attention to thieves, shapeshifters, and invisible opponents.

DC 21 Craft (alchemy); *Type:* Pellet; *Rarity:* Uncommon; *Price:* 25 gp; *Weight:* 1 lb.; *Alchemical Formula:* Azoth (any), Sulfur (any), Transmutation

Earth Sphere: This grenade targets a grid intersection. It bursts, doing 1d4 + 1 points of bludgeoning damage to all targets adjacent to the intersection, and scattering dirt and stone over the ground. This creates difficult terrain in that area.

DC 24 Craft (alchemy); *Type:* Grenade; *Rarity:* Uncommon; *Price:* 150 gp; *Weight:* 1 lb.; *Alchemical Formula:* Rare Earth, Earth (any), Sulfur (any), Strength

Fire Interruption Gas: This grenade instantly extinguishes all fires in a 10-foot-by-10-foot square. Any fire in the square is extinguished. However it does this by displacing all the available oxygen. The entire square is completely filled with opaque smoke that acts as an asphyxiant. This persists until dispersed based on prevailing conditions, usually after one minute (q.v. Gas Dispersion). If the grenade is used and there is no fire, there is no reaction and the grenade is wasted.

DC 25 Craft (alchemy); *Type:* Grenade; *Rarity:* Rare; *Price:* 25 gp; *Weight:* 1 lb.; *Alchemical Formula:* Mercury (any) (x2), Salt (any) (x2)

Fireburst Pellet: When this pellet is thrown into a nonmagical flame, it explodes in searing bursts and gouts of flame. All creatures that are standing within 10 feet of the flame suffer 2d4 + 2 points of damage. Targets that succeed at a DC 14 Reflex save take half damage.

DC 20 Craft (alchemy); *Type:* Pellet; *Rarity:* Uncommon; *Price:* 10 gp; *Weight:* 1 lb.; *Alchemical Formula:* Fire (any) (x2), Sulfur (any)

Firestone (5): When struck sharply, this stone bursts into flame, doing 1d6 points of fire damage to all targets in a single five-foot square and igniting any flammable objects. Fires lit by a firestone then burn normally.

DC 25 Craft (alchemy); *Type:* Stone; *Rarity:* Uncommon; *Price:* 100 gp; *Weight:* 5 lb.; *Alchemical Formula:* Rare Earth, Ruby, Fire (any)

Flame Globe: When this grenade strikes a target, it does 2d6 points of fire damage and 2 points of splash damage to adjacent targets. It burns for three rounds, doing 1d6 points of fire damage each round.
The target may attempt to extinguish the flames to prevent the additional rounds of damage. A successful DC 15 Reflex save accomplishes this. Dropping to the ground and rolling about provides a +2 circumstance bonus to the roll. Immersion in water extinguishes the fire.
If targeting a grid intersection, it fills a five-foot-radius area with flame. These flames burn anyone who stands in these spaces, doing 1d6 points of fire damage. You may attempt to avoid the damage by passing through the square and succeeding at a DC 16 Reflex save.

DC 30 Craft (alchemy); *Type:* Grenade; *Rarity:* Very Rare; *Price:* 500 gp; *Weight:* 1 lb.; *Alchemical Formula:* Emerald, Ruby, Fire (any)

Flaming Morass: When this strikes a surface or a target, this flares out in a 20-foot radius. Anyone within this area takes 1d4 points of fire damage. Sticky flaming goo shoots everywhere. This covers surfaces and makes movement difficult. Terrain within the area of effect is considered difficult. This lasts for two rounds before burning itself up. Each round anyone within the area of affect takes 1d4 points of fire damage.

DC 30 Craft (alchemy); *Type:* Grenade; *Rarity:* Very Rare; *Price:* 500 gp; *Weight:* 1 lb.; *Alchemical Formula:* Emerald, Jade, Onyx, Ruby, Fire (any)

Flash Pellets: When thrown, this causes a click and draws attention. Then a bright stunning light appears. Anyone unprepared within 60 feet who fails a DC 13 Reflex save gains the blinded condition for 1d3 rounds.

DC 25 Craft (alchemy); *Type:* Pellet; *Rarity:* Uncommon; *Price:* 50 gp; *Weight:* 1 lb.; *Alchemical Formula:* Rare Earth, Fire (any), Salt (any), Light

Frost Sap: This flask contains two different substances that mix and adhere when they strike their target. Upon striking the target, it does 1d6 points of cold damage. The next round the target takes another 1d6 points of cold damage. It does no splash damage.
The substance is sticky and hard to remove but may be scraped off as a full-round action with a successful DC 15 Reflex save.

DC 25 Craft (alchemy); *Type:* Grenade; *Rarity:* Uncommon; *Price:* 40 gp; *Weight:* 1 lb.; *Alchemical Formula:* Salt (any), Sulfur (any), Water (any), Cold

Frozen Fire: This grenade sprays out a mist when it strikes a target. The mist instantly catches fire, burning the target for 1d6 points of fire damage and doing 1 point of splash fire damage. The next round, the remaining liquid then gets very cold, damaging the target for another 1d6 points of cold damage and doing 1 point of cold damage to those initially splashed.
The liquid mist can't be scraped off, but a full-round action using a mild alcohol or solvent solution to clean it off eliminates it and prevents the additional damage.

DC 26 Craft (alchemy); *Type:* Grenade; *Rarity:* Rare; *Price:* 75 gp; *Weight:* 1 lb.; *Alchemical Formula:* Malachite, Ruby, Fire (any), Cold

Frozen Prison: When this grenade strikes a target, the target is quickly trapped in a layer of ice. If the target succeeds at a DC 16 Reflex save, they can spend their next full-round action breaking out. If it fails, they are trapped for two minutes, gaining the helpless condition. Because they are encased in ice, any attacks against them instead damage the ice, which frees them. The ice has hardness 0 and 9 hit points. Each round during those two minutes they may attempt a DC 21 Strength check or a DC 30 Escape Artist check to escape.
This affects only man-sized creatures or smaller. Larger or bigger creatures receive their size bonus both on the saving throw and their chance to escape.
While imprisoned, the cold saps 1 hit point from the target per round. In very cold or wet areas, the prison might trap people for double or even quadruple normal duration. Each additional hit with a frozen prison grenade adds +1 to the break DC and +2 to the Escape Artist DC and increases the ice hit point total by 9. If already affected by *frozen prison*, they receive no saving throw to avoid the effect. Additional grenades reset the two-minute duration.

DC 26 Craft (alchemy); *Type:* Grenade; *Rarity:* Rare; *Price:* 500 gp; *Weight:* 1 lb.; *Alchemical Formula:* Amethyst, Onyx, Water (any), Cold (x2)

Glow Glue: This sticky substance is thrown against a single target. If it hits the target, that target begins to glow with a pale outline. The alchemist can determine the color. This allows you to notice the target in darkness, hiding behind partial cover, protected by partial concealment, or when invisible. It is a simple luminescent glow and provides only enough light in one square to see by. It causes no damage to the target struck.

DC 20 Craft (alchemy); *Type:* Grenade; *Rarity:* Uncommon; *Price:* 35 gp; *Weight:* 1 lb.; *Alchemical Formula:* Earth (any), Water (any), Light

Gravity Globe: This grenade subjects the target to increased weight. The target must make a DC 16 Fortitude save. Targets in splash range make a DC 12 Fortitude save. On a failed save, the target suffers from crushing gravity. This affects the target as if it had a heavy encumbrance value.

DC 30 Craft (alchemy); *Type:* Grenade; *Rarity:* Very Rare; *Price:* 500 gp; *Weight:* 1 lb.; *Alchemical Formula:* Emerald, Jade, Sapphire, Turquoise, Stasis

Knockout Globe: When this powerful globe shatters, it fills a single five-foot square with a powerful transparent gas. Anyone exposed to this gas must succeed at a DC 12 Fortitude save or fall unconscious for 1d4 + 1 rounds. It disperses naturally in three minutes (q.v. Gas Dispersion Rates).

DC 28 Craft (alchemy); *Type:* Grenade; *Rarity:* Rare; *Price:* 200 gp; *Weight:* 1 lb.; *Alchemical Formula:* Emerald, Moonstone, Sapphire, Air (any), Toxin

Lethargy Globe: When thrown, this bursts in a five-foot-radius cloying cloud of mist. The target must succeed at a DC 16 Fortitude save or be affected by a *slow* effect, as the spell. Everyone adjacent to the target must succeed at a DC 14 Fortitude save or also be *slowed* as the spell. If targeting a grid intersection, all adjacent targets save versus DC 14. The gas disperses in one round.

DC 30 Craft (alchemy); *Type:* Grenade; *Rarity:* Very Rare; *Price:* 1,000 gp; *Weight:* 1 lb.; *Alchemical Formula:* Agate, Jade, Air (any), Stasis

Levitation Grenade: When this strikes, a glowing fluid covers the target. If targeted at an intersection, it affects four five-foot squares. All gravity in this square or for the target is reversed for 1d4 + 1 rounds. Targets fall to the ceiling, taking falling damage as normal, but then may fight and act on the ceiling, at least until the grenade effect ends. Targets entering the area of effect have the same occur to them, but the effect ends if they leave the area of effect. Then the targets fall, taking falling damage again.

DC 35 Craft (alchemy); *Type:* Grenade; *Rarity:* Rare; *Price:* 200 gp; *Weight:* 1 lb.; *Alchemical Formula:* Emerald, Rare Earth, Sapphire, Flight

Liquid Ice: Also known as "alchemist's ice," this sealed jar contains crystalline blue fluid that immediately starts to hiss and evaporate once opened. During the 1d6 rounds after it is opened but before it evaporates completely, you can use it to freeze a liquid or to coat an object in a thin layer of ice. You can also throw liquid ice as a splash weapon. A direct hit deals 1d6 points of cold damage; creatures within five feet of where it hits take 1 point of cold damage from the splash.

DC 25 Craft (alchemy); *Type:* Grenade; *Rarity:* Uncommon; *Price:* 40 gp; *Weight:* 1 lb.; *Alchemical Formula:* Sulfur (any), Water (any), Cold

Mephitic Smoke: This shatters when it strikes a target, spewing flaming smoke out to a maximum of a 20-foot radius. Everyone within the area of effect takes 1d4 fire damage, and the area is filled with a thick, black, choking smoke. The smoke is opaque and anyone inside must succeed at a DC 16 Fortitude save or gain the sickened condition. It disperses naturally in three minutes (q.v. Gas Dispersion Rates).

DC 35 Craft (alchemy); *Type:* Grenade; *Rarity:* Very Rare; *Price:* 150 gp; *Weight:* 1 lb.; *Alchemical Formula:* Air (any), Fire (any), Salt (any), Toxin

Misery Vial: This cursed grenade is a small sphere covered in enchanted runes. Upon striking the target, the grenade shatters and splatters the target with a grimy light oil.
On the next round, the target must make a DC 16 Will save. Failure means the curse takes hold and, for the next 1d4 + 4 rounds, the target takes twice the damage it inflicts on others. Rents and sympathetic wounds of similar types appear on the target's flesh. There is no splash damage.
The target must be a living creature and the effect can be dispelled by a *dispel magic*, *remove curse*, or stronger.

DC 25 Craft (alchemy); *Type:* Grenade; *Rarity:* Very Rare; *Price:* 450 gp; *Weight:* 1 lb.; *Alchemical Formula:* Diamond, Emerald, Azoth (any), Decay

Mitelight: This grenade creates a buzzing column of glowing gnats and mites. Anyone in the square with the mites must succeed at a DC 16 Will save or be dazed for one round. In any case, the target is dazzled for 1d4 + 1 rounds. The cloud is semi-opaque and lasts for 1d4 + 1 rounds, provides partial concealment, and sheds dim light out to 10 feet.

DC 25 Craft (alchemy); *Type:* Grenade; *Rarity:* Uncommon *Price:* 80 gp; *Weight:* 1 lb.; *Alchemical Formula:* Rare Earth, Air (any), Fire (any), Light

Nightblinder: This grenade has no effect on normal sighted creatures. However, if it strikes a creature with low-light vision or darkvision, they must succeed at a DC 16 Fortitude save and anyone adjacent to the target must succeed at a DC 12 Fortitude save. If failed, it disables their special sight for the duration of a minute. They can still see in the normal spectrum of light.

DC 25 Craft (alchemy); *Type:* Grenade; *Rarity:* Rare; *Price:* 100 gp; *Weight:* 1 lb.; *Alchemical Formula:* Rare Earth, Fire (any), Mercury (any), Sulfur (any)

Noisemaker: When struck against a hard surface, these make a terrible racket — not enough to deafen targets but enough to draw the attention of anyone within 60 feet. Anyone attempting a Stealth skill check for stealthy movement receives a +4 circumstance bonus, and targets that fail a DC 16 Fortitude save automatically fail their Perception check to notice the target.
Note that the noise reaction continues for several moments and likely draws the attention of wandering or nearby monsters. The encounter chance is increased after noisemakers are used.

DC 20 Craft (alchemy); *Type:* Pellet; *Rarity:* Uncommon; *Price:* 20 gp; *Weight:* 1 lb.; *Alchemical Formula:* Iron, Air (any), Earth (any), Sulfur (any), Stealth

Puppet Blood: When this strikes a target, the target is coated in an adhesive oil. Immediately, tendrils of gooey paste writhe toward the ceiling. If there is a surface above the victim within 50 feet, the victim must succeed at a DC 15 Reflex save or be immobilized and pulled up toward the ceiling. Even if they succeed at their check and remain on the ground, they have a –4 penalty to Dexterity.

Dealing 15 points of damage to the goo with a slashing weapon or making a successful DC 17 Strength check lets a character break free. No attack roll is needed. If a creature attempts to cast a spell, they must succeed at a DC 15 + spell level concentration check to do so.

Breaking free also involves a fall to the floor, doing 1d6 damage per 10 feet. The goop itself dissolves in 1d4 + 1 rounds, dropping the victim, prepared or not.

DC 30 Craft (alchemy); *Type:* Grenade; *Rarity:* Very Rare; *Price:* 150 gp; *Weight:* 1 lb.; *Alchemical Formula:* Azoth (any), Earth (any), Salt (any), Stasis

Putrid Sphere: When thrown, this grenade bursts into a flesh-eating liquid that does 2d8 + 3 points of negative energy damage to the target and 1d4 + 1 points of negative energy splash damage. Targets hit must succeed at a DC 16 Fortitude save or take 1d4 + 1 Constitution damage. Targets splashed must succeed at a DC 12 Fortitude save or take 1 point of Constitution damage.

DC 28 Craft (alchemy); *Type:* Grenade; *Rarity:* Uncommon; *Price:* 600 gp; *Weight:* 1 lb.; *Alchemical Formula:* Onyx, Ruby, Azoth (any), Decay

Pyrotechnic Dazzler: When thrown, this small pellet produces a dazzling flash of pulsing light. Everyone within sight of where the dazzler strikes must succeed at a DC 16 Fortitude save or gain the dazzled condition for 1d4 + 1 rounds.

DC 20 Craft (alchemy); *Type:* Pellet; *Rarity:* Uncommon; *Price:* 50 gp; *Weight:* 1 lb.; *Alchemical Formula:* Rare Earth, Fire (any 2) *or* Light, Sulfur (any)

Sabotage Pulse: This grenade disables constructs. Any non-construct target hit takes 1d4 points of electrical damage. Constructs when hit take 1d8 + 2 points of force damage and immediately take 3d8 + 6 points of special damage that acts as nonlethal damage. Even though constructs cannot take nonlethal damage, this damage acts in all ways like nonlethal damage up to and including the construct "shutting down" if the damage exceeds its current hit points. However, unlike nonlethal damage, once shut down, the construct stays shut down for 1d3 rounds, and then all of this damage is instantly removed.

DC 28 Craft (alchemy); *Type:* Grenade; *Rarity:* Rare; *Price:* 600 gp; *Weight:* 1 lb.; *Alchemical Formula:* Diamond, Platinum, Rare Earth, Azoth (any), Electricity

Shadow Shell: This grenade is filled with an inky, dark, liquid. If it strikes a target, it does 1d6 + 1 points of negative energy damage. The target must succeed at a DC 16 Fortitude save or suffer 1d4 + 1 points of Strength damage and become blinded for one round.

DC 28 Craft (alchemy); *Type:* Grenade; *Rarity:* Rare; *Price:* 200 gp; *Weight:* 1 lb.; *Alchemical Formula:* Fire (any), Mercury (any), Disease, Decay

Shrieking Betty: When this grenade is thrown, it causes a deafening shrieking sound that lasts for three rounds. While the grenade is going, all targets with a 10-foot radius of the grenade have the deafened condition.

DC 20 Craft (alchemy); *Type:* Grenade; *Rarity:* Uncommon; *Price:* 30 gp; *Weight:* 1 lb.; *Alchemical Formula:* Air (any), Salt (any), Sulfur (any)

Sleepsmoke: This releases a vapor that will not actually put anyone to sleep due to how quickly it disperses. It produces a vapor on a direct hit. A failed DC 20 Fortitude save causes a single target to gain the stunned condition for one round and then become disoriented and confused, gaining the sickened condition for 1d4 rounds.

DC 25 Craft (alchemy); *Type:* Grenade; *Rarity:* Uncommon; *Price:* 50 gp; *Weight:* 1 lb.; *Alchemical Formula:* Salt (any), Sulfur (any), Water (any), Stasis

Slickshell: This is the grenade version of *alchemical grease*. It is a quick-drying oil that is extremely slick. When thrown at a surface, it covers a single five-foot-by-five-foot square. Anyone standing in, entering, or leaving that square must make a DC 14 reflex save or fall prone. The oil dries and becomes useless in 1d4 rounds.

DC 20 Craft (alchemy); *Type:* Grenade; *Rarity:* Uncommon; *Price:* 10 gp; *Weight:* 1 lb.; *Alchemical Formula:* Sulfur (any), Water (any), Agility, Stasis

Slime Bane: This mixture is designed to dissolve the bonds of any ooze, pudding, or slime-like creature. On a successful hit, it does 2d8 + 2 points of damage to any creature with the ooze type. On the following round, a DC 16 Fortitude save must be made or it takes another 1d8 damage. It does only 1d4 points of damage against all other creatures.

DC 25 Craft (alchemy); *Type:* Grenade; *Rarity:* Uncommon; *Price:* 15 gp; *Weight:* 1 lb.; *Alchemical Formula:* Earth (any), Salt (any), Sulfur (any), Decay

Smoke Pellet: When thrown, this pellet creates thick clouds of opaque smoke that covers a single 10-foot-cube area for two rounds. This fog blocks vision, providing total concealment to anything more than five feet away; otherwise, it provides partial concealment. The alchemist sets the color of the smoke.

DC 20 Craft (alchemy); *Type:* Pellet; *Rarity:* Uncommon; *Price:* 25 gp; *Weight:* 1 lb.; *Alchemical Formula:* Rare Earth, Air (any), Earth (any), Salt (any), Stealth

Snarlweave: This small item creates a shockwave that causes all plants within a 10-foot-square area to begin writhing and affects anyone in the area as if subject to an *entangle* spell for 1d4 + 1 rounds.

DC 25 Craft (alchemy); *Type:* Stone; *Rarity:* Uncommon; *Price:* 200 gp; *Weight:* 1 lb.; *Alchemical Formula:* Earth (any), Salt (any), Sulfur (any), Plant

Spore Stone: This is not an actual stone, but a calcified shell around spores. When thrown on the ground, it releases a cloud of spores that cover a five-foot radius from detonation. All who enter this cloud must succeed at a DC 16 Fortitude save or gain the nauseated condition for 1d4 rounds. If the creature leaves the cloud, the effect ends at the start of their next turn.

DC 25 Craft (alchemy); *Type:* Stone; *Rarity:* Uncommon; *Price:* 50 gp; *Weight:* 1 lb.; *Alchemical Formula:* Earth (any), Water (any), Plant, Toxin

Sticky Mist: This grenade covers a 10-foot-square area in mist for two rounds. Anyone caught within this mist or passing through it during the two rounds is affected. After two rounds, the mist begins to harden, sticking fast for one hour. Those covered in the mist have a –4 penalty to Dexterity. They must also succeed at a DC 17 Reflex save or be considered staggered. Even if they succeed, their movement is still halved.

Taking a round to escape allows a creature to break the bonds of the mist by making a DC 17 Strength check. The mist can be scraped or burnt off. Sticky mist has hardness 0 and 20 hp. Any attacks made on the mist do half their damage to any target trapped by the mist.

If a creature attempts to cast a spell, it must succeed at a DC 15 + spell level concentration check to do so.

DC 28 Craft (alchemy); *Type:* Grenade; *Rarity:* Rare; *Price:* 400 gp; *Weight:* 1 lb.; *Alchemical Formula:* Emerald, Turquoise, Air (any), Strength

Stink Bomb: This bomb fills a 10-foot-square area with a thick disgusting stench. This stench is completely transparent and provides no obfuscation of any kind. Anyone within this area must succeed at a DC 16 Fortitude save or gain the sickened condition. This lasts the number of rounds the target is in the cloud and the round after they leave. The cloud disperses in 2d4 rounds if not sooner by prevailing conditions.

DC 23 Craft (alchemy); *Type:* Grenade; *Rarity:* Uncommon; *Price:* 50 gp; *Weight:* 1 lb.; *Alchemical Formula:* Sulfur (any), Decay, Toxin

Stun Gas: This is a clear red liquid that instantly evaporates when exposed to air, forming a gas cloud. When thrown, it creates a 10-foot-radius sphere of gas that dissipates in one round. During that round, the gas cloud is opaque, providing total concealment.

Anyone caught inside must make a DC 14 Fortitude save or be stunned for 1d4 + 1 rounds.

DC 25 Craft (alchemy); *Type:* Grenade; *Rarity:* Uncommon *Price:* 600 gp; *Weight:* 1 lb.; *Alchemical Formula:* Air (any), Salt (any), Sulfur (any), Stasis

Tanglefoot Bag: A *tanglefoot bag* is a small sack filled with tar, resin, and other sticky substances. When you throw a *tanglefoot bag* at a creature (as a ranged touch attack with a range increment of 10 feet), the bag comes apart and goo bursts out, entangling the target and then becoming tough and resilient upon exposure to air. An entangled creature takes a –2 penalty on attack rolls and a –4 penalty to Dexterity and must make a DC 15 Reflex save or be glued to the floor, unable to move. Even on a successful save, it can move only at half speed. Huge or larger creatures are unaffected by a *tanglefoot bag*. A flying creature is not stuck to the floor, but it must make a DC 15 Reflex save or be unable to fly (assuming it uses its wings to fly) and fall to the ground. A *tanglefoot bag* does not function underwater. A creature that is glued to the floor (or unable to fly) can break free by making a DC 17 Strength check or by dealing 15 points of damage to the goo with a slashing weapon. A creature trying to scrape goo off itself, or another creature assisting, does not need to make an attack roll; hitting the goo is automatic, after which the creature that hit makes a damage roll to see how much of the goo was scraped off. Once free, the creature can move (including flying) at half speed. If the entangled creature attempts to cast a spell, it must make a concentration check with a DC of 15 + the spell's level or be unable to cast the spell. The goo becomes brittle and fragile after 2d4 rounds, cracking apart and losing its effectiveness. An application of *universal solvent* to a stuck creature dissolves the alchemical goo immediately.

DC 25 Craft (alchemy); *Type:* Grenade; *Rarity:* Common; *Price:* 50 gp; *Weight:* 4 lbs.; *Alchemical Formula:* Rare Earth, Mercury (any), Stasis

Tanglefoot Bag, Acidic: This is a small bag filled with acidic adhesive. It works much like a *tanglefoot bag*. When it strikes a creature, the bag comes apart, and the goo inside bursts out, entangling the target and hardening in air. Anyone struck by the bag has a penalty of –4 points to their Dexterity. They also take 1d4 + 1 points of damage per round while under the effects of the bag. They also must succeed at a DC 15 Reflex save or be immobilized. Even if the target succeeds, their movement is still impaired, moving at one-half speed
A creature can deal 15 points of damage to the goo with a slashing weapon or make a successful DC 17 Strength check to break free. No attack roll is needed.
If a creature attempts to cast a spell, it must succeed at a DC 15 + spell level Concentration check to do so.
An *acidic tanglefoot bag* does not function underwater. The bag dissolves in two rounds, the goo melting away.

DC 28 Craft (alchemy); *Type:* Grenade; *Rarity:* Rare; *Price:* 200 gp; *Weight:* 4 lbs.; *Alchemical Formula:* Rare Earth, Mercury (any), Acid, Stasis

Teleportation Grenade: When this grenade strikes an area, all creatures within the detonation zone of a five-foot radius are randomly teleported five to 40 feet. Determine direction by rolling a 1d8. Determine distance in feet by rolling a 1d8 and multiplying by 5. Targets that end up in solid areas or areas occupied by other creatures take 4d6 damage and are shunted to the nearest open space. In any case, the experience is jarring, and targets must succeed at a DC 16 Fortitude save or be nauseated for 1d3 rounds. Rumors exist of more powerful versions of this grenade that slay anyone by teleporting them inside solid objects.

DC 35 Craft (alchemy); *Type:* Grenade; *Rarity:* Very Rare; *Price:* 500 gp; *Weight:* 1 lb.; *Alchemical Formula:* Diamond, Emerald, Pearl, Transportation

Thunder Globe: When this stone strikes a hard surface, it creates a thunderous clap. Each creature within a 20-foot-radius spread takes 1d8 sonic damage and must succeed at a DC 15 Fortitude save or be deafened for one hour. A deafened creature, in addition to the obvious effects, takes a –4 penalty on initiative and has a 20% chance to miscast and lose any spell with a verbal component that it tries to cast.
Since you don't need to hit a specific target, you can simply aim at a particular five-foot square.

DC 30 Craft (alchemy); *Type:* Stone; *Rarity:* Very Rare; *Price:* 100 gp; *Weight:* 1 lb.; *Alchemical Formula:* Rare Earth, Sapphire, Air (any), Salt (any), Strength, Prowess

Thunderstone (5): When a thunderstone strikes a hard surface (or is struck hard), it creates a deafening bang that is treated as a sonic attack. Each creature within a 10-foot-radius spread must make a DC 15 Fortitude save or be deafened for one hour. A deafened creature, in addition to the obvious effects, takes a –4 penalty on initiative and has a 20% chance to miscast and lose any spell with a verbal component that it tries to cast.
Since you don't need to hit a specific target, you can simply aim at a particular five-foot square.

DC 25 Craft (alchemy); *Type:* Stone; *Rarity:* Common; *Price:* 150 gp; *Weight:* 1 lb.; *Alchemical Formula:* Rare Earth, Sapphire, Salt (any), Strength

Void Bomb: This more advanced version of a demi-bomb creates a literal black hole. When thrown, they spin up in the air and beep until the start of the thrower's next turn. Anyone standing in the square the grenade lands in when it goes off is obliterated. A black hole then occupies that square for 1d3 + 1 rounds. Anyone passing adjacent to this square must succeed at a DC 22 Fortitude save to avoid getting sucked into the square and killed. Anyone passing within 20 feet must succeed at a DC 16 fortitude save or be pulled one square toward the black hole. Grabbing hold of something solid provides a +8 circumstance bonus to the saving throw, but you must take a standard action focused on holding on to gain this bonus.

DC 35 Craft (alchemy); *Type:* Grenade; *Rarity:* Very Rare; *Price:* 1,000 gp; *Weight:* 1 lb.; *Alchemical Formula:* Diamond, Emerald, Onyx, Rare Earth, Azoth (any), Planar

Voltaic Orb: This grenade bursts and covers a single five-foot square in a hemisphere of cackling electricity that lasts for 1d4 + 1 rounds. Any targets adjacent to the sphere take 1d4 points of electrical damage each round. Any target in the sphere takes 2d4 points of electrical damage each round. If the target surrounded by the hemisphere leaves the hemisphere, or if anyone attempts to enter, they take 6d4 + 6 points of electrical damage.

DC 32 Craft (alchemy); *Type:* Grenade; *Rarity:* Rare; *Price:* 600 gp; *Weight:* 1 lb.; *Alchemical Formula:* Emerald, Ruby, Sapphire, Electricity

Wind Sphere: This grenade explodes and covers a 20-square-foot area. It creates tumultuous winds that swirl around the area. This clears out any standing gases and causes all ranged attacks that pass through this area to suffer a –6 circumstance penalty. It also penalizes attempts to make Dexterity checks by –4, and passing through the area requires a successful DC 12 Acrobatics check to avoid being knocked prone. These winds last for 1d4 rounds.

DC 24 Craft (alchemy); *Type:* Grenade; *Rarity:* Uncommon; *Price:* 200 gp; *Weight:* 1 lb.; *Alchemical Formula:* Emerald, Jade, Sapphire, Air (any), Strength

INCENSE

These are organic materials that have heat applied to release a scent or smoke. Incense is made from aromatic flora material. Incense comes in one duration, taking 1 move action to light and burning for one hour. Their effects begin one full round after they are lit.

Incense affects an area. Incense in an open area has a 15-foot radius of effect; however, if the area is enclosed or if the air is particularly still, it can affect a maximum radius of 25 feet.

Incense can be snuffed out by ordinary means. After being doused, crushed, or covered, the effects of incense end in 1d4 + 1 rounds.

Incense is found in bundles of 2d3 sticks or cones. When crafting these items, the alchemical formulas below produce a batch of six sticks unless otherwise noted.

TABLE 3–4: INCENSE

Name	Craft (alchemy) DC	Price	Weight
Aromatherapy	22	150 gp	0.05 lb.
Beastbane	16	60 gp	0.05 lb.
Healing	22	300 gp	0.05 lb.
Insanity	25	250 gp	0.05 lb.
Phasebound	22	300 gp	0.05 lb.
Phasic Disruption	25	150 gp	0.05 lb.
Poison	28	500 gp	0.05 lb.
Prognostication	25	250 gp	0.05 lb.
Sleep	20	200 gp	0.05 lb.
Spellbreaker	22	100 gp	0.05 lb.
Stinkstuff	16	60 gp	0.05 lb.
Thoughtfocus	16	60 gp	0.05 lb.
Trollbane	18	50 gp	0.05 lb.
Unfettered Joy	18	50 gp	0.05 lb.
Verminbane	16	50 gp	0.05 lb.
War	22	50 gp	0.05 lb.
Wolfsbane	18	100 gp	0.05 lb.

Aromatherapy Incense: There are a variety of these incenses, with each providing a minor alchemical bonus of a certain type to an ability score or skill. Anyone who mediates for one minute within the range of this incense receives a +1 alchemical bonus to the specific statistic or a +2 alchemical bonus to a specific skill.
This specific statistic or skill must be selected when the item is created; e.g., the alchemist could create an *aromatherapy of strength* and gain a +1 alchemical bonus to Strength after meditating.
The effects of this incense last for one hour.

DC 22 Craft (alchemy); *Rarity:* Common; *Price:* 150 gp; *Weight:* —; *Alchemical Formula:* Rare Earth, Mercury (any), Salt (any), Plant

Beastbane Incense: This produces a cloud and scent that animals find distasteful. Any animal must succeed at a DC 16 Fortitude save in order to enter the cloud. Magical beasts must save as well; however, they receive a +4 racial bonus to their saving throw. Once within the cloud, all animals receive a –1 alchemical penalty to attack rolls and saving throws. Attacking any animal negates the need for them to make a saving throw to enter the cloud.

DC 16 Craft (alchemy); *Rarity:* Uncommon; *Price:* 60 gp; *Weight:* —; *Alchemical Formula:* Rare Earth, Air (any), Fire (any), Mercury (any), Emotion

Healing Incense: This incense produces a golden cloud that smells of lavender. All those within the area of effect of this incense are soothed and calmed. Any healing they receive is doubled.

DC 22 Craft (alchemy); *Rarity:* Rare; *Price:* 300 gp; *Weight:* —; *Alchemical Formula:* Jade, Rare Earth, Healing *or* Plant

Insanity Incense: This incense produces a vapor that clouds the minds of those who enter its radius. Those that fail a DC 16 Will save are subject to *confusion* as the spell.

DC 25 Craft (alchemy); *Rarity:* Rare; *Price:* 250 gp; *Weight:* —; *Alchemical Formula:* Rare Earth, Mercury (any), Mind

Phasebound Incense: While this incense burns, it produces light smoke of a pleasant scent but has no other obvious effect. However, for anyone who is not located on the Prime Material Plane where the incense burns notices a golden cloud pouring out from the incense. This cloud is viscous and solid. Anyone covered by this smoke is forced from other planes into the Prime Material.
This prevents blinking, etherealness, astral travel, shadow walking, phasing, and other forms of dimensional travel. Outside of the radius, in other dimensions the cloud appears as a solid wall filling the area it covers. Anyone engaged in physically occupying more than one plane at once is shunted into the Prime Material Plane. If the creature is normally multi- or extraplanar, it is unable to enter the area. If the effect causing the planar shift is magical, it is dispelled. Extra-dimensional items are rendered inert for one minute after leaving the cloud.

DC 22 Craft (alchemy); *Rarity:* Rare; *Price:* 300 gp; *Weight:* —; *Alchemical Formula:* Jade, Rare Earth, Azoth (any), Planar, Stasis

Phasic Disruption Incense: This incense burns a purple cloud that smells of metallic silver. Any creature out of phase with the Prime Material Plane, such as an ethereal or incorporeal creature, suddenly finds itself corporeal while within the area of this incense. They are subject to any and all attacks from creatures on the Prime Material. However, there is no compulsion on them staying within range of the incense; they may enter and leave freely. It does not affect anything other than ethereal or incorporeal creatures and has no effect other than making them vulnerable to physical attacks.

DC 25 Craft (alchemy); *Rarity:* Rare; *Price:* 300 gp; *Weight:* —; *Alchemical Formula:* Onyx, Rare Earth, Silver, Azoth (any), Planar, Stasis

Poison Incense: Anyone who catches a whiff of this deadly incense must make a DC 16 Fortitude save or suffer the effects of *poison*, as per the spell.

DC 28 Craft (alchemy); *Rarity:* Rare; *Price:* 500 gp; *Weight:* —; *Alchemical Formula:* Rare Earth, Air (any), Water (any), Toxin

Prognostication Incense: Those who burn this incense receive a +2 (or +10%) Alchemical bonus on any rolls to succeed at divination spells cast within the area of effect of the incense.

DC 25 Craft (alchemy); *Rarity:* Uncommon; *Price:* 250 gp; *Weight:* —; *Alchemical Formula:* Rare Earth, Air (any), Fire (any), Sulfur (any), Prophecy *or* Perception

Sleep Incense: Anyone who smells this pleasant incense must make a DC 16 Fortitude save or fall fast asleep. This sleep is natural and may be ended normally. If the target stays in range of the incense, they must make a saving throw every round.

DC 20 Craft (alchemy); *Rarity:* Uncommon; *Price:* 200 gp; *Weight:* —; *Alchemical Formula:* Moonstone, Rare Earth, Air (any), Stasis

Spellbreaker Incense: This creates a cloud that disturbs concentration. Any spell cast triggers a DC 15 + spell level Concentration check. On a failure, the spell fails.

DC 22 Craft (alchemy); *Rarity:* Rare; *Price:* 100 gp; *Weight:* —; *Alchemical Formula:* Rare Earth, Air (any), Fire (any), Water (any)

Stinkstuff Incense: This incense smells like garbage and rotting meat. After lighting this incense, 2d10 rats or other appropriate vermin arrive within 1d10 + 1 rounds. They are not under the control of the summoner and are somewhat agitated by the scent of the incense.

DC 16 Craft (alchemy); *Rarity:* Uncommon; *Price:* 60 gp; *Weight:* —; *Alchemical Formula:* Rare Earth, Air (any), Fire (any), Decay

Thoughtfocus Incense: This pleasant-smelling incense is an aid to the mind. Any Intelligence-based check made while exposed to this incense is given a +2 alchemical bonus.

DC 16 Craft (alchemy); *Rarity:* Uncommon; *Price:* 60 gp; *Weight:* —; *Alchemical Formula:* Rare Earth, Mercury (any), Mind

Trollbane Incense: This produces a greasy, thin, green cloud that smells pungent. While unpleasant to all, it is especially repulsive to trolls, which must succeed at a DC 16 Fortitude save to even approach. Once within the cloud, trolls receive a –1 alchemical penalty to attack rolls and saving throws. Attacking any troll negates the need for them to make a saving throw to enter the cloud.

DC 18 Craft (alchemy); *Rarity:* Uncommon; *Price:* 50 gp; *Weight:* —; *Alchemical Formula:* Rare Earth, Earth (any), Fire (any), Mercury (any)

Unfettered Joy Incense: This produces a scent cloud that affects any being who is not under the effects of an oath, geas, or any other form of behavioral coercion. When they breathe the gas, they begin to laugh joyously, though the people in the cloud may choose to stifle this laughter a moment after it begins.

DC 18 Craft (alchemy); *Rarity:* Uncommon; *Price:* 50 gp; *Weight:* —; *Alchemical Formula:* Rare Earth, Air (any), Fire (any), Emotion

Verminbane Incense: This produces a cloud and scent that vermin find distasteful. Any vermin must succeed at a DC 16 Fortitude save in order to enter the cloud. Once within the cloud, all vermin receive a –1 alchemical penalty to attack rolls and saving throws. Attacking any vermin negates the need for them to make a saving throw to enter the cloud.

DC 16 Craft (alchemy); *Rarity:* Uncommon; *Price:* 50 gp; *Weight:* —; *Alchemical Formula:* Rare Earth, Air (any), Sulfur (any), Water (any), Emotion

War Incense: This produces a red-tinged cloud of smoke that spells like blood. All those within the area of effect of this incense are affected by bloodlust and are given a +1 alchemical bonus to hit and a +1 alchemical bonus to damage. This effect lasts for three minutes after leaving the incense. A person may be affected by this incense only once in a 24-hour period.

DC 22 Craft (alchemy); *Rarity:* Rare; *Price:* 50 gp; *Weight:* —; *Alchemical Formula:* Earth, Earth, Mercury, Rare Earth

Wolfsbane Incense: This incense burns for eight hours. While it is burning, it gives those within the cloud the ability to resist lycanthropic change. It provides a 50% chance that the change will not occur. This works on both willing and unwilling targets. Once suppressed, the ability to change is lost for 24 hours.

DC 18 Craft (alchemy); *Rarity:* Uncommon; *Price:* 50 gp; *Weight:* —; *Alchemical Formula:* Rare Earth, Silver, Air (any), Mercury (any), Emotion

LIQUIDS AND TONICS

Liquids and tonics are usually found in simple glass vials, bottles, or jars with one dose. These are usually labeled. Unfortunately these labels usually have nothing but exaggerated claims of their effectiveness. Since these are manufactured for a profit, they are usually branded with the name of a local alchemist. Until consumed, it is difficult to determine the effects of these substances, so imbibe those that are unlabeled at your own risk. Liquids of the same type, make, and manufacture will be somewhat similar, though formulation varies greatly from alchemist to alchemist.

Unless otherwise noted in the descriptions of the individual tonics listed below, the effects last for 1d4 + 4 minutes. The whole dose must be consumed for any effect.

TABLE 3–5: LIQUIDS AND TONICS

Name	Craft (alchemy) DC	Price	Weight
Air Crystal	20	50 gp	0.1 lb.
Alchemist's Kindness (20)	20	20 gp	0.1 lb.
Amnesia Tonic	18	25 gp	0.1 lb.
Analgesic	21	5 gp	0.1 lb.
Antiemetic Snuff	25	50 gp	0.1 lb.
Antiplague	25	50 gp	0.1 lb.
Antitoxin	25	50 gp	0.1 lb.
Bast's Kindness	20	3 gp	0.1 lb.
Bone Bomb	20	50 gp	0.1 lb.
Dead Water	25	100 gp	0.1 lb.
Death Flame	20	50 gp	0.1 lb.
Dragon's Heart	25	50 gp	0.1 lb.
Elf's Heart	25	50 gp	0.1 lb.
Embalming Fluid	25	50 gp	10 lbs.
Emetic	25	50 gp	0.1 lb.
Endurance Booster	20	50 gp	0.1 lb.
Energy Drink	15	400 gp	0.1 lb.
False Slumber	22	600 gp	0.1 lb.
Fool's Water	25	50 gp	0.1 lb.
Fruity Mouth Paste	20	100 gp	0.1 lb.
Lifeline	25	250 gp	0.1 lb.
Liquid Breath	30	100 gp	0.1 lb.
Low-Light Tonic	25	100 gp	0.1 lb.
Oasis Refreshment	22	80 gp	0.1 lb.
Olfactory Acuity	24	25 gp	0.1 lb.
Olfactory Dulling	18	5 gp	0.1 lb.
Piling	15	50 gp	0.1 lb.
Slumber Swig	15	200 gp	0.1 lb.
Smelling Salts	25	25 gp	0.1 lb.
Sweet Rest	20	75 gp	0.1 lb.
Thief's Heart	25	50 gp	0.1 lb.

Air Crystal: These unpleasant tasting, alchemically grown crystals release breathable air when chewed. A pouch of air crystals provides one minute of breathable air. Placing air crystals in your mouth takes a standard action; chewing them each round is a free action. Any attempt to speak while chewing air crystals negates any remaining duration.

DC 20 Craft (alchemy); *Rarity:* Uncommon; *Price:* 50 gp; *Weight:* —; *Alchemical Formula:* Amethyst, Air (any) (x3)

Alchemist's Kindness (20): Favored by young rakes and other well-to-do inebriates, this crystalline powder resembles salt. Mixed with water, it makes a fizzing cocktail that eliminates the effects of a hangover within 10 minutes of drinking it.

DC 20 Craft (alchemy); *Rarity:* Common; *Price:* 20 gp; *Weight:* —; *Alchemical Formula:* Rare Earth, Earth (any), Sulfur (any)

Amnesia Tonic: This tonic causes the user to have difficulty remembering the previous day after sleeping. Upon waking, the drinker must struggle to remember any events from the previous period of wakefulness. A successful DC 18 Will save allows the imbiber to recover a single piece of information. The DC may be increased to recover more specific information.

DC 18 Craft (alchemy); *Rarity:* Uncommon; *Price:* 25 gp; *Weight:* —; *Alchemical Formula:* Mercury (any), Water (any), Memory

Analgesic: This is an alchemist's painkiller. It can increase a save versus a pain-related effect with a +2 alchemical bonus or allow a person to continue to function down to –3 hit points. Effects related to reaching 0 hit points don't take effect until the imbiber reaches –3 hit points. It can also provide relief for migraines and post-surgical pain.

DC 21 Craft (alchemy); *Rarity:* Common; *Price:* 5 gp; *Weight:* —; *Alchemical Formula:* Fire (any), Water (any), Body

Antiemetic Snuff: This snuff can be used to shake off the effects of nausea. If you take it before being exposed to an effect that would give you the nauseated condition and allows a saving throw, you attempt two saving throws against the effect and take the higher result. A single dose provides this benefit for one hour.

DC 25 Craft (alchemy); *Rarity:* Common; *Price:* 50 gp; *Weight:* —; *Alchemical Formula:* Rare Earth, Earth (any), Salt (any), Body

Antiplague: If you drink a vial of this foul-tasting, milky tonic, you gain a +5 alchemical bonus on Fortitude saving throws against disease for the next hour. If already infected, you may also make two saving throws (without the +5 bonus) that day and use the better result.

DC 25 Craft (alchemy); *Rarity:* Uncommon; *Price:* 50 gp; *Weight:* —; *Alchemical Formula:* Earth (any), Fire, Sulfur, Disease, Healing

Antitoxin: This is not the antidote to poison, but a range of counteragents for a variety of toxins. If you drink a vial of antitoxin, you gain a +5 alchemical bonus on Fortitude saving throws against poison for one hour.

DC 25 Craft (alchemy); *Rarity:* Uncommon; *Price:* 50 gp; *Weight:* —; *Alchemical Formula:* Earth (any), Sulfur (any), Water (any), Protection, Toxin

Bast's Kindness: This tonic dramatically reduces the chances of conception during sexual intercourse if taken daily for one month by either party. The effects last as long as it is taken daily thereafter. Each bottle contains 30 doses.

DC 20 Craft (alchemy); *Rarity:* Uncommon; *Price:* 3 gp; *Weight:* —; *Alchemical Formula:* Water (any)

Bone Bomb: When this is applied to an inanimate skeleton, it causes several effects. The bones take on a glossy sheen, and they become easier to damage.
If the skeleton is raised from the dead, it suffers a –2 alchemical penalty to natural armor. The bones shatter if the skeleton is destroyed.
Everyone adjacent to the skeleton must make a DC 16 Reflex save or take 1d4 points of piercing damage per hit die of the skeleton.

DC 20 Craft (alchemy); *Rarity:* Uncommon; *Price:* 50 gp; *Weight:* —; *Alchemical Formula:* Rare Earth, Azoth (any), Mercury (any), Decay

Dead Water: When this is added to water, it instantly removes all the oxygen from the liquid in a 10-foot cube. Still waters will remain oxygen deprived for 24 hours. More active waters clear themselves out in a few rounds, usually six. Water-breathing creatures in the area immediately begin to suffocate.

DC 25 Craft (alchemy); *Rarity:* Uncommon; *Price:* 100 gp; *Weight:* —; *Alchemical Formula:* Iron, Rare Earth, Water (any), Salt (any)

Death Flame: This fluid is applied to unintelligent undead. When undead coated in this fluid are struck in combat, they explode into flame. This greenish-blue flame does no damage to them, but any attack they make does an additional 1d6 points of fire damage for one minute.

DC 20 Craft (alchemy); *Rarity:* Uncommon; *Price:* 50 gp; *Weight:* —; *Alchemical Formula:* Onyx, Azoth (any), Fire (any), Sulfur (any)

Dragon's Heart: This provides a +1 alchemical bonus to Fortitude saves for one hour.

DC 25 Craft (alchemy); *Rarity:* Uncommon; *Price:* 50 gp; *Weight:* —; *Alchemical Formula:* Rare Earth, Earth (any), Salt (any), Body

Elf's Heart: This provides a +1 alchemical bonus to Will saves for one hour.

DC 25 Craft (alchemy); *Rarity:* Uncommon; *Price:* 50 gp; *Weight:* —; *Alchemical Formula:* Rare Earth, Salt (any), Water (any), Mind

Embalming Fluid: This fluid is used to preserve corpses, whether for later dissection, taxidermy, necromancy, or magic such as *raise dead*. Embalming fluid is technically a poison, and using it makes a corpse unpalatable to most animals and vermin, though corpse-eating undead don't mind the taste. Treating a corpse with embalming fluid takes one hour and a successful DC 25 Heal check. The embalmed corpse decays at half the normal rate (each day dead counts as half a day for the purpose of *raise dead*).

DC 25 Craft (alchemy); *Rarity:* Common; *Price:* 50 gp; *Weight:* 10 lbs.; *Alchemical Formula:* Rare Earth, Earth (any), Salt (any), Water (any), Stasis

Emetic: This liquid induces vomiting. If opened after being swallowed whole by a creature, this causes the creature to vomit you out unless it passes a DC 16 Fortitude save. The creature is sick and gains the nauseated condition for 1d4 + 1 rounds.
If imbibed after ingesting a poison, this gives a second save with a +5 alchemical bonus to the saving throw. There are 10 doses in a vial. If some doses of this have been used and then it is used on a creature who swallows you, the DC to resist vomiting is decreased by 1 for each dose already used.

DC 25 Craft (alchemy); *Rarity:* Uncommon; *Price:* 50 gp; *Weight:* —; *Alchemical Formula:* Rare Earth, Water (any)

Endurance Booster: This tonic grants the imbiber the Endurance feat for one hour. After this hour they gain the fatigued condition when they crash. If the imbiber was fatigued when they took this tonic, then when it wears off they become exhausted. 25% of the people who drink this tonic react strongly to it, and it lasts 1d4 hours for them. This is only rolled the first time an imbiber takes an *endurance booster*.

DC 20 Craft (alchemy); *Rarity:* Uncommon; *Price:* 50 gp; *Weight:* —; *Alchemical Formula:* Rare Earth, Sulfur (any) (x2), Strength

Energy Drink: This liquid banishes any sort of fatigue or exhaustion in the user. However, if the user engaged in further activity that causes fatigue, it accumulates as normal. The consumption of another beverage can also banish this fatigue. After 24 hours, the imbiber becomes completely overwhelmed and must sleep for eight hours + four hours per drink beyond the first. If four or more are consumed within a week or more than one is consumed in a 24-hour period, the player must succeed at a DC 5 Constitution check or suffer 1d4 Constitution damage.

DC 15 Craft (alchemy); *Rarity:* Uncommon; *Price:* 400 gp; *Weight:* —; *Alchemical Formula:* Air (any), Fire (any), Mercury (any), Sulfur (any), Strength, Body

False Slumber: When consumed, this tonic causes the imbiber to fall into a deep sleep for (2d6 + 4) x 10 minutes. The character cannot be awakened short of a *dispel magic* or stronger. Another side effect of this tonic is that the user appears to be dead: her heartbeat slows, her skin turns gray, and she becomes nonresponsive.

DC 22 Craft (alchemy); *Rarity:* Rare; *Price:* 600 gp; *Weight:* —; *Alchemical Formula:* Rare Earth, Mercury (any), Salt (any), Stasis

Fool's Water: This substance appears to be a totally normal vial of water. When poured out of the vial, however, it flows uphill until it reaches the highest surface nearby. Surface tension keeps it attached to the surface it is poured on. It pools on this surface, and if possible, it begins to drip upward toward the sky.
This can be poured on a wall inside a closed chamber, in which case, it climbs and finds the highest point on the ceiling. It is water, so if it encounters a crevice, it flows through that crevice just as normal water would. If opened outside, it flows upward into the sky.

DC 25 Craft (alchemy); *Rarity:* Rare; *Price:* 50 gp; *Weight:* —; *Alchemical Formula:* Rare Earth, Air (any), Mercury (any), Flight

Fruity Mouth Paste: This liquid coats the inside of the imbiber's mouth. This allows them to hold toxic substances within their mouth for up to an hour without receiving any negative effects. Note that if the user swallows the toxic substance, it affects them normally. But even the most toxic chemicals may be held in the mouth for the duration. This is useful for spitting a poison spray at opponents.

DC 20 Craft (alchemy); *Rarity:* Rare; *Price:* 100 gp; *Weight:* —; *Alchemical Formula:* Rare Earth, Earth (any), Salt (any), Toxin

Lifeline: When consumed, this liquid tonic affects the imbiber for 24 hours. If at any time during that period the imbiber falls under 0 hit points, they automatically stop bleeding. If at exactly 0 hit points, you may still take actions. If below 0 hit points, you gain the staggered condition instead of falling unconscious. You still die at whatever final threshold your game uses for death.

DC 25 Craft (alchemy); *Rarity:* Rare; *Price:* 250 gp; *Weight:* —; *Alchemical Formula:* Emerald, Jade, Life

Liquid Breath: This fills the lungs with a highly oxygenated liquid. While filled in this manner, the imbiber is able to breathe in oxygenated liquids such as water and is immune to the nonlethal environmental pressure and effects due to depths; e.g., the bends. This lasts for two hours. Note that 1d6 rounds after imbibing this substance, the user can no longer breathe air.

DC 30 Craft (alchemy); *Rarity:* Very Rare; *Price:* 100 gp; *Weight:* —; *Alchemical Formula:* Sapphire, Air (any), Water (any), Body

Low-Light Tonic: This tonic grants the imbiber low-light vision.

DC 25 Craft (alchemy); *Rarity:* Rare; *Price:* 100 gp; *Weight:* —; *Alchemical Formula:* Rare Earth, Mercury (any), Sulfur (any), Perception

Oasis Refreshment: This wonderful liquid prevents all negative effects from heat, sunstroke, and dehydration for 12 hours. If the user already has penalties from the effects of the sun, these are negated. The liquid rehydrates the imbiber, and they are protected from the environment for six hours.

DC 22 Craft (alchemy); *Rarity:* Uncommon; *Price:* 80 gp; *Weight:* —; *Alchemical Formula:* Salt (any), Sulfur (any), Water (any), Body

Oil, Fire-Breathing: This hard-to-light oil burns well at a low temperature. It is often used by jesters and other fire-breathing entertainers. Those untrained with the oil and wielding a flame source can breathe out a one-foot cone that is five feet wide at the end and deals 1d3 points of fire damage to a creature adjacent to you on a hit. A fumble means that you accidentally burn yourself for 1d6 points of fire damage. There are 10 doses per vial.

DC 15 Craft (alchemy); *Rarity:* Uncommon; *Price:* 50 gp; *Weight:* —; *Alchemical Formula:* Fire (any) (x2), Salt (any), Water (any)

Olfactory Acuity Tonic: This gives the user a preternatural sense of smell. They gain the Scent extraordinary ability. They receive an alchemical bonus to Survival checks made to track equal to half their level + 4.

DC 24 Craft (alchemy); *Rarity:* Rare; *Price:* 25 gp; *Weight:* —; *Alchemical Formula:* Air (any), Earth (any), Salt (any), Perception

Olfactory Dulling Tonic: This nullifies the imbibers sense of smell for one hour, making him or her immune to stench attacks and giving a +1 alchemical bonus on saves versus any noxious gas that causes nausea, vomiting, or illness.

DC 18 Craft (alchemy); *Rarity:* Common; *Price:* 5 gp; *Weight:* —; *Alchemical Formula:* Earth (any), Salt (any)

Piling Tonic: When this tonic is dumped out onto the floor, all light loose material within a 20-foot radius is gathered into a pile. This includes dust, fluff, and loose objects of one pound or less. There is no limit to how much the potion can attract, but the objects must be non-living and unconstrained. Coins in a box, bag, drawer, or behind a door are not affected. It takes 10 minutes for everything to roll to the center near the liquid. It is advised to stand back. As soon as the gathering is over, the items may be redistributed freely.

DC 15 Craft (alchemy); *Rarity:* Rare; *Price:* 50 gp; *Weight:* —; *Alchemical Formula:* Iron, Silver, Rare Earth, Azoth (any)

Slumber Swig: When this is consumed or inhaled, the imbiber falls asleep for eight hours. They may resist if they succeed at a DC 26 Fortitude save. They may make another check each hour with a cumulative +2 bonus to wake up; i.e., after four hours, the drinker attempts to wake up, and must succeed at a DC 18 Fortitude save. Note that this must be held over the mouth for one round or imbibed to have an effect.

DC 15 Craft (alchemy); *Rarity:* Uncommon; *Price:* 200 gp; *Weight:* —; *Alchemical Formula:* Rare Earth, Mercury (any), Water (any), Stasis

Smelling Salts: These sharply scented gray crystals cause people inhaling them to regain consciousness. *Smelling salts* grant you a new saving throw to resist any spell or effect that has already rendered you unconscious or staggered. If exposed to *smelling salts* while dying, you immediately become conscious and staggered, but must still make stabilization checks each round; if you perform any standard action (or any other strenuous action), you take 1 point of damage after completing the act and fall unconscious again. A container of *smelling salts* has dozens of uses if stoppered after each use but depletes in a matter of hours if left open.

DC 25 Craft (alchemy); *Rarity:* Uncommon; *Price:* 25 gp; *Weight:* —; *Alchemical Formula:* Rare Earth, Salt (any), Sulfur (any)

Sweet Rest: When imbibed, this effervescent solution causes a heavy warmth to spread from your stomach outward to your limbs, resulting in feelings of security and well-being. If you sleep for at least one hour after consuming the solution, the next time within the next 24 hours that you attempt a saving throw to remove a temporary negative level, you can roll the save twice and use the better result.

DC 20 Craft (alchemy); *Rarity:* Rare; *Price:* 75 gp; *Weight:* —; *Alchemical Formula:* Rare Earth, Salt (any), Sulfur (any), Healing

Thief's Heart: This provides a +1 alchemical bonus on Reflex saves for one hour.

DC 25 Craft (alchemy); *Rarity:* Uncommon; *Price:* 50 gp; *Weight:* —; *Alchemical Formula:* Rare Earth, Air (any), Fire (any), Salt (any), Agility

OINTMENTS AND PASTES

Ointments and pastes are substances that produce an alchemical effect when they are smeared over a surface. They take a full-round action to apply. Ointments are applied to the skin and pastes to objects.

Note that in order to apply an ointment to the skin, clothing and armor must be removed.

Unless otherwise noted, ointments and pastes have a duration of one hour. Like magical oils, unless otherwise noted, these may be rinsed off with a mild alcohol solution such as wine if there is a desire to end their effects early.

TABLE 3–6: OINTMENTS AND PASTES

Name	Craft (alchemy) DC	Price	Weight
Alchemical Glue	20	20 gp	0.5 lb.
Alchemical Grease (5)	15 gp	25	0.5 lb.
Armor Malleability	25	550 gp	0.1 lb.
Blessing	20	300 gp	0.1 lb.
Brittle Cream	20	150 gp	0.1 lb.
Buoyancy	14	400 gp	0.1 lb.
Clarity	22	400 gp	0.1 lb.
Counterscent	23	25 gp	0.1 lb.
Durability	20	100 gp	0.1 lb.
Flame Paste	25	150 gp	0.1 lb.
Icewalking	30	375 gp	0.1 lb.
Insect Repellent	15	50 gp	0.1 lb.
Insulating Paste	25	100 gp	0.1 lb.
Lockstick	22	50 gp	0.1 lb.
Magic Aura	15	50 gp	0.1 lb.
Nightingale	16	25 gp	0.1 lb.
Orcus' Protection	22	100 gp	0.1 lb.
Protection	18	650 gp	0.1 lb.
Quieting	25	250 gp	0.1 lb.
Scarsalve	20	10 gp	1 lb.
Shrieking Paste	20	50 gp	0.1 lb.
Sun Cream	20	10 gp	0.5 lb.
Toxinshield	22	125 gp	0.1 lb.
Trollkiller	25	300 gp	0.1 lb.
Weapon Blanch, Adamantine (5)	25	500 gp	2.5 lbs.
Weapon Blanch, Cold Iron (5)	20	100 gp	2.5 lbs.
Weapon Blanch, Ghost Salt	25	200 gp	0.5 lb.
Weapon Blanch, Silver (10)	20	50 gp	5 lbs.
Woodbronzer	15	60 gp	0.1 lb.

Alchemical Glue: This glue is stored as two flasks of syrupy liquid. When mixed together and allowed to cure, they form a strong bond. The glue is sufficient to coat one square foot of surface or (because of waste, spills, and inaccurate mixing) up to 20 smaller applications of approximately two square inches each. The glue is tacky after one minute and fully cured after one hour. Pulling apart a large glued surface (at least one square foot) requires a DC 20 Strength check for tacky glue or DC 25 for cured glue. Pulling apart a small glued surface (anything less than one square foot) is a DC 15 Strength check for tacky glue or DC 20 for cured glue.

DC 20 Craft (alchemy); *Rarity:* Common; *Price:* 20 gp; *Weight:* 0.5 lb.; *Alchemical Formula:* Rare Earth, Earth (any), Salt (any), Water (any)

Alchemical Grease (5): Each pot of this slick black goo has sufficient contents to cover one Medium creature or two Small ones. If you coat yourself in *alchemical grease*, you gain a +5 alchemical bonus on Escape Artist checks, on combat maneuver checks made to escape a grapple, and to your CMD to avoid being grappled; this lasts for four hours or until you wash it off.

DC 15 Craft (alchemy); *Rarity:* Common; *Price:* 25 gp; *Weight:* —; *Alchemical Formula:* Salt (any), Water (any), Agility *or* Plant

Armor Malleability Paste: This useful paste has a sharp acrid odor. Its purpose is to remove some of the inherent stiffness in armor. The magics that allow it to work do so by weakening the armor itself.

Once applied, it improves the chances of moving stealthily and easily in the armor. The armor check penalty for acrobatics and Stealth checks is reduced by 2. It also allows anyone wearing the armor to treat it as if it were less restrictive and encumbering. For any armor that restricts movement, it provides an additional five feet of movement per round up to the character's maximum speed.

Every time this paste is applied to the armor, it permanently lower the hardness of the item by one, and does 1d4 points of damage to the item bypassing hardness.

DC 25 Craft (alchemy); *Rarity:* Uncommon; *Price:* 550 gp; *Weight:* —; *Alchemical Formula:* Rare Earth, Water (any), Body, Stealth

Blessing Ointment: Using this ointment grants the user a +2 deflection bonus to AC and gives the user a +2 resistance bonus to saves for one hour.

DC 20 Craft (alchemy); *Rarity:* Uncommon; *Price:* 300 gp; *Weight:* —; *Alchemical Formula:* Rare Earth, Salt (any), Sulfur (any), Protection

Brittle Cream: When spread over any object, this paste reduces hardness by 3 and lowers the break DC by 2 points. It affects one medium-sized object or equivalent.

DC 20 Craft (alchemy); *Rarity:* Uncommon; *Price:* 150 gp; *Weight:* —; *Alchemical Formula:* Earth (x5), Mercury (x5), Rare Earth, Rare Earth

Buoyancy Ointment: Coating a person or object with this oil provides a natural buoyancy and causes the target to float in water for 2d4 + 6 hours. One jar of ointment is sufficient to cover 30 square feet or one Medium creature. The users get a +10 alchemical bonus on any Swim checks made to stay afloat.

DC 14 Craft (alchemy); *Rarity:* Uncommon; *Price:* 400 gp; *Weight:* —; *Alchemical Formula:* Rare Earth, Air (any) (x2), Water (any)

Clarity Ointment: This cream-colored ointment has no efficacy on its own of any sort, but when it is used in conjunction with spells affecting vision such as *clairvoyance* or *arcane sight*, it doubles range and effect.

DC 22 Craft (alchemy); *Rarity:* Uncommon; *Price:* 400 gp; *Weight:* —; *Alchemical Formula:* Rare Earth, Mercury (any), Sulfur (any), 2 Perception *or* 1 Prophecy

Counterscent Ointment: When applied, this ointment neutralizes and masks any odors produced for one man-sized creature for two hours. During that time, the user exudes no scent or odor. This makes tracking more difficult and adds +5 to the DC required to track the target.

DC 23 Craft (alchemy); *Rarity:* Common; *Price:* 25 gp; *Weight:* —; *Alchemical Formula:* Air (any), Fire (any), Salt (any), Stealth

Durability Paste: When spread over any material, this paste increases the hardness of the material by 3 and raises the break DC by 2 for one hour. It can affect one medium-sized object or equivalent.

DC 20 Craft (alchemy); *Rarity:* Uncommon; *Price:* 100 gp; *Weight:* —; *Alchemical Formula:* Rare Earth, Earth (any), Salt (any), Decay

Flame Paste: This thick paste concentrates flame and burns extremely hot. It can be applied in any one-square-foot configuration; e.g., a line one inch high and 12 feet long or a one-foot square. It burns extremely hot, doing 3d6 + 3 damage per round and ignoring half hardness of whatever material it is spread on. It must be applied thinly because it does not splatter or burn well upon initial exposure to air. It must set for one round. *Flame paste* burns for three rounds.

While *flame paste* does burn hotter, it will not spread itself. When using the fire rules, simply apply increasing damage to the object and, if it burns hotter, allow the possibility of igniting very close nearby flammable materials.

DC 25 Craft (alchemy); *Rarity:* Uncommon; *Price:* 150 gp; *Weight:* —; *Alchemical Formula:* Iron, Rare Earth, Silver, Fire (any)

Icewalking Paste: When applied to your hands and feet, this paste adheres to ice and allows you to cross and climb on icy surfaces as if under the influence of a *spider climb* spell.

DC 30 Craft (alchemy); *Rarity:* Very Rare; *Price:* 375 gp; *Weight:* —; *Alchemical Formula:* Moonstone, Rare Earth, Air (any), Agility

Insect Repellent Ointment: This ointment can be applied to the skin to repel small biting insects. Tiny or smaller insects are held at bay for four hours. Larger insects or swarms must succeed at a DC 14 Will save to approach. If the character attacks the insects or intentionally agitates them, the insects automatically make their saving throws.

DC 15 Craft (alchemy); *Rarity:* Uncommon; *Price:* 50 gp; *Weight:* —; *Alchemical Formula:* Rare Earth, Salt (any), Protection

Insulating Paste: When applied to the interior of armor, this paste gives the user a +5 alchemical bonus to all saves versus cold weather for 24 hours. It also gives a +2 alchemical bonus to all saves versus magical cold and cold attacks. It makes the armor stiffer, increasing the armor check penalty by 1.

DC 25 Craft (alchemy); *Rarity:* Uncommon; *Price:* 100 gp; *Weight:* —; *Alchemical Formula:* Rare Earth, Earth (any), Fire (any), Cold

Lockstick Paste: When applied to a lock, this substance makes the lock more difficult to pick. Picks slide off, and gears and pins become more difficult to manipulate. Disable device checks made to open the lock it is applied to suffer a –5 alchemical penalty.

DC 22 Craft (alchemy); *Rarity:* Uncommon; *Price:* 50 gp; *Weight:* —; *Alchemical Formula:* Rare Earth, Earth (any), Salt (any), Protection

Magical Aura Ointment: Nonmagical items covered in this ointment detect as magical. When you create this ointment, you can determine the type of aura that this ointment creates.

DC 15 Craft (alchemy); *Rarity:* Uncommon; *Price:* 50 gp; *Weight:* —; *Alchemical Formula:* Rare Earth, Azoth (any), Mercury (any), Transmutation

Nightingale Paste: When spread over a 10-foot-by-10-foot section of floor, this paste makes a loud squeaking noise, alerting nearby listeners. Surfaces covered with this paste give a –10 alchemical penalty to Stealth checks. This paste lasts indefinitely but heavy foot traffic causes it to come off.

DC 16 Craft (alchemy); *Rarity:* Uncommon; *Price:* 25 gp; *Weight:* —; *Alchemical Formula:* Air (any), Mercury (any), Stealth

Orcus' Protection Ointment: This ointment is formulated to provide protection from sunlight for light-sensitive humanoids and undead. It is a thick white ointment that provides 24 hours of protection. While under the protection of this ointment, drow armor and weapons do not decay, sub-world creatures do not receive penalties for fighting during the day, and vampires no longer take damage from the sun. Note that direct bright sun exposure might still have an effect, and radiant damage and sunlight spells affects the target as a normal aboveground creature.

DC 22 Craft (alchemy); *Rarity:* Rare; *Price:* 100 gp; *Weight:* —; *Alchemical Formula:* Gold, Onyx, Rare Earth, Mercury (any), Protection

Protection Ointment: This light blue ointment improves saving throws by providing a +2 alchemical bonus to all saving throws for eight hours.

DC 18 Craft (alchemy); *Rarity:* Uncommon; *Price:* 650 gp; *Weight:* —; *Alchemical Formula:* Rare Earth, Earth (any), Fire (any), Water (any), Protection

Quieting Paste: This paste is an oily black color, with a sharp metallic smell. Its purpose is to reduce the noise that armors and clothing make. The armor check penalty for Stealth checks is reduced by 2.

DC 25 Craft (alchemy); *Rarity:* Uncommon; *Price:* 250 gp; *Weight:* —; *Alchemical Formula:* Rare Earth, Sapphire, Mercury (any), Stealth

Scarsalve: When applied to scarred areas of the body, *scarsalve* causes those scars to fade from view for one day. A character who gains benefits from having visible scars loses those benefits while under the effects of *scarsalve* but also gains a +2 alchemical bonus on Disguise checks.

DC 20 Craft (alchemy); *Rarity:* Uncommon; *Price:* 10 gp; *Weight:* 1 lb.; *Alchemical Formula:* Air (any), Mercury (any), Salt (any), 2 Body *or* 1 Healing

Shrieking Paste: Once this paste is exposed to air, after one round it begins to shriek as loudly as a shrieker. It continues to do so for a full minute.

DC 20 Craft (alchemy); *Rarity:* Uncommon; *Price:* 50 gp; *Weight:* —; *Alchemical Formula:* Air (x2), Earth, Rare Earth

Sun Cream: Each application of this alchemical solution — typically compounded in combination with substances found in desert flowers, fruits, and roots — heals 1d4 points of nonlethal damage that the target takes from heat exposure. If you succeed at a DC 20 Heal check while applying *sun cream*, you may add your Wisdom modifier to the nonlethal damage healed. A creature cannot benefit from more than one application of *sun cream* in a 24-hour period.

DC 20 Craft (alchemy); *Rarity:* Uncommon; *Price:* 10 gp; *Weight:* 0.5 lb.; *Alchemical Formula:* Earth, Mercury (any), Salt (any)

Toxinshield Ointment: This ointment produces a waxy coating on your skin that protects you from contact poisons. Note that this works well on most flesh and lasts for one hour; on areas that move frequently, such as hands, it lasts for a 2d4 + 2 minutes.

DC 22 Craft (alchemy); *Rarity:* Rare; *Price:* 125 gp; *Weight:* —; *Alchemical Formula:* Rare Earth, Salt (any), Water (any), Toxin

Trollkiller Paste: When applied to a weapon, the paste covering causes damage that is difficult to heal on a successful strike. The edges of the wound are corrupted, and natural healing processes are inhibited. Damage caused can only be healed magically and by natural healing. Regeneration cannot heal this damage. Wounds caused by this weapon are always lethal damage. The paste lasts for one hour.

DC 25 Craft (alchemy); *Rarity:* Uncommon; *Price:* 300 gp; *Weight:* —; *Alchemical Formula:* Onyx, Rare Earth, Earth (any), Fire (any), Decay

Weapon Blanch, Adamantine (5): These silver, alchemical powders have a gritty consistency, appearing at first glance to be simple metal shavings. When poured on a weapon and placed over a hot flame for a full round, they melt and form a temporary coating on the weapon. The blanching gives the weapon the ability to bypass adamantine damage reduction. The blanching remains effective until you make a successful attack with the weapon. Each dose of blanching can coat one weapon or up to 10 pieces of ammunition. Only one kind of *weapon blanch* can be on a weapon at one time, though a weapon made of one special material (such as adamantine) can have a different material blanch (such as silver), and counts as both materials for the first successful hit.

DC 25 Craft (alchemy); *Rarity:* Rare; *Price:* 500 gp; *Weight:* 2.5 lbs.; *Alchemical Formula:* Adamantine, Diamond, Rare Earth, Mercury (any), Water (any)

Weapon Blanch, Cold Iron (5): These silver, alchemical powders have a gritty consistency, appearing at first glance to be simple metal shavings. When poured on a weapon and placed over a hot flame for a full round, they melt and form a temporary coating on the weapon. The blanching gives the weapon the ability to bypass cold iron damage reduction. The blanching remains effective until you make a successful attack with the weapon. Each dose of blanching can coat one weapon or up to 10 pieces of ammunition. Only one kind of *weapon blanch* can be on a weapon at one time, though a weapon made of one special material (such as adamantine) can have a different material blanch (such as silver), and counts as both materials for the first successful hit.

DC 20 Craft (alchemy); *Rarity:* Common; *Price:* 100 gp; *Weight:* 2.5 lbs.; *Alchemical Formula:* Iron, Rare Earth, Mercury (any), Water (any)

Weapon Blanch, Ghost Salt: This gritty alchemical powder is made from exotic minerals mixed with an infusion crafted from the ectoplasmic remains of destroyed incorporeal undead. When rubbed onto a weapon that is then placed over a hot flame for a full round, ghost salt melts and forms a temporary coating on the weapon. The blanching gives the weapon the ability to do full damage to incorporeal creatures, even if the weapon itself is nonmagical. An application of ghost salt remains effective until the weapon makes a successful attack. Each dose of *weapon blanch* can coat one weapon or up to 10 pieces of ammunition. Only one kind of weapon blanch can be on a weapon at one time.

DC 25 Craft (alchemy); *Rarity:* Rare; *Price:* 200 gp; *Weight:* 0.5 lb.; *Alchemical Formula:* Rare Earth, Silver, Azoth (from 2 sources), Mercury (any), Water (any)

Weapon Blanch, Silver (10): These silver, alchemical powders have a gritty consistency, appearing at first glance to be simple metal shavings. When poured on a weapon and placed over a hot flame for a full round, they melt and form a temporary coating on the weapon. The blanching gives the weapon the ability to bypass silver damage reduction. The blanching remains effective until you make a successful attack with the weapon. Each dose of blanching can coat one weapon or up to 10 pieces of ammunition. Only one kind of *weapon blanch* can be on a weapon at one time, though a weapon made of one special material (such as adamantine) can have a different material blanch (such as silver), and counts as both materials for the first successful hit.

DC 20 Craft (alchemy); *Rarity:* Common; *Price:* 50 gp; *Weight:* 5 lbs.; *Alchemical Formula:* Rare Earth, Silver, Mercury (any), Water (any)

Woodbronzer: When applied to any wooden object, it strengthens and protects wood, increasing the hardness of wood by 5 and adding 2 to the break DC. This substance affects only rigid, porous, organic materials (e.g., wood, coral).

DC 15 Craft (alchemy); *Rarity:* Uncommon; *Price:* 60 gp; *Weight:* —; *Alchemical Formula:* Iron, Rare Earth, Earth (any), Plant

POWDERS

Unless otherwise noted, powders appear as a dry thick bulk solid composed of unconstrained flowing particles that move freely when shifted. Powders are often very fine and tend to clump. Color and consistency may vary. Powders are delivered to the target by a variety of methods. They may be sprinkled, added to food or drink, delivered by blowgun, or thrown.

Powders delivered via blowgun have a range of 10 feet maximum, affecting the first target in front of the alchemist. The alchemist may shorten this range and strike two creatures both adjacent to each other and the alchemist, giving them both a +2 circumstance bonus to their saving throws if any. The user must have proficiency with the exotic blowgun in order to deliver powder this way; otherwise, in addition to the hit penalty, on a natural roll of 1 the powder affects the user. Powders may also be thrown like grenades with a range of increment of 10 feet. A direct hit is necessary to affect a single target. Any miss and the powder is harmless.

To be thrown as a grenade-like weapon, the powder must be prepared this way specifically ahead of time and contained in a light, breakable shell. Otherwise, they are loose piles of powder suitable for sprinkling or for use in a blowgun. In order to hit a target with a powder thrown as a grenade-like weapon, they do not need to penetrate armor unless specifically noted. A simple touch attack will strike true. Powders must score a direct hit, otherwise they dissipate harmlessly. There is no splash effect.

On a miss, the powder lands somewhere harmlessly, ruined.

On contact, the target immediately makes any save if applicable, but the powder does not take effect immediately. Its effects begin at the start of the next round. Unless otherwise noted, the effects of powder lasts for 1d4 + 1 rounds.

TABLE 3–7: POWDERS

Name	Craft (alchemy) DC	Price	Weight
Absorption	15	400 gp	0.2 lb.
Acid-Neutralizing	20	20 gp	0.2 lb.
Avian Repellent	10	150 gp	0.2 lb.
Blandness	15	150 gp	0.2 lb.
Bloodhound Lure	20	20 gp	0.2 lb.
Cleanliness	18	50 gp	0.2 lb.
Clouded Vision	15	25 gp	0.2 lb.
Contrariness	25	50 gp	0.2 lb.
Convulsive Cachinnate	20	100 gp	0.2 lb.
Deathsight	12	30 gp	0.2 lb.
Defoliant	25	30 gp	0.2 lb.
Dehydration	20	60 gp	0.2 lb.
De-Icing	20	30 gp	0.2 lb.
Delirium	19	20 gp	0.2 lb.
Desalination	12	50 gp	0.2 lb.
Dire	24	150 gp	0.2 lb.
Dousing	15	10 gp	0.2 lb.
Enfeeblement	20	400 gp	0.2 lb.
Fatigue	20	400 gp	0.2 lb.
Fertilizing	20	25 gp	0.2 lb.
Frailty	20	350 gp	0.2 lb.
Frothing	20	20 gp	0.2 lb.
Ground Fog	22	100 gp	0.2 lb.
Hallucinations	16	30 gp	0.2 lb.
Incendiary (10)	15	10 gp	2 lbs.
Insect Repellent	12	300 go	0.2 lb.
Itching	20	25 gp	0.2 lb.
Madness	28	250 gp	0.2 lb.
Magic Detection	21	250 gp	0.2 lb.
Nausea	15	30 gp	0.2 lb.
Nullifying	22	75 gp	0.2 lb.

Name	Craft (alchemy) DC	Price	Weight
Obscuring	25	500 gp	0.2 lb.
Paralysis	25	100 gp	0.2 lb.
Pesticide	16	10 gp	0.2 lb.
Piquant	15	100 gp	0.2 lb.
Powdered Water	10	30 gp	0.2 lb.
Razor	25	50 gp	0.2 lb.
Smoke	10	3 gp	0.2 lb.
Snap	18	5 gp	0.2 lb.
Sneezing	13	60 gp	2 lbs.
Spoilage	15	100 gp	0.2 lb.
Trail Dispersion	18	600 gp	0.2 lb.
Vertigo	15	40 gp	0.2 lb.

Absorption Powder: This powder is powerfully absorbent. When added to a liquid such as water or acid, it absorbs it all up to 100 cubic feet, leaving a thick, inert, paste-like mud.

DC 15 Craft (alchemy); *Rarity:* Uncommon; *Price:* 400 gp; *Weight:* —; *Alchemical Formula:* Rare Earth, Air (any), Earth (any), Salt (any)

Acid-Neutralizing Powder: This powder instantly neutralizes any acids or solvents it comes into contact with, absorbing them and causing them to cease damaging effects immediately. A character may spend a round applying it to themselves to eliminate ongoing acid or solvent damage.

DC 20 Craft (alchemy); *Rarity:* Uncommon; *Price:* 20 gp; *Weight:* —; *Alchemical Formula:* Air (any), Earth (any), Salt (any), Acid

Avian Repellent Powder: This powder is particularly effective at repelling small birds. Each dose covers one acre and prevents any creature smaller than an eagle from landing there for one year.

DC 10 Craft (alchemy); *Rarity:* Uncommon; *Price:* 150 gp; *Weight:* —; *Alchemical Formula:* Rare Earth, Air (any), Salt (any), Protection

Blandness Powder: When applied to anything edible, this powder removes any distinctive smell or taste. This destroys any olfactory or gustatory properties of the item. This can be used to disguise the taste or smell of poisons or to neutralize the odor of a body, drugs, or the shoes of teenagers. There is enough to cover the smell of one corpse or six plates of food.

DC 15 Craft (alchemy); *Rarity:* Very Rare; *Price:* 150 gp; *Weight:* —; *Alchemical Formula:* Rare Earth, Earth (any), Salt (any), Illusion

Bloodhound Lure: This powder draws the attention of animals. Anyone covered in this powder is easily detectable by any natural animal. Animals receive a +4 alchemical bonus to all Perception and Survival checks against the creature. In combat, all animals favor anyone covered in this powder.

DC 20 Craft (alchemy); *Rarity:* Common; *Price:* 20 gp; *Weight:* —; *Alchemical Formula:* Air (any), Earth (any), Emotion

Cleanliness Powder: A quick dusting of this powder leaves clothes and materials clean and dry. It removes mud, blood, stains — any substance marring the surface of the clothing and fabric — yet this dust is not abrasive and leaves no marks.

DC 18 Craft (alchemy); *Rarity:* Uncommon; *Price:* 50 gp; *Weight:* —; *Alchemical Formula:* Silver, Rare Earth, Salt (any), Sulfur (any)

Clouded Vision Powder: On a successful use, this powder causes 1d4 + 1 rounds of blindness on a failed DC 10 Fortitude save. In order for this powder to work, it must target the eyes and so it carries a –5 to hit penalty against the target's touch AC and does not work against any humanoid wearing a full helm.

DC 15 Craft (alchemy); *Rarity:* Common; *Price:* 25 gp; *Weight:* —; *Alchemical Formula:* Earth (any), Fire (any), Mercury (any), Illusion, Light

Contrariness Powder: When successfully used against a target, this produces a specific insanity that alters behavior. If a DC 16 Will save is failed, then the target behaves in some respect opposite the way they normally would. Their alignment may reverse or they may attack their allies instead of their opponents. The powder lasts for 1d6 + 4 rounds before the effect wears off.
There is a small chance upon repeated usage that the effect could become permanent.

DC 25 Craft (alchemy); *Rarity:* Uncommon; *Price:* 50 gp; *Weight:* —; *Alchemical Formula:* Rare Earth, Air (any), Earth (any), Mercury (any), Mind

Convulsive Cachinnate Powder: When a target is dosed with this powder, they are seized with an overwhelming compulsion to laugh. Everything becomes hilarious. They may succeed at a DC 16 Will Save to avoid the effects. If the saving throw fails, the target begins laughing uncontrollably, falling prone on the ground. This lasts only for one round. After this round, they may stand up again, but they continue to laugh for the next 1d4 + 1 rounds. While laughing, they receive a –2 circumstance penalty on all attack and damage rolls.
This only affects targets of intelligence 4 or higher.

DC 20 Craft (alchemy); *Rarity:* Uncommon; *Price:* 100 gp; *Weight:* —; *Alchemical Formula:* Rare Earth, Air (any), Mercury (any), Emotion

Deathsight Powder: When this dust is inhaled or consumed, it causes the target to perceive all living creatures as walking corpses. Flesh appears to be rotting and sloughing off, gait is unsteady, and the process of decay has set in on every living creature the target sees. The target is under no compulsion to act hostilely toward the visions and perceives all other visual and auditory stimuli as normal; i.e., he hears their speech and sees their reactions as normal.
The powder tastes like bananas and cumin and flavors food and drink accordingly.

DC 12 Craft (alchemy); *Rarity:* Uncommon; *Price:* 30 gp; *Weight:* —; *Alchemical Formula:* Air (any), Mercury (any), Salt (any), Illusion

Defoliant Powder: This is a whitish powder used to kill plants. This kills most small plants within 24 hours. One dose is enough to cover five square feet or one large plant. Trees and various other large leafy plants die off over the following week.
This powder also has a damaging effect on any creature of the plant type. If targeted with this powder, they take 1d6 points of damage this round, and 1d6 points of damage the next. They receive a DC 14 Fortitude save to avoid the secondary damage the next round.

DC 25 Craft (alchemy); *Rarity:* Uncommon; *Price:* 30 gp; *Weight:* —; *Alchemical Formula:* Earth (any), Salt (any), Plant, Decay

Dehydration Powder: This horrible powder dehydrates the target. If an organic living target is hit by this powder, they instantly become dehydrated as the powder absorbs water from their body through their pores and skin. The target must make a DC 16 Fortitude save or immediately take 2d6 points of nonlethal damage and gain the fatigued condition.
They must repeat this save in an hour if they do not acquire any water in the interim. If used on organic corporeal undead that fail their save, it desiccates the corpse. This causes those undead to become weak to fire. Creatures subject to this powder feel as if they are dying of thirst and unless they succeed at a DC 12 Will save, they stop what they are doing and drink any available liquid — even poison.

DC 20 Craft (alchemy); *Rarity:* Uncommon; *Price:* 60 gp; *Weight:* —; *Alchemical Formula:* Rare Earth, Fire (any), Salt (any), Death, Decay

De-icing Powder: This powder is heavy, but when dispersed over ice, it instantly melts one 10-foot-by-10-foot square to form a non-slick slurry. This can be used on solid ice to provide traction, but caution must be used if the surface of the ice is thin, as it increases the chance that you fall through.
It also melts a solid cubic foot of ice and does 1d6 + 2 points of damage to creatures with the cold subtype. If a creature happens to be made of ice, it deals 2d6 + 4 points of damage.

DC 20 Craft (alchemy); *Rarity:* Uncommon; *Price:* 30 gp; *Weight:* —; *Alchemical Formula:* Fire (any), Mercury (any), Salt (any)

Delirium Powder: When a target is hit with this powder, it must make a DC 18 Will save. If the save fails, they begin to babble and speak randomly in any languages they know. Topics selected are random and may include the weather, dreams, fantasies, complaints, or even secret or useful information (10% chance per round). This effect lasts for 2d4 rounds.
A target knows what happened but is unable to stop themselves. They may become hostile immediately after the powder wears off.

DC 19 Craft (alchemy); *Rarity:* Uncommon; *Price:* 20 gp; *Weight:* —; *Alchemical Formula:* Air (any), Mercury (any), Salt (any), Control

Desalination Powder: This wonderful powder turns one gallon of saltwater into green, brackish, foul freshwater. It is safe to drink.

DC 12 Craft (alchemy); *Rarity:* Uncommon; *Price:* 50 gp; *Weight:* —; *Alchemical Formula:* Rare Earth, Silver, Sulfur (any)

Dire Powder: A target hit by this powder must make a DC 20 Will save. On a failure, they develop an insatiable bloodlust and immediately attack the nearest target. If multiple targets from the victim are equidistant, then select the target randomly. This powder lasts for 2d8 + 2 rounds. The victims continue to attack the nearest target until incapacitated or until the effect ends.

DC 24 Craft (alchemy); *Rarity:* Rare; *Price:* 150 gp; *Weight:* —; *Alchemical Formula:* Rare Earth, Mercury (any), Salt (any), Water (any), Emotion

Dousing Powder: This dark-gray powder is used to extinguish fires. When spread or dumped on a small flame, it immediately snuffs it out. It can be used to automatically prevent continuing fire damage. It automatically extinguishes a fire in a five-foot square. If using the optional fire rules (see **Table 1–6: Fire Progression**), reduce the severity of a fire in a five-foot square by one level.
It also causes damage to creatures made of living fire. When used upon any creature made of fire or with the elemental fire subtype, it does 2d8 + 2 points of damage.

DC 15 Craft (alchemy); *Rarity:* Uncommon; *Price:* 10 gp; *Weight:* —; *Alchemical Formula:* Water (any), Salt (any) (x2)

Enfeeblement Powder: A target hit with this dust must make a DC 18 Fortitude save. On a failed save, it experiences terrible weakness for one minute. This weakness is debilitating, giving them an alchemical Strength penalty of 1d6 + 4 points. A creature's Strength cannot be lowered below 1 using this powder.

DC 20 Craft (alchemy); *Rarity:* Uncommon; *Price:* 400 gp; *Weight:* —; *Alchemical Formula:* Onyx, Platinum, Rare Earth, Water (any), Decay

Fatigue Powder: A target hit by this dust must make a DC 16 Fortitude save. On a failed save, the target gains the exhausted condition. A successful save means they gain the fatigued condition.

DC 20 Craft (alchemy); *Rarity:* Uncommon *Price:* 400 gp; *Weight:* —; *Alchemical Formula:* Onyx, Platinum, Rare Earth, Fire (any), Stasis

Fertilizing Powder: This enriches soil, providing basic nutrition for plants. They are more likely to produce strong plants and good harvests. One dose is enough for an acre, and it must be applied weekly. Proper application of this powder increases the crop yield by 25%.

DC 20 Craft (alchemy); *Rarity:* Common; *Price:* 25 gp; *Weight:* —; *Alchemical Formula:* Earth (any), Plant (any), Sulfur (any)

Frailty Powder: When a target is affected by this powder, their immune system becomes heavily compromised. All Fortitude saves the target makes have their DC increased by 4. Anyone within range of splash damage has their Fortitude save DCs increased by 1. This is an alchemical penalty and does not stack. This effect lasts for one minute.

DC 20 Craft (alchemy); *Rarity:* Uncommon; *Price:* 350 gp; *Weight:* —; *Alchemical Formula:* Iron, Onyx, Rare Earth, Water (any), Decay

Frothing Powder: This dry, salty powder causes any water it is dispersed in to froth and boil violently. This attracts any nearby water predators or animals for a great distance, up to a quarter of a mile. Any animals caught in the 10-foot cube the powder creates are burned and harmed by the boiling effect, taking 3d6 fire damage per round. A successful DC 16 Fortitude save allows half damage.

A slow disturbance begins in the water on the first round after the powder is applied. The water then boils and roils violently for the next 1d4 + 1 rounds.

DC 20 Craft (alchemy); *Rarity:* Uncommon; *Price:* 20 gp; *Weight:* —; *Alchemical Formula:* Earth (any), Fire (any) (x2), Water (any)

Ground Fog Powder: When this powder is thrown on the ground, it covers a 250-square-foot area (50 feet by 50 feet) in a low, rolling fog. It flows along the ground, rolling downstairs and cascading into pits. The fog is in constant motion. Stealthy or invisible creatures are not revealed, though anyone attempting to determine what area they are in gains a +2 circumstance bonus to spot invisible or hidden Medium or larger creatures.

The ground is not visible beneath the fog. The fog has a height of three to four feet and covers anything on the floor completely. It is particularly effective at allowing creatures in gaseous form to hide, granting them a +10 circumstance bonus to Stealth checks.

DC 22 Craft (alchemy); *Rarity:* Uncommon; *Price:* 100 gp; *Weight:* —; *Alchemical Formula:* Rare Earth, Air (any), Sulfur (any), Water (any), Stealth

Hallucination Powder: On a successful use of this powder, the subject must succeed at a DC 16 Will save or the victim experiences 1d4 + 1 rounds of terrifying hallucinations. This produces a result in the victim similar to fear. Spellcasting and combat are impossible, but the target may defend himself normally. The subject gains the cowering condition for the duration.

Bizarre psychology renders the power ineffective. It works only on humanoid and animal type creatures; magical beasts and monstrous humanoids get a +4 bonus to saves versus the powder, and all others are immune. Using or making this powder carries a 1% chance that the user could go insane, as per *insanity*, unless they have poison use.

DC 16 Craft (alchemy); *Rarity:* Uncommon; *Price:* 30 gp; *Weight:* —; *Alchemical Formula:* Air (any), Earth (any), Mercury (any), Illusion

Incendiary Powder (10): This is a quick-burning powder used in the construction of fuses and bombs. If an ounce is exposed to open flame, it flares up and does 1d4 points of damage per ounce to anyone holding the powder. Large quantities of it can be quite dangerous near open flame, but by itself it makes a poor weapon — if thrown on a person who is currently on fire, if they fail a DC 16 Reflex save, it does 1d4 points of damage per ounce. No more than two ounces of the loose dust can be thrown for this effect. Larger amounts can do more damage; however, when using too much of the loose powder, it puts itself out and prevents increased efficacy. Use the following table as reference for questions concerning damage caused by large amounts of incendiary powder:

TABLE 3–8: INCENDIARY POWDER AMOUNTS

Size		Cost	Damage
Mini-Keg	32 ounces	32 gp	3d6
Keg	64 ounces	64 gp	4d6
Gallon	128 ounces	128 gp	6d6
Rundlet (18 Gallons)	2,304 ounces	2,300 gp	8d6
Barrel (32 Gallons)	4,096 ounces	4,100 gp	12d6

DC 15 Craft (alchemy); *Rarity:* Common; *Price:* 10 gp; *Weight:* —; *Alchemical Formula:* Fire (any), Salt (any), Sulfur (any)

Insect Repellent Powder: This powder is particularly effective at repelling small insects. Each dose covers one acre and prevents any insect smaller than a large beetle from entering for one year.

DC 12 Craft (alchemy); *Rarity:* Uncommon; *Price:* 300 gp; *Weight:* —; *Alchemical Formula:* Rare Earth, Earth (any), Salt (any)

Itching Powder: This powder causes severe irritation, giving the target a –2 circumstance penalty to all attacks, damage, and other rolls until they take one full-round action to wash off the powder.

DC 20 Craft (alchemy); *Rarity:* Uncommon; *Price:* 25 gp; *Weight:* —; *Alchemical Formula:* Earth (any) (x2), Fire (any), Pain

Magic Detection Powder: The application of this powder causes any magical item, ward, creature, or aura to glow. The color and strength of the glow indicates the type and strength of the magic as *detect magic*. This grants a +10 alchemical bonus to identifying the item and allows characters without *detect magic* to attempt the check to identify.

DC 21 Craft (alchemy); *Rarity:* Uncommon; *Price:* 250 gp; *Weight:* —; *Alchemical Formula:* Diamond, Gold, Rare Earth, Azoth (any)

Madness Powder: On a successful use of this power, victims must make a DC 16 Will save or go insane, as per *insanity*. *Remove curse*, *remove disease*, and *neutralize poison*, in addition to spells that normally cure *insanity*, all cure the subject.

DC 28 Craft (alchemy); *Rarity:* Rare; *Price:* 250 gp; *Weight:* —; *Alchemical formula:* Moonstone, Onyx, Pearl, Rare Earth, Mind

Nausea Powder: A successful use of this powder causes retching and nausea for 1d4 + 1 rounds. Targets must succeed at a DC 14 Fortitude save or gain the sickened condition for the duration.

DC 15 Craft (alchemy); *Rarity:* Common; *Price:* 30 gp; *Weight:* —; *Alchemical Formula:* Earth (any), Fire (any), Water (any), Toxin

Nullifying Powder: This powder neutralizes alchemical reactions. It stops acid from continuing to do damage, puts out small fires, calms violent turbulent waters, and even calms upset stomachs. It affects one target except in the case of calming turbulent waves, where it affects a 300-foot radius.

DC 22 Craft (alchemy); *Rarity:* Uncommon; *Price:* 75 gp; *Weight:* —; *Alchemical Formula:* Rare Earth, Air (any), Azoth (any), Earth (any), Fire (any), Mercury (any), Salt (any), Sulfur (any)

Obscuring Powder: This gray, ash-like powder has no remarkable qualities. If dashed upon the ground, it creates a 60-foot-diameter cloud that limits vision to less than one foot. The air is filled with an acrid odor that nullifies the scent ability, and it is difficult to hear sounds within the cloud. Targets within the cloud have total concealment. The cloud lasts for 1d4 minutes and can be dispersed earlier by a strong wind.

DC 25 Craft (alchemy); *Rarity:* Uncommon; *Price:* 500 gp; *Weight:* —; *Alchemical Formula:* Rare Earth, Air (any), Sulfur (any), Stealth

Paralysis Powder: On a successful use, this requires the victim to succeed at a DC 12 Fortitude save or become paralyzed for 1d4 + 1 rounds. Targets may make a new save as a full-round action on their turn. Movement and speech become impossible.

DC 25 Craft (alchemy); *Rarity:* Uncommon; *Price:* 100 gp; *Weight:* —; *Alchemical Formula:* Rare Earth, Mercury (any), Salt (any), Stasis

Pesticide Powder: This powder causes diminutive vermin to die. When spread around an area, vermin pick up the powder on their extremities and transport it back to their lair. When they clean it off, it causes fatal damage to the surrounding vermin and they die. This is also harmful to small children and pets. Creatures that are Tiny or Small that pass through an area are affected by the pesticide poison. Pesticide is a contact poison with a Fortitude DC 16, with a six-hour onset. It does 1d2 Constitution damage and 1d4 Intelligence damage.

DC 16 Craft (alchemy); *Rarity:* Uncommon; *Price:* 10 gp; *Weight:* —; *Alchemical Formula:* Rare Earth, Salt (any), Death

Piquant Powder: When applied to anything edible, this powder increases any distinctive smell or taste by a factor of ten. It allows the eater of the food to fully experience each unique flavor and odor in the food. It also intensifies the smell of toxins and poor preparation. There is enough to use on six meals. This grants a +8 alchemical bonus to detect any poisons, toxins, or alterations to the food.

DC 15 Craft (alchemy); *Rarity:* Uncommon; *Price:* 100 gp; *Weight:* —; *Alchemical Formula:* Rare Earth, Mercury (any), Earth (any), Salt (any), Sulfur (any), Perception

Powdered Water: When a single drop of water is added to this white sparkling powder, it turns into a gallon of pure water. After the water is added, the mixture must be agitated, and it produces a fair bit of heat. The powder is often added to a gallon size container before reconstitution for ease of use.

Powdered water is useful to save weight on long treks and can be made in large enough quantities to ship to arid locals. It is difficult to transport by sea, as it must be kept dry.

A person in desperate need may swallow a dose and gain the equivalent of one quart of liquid. The extra is neutralized by the stomach acid.

DC 10 Craft (alchemy); *Rarity:* Rare; *Price:* 30 gp; *Weight:* —; *Alchemical Formula:* Salt (any) (x2), Water (any) (x2)

Razor Powder: Razor-sharp crystals form when this powder is spread over an area. You can cover a single five-foot square with a standard action, or four squares with a full-round action. Anyone entering this five-foot-square area takes 1d8 damage from cuts. You can avoid the damage by treating the terrain as difficult. The crystals dissolve after one hour. This powder is found with enough for 1d8 + 2 applications and is crafted with enough for 10 applications.

DC 25 Craft (alchemy); *Rarity:* Uncommon; *Price:* 50 gp; *Weight:* —; *Alchemical Formula:* Diamond, Iron, Rare Earth, Salt (any)

Smoke Powder: When added to fire, this simple powder changes the color of the fire or produces smoke of any color the alchemist wishes. The smoke does not increase in volume or provide any sort of cover.

DC 10 Craft (alchemy); *Rarity:* Common; *Price:* 3 gp; *Weight:* —; *Alchemical Formula:* Plant

Snap Powder: One dose of this powder is enough to cover a five-foot-square area. Any creature that weighs more than 20 pounds sets off tiny explosions and sparkling lights when moving through the area. Anyone attempting to move quietly or in the shadows is almost instantly discovered; Stealth checks have a –40 penalty.
If these are set off by another creature, they draw a lot of attention and may increase your ability to move unnoticed, providing a +6 circumstance bonus to Stealth checks.

DC 18 Craft (alchemy); *Rarity:* Uncommon; *Price:* 5 gp; *Weight:* —; *Alchemical Formula:* Light

Sneezing Powder: This coarse, yellowish-red powder is a splash weapon that causes uncontrollable sneezing for 1d4 + 1 rounds. Anyone standing in the square of impact must succeed on a DC 12 Fortitude save to resist the powder, while those in adjacent squares must make DC 8 Fortitude saves. Creatures affected by sneezing powder must make a DC 10 Fortitude save every round for the duration or be staggered until their next turn.

DC 25 Craft (alchemy); *Rarity:* Common; *Price:* 60 gp; *Weight:* 2 lbs.; *Alchemical Formula:* Rare Earth, Air (any), Salt (any), Sulfur (any), Toxin

Spoilage Powder: When sprinkled over food, this powder causes it to rapidly spoil. It is not instant, but within the hour a cubic foot of food spoils. Within a day, 100 cubic feet can be spoiled.

DC 15 Craft (alchemy); *Rarity:* Uncommon; *Price:* 10 gp; *Weight:* —; *Alchemical Formula:* Salt (any), Decay

Trail Dispersion Powder: A good dusting of this powder removes a tracker's ability to follow a trail using normal sensory methods. Dogs become distracted and lose the scent, and tracks appear confusing and difficult to follow. This increases the tracking DC by 20. One container is enough to provide 1d6 + 4 uses when found and is crafted with 10 uses.

DC 18 Craft (alchemy); *Rarity:* Uncommon; *Price:* 600 gp; *Weight:* —; *Alchemical Formula:* Plant, Stealth

Vertigo Powder: On a successful use of this powder, the subject must succeed at a DC 16 Will save or they experience severe dizziness for 1d4 + 1 rounds. If the victim does not immediately sit or lie down, there is a 50% chance each round that they fall prone. If this occurs, they may make a DC 10 Reflex save to avoid falling prone, but they lose their action for the round.
An unusual sense of balance can render this powder ineffective. It works only on humanoids and animal creature types; magical beasts get a +4 racial bonus to saves, and all others creature types are immune.

DC 15 Craft (alchemy); *Rarity:* Uncommon; *Price:* 40 gp; *Weight:* —; *Alchemical Formula:* Rare Earth, Air (any), Illusion

SOLVENTS

Solvents are substances that weaken or break down materials to which they are applied. Acids work by bonding with the substances they contact, causing them to dissolve. Bases work in the opposite manner, but with a similar effect, so they are treated as functionally identical to solvents. Damage caused by solvents is acid damage.

Solvents are not represented by name, but by a class. Each type has a varying damage, type, and efficacy. The alchemist must master each solvent grade in order, starting first with Solvent Type A, then B, and so on. Once the alchemist masters the various solvent grades, he or she may make special organic and inorganic solvents that affect only the appropriate materials of that type. Upon crafting one of each, the character may mix them to create the legendary alkahest or universal solvent, which is able to dissolve any substance practically instantly.

Solvents used in combat have a very small (one-foot) splash radius that rarely affects anyone but their target. Only those grappling the target or sharing a space with the target takes splash damage. On a direct hit, the solvents continue to apply their damage for 1d6 rounds determined randomly. Solvents assume one full eight-ounce dose of the solvent, with times to dissolve items adjusted by the quantity of solvent; i.e., if 16 ounces of a solvent are used, items dissolve twice as fast. Greater amounts of solvent do not increase damage in combat; i.e., once affected by a solvent, throwing more only allows a new duration roll but does not increase the ongoing damage. Solvents in most cases ignore item hardness, except for certain special cases like glass or crystal.

A target may take an action to wash with an astringent such as wine or vinegar or even large amounts of water to stop ongoing solvent damage.

Using solvents is not without risk. Solvents are carried safely only in glass or crystal vials due to their tendency to dissolve any other substances. If the alchemist is subject to any shock such as a fall or takes any sonic damage and fails their save, each vial must make the appropriate saving throw using the alchemist's modifiers. For every vial that fails, the alchemist is subject to the full value of the damage.

TABLE 3–9: SOLVENTS

Name	DC	(R)gp	Ttc	(C)gp	Damage/Round	Organic Matter*	Leather/Rope*	Wood*	Bone*	Stone*	Gems*	Metal*
Alchemical Solvent	20	20 gp	4 hours	10 gp	0	—	—	—	—	—	—	—
Solvent Type A	15	25 gp	4 hours	10 gp	1d4	2 minutes	6 minutes	12 minutes	24 minutes	12 hours	—	—
Solvent Type B	20	50 gp	1 day	25 gp	1d6	1 minute	4 minutes	9 minutes	12 minutes	10 days	12 days	—
Solvent Type C	22	100 gp	2 days	50 gp	2d4	5 rounds	2 minutes	6 minutes	9 minutes	6 hours	10 days	12 days
Solvent Type D	25	200 gp	4 days	100 gp	3d4	3 rounds	1 minute	2 minutes	6 minutes	9 minutes	6 hours	10 days
Solvent Type E	26	500 gp	10 days	250 gp	3d6	1 round	5 rounds	1 minute	2 minutes	3 minutes	9 minutes	6 Hours
Organic Solvent	28	1,000 gp	20 days	500 gp	6d6	instant	1 round	1 round	2 rounds	—	—	—
Inorganic Solvent	28	1,000 gp	20 days	500 gp	6d6**	—	—	—	—	instant	1 round	1 round
Universal Solvent	—	10,000 gp	—	—	8d10	instant	instant	instant	instant	instant	instant	instant
Digestive Acids												
Tiny	—	—	—	—	1d6 – 4	6 hours	12 hours	1 day	—	—	—	—
Small	—	—	—	—	1d4 – 1	3 hours	6 hours	12 hours	1 day	—	—	—
Medium	—	—	—	—	1d4	6 minutes	12 minutes	6 hours	12 hours	1 day	—	—
Large	—	—	—	—	1d4	3 minutes	6 minutes	12 minutes	6 hours	12 hours	—	—
Huge	—	—	—	—	1d6	1 minute	2 minutes	6 minutes	12 minutes	6 hours	—	—
Gargantuan	—	—	—	—	2d6	5 rounds	1 minute	2 minutes	6 minutes	12 minutes	1 day	—

* Time to dissolve one cubic foot of material.
** Affects only inorganic creatures such as constructs

Alchemical Solvent: This bubbling purple gel eats through adhesives. Each vial can cover a single five-foot square. It destroys most normal adhesives (such as tar, tree sap, or glue) in a single round but takes 1d4 + 1 rounds to deal with more powerful adhesives (*alchemical glue*, *tanglefoot bags*, spider webbing, and so on). It has no effect on fully magical adhesives such as *sovereign glue*.

DC 20 Craft (alchemy); *Rarity:* Common; *Price:* 20 gp; *Weight:* 1 lb.; *Alchemical Formula:* Fire (any), Mercury (any), Sulfur (any), Decay

Solvent Type A: This weak solvent does 1d4 points of acid damage on a direct hit for 1d6 rounds. It causes no splash damage.

DC 15 Craft (alchemy); *Rarity:* Uncommon; *Price:* 25 gp; *Weight:* 1 lb.; *Alchemical Formula:* Earth (any), Fire (any), Mercury (any), Sulfur (any), Acid

Solvent Type B: This moderate solvent does 1d6 points of acid damage on a direct hit for 1d6 rounds. Anyone standing within a five-foot radius takes 1 point of acid splash damage.

DC 20 Craft (alchemy); *Rarity:* Uncommon; *Price:* 50 gp; *Weight:* 1 lb.; *Alchemical Formula:* Earth (any), Fire (any), Mercury (any), Sulfur (any), Acid (x2)

Solvent Type C: This strong solvent does 2d4 points of acid damage for 1d6 rounds on a direct hit. Anyone standing within a five-foot radius takes 1d4 points of acid splash damage.

DC 22 Craft (alchemy); *Rarity:* Uncommon; *Price:* 100 gp; *Weight:* 1 lb.; *Alchemical Formula:* Emerald, Earth (any), Fire (any), Mercury (any), Sulfur (any), Acid (x2), Decay

Solvent Type D: This powerful solvent does 3d4 points of acid damage for 1d6 rounds on a direct hit. Anyone standing within a five-foot radius takes 1d4 + 1 points of acid splash damage.

DC 25 Craft (alchemy); *Rarity:* Rare; *Price:* 200 gp; *Weight:* 1 lb.; *Alchemical Formula:* Emerald, Pearl, Earth (any), Fire (any), Mercury (any), Sulfur (any), Acid (x2), Decay (x2)

Solvent Type E: This dangerous and expensive solvent does a substantial 3d6 points of acid damage for 1d6 rounds on a direct hit. Anyone standing within a five-foot radius takes 1d6 + 1 acid splash damage.

DC 26 Craft (alchemy); *Rarity:* Rare; *Price:* 500 gp; *Weight:* 1 lb.; *Alchemical Formula:* Emerald, Pearl, Ruby, Earth (any), Fire (any), Mercury (any), Sulfur (any), Acid (x2), Decay (x2), Death

Organic Solvent: This powerful solvent does 6d6 points of acid damage to all living and organic creatures for 1d6 rounds on a direct hit. Anyone standing within a five-foot radius takes 2d6 + 2 acid splash damage. It dissolves any organic material at the rate of one cubic foot per round. This solvent must be contained in any glass, ceramic, or metal container. It has no effect on inorganic material.

DC 28 Craft (alchemy); *Rarity:* Very Rare; *Price:* 1,000 gp; *Weight:* 1 lb.; *Alchemical Formula:* Emerald, Pearl, Ruby, Turquoise, Acid, Plant

Inorganic Solvent: This substance dissolves any inorganic material at the rate of one cubic foot per round. It must be carried in an organic container such as a wooden vial, animal bladder, or wineskin. This solvent has no effect on organic material of any kind.
If used against any construct or animate object, it does 6d6 points of acid damage for 1d6 rounds on a direct hit. Any construct or animate object standing within a five-foot radius takes 2d6 + 2 acid splash damage.

DC 28 Craft (alchemy); *Rarity:* Very Rare; *Price:* 1,000 gp; *Weight:* 1 lb.; *Alchemical Formula:* Agate, Jade, Ruby, Turquoise, Azoth (any), Acid

Universal Solvent (Alkahest): This horrible substance is not made in a lab because it is too volatile to exist for very long. It destroys all matter it comes into contact with — it is the alkahest. It is made by mixing together the organic and inorganic solvent.
For one round after they are mixed together, the substance is inert. After this time period, it begins to dissolve anything it comes in contact with. It dissolves one cubic foot a second for 6d10 seconds.
A splash of this substances does 8d6 + 8 points of acid damage and a direct hit results in 24d6 points of acid damage for 1d6 rounds. If this kills a creature, they are completely disintegrated and can be brought back from the dead only with a *miracle* or *wish*.
There is no antidote.

DC — Craft (alchemy); *Rarity:* Very Rare; *Price:* — gp; *Weight:* 1 lb.; *Alchemical formula:* Organic Solvent (1 dose), Inorganic Solvent (1 dose), Azoth (any)

TINCTURES

A tincture is an extract formed using substance soaked in alcohol. These are not always consumed. They are often added to other liquids and substances both magical and alchemical for their effects.

The creation process is a little different than the standard alchemical creation techniques, being that it takes time for the alcohol to work on the substance. In addition to the crafting time, it takes six weeks for the tincture to soak before it becomes effective. The alchemist may engage in any activity he wishes during this time.

The duration for a tincture is permanent unless otherwise noted.

It usually takes 1 standard action to imbibe or apply a tincture, but it takes a few seconds before the tincture takes effect. Tinctures take effect at the start of the alchemist's next turn after activation.

TABLE 3–10: TINCTURES

Name	Craft (alchemy) DC	Price
Tincture of Antemortem	12	25 gp
Tincture of Extension	24	250 gp
Tincture of Far Reaching	24	250 gp
Tincture of Fire	18	150 gp
Tincture of Health (50)	10	10 gp
Tincture of Lethality	25	200 gp
Tincture of Magnification	25	1,000 gp
Tincture of Poisonflesh	25	315 gp
Tincture of Purification (50)	8	10 gp
Tincture of Putrefaction (50)	8	10 gp
Tincture of Sanguineness	22	100 gp
Tincture of Slumber	34	450 gp
Tincture of the Clouded Mind	28	200 gp
Tincture of Transference	26	2,500 gp
Tincture of Witch Bane	12	3 gp
Tincture of Wolfsbane (50)	9	10 gp

Tincture of Antemortem: This tincture does nothing until the drinker expires and stays active for the drinker for one minute. Once that occurs, the tincture slows all mental and bodily processes, suspending the body a moment before death. Note that any further damage after this point results in death. Healing effects can be used during this time as normal, though the body does not visibly heal until the suspended animation ends.

This state of suspended animation lasts for 24 hours. This state can be extended by 12 hours if the body is kept out of the light of the sun. If no healing has been performed, the creature is 1 point away from death and unstable.

DC 12 Craft (alchemy); *Rarity:* Uncommon; *Price:* 25 gp; *Weight:* —; *Alchemical Formula:* Salt (any), Plant, Stasis

Tincture of Extension: When this tincture is added to a magic potion or other liquid, the duration of the effect is extended by 50%. The magic potion or liquid is not included in the casting cost.

DC 24 Craft (alchemy); *Rarity:* Very Rare; *Price:* 250 gp; *Weight:* —; *Alchemical Formula:* Rare Earth, Azoth (any) (x2), Salt (any)

Tincture of Far Reaching: When this tincture is added to a magic potion or other liquid, the range of the effect (such as *oil of fire breathing*) is extended by 50%.

DC 24 Craft (alchemy); *Rarity:* Very Rare; *Price:* 250 gp; *Weight:* —; *Alchemical Formula:* Rare Earth (5), Azoth (any) (x2), Sulfur (any)

Tincture of Fire: This tincture is added to other liquids or foods as an incapacitating element, though some people voluntarily imbibe such substances.

If anyone eats or sips some liquid or food contaminated with this tincture, they must make a DC 16 Fortitude save or fall prone writhing from the heat of the substance for 1d8 + 1 rounds. Each round they take a point of fire damage.

If this tincture is consumed straight and not diluted in another substance, then the imbiber must succeed at a DC 5 Fortitude save or die from respiratory or heart failure. If they survive, they are incapacitated for 3d4 rounds, taking one point of fire damage per round.

DC 18 Craft (alchemy); *Rarity:* Uncommon; *Price:* 150 gp; *Weight:* —; *Alchemical Formula:* Rare Earth, Fire (any) (x2), Salt (any)

Tincture of Health (50): This tincture enhances the respiratory functions and reduces inflammation of the bronchial passages. This tincture fight infections in the chest and lungs.

When taken, this provides a +2 circumstance bonus on the next saving throw versus disease a character must make while diseased.

DC 10 Craft (alchemy); *Rarity:* Common; *Price:* 10 gp; *Weight:* 2.5 lbs.; *Alchemical Formula:* Earth (any), Sulfur (any), Healing

Tincture of Lethality: When added to any poison, this tincture affects the body's natural defenses, making it harder to resist. Any poison with this tincture added to it has a +2 alchemical bonus to the saving throw DC of the poison.

DC 25 Craft (alchemy); *Rarity:* Very Rare; *Price:* 200 gp; *Weight:* —; *Alchemical Formula:* Rare Earth, Salt (any), Water (any), Death

Tincture of Magnification: This tincture is intended to be mixed with a magical liquid. When combined, this tincture causes the magical liquid to have maximum effect. This means that the duration is the longest possible duration and any numeric effects are not rolled but given their maximum values. For example, when mixed with a *potion of cure light wounds* made by a 3rd-level cleric, the potion heals 11 points of damage.

DC 25 Craft (alchemy); *Rarity:* Very Rare; *Price:* 1,000 gp; *Weight:* —; *Alchemical Formula:* Diamond, Platinum, Azoth (any) (x2)

Tincture of Poisonflesh: When mixed with up to three doses of poison, this powerful tincture turns your very flesh to the poison you mixed it with. When it is consumed, roll a DC 14 Fortitude save. Failure means you feel ill and gain the sickened condition for the duration of the tincture. You are immune to the type of poison contained within the tincture for the duration. The cost varies based on the cost of the poison. The price is equal to the price of three doses of the poison, plus 315 gold for essences and Rare Earths.

If you are bitten or attacked and swallowed, the attacker is affected by the poison that flows in your flesh. They must make a save versus the poison you ingested as if they had been attacked with it. If they fail, they experience the effects of the poison that you ingested.

DC 25 Craft (alchemy); *Rarity:* Very Rare; *Price:* 315 gp; *Weight:* —; *Alchemical Formula:* Agate, Malachite, Rare Earth, Salt (any), Toxin

Tincture of Purification (50): This tincture purifies one gallon of water, removing all bacteria and impurities. It will not prevent the water from recontamination nor will it have any effect on magically polluted water. This tincture can be used to create the pure water necessary for the creation of potions.

DC 8 Craft (alchemy); *Rarity:* Common; *Price:* 10 gp; *Weight:* 2.5 lbs.; *Alchemical Formula:* Fire (any), Sulfur (any), Purity

Tincture of Putrefaction (50): This tincture instantly putrefies one gallon of water, making it unfit for consumption. Anyone who drinks water ruined with this tincture becomes violently ill and spends the next 2d4 rounds uncontrollably retching, gaining the nauseated condition.

DC 8 Craft (alchemy); *Rarity:* Common; *Price:* 10 gp; *Weight:* 2.5 lbs.; *Alchemical Formula:* Earth (any), Fire (any), Decay

Tincture of Sanguineness: When this tincture is added to any poison, it has the side effect of causing bleeding. If the character fails a save versus the poison, the wound damaged by the poison bleeds for 1 point of damage every round that the poison's effects continue. It the poison was ingested, the character instead takes 2d8 damage from internal bleeding.

DC 22 Craft (alchemy); *Rarity:* Rare; *Price:* 100 gp; *Weight:* —; *Alchemical Formula:* Iron, Malachite, Onyx, Rare Earth

Tincture of Slumber: When added to any poison or liquid, this tincture causes the target to slumber. They must make a DC 16 Fortitude save or fall asleep. This has no affect when combined with a poison that already causes sleep. They sleep for eight hours and then must again make another save, this time a DC 20 Fortitude save. Failing that, they fall into a coma and can be awakened only by a *cure disease* or *remove curse* spell.

DC 34 Craft (alchemy); *Rarity:* Very Rare; *Price:* 450 gp; *Weight:* —; *Alchemical Formula:* Moonstone, Pearl, Platinum, Rare Earth, Stasis

Tincture of the Clouded Mind: When mixed with up to four doses of poison, this tincture adds a side effect of confusion to the poison. If the target fails the save versus the poison, they must make a second Fortitude save at the same difficulty to resist this tincture. If this save fails, the imbiber takes an alchemical penalty of –2 to all saving throws and the user must succeed at a Concentration check of DC 15 + spell level to cast spells.

DC 28 Craft (alchemy); *Rarity:* Rare; *Price:* 200 gp; *Weight:* —; *Alchemical Formula:* Rare Earth, Mercury (any), Water (any), Mind

Tincture of Transference: This tincture is intended to be added to a magical liquid. When consumed, the magical liquid does not affect the imbiber but instead affects the target, determined by the organic essence added to the mixture as well as the thoughts of the imbiber. The target must be within 100 miles, and no saving throw is allowed. The liquid always affects the target who saves versus the substance or has the substance affect them as normal. There is always a small chance (1%) that this tincture fails to function, and the magical liquid may affect the imbiber.

DC 26 Craft (alchemy); *Rarity:* Rare; *Price:* 2,500 gp; *Weight:* —; *Special Requirement*: Hair, nail, or blood of target; *Alchemical Formula:* Agate, Diamond, Pearl, Platinum, Azoth (any)

Tincture of Witch Bane: When given to someone under the effect of an enchantment effect, this tincture immediately allows a save with a +1 alchemical bonus. If the save is successful, the enchantment effect immediately ends.

DC 12 Craft (alchemy); *Rarity:* Uncommon; *Price:* 3 gp; *Weight:* —; *Alchemical Formula:* Moonstone, Sulfur (any)

Tincture of Wolfsbane (50): This is a curative tincture. It has several effects depending on application. When added to water and drunk, this tincture acts as a diuretic and diaphoretic. In addition to causing urination and excessive sweating, it also provides a +2 alchemical bonus to any saves against lycanthropy if infected. This tincture can also be applied externally to heal wounds, bruises, arthritis, and irritations. It heals 1d4 points of damage when used this way.
If the alchemist fails a DC 9 Craft (alchemy) check when applying this tincture, the tincture was prepared or applied incorrectly. You cannot take a 10 on this check due to the assumed danger of lycanthropy. If applied externally, the tincture deals 2d4 damage and no natural healing occurs that day due to blistering and inflammation. If taken internally, it can cause bleeding and possible death. Make a DC 12 Fortitude save three times. For each one that fails, take 1d4 damage. If all three saves fail, your heart becomes damaged and you die unless you pass a DC 12 Fortitude save.

DC 9 Craft (alchemy); *Rarity:* Common; *Price:* 10 gp; *Weight:* 2.5 lbs.; *Alchemical Formula:* Fire (any), Sulfur (any), Body, Plant

CHAPTER FOUR: MAGIC ITEMS

Alchemists have discovered many unique magic items and ways to use materials. They follow all standard rules for magic item creation, using Spellcraft or the associated craft skill required. Like any spellcaster, they must possess the appropriate feats and spells required to cast. However, if an alchemist possesses the correct essences of a creature, then not only can they lower the crafting cost of the item, they can also bypass the spell requirement. This does not reduce the time needed to craft the item.

SPELL-BASED POTIONS

Potions are spells put into physical consumable form. It's often thought that potions are only able to be created containing the power of the weaker spells. This is not true. The ability to take more powerful spells and contain them within potions exists. In order to do so, you must have specialized knowledge, in the form of the feat Brew Improved Potion. Creating potions of such a powerful nature is more complicated than just brewing the potions. In addition to the cost, each potion requires the use of 1 essence per 1,000 gold pieces (or portion thereof) of its cost. The essence, or one of its sub-essences, either must match one of the type descriptors of the spell contained within the potion or must be an Azoth essence.

NEW FEAT

Brew Improved Potion (Item Creation)
You can create more powerful potions.
Prerequisite: Caster level 7th, Brew Potion
Benefit: You can create a potion of any 6th-level or lower spell that you know and that targets one or more creatures or objects. Brewing a potion takes two hours if its base price is less than 250 gp; otherwise, brewing a potion takes one day for each 1,000 gp in its base price. When you create a potion, you set the caster level, which must be sufficient to cast the spell in question and no higher than your own level. To brew a potion, you must use up raw materials costing one-half this base price. See the magic item creation rules in **Magic Items** for more information. If the potion is 4th level or higher, you must include one essence for every 1,000 gp of the base price of the potion, or portion thereof. The essence, or one of its sub-essences, either must match one of the type descriptors of the spell contained within the potion or must be an Azoth essence.

When you create a potion, you make any choices that you would normally make when casting the spell. Whoever drinks the potion is the target of the spell.

Special: An alchemist can brew potions of any formulae he knows (up to 6th level), using his alchemist level as his caster level. The spell must be one that can be made into a potion. The alchemist does not need to meet the caster level prerequisites for this feat.

Normal: You cannot craft potions above 4th level

The price of a potion is equal to the level of the spell × the creator's caster level × 50 gp. If the potion has a material component cost, it is added to the base price and cost to create. **Table 4–1** below gives sample prices for potions created at the lowest possible caster level for each spellcasting class. Note that some spells appear at different levels for different casters. The level of such spells depends on the caster brewing the potion. This cost is on top of the requirement to attain essences.

TABLE 4–1: BREW IMPROVED POTION COSTS BY CLASS AND LEVEL

Spell Level	Cleric, Druid, Wizard	Sorcerer	Bard	Alchemist	Paladin, Ranger
0	25 gp	25 gp	25 gp	—	—
1st	50 gp	50 gp	50 gp	50 gp	50 gp
2nd	300 gp	400 gp	400 gp	400 gp	400 gp
3rd	750 gp	900 gp	1,050 gp	1,050 gp	1,050 gp
4th	1,400 gp	1,600 gp	2,000 gp	2,000 gp	2,600 gp
5th	2,250 gp	2,500 gp	3,250 gp	3,250 gp	—
6th	3,300 gp	3,600 gp	4,800 gp	4,800 gp	—

Potions are like spells cast upon the imbiber. The character taking the potion doesn't get to make any decisions about the effect — the caster who brewed the potion has already done so. The imbiber of a potion is the effective target and the caster of the effect (though the potion indicates the caster level, the drinker still controls the effect).

The person applying an oil is the effective caster, but the object is the target.

WONDROUS ITEMS

Essences can also be used to aid in the crafting of magical items to reduce the crafting cost. The essence, or one of its sub-essences, either must match one of the type descriptors of the item, a spell used in the crafting of the item, a material component of a spell used in the crafting of the item, or must be an Azoth essence. Rare Earth can also be used to reduce crafting costs in this way.

CANDLES

Candles are most often made from animal fat. Candles usually have wicks, though primitive tallow candles can be made.

Candles can be snuffed out by ordinary means. The effects of candles are canceled immediately once snuffed out. Note that the effects candles produce (arcane warding, protection, etc.) do not prevent warded creatures or effects from putting the candles out.

TABLE 4–2: CANDLES

Name	Price
Arcane Warding Candle	1,800 gp
Black Candle	4,500 gp
Blade Candle	300 gp
Blinking Candle	10,500 gp
Blue Candle	1,500 gp
Brilliant Candle	50 gp
Detonating Candle	1,200 gp
Divination Candle	27,500 gp
Flame Arrow Candle	750 gp
Gold Candle	26,000 gp
Holy Candle	6,000 gp
Radiant Candle	6,000 gp
Reflection Candle	1,500 gp
Sanctuary Candle	500 gp
Shielding Candle	750 gp
Slaying Candle	375 gp
Vision Candle	5,000 gp
Wizardry Candle	20,000 gp

ARCANE WARDING CANDLE
Aura Moderate Abjuration; **CL** 11th
Slot None; **Price** 1,800 gp; **Weight** 0.5 lb.

DESCRIPTION
This creates a shimmering globe with a 10-foot radius centered on the candle. It surrounds the wielder and excludes all spell effects of 4th level or lower. The area or effect of any such spells does not include the area covered by the candle. Excluded effects include spell-like abilities and spells or spell-like effects from items. Any spell may be cast from within the globe. Spells of 5th level or higher are not affected by the globe, and the candle will be destroyed by a *mage's disjunction* spell. Anyone may enter or leave the area of effect of the candle without penalty. This candle burns for one minute.

CONSTRUCTION
Requirements Craft Wondrous Item, *globe of invulnerability*; **Cost** 900 gp; **Rarity:** Very Rare
Alchemical Formula: Azoth (any), Fire (any), Protection

BLACK CANDLE
Aura Moderate Necromancy [Evil]; **CL** 5th
Slot None; **Price** 4,500 gp; **Weight** 0.5 lbs.

DESCRIPTION
This dark candle burns for one hour with a purple flame. When lit, it allows a curse to be bestowed for every 10 minutes it is lit. The target of a curse receives a DC 20 Will Saving Throw. On a failure, the holder of the candle can choose which curse affects the target. Curses include suffering, which reduces a single stat by −6, or poverty, which renders all held or touched coins and gems to clay. They return to their normal value once out of the possession of the cursed person for 24 hours. If used to purchase goods, the worthless coins return to the user in an hour. The curse first applies at the end of the first 10 minutes. The same person can be targeted with each curse the candle can bestow.

CONSTRUCTION
Requirements Craft Wondrous Item, *bestow curse*; **Cost** 2,250 gp; **Rarity:** Rare
Alchemical Formula: Fire (any), Salt (any), Sulfur (any), Death

BLADE CANDLE
Aura faint evocation [fire]; **CL** 3rd
Slot None; **Price** 300 gp; **Weight** 0.5 lbs.

DESCRIPTION
When lit, the flame of this candle springs out to a length of three feet. It burns for one minute. The candle may be picked up as a hilt and wielded as a scimitar. It does 1d8 + 3 fire damage on a successful touch attack. Strength bonuses to damage do not apply to attacks made with the blade.

CONSTRUCTION
Requirements Craft Wondrous Item, *flame blade*; **Cost** 150 gp; **Rarity:** Uncommon
Alchemical Formula: Fire (any), Mercury (any), Transportation

BLINKING CANDLE
Aura faint transmutation; **CL** 7th
Slot None; **Price** 10,500 gp; **Weight** 0.5 lbs.

DESCRIPTION
The person holding this candle begins blinking in all respects identical to the spell *blink*, with one exception. The spell effect ends if they set down the candle. When set down, the candle does not blink on its own. The wielder is affected by the spell only when the candle is held. It burns for one minute. Physical attacks against you have a 50% miss chance, and you gain all the other features, penalties, and aspects of the spell *blink* while grasping the candle.

CONSTRUCTION
Requirements Craft Wondrous Item, *blink*; **Cost** 5,250 gp; **Rarity:** Rare
Alchemical Formula: Fire (any), Mercury (any), Planar

BLUE CANDLE

Aura faint abjuration; **CL** 3rd
Slot None; **Price** 1,500 gp; **Weight** 0.5 lbs.

DESCRIPTION

While this candle burns, it projects a blue aura. It burns for six hours. This aura is of the type set by the *protection* spell used to craft the candle and cannot be changed; i.e., *blue candle of protection from evil*, etc. Any creature within the sphere is protected as if by a *protection* spell of the type cast into the candle. Creatures that the candle protects against must succeed at a DC 12 Will save to enter the area of the candle. Once they succeed at this save, they may enter the area of the candle but are still affected by the *protection* spell on the creatures within the boundary of the candle.

CONSTRUCTION

Requirements Craft Wondrous Item, *protection from good/evil/law/chaos*; **Cost** 750 gp; **Rarity:** Rare
Alchemical Formula: Fire (any), Salt (any), Planar

BRILLIANT CANDLE

Aura faint evocation [light]; **CL** 3rd
Slot None; **Price** 50 gp; **Weight** 0.5 lbs.

DESCRIPTION

This candle burns for six hours. It produces light equivalent to a *continual flame* spell. If this candle is countered and extinguished by magical darkness, it may simply be relit.

CONSTRUCTION

Requirements Craft Wondrous Item, *continual flame*; **Cost** 25 gp; **Rarity:** Rare
Alchemical Formula: Fire (any), Light
Small alterations to the formula may be made to produce a candle that emanates *darkness* as the spell in the same manner. The alchemical formula for this version of the item is Water (any), Light.

DETONATING CANDLE

Aura moderate evocation; **CL** 8th
Slot None; **Price** 1,200 gp; **Weight** 0.5 lbs.

DESCRIPTION

This candle burns for 1d8 + 4 rounds, then explodes in a sphere of flame. The flame extends 15 feet out from the center of the candle (covering a 30-foot diameter). It does 8d6 points of fire damage to all targets in the blast and destroys the candle. A successful DC 16 Reflex save halves the damage. You may trim the wick on this candle to reduce the burning duration by one or more. If, however, the random duration is rolled and results in being a duration of 0 or less, then the candle explodes instantly upon being lit.

CONSTRUCTION

Requirements Craft Wondrous Item, *fireball*; **Cost** 600 gp; **Rarity:** Uncommon
Alchemical Formula: Fire (any), Earth (any), Memory

DIVINATION CANDLE

Aura Strong Divination; **CL** 13th
Slot None; **Price** 27,500 gp; **Weight** 0.5 lbs.

DESCRIPTION

When this candle is lit, it allows the wielder to cast a single spell from the school of Divination that the wielder can normally cast that they do not have prepared. The character may instead choose to cast a single Divination spell that they have prepared without having it vanish from memory.
The candle burns for an hour. Each time this ability is used, the candle burns down and loses 10 minutes of burning time.

CONSTRUCTION

Requirements Craft Wondrous Item, *limited wish*; **Cost** 13,750 gp; **Rarity:** Very Rare
Alchemical Formula: Fire (any), Mercury (any), Perception, Prophecy

FLAME ARROW CANDLE

Aura faint evocation; **CL** 5th
Slot None; **Price** 750 gp; **Weight** 0.5 lbs.

DESCRIPTION

This candle burns for 10 minutes. Once lit, this candle affects any arrow fired within five feet of the candle as the spell *flame arrow*. A lick of flame leaps up and lights the arrow once it is released. Each piece of ammunition fired within five feet of the candle does an additional 1d6 fire damage and can easily ignite a flammable object or structure, but won't ignite creatures.

CONSTRUCTION

Requirements Craft Wondrous Item, *flame arrow*; **Cost** 375 gp; **Rarity:** Uncommon
Alchemical Formula: Fire (any), Mercury (any), Flight

GOLD CANDLE

Aura moderate conjuration [healing]; **CL** 11th
Slot None; **Price** 26,000 gp; **Weight** 0.5 lbs.

DESCRIPTION

This candle burns for 10 minutes. When lit, anyone within a 30-foot radius of this candle is healed for 1d4 + 1 hit points per round. This healing is positive energy and deals a similar amount of damage to undead. Note that this affects any creatures within the range of the light.

CONSTRUCTION

Requirements Craft Wondrous Item, *heal;* **Cost** 13,000 gp; **Rarity:** Rare
Alchemical Formula: Gold, Fire (any), Healing, Life

HOLY CANDLE

Aura faint necromancy; **CL** 5th
Slot None; **Price** 6,000 gp; **Weight** 0.5 lbs.

DESCRIPTION

This candle burns for six hours. Once lit, this candle repels undead within a 10-foot radius of the candle. Undead must succeed at a DC 14 Will save or they are unable to enter the range of the candle. Undead must attempt this save every round. Attacking the undead or forcing them to enter the radius of the effect cancels the effect for the round.

CONSTRUCTION

Requirements Craft Wondrous Item, *hide from undead*; **Cost** 3,000 gp; **Rarity:** Rare
Alchemical Formula: Silver, Fire (any), Life

RADIANT CANDLE

Aura moderate necromancy; **CL** 10th
Slot None; **Price** 6,000 gp; **Weight** 0.5 lbs.

DESCRIPTION

This candle burns for one hour. Once lit, this candle scalds undead within a 30-foot radius of the candle. Any skeletons, zombies, ghouls, shadows, and undead with 3 hit dice or fewer take 2d6 points of positive energy damage per round. Any wights, ghasts, or undead with 4 or 5 hit dice take 1d6 points of positive energy damage per round. Any other undead take 1d4 points of positive energy damage per round.
A character with the ability to channel to harm undead that lights and holds the candle has their ability to channel to harm undead increased by two levels. This affects only their ability to channel to harm undead.

CONSTRUCTION

Requirements Craft Wondrous Item, *disrupt undead*; **Cost** 3,000 gp; **Rarity:** Uncommon
Alchemical Formula: Gold, Fire (any), Life

REFLECTION CANDLE

Aura moderate illusion; **CL** 5th
Slot None; **Price** 1,500 gp; **Weight** 0.5 lbs.

DESCRIPTION

This candle burns for six hours. When this candle is lit, the smoke forms into an image that matches the appearance of the person who lit the candle exactly. The image can move about, speak, and act as the igniter wishes within a 30-foot radius of candle. The appearance is copied exactly, but the image remains made of smoke and insubstantial, unable to attack, move an object, or affect the environment in any way. The form cannot cast spells. The igniter can control the image from up to a half mile away. If they wish to concentrate, taking no other action, they can see and hear the location where the reflected form resides. Controlling the image requires a move action.

CONSTRUCTION

Requirements Craft Wondrous Item, *major image*; **Cost** 750 gp; **Rarity:** Very Rare
Alchemical Formula: Fire (any), Mercury (any), Body, Illusion

SANCTUARY CANDLE

Aura faint abjuration; **CL** 1st
Slot None; **Price** 500 gp; **Weight** 0.5 lbs.

DESCRIPTION

This candle burns for one hour. This candle wards the user from notice and attack. Anyone attempting to attack the user must succeed at a DC 16 Will save or they find themselves unable to strike the holder of this candle. Anyone who has succeeded at this save once no longer needs to make it, and they may attack the user freely. Creatures and opponents may make as many attempts to attack the holder as they wish. This ability is similar to the spell *sanctuary*.

CONSTRUCTION

Requirements Craft Wondrous Item, *sanctuary*; **Cost** 250 gp; **Rarity:** Rare
Alchemical Formula: Gold, Fire (any), Protection

SHIELDING CANDLE

Aura faint abjuration; **CL** 1st
Slot None; **Price** 750 gp; **Weight** 0.5 lbs.

DESCRIPTION

This candle burns for an hour. When this candle is lit and held, a floating circle of force floats nearby and protects the user as the spell *shield*. Note that the candle must be held for it to have an effect.

CONSTRUCTION

Requirements Craft Wondrous Item, *shield*; **Cost** 375 gp; **Rarity:** Uncommon
Alchemical Formula: Fire (any), Armor, Body

SLAYING CANDLE

Aura faint enchantment; **CL** 5th
Slot None; **Price** 375 gp; **Weight** 0.5 lbs.

DESCRIPTION

The candle burns for one minute. Once lit, this candle affects only a single target. After the target is killed, the candle withers, cracks, and turns to dust. Once lit, this candle produces a spectral flame that affixes to an indicated foe within 50 feet of the candle. All allies within 50 feet of the candle flame gain a +2 insight bonus to hit the targeted foe, and the foe receives a −1 circumstance penalty to all attack rolls and skill checks.

CONSTRUCTION

Requirements Craft Wondrous Item, *heroism*; **Cost** 187 gp 5 sp; **Rarity:** Rare
Alchemical Formula: Rare Earth, Fire (any), Body

VISION CANDLE

Aura faint evocation; **CL** 5th
Slot None; **Price** 5,000 gp; **Weight** 0.5 lbs.

DESCRIPTION

The candle burns for six hours. The light of this candle turns all invisible things within a 10-foot radius visible. This terminates any magical invisibility. This has no effect on naturally invisible or hidden creatures. *Invisibility* does not function within range of the candle.

CONSTRUCTION

Requirements Craft Wondrous Item, *invisibility purge*; **Cost** 2,500 gp; **Rarity:** Uncommon
Alchemical Formula: Rare Earth, Air (any), Fire (any), Perception

WIZARDRY CANDLE

Aura faint magic; **CL** 11th
Slot None; **Price** 20,000 gp; **Weight** 0.5 lbs.

DESCRIPTION

This candle burns for six hours. Any use, even for 15 minutes, burns down a full hour of the candle. When lit while preparing spells, this allows any prepared spellcaster or alchemist to prepare three additional 1st-level spells or extracts, two additional 2nd-level spells or extracts, or one additional 3rd-level spell or extract.

CONSTRUCTION

Requirements Craft Wondrous Item, *mage's lucubration*; **Cost** 10,000 gp; **Rarity:** Uncommon
Alchemical Formula: Gold, Onyx, Azoth (any), Fire (any)

CUSPS, EYES, AND SPECTACLES

Cusps are gem-like hemispheres found in pairs that are placed over the eyes where they affix themselves. It takes a full round to apply these to the face, after which the character has a –4 circumstance penalty on all vision-based perception skill checks, attack rolls, and vision-based saves, until their vision adjusts to the cusps one minute later. These may be worn for one hour before the eye fatigue becomes too great. They must be removed to allow the eyes to rest; if not, the user can continue to use them for a second hour, but then they become blind for 1d4 days. Six hours passing is enough time for the eyes to recover. The hour the cusps are used need not be consecutive — if used for fewer than 10 minutes, an hour is enough to allow the eyes to recover.

Spectacles are crystal discs in a frame placed over where the eyes rest. There is a 25% chance when they are found that they have ear hooks. For an extra 10 gp, these can be constructed with ear hooks. This allows the lenses to be used hands-free.

These can cause eye fatigue if used for longer than five minutes, giving the character a –4 circumstance penalty on all vision-based Perception skill checks, attack rolls, and vision-based saves. The strain on the eyes requires an hour recovery time between uses to avoid the eye fatigue from beginning immediately upon putting the spectacles on.

Eyes may be worn without constraint and appear much like spectacles.

TABLE 4–3: CUSPS, EYES, AND SPECTACLES

Name	Price
Cusp of Antimagic	198,000 gp
Cusps of Blasting	12,000 gp
Cusps of Enthrallment	10,800 gp
Cusps of Illusion Detection	90,000 gp
Cusps of Precognition	45,400 gp
Eyes of Night Vision	10,800 gp
Eyes of Shade	56,000 gp
Eyes of Skysight	10,000 gp
Eyes of the Withering Gaze	360,000 gp
Spectacles of Comprehension	3,000 gp
Spectacles of Life Sight	40,000 gp
Spectacles of Secret Door Detection	22,500 gp

CUSP OF ANTIMAGIC
Aura faint abjuration; **CL** 11th
Slot eyes; **Price** 198,000 gp; **Weight** 1 lb.

DESCRIPTION
This is not two cusps, but rather one large cusp that sits over the bridge of the nose and covers both eyes and a substantial portion of the wearer's forehead. As soon as they are applied, anything within the arc of the cusps is bathed in an antimagic field. At the end of each of their turns, the user can select one 150-foot cone-related area to be looking at, and that area is covered in the field and no magic can function. Note that this covers the user's entire field of vision, so although they can use magic, anything that affects them or needs a target they can see will be nullified by the antimagic field. Due to the extreme focus of the user's vision and lack of peripheral vision, all attacks from outside the cone are considered to be from an invisible source unless the user has additional eyes that can look in separate directions from the primary eyes or the All-Around Vision ability.

CONSTRUCTION
Requirements Craft Wondrous Item, *antimagic field*; **Cost** 99,000 gp; **Rarity:** Rare
Alchemical Formula: Diamond, Gold, Azoth (any) (x3), Planar, Prowess, Purity

CUSPS OF BLASTING
Aura faint evocation [fire]; **CL** 3rd
Slot eyes; **Price** 10,000 gp; **Weight** 1 lb.

DESCRIPTION
When worn, these allow the user to fire blasts of fire from their eyes. As a standard action, the user can make a ranged touch attack against a target within 30 feet. On a hit, the target takes 4d6 fire damage.

CONSTRUCTION
Requirements Craft Wondrous Item, *scorching ray*; **Cost** 5,000 gp; **Rarity:** Rare
Alchemical Formula: Fire (any), Light, Mind, Strength

CUSPS OF ENTHRALLMENT
Aura faint illusion; **CL** 3rd
Slot eyes; **Price** 10,800 gp; **Weight** 1 lb.

DESCRIPTION
These powerful cusps allow the user to mesmerize a single target. At will, the user may as a standard action attempt to affect one target with either the spell *hypnotism* or create a *hypnotic pattern* originating from the cusps. Both of these require the user to concentrate on the effect with a move action to maintain it; not taking this action frees the target. They may affect a single target of up to 2d4 + 3 hit dice. Obvious threats or nearby combat prevent *hypnotism* from working, but only provides another saving throw for *hypnotic pattern*. Either effect fails if the target succeeds at a DC 16 Will saving throw.

CONSTRUCTION
Requirements Craft Wondrous Item, *hypnotism, hypnotic pattern*; **Cost** 5,400 gp; **Rarity:** Rare
Alchemical Formula: Diamond, Mercury (any), Control, Illusion

CUSPS OF ILLUSION DETECTION
Aura moderate divination; **CL** 11th
Slot eyes; **Price** 120,000 gp; **Weight** 1 lb.

DESCRIPTION
Anything you view while wearing these cusps is revealed as it really is, as if by *true seeing*. You can see through normal and magical darkness, illusions, spells that obscure creatures such as *blur* or *mirror image* and displacement effects. It does not penetrate solid objects.

CONSTRUCTION
Requirements Craft Wondrous Item, *true seeing*; **Cost** 60,000 gp; **Rarity:** Rare
Alchemical Formula: Ruby, Mercury (any), Illusion, Perception

CUSPS OF PRECOGNITION
Aura strong divination; **CL** 17th
Slot eyes; **Price** 45,400 gp; **Weight** 1 lb.

DESCRIPTION
Whoever looks through these cusps sees the next several moments happen in advance. If the wearer spends a full round action looking through these cusps, they receive a +2 insight bonus on initiative, attack rolls, saves, skill and ability checks, along with a +2 dodge bonus to armor class for the next two rounds.

The cusps show several possible likely futures of several universes simultaneously, so it is impossible to predict if a door has a specific kind of trap. To use these in a non-combat situation, a minute of study must be completed to acquire the same bonus.

CONSTRUCTION
Requirements Craft Wondrous Item, *time stop*; **Cost** 22,700 gp; **Rarity:** Rare
Alchemical Formula: Moonstone, Sulfur (any), Dream, Prophecy

EYES OF NIGHT VISION
Aura faint transmutation; **CL** 3rd
Slot eyes; **Price** 10,800 gp; **Weight** 1 lb.

DESCRIPTION: When worn, these cusps allow the user to see in dim light and darkness as if it was bright light. The range on these cusps is unlimited. Vision when wearing these cusps is in shades of gray, making color impossible to distinguish.

CONSTRUCTION
Requirements Craft Wondrous Item, *darkvision*; **Cost** 5,400 gp; **Rarity:** Rare
Alchemical Formula: Air (any), Mercury (any), Perception

EYES OF SHADE
Aura faint evocation [darkness]; **CL** 3rd
Slot eyes; **Price** 56,000 gp; **Weight** 1 lb.

DESCRIPTION
These lenses fit securely over the user's eyes, shading them from sunlight, light, and other light-based effects. Unlike normal cusps, these may be worn constantly. The wearer receives a +4 circumstance bonus on saving throws against any blinding, dazzling, or other sight-based effects, any penalties due to bright light, or any illusions relying on visual mesmerization or patterns. When removed, the wearer treats dim light as darkness and bright light as dim light for one minute.

CONSTRUCTION
Requirements Craft Wondrous Item, *darkness*; **Cost** 27,000 gp; **Rarity:** Rare
Alchemical Formula: Jade, Platinum, Fire (any), Light

EYES OF SKYSIGHT
Aura faint divination; **CL** 11th
Slot eyes; **Price** 10,000 gp; **Weight** 1 lb.

DESCRIPTION
When these cusps are worn, they negate any vision impairments or obstructions within one-half mile, such as clouds, fog, hail, mists, or any obscuring vapor. It doubles the distance you can see in bright light and doubles the distance of dim light. It only has these effects. Sandstorms, fogs, mists, and particulate matter are completely transparent to the wearer, providing no cover or concealment.

CONSTRUCTION
Requirements Craft Wondrous Item, *true seeing*; **Cost** 5,000 gp; **Rarity:** Rare
Alchemical Formula: Air (any), Illusion, Perception

EYES OF THE WITHERING GAZE
Aura faint necromancy; **CL** 9th
Slot eyes; **Price** 360,000 gp; **Weight** 1 lb.

DESCRIPTION
As a standard action, the viewer may meet the gaze of any target. That target must succeed at a DC 16 Will save or become paralyzed. The target may repeat this save at the end of every turn to free themselves. If the target succeeds at that save when the user gazes at them, they must make a second DC 20 Will save or become frightened. If it succeeds at this second save, it is shaken.

CONSTRUCTION
Requirements Craft Wondrous Item, *hold monster, cause fear*; **Cost** 180,000 gp; **Rarity:** Very Rare
Alchemical Formula: Mercury (any), Fear, Stasis

SPECTACLES OF COMPREHENSION
Aura faint divination; **CL** 3rd
Slot eyes; **Price** 3,000 gp; **Weight** 1 lb.

DESCRIPTION
The wearer of these spectacles is able to read any writing, working as a visual only version of *comprehend languages*.

CONSTRUCTION
Requirements Craft Wondrous Item, *comprehend languages*; **Cost** 1,500 gp; **Rarity:** Rare
Alchemical Formula: Azoth (any), Mercury (any), Perception

SPECTACLES OF LIFE SIGHT
Aura faint necromancy; **CL** 7th
Slot eyes; **Price** 40,000 gp; **Weight** 1 lb.

DESCRIPTION
These spectacles give you an indication of the relative health of any creature you can see. It does not give numerical information, but you can tell if a target is healthy (100% health), lightly wounded (76%–99% health), wounded (51%–75% health), bloodied (26%–50% health), seriously wounded (11%–25% health), near death (0%–10% health), dying, or dead. You can also tell if a creature is regenerating, undead or unconscious, in possession of temporary hit points, healing, or losing hit points.

CONSTRUCTION
Requirements Craft Wondrous Item, *deathwatch*; **Cost** 20,000 gp; **Rarity:** Rare
Alchemical Formula: Air (any), Fire (any), Perception

SPECTACLES OF SECRET DOOR DETECTION
Aura faint divination; **CL** 5th
Slot eyes; **Price** 22,500 gp; **Weight** 1 lb.

DESCRIPTION
When used, these spectacles allow the wearer to see incredibly fine detail. This grants a +15 competence bonus to Perception checks to detect traps and secret doors.

These lenses quickly cause eye fatigue. The one minute they can be used allows the user to inspect a 10-foot-cube area, including floors, walls, and ceilings. If examining a single surface, you may cover 600 square feet, or six 10-foot square walls. The user must rest their eyes for six minutes before using the cusps again.

CONSTRUCTION
Requirements Craft Wondrous Item, *detect secret doors, clairvoyance*; **Cost** 11,250 gp; **Rarity:** Rare
Alchemical Formula: Earth (any), Water (any), Perception

DUSTS

Dusts appear as collections of fine, granular, light, metallic particles. They do not clump. Color and constancy may vary, but they usually are metallic in nature. Dusts are delivered to the target by a variety of methods. They may be sprinkled, added to food or drink, delivered by blowgun, or thrown.

Dusts are heavy and are relatively dense. Dusts delivered via blowgun have a range of 20 feet maximum and affect all targets in a 15-foot-wide cone at that distance. The user must have proficiency with the blowgun in order to deliver dusts this way; otherwise, in addition to the hit penalty, on a natural roll of 1 the dust affects the user. Dusts may also be thrown like grenades with a range increment of 20 feet. A dust thrown as a grenade affects all targets within a five-foot radius. You must specifically prepare a dust this way ahead of time to be thrown as a grenade-like weapon. Each attack made this way counts as a single use of the dust.

In order to hit a target with a dust thrown as a grenade-like weapon, they do not need to penetrate armor, unless specifically noted; a touch attack is all that is necessary to hit. Dusts affect all targets within a five-foot radius. You can choose to target a surface: In this case, hit AC 5 with a dust and it still affects all creatures nearby. On a miss, the dust must land somewhere. Roll a 1d8 for direction. For each range increment thrown, the missile travels five feet in the direction indicated on the d8.

TABLE 4–4: DUSTS

Name	Price		Name	Price
Dust of Amnesia	7,000 gp		Dust of Instant Ice	1,400 gp
Dust of Arcane Weakness	8,100 gp		Dust of Lightness	1,500 gp
Dust of Blending	1,400 gp		Dust of Looping	12,000 gp
Dust of Blight	1,500 gp		Dust of Maladweomer	22,750 gp
Dust of Blighted Bones	3,300 gp		Dust of Mind Dulling	22,500 gp
Dust of Blindness	2,400 gp		Dust of Non-Detection	750 gp
Dust of Blood Leech	4,950 gp		Dust of Panic	16,500 gp
Dust of Burning 1,500 gp			Dust of Paralyzation	31,500 gp
Dust of Catastrophe	12,000 gp		Dust of Planar Severance	30,000 gp
Dust of Cloud Dispersal	4,500 gp		Dust of Redirection	11,250 gp
Dust of Clouds	22,500 gp		Dust of Rending Protections	33,000 gp
Dust of Confusion	14,000 gp		Dust of Revealing	3,300 gp
Dust of Consumption	500 gp		Dust of Roughage	12,750 gp
Dust of Decay	15,000 gp		Dust of Rust	1,400 gp
Dust of Deformity	6,000 gp		Dust of Slayerbane	6,000 gp
Dust of Deliquescence	33,000 gp		Dust of Sleep	22,500 gp
Dust of Deprivation	1,500 gp		Dust of Sneezing 15,000 gp	
Dust of Detect Illusion	3,300 gp		Dust of Solid Vapor	13,500 gp
Dust of Dispelling	13,500 gp		Dust of Spirit Binding	45,500 gp
Dust of Distraction 8,400 gp			Dust of the Grave	28,000 gp
Dust of Echoes	11,200 gp		Dust of the Sparkling Mind	45,000 gp
Dust of Fertile Growth	750 gp		Dust of Toxin Adherence	1,400 gp
Dust of Fury	13,500 gp		Dust of Turn Resistance	7,650 gp

DUST OF AMNESIA

Aura faint transmutation; **CL** 7th
Slot none; **Price** 7,000 gp; **Weight** —

DESCRIPTION

This dust causes the target to suffer complete memory loss for 2d6 minutes on a failed DC 20 Will Save. They will not know their name, where they are from, what they are doing, or any single fact about their lives. They are still able to breathe, eat, fight, cook, and cast spells. They continue to know how to perform any skills they possessed before except for skills involving lore, and they lose access to all knowledge skills. Some people affected by this dust never recover. There is a small chance that the memory loss could become permanent until the application of an appropriate cure spell. Each bag of dust is found with 1d4 + 1 pinches available; newly crafted bags have five pinches.

CONSTRUCTION

Requirements Craft Wondrous Item, *modify memory*; **Cost** 3,500 gp;
Rarity: Rare
Alchemical Formula: Earth (any), Mercury (any), Salt (any), Memory

DUST OF ARCANE WEAKNESS

Aura strong abjuration; **CL** 18th
Slot none; **Price** 8,100 gp; **Weight** —

DESCRIPTION

A target struck by this dust must make a DC 20 Will saving throw. On a failed save, the target's spiritual pattern is weakened. They receive a –8 alchemical penalty on any saving throws versus the next spell cast against them in the next minute or, if the spell causes damage, they do not receive a saving throw versus the damage and they take double damage from the spell as if they are vulnerable.

CONSTRUCTION

Requirements Craft Wondrous Item, *mage's disjunction*; **Cost** 4,050 gp;
Rarity: Very Rare
Alchemical Formula: Iron, Azoth (any), Earth (any)

DUST OF BLENDING

Aura moderate illusion; **CL** 7th
Slot none; **Price** 1,400 gp; **Weight** —

DESCRIPTION

This dust is not found as loose grains or powder; instead, it is found in the form of a golden, crumbly, dirt-like cake approximately four inches in diameter and up to one inch thick. When thrown at a creature or object, the dust explodes in a shower of sparks and magic. The target begins to blend like a chameleon with the area, providing full concealment to the target and a +20 alchemical bonus to Stealth checks. Each cake can affect one man-sized creature or object.

This effect lasts for 2d6 + 3 minutes. If actively moving or marching or if other strenuous activity is engaged in, there is a 1-in-10 chance per minute that the dust can be shaken off. The dust may be removed and washed off at will. Creatures that are moving or fighting are easier to detect, receiving partial concealment and a +10 alchemical bonus to Stealth checks.

CONSTRUCTION

Requirements Craft Wondrous Item, *improved invisibility*; **Cost** 700 gp;
Rarity: Rare
Alchemical Formula: Earth (any), Mercury (any), Stealth

DUST OF BLIGHT

Aura faint necromancy; **CL** 3rd
Slot none; **Price** 1,500 gp; **Weight** —

DESCRIPTION

Targets hit by the dust must succeed at a DC 20 Fortitude save or lose the ability to heal for 10 minutes. Spells such as *cure light wounds* fail to heal the target, regeneration and fast healing stop, a potion that heals has no effect, and even magical items such as a *ring of regeneration* cease to work. After the duration expires, healing again functions normally. Each bag of dust is found with 1d8 + 2 pinches available; newly crafted dusts have a full 10 pinches.

CONSTRUCTION

Requirements Craft Wondrous Item, *ray of enfeeblement*; **Cost** 750 gp;
Rarity: Rare
Alchemical Formula: Iron, Rare Earth, Earth (any), Death, Stasis

DUST OF BLIGHTED BONES

Aura moderate necromancy [evil]; **CL** 11th
Slot none; **Price** 3,300 gp; **Weight** —

DESCRIPTION

This horrible dust causes a terrible bone disease to take root within the target. A saving throw DC 22 Fortitude save negates the effect of the dust. On a failed save, over the next 1d6 + 1 days, the targets bones slowly melt into jelly, causing an excruciating death.

During this time, the person takes double damage from all attacks and quadruple damage from falling and bludgeoning attacks. This begins 2d3 minutes after first exposure to the dust. At the end of the course of the disease, the target's bones turn to jelly. A target without a spine can no longer move. Their brain slowly dies as the skull is no longer solid enough to keep the brain together. The target can look forward to a very slow, excruciating, painful, messy demise.

A *heal, remove curse, limited wish,* or *wish* ends the effect. *Cure disease* resets the progression of the disease but does not end the effect. *Dispel magic* ends the effect but does not reset the progression of the disease, leaving the bones in their weakened state.

CONSTRUCTION

Requirements Craft Wondrous Item, *harm*; **Cost** 1,650 gp; **Rarity:** Very Rare
Alchemical Formula: Earth (any), Death, Decay, Disease, Toxin

DUST OF BLINDNESS

Aura faint necromancy; **CL** 3rd
Slot none; **Price** 2,400 gp; **Weight** —

DESCRIPTION

Targets struck by this dust are blinded. There is no save. The condition lasts for 2d6 minutes. Each bag of dust is found with 2d4 pinches of dust; newly crafted dusts have a full eight pinches.

CONSTRUCTION

Requirements Craft Wondrous Item, *blindness*; **Cost** 1,200 gp; **Rarity:** Rare
Alchemical Formula: Earth (any), Mercury (any), Stasis

DUST OF BLOOD LEECH

Aura moderate necromancy; **CL** 9th
Slot none; **Price** 4,950 gp; **Weight** —

DESCRIPTION

This heinous dust draws a creature's blood out through its skin. It leeches the blood from the veins, flesh, and even the very bone marrow of the targets. When used, it forms a cloud 40 feet wide by 40 feet long by 20 feet high. Anyone in this cloud has the dust adhere to their skin as it begins to leech blood from their body and causes immediate weakness. Strength and Dexterity scores take a penalty equal to half the target's ability score for all who are caught within the cloud. Each round thereafter until death, the victims must make a saving throw DC 16 Fortitude. On the first failed save, the target falls prone and gains the staggered condition. The second failed save causes paralysis. The third failed save results in death. The only cure for the dust is holy water, or a *dispel magic* or a *wish* spell. Survivors recover 1 point of their lost ability scores per day.

CONSTRUCTION

Requirements Craft Wondrous Item, *enervation, cloudkill*; **Cost** 2,475 gp;
Rarity: Rare
Alchemical Formula: Iron, Earth (any), Body, Decay, Stasis

DUST OF BREACHING

Aura faint transmutation; **CL** 11th
Slot none; **Price** 3,300 gp; **Weight** —

DESCRIPTION

When this dust is flung against any magical or nonmagical physical barrier up to 10 feet thick, an opening appears. It slowly grows into a five-foot-radius cylinder over the course of the round. This opening persists for one round, after which it closes instantly. Anything can pass through this space in the barrier. Creatures may enter or exit, arrows or spells may be cast through this space, and it can be seen through with no difficulty. The barrier is unharmed by any of this activity. Any barrier may be affected, whether a *wall of fire*, a *wall of iron*, a dungeon wall, an *antimagic shell* or even a *prismatic sphere*.

If anyone is within the portal at the end of the round, they must succeed at a DC 20 Fortitude save or die. On a successful save, they take 5d8 points of damage and get shunted to one side or the other of the barrier. The side of the barrier is determined randomly.

CONSTRUCTION

Requirements Craft Wondrous Item, *disintegrate*; **Cost** 1,650 gp; **Rarity:** Rare
Alchemical Formula: Malachite, Azoth (any), Earth (any), Planar

DUST OF BURNING

Aura faint evocation; **CL** 3rd
Slot none; **Price** 1,500 gp; **Weight** —

DESCRIPTION

When spread over an object, this dust makes that object flammable. It works on such objects as wet wood and leaves, but it also makes sand, stone, bricks, and other nonflammable objects burn as wood would burn. The object decays and burns in a normal manner. Objects on fire via use of this dust cannot be put out by any normal nonmagical means. When found, there are 1d6 + 4 pinches; when crafting, it has the full allotment of 10 doses.

CONSTRUCTION

Requirements Craft Wondrous Item, *produce flame*; **Cost** 750 gp; **Rarity:** Rare
Alchemical Formula: Earth (any), Fire (any), Transmutation

DUST OF CATASTROPHE

Aura faint transmutation; **CL** 5th
Slot none; **Price** 12,000 gp; **Weight** —

DESCRIPTION

When targets are struck by this dust, they must make a DC 18 Reflex save. On a successful save, they are slowed for one minute. On a failed save, they drop anything held and fall prone. For one minute, targets are unable to attack with missile weapons (they drop the ammunition, fumbling it to the ground), make melee attacks with a −2 luck penalty, and must save once per round versus a DC 14 Reflex save or drop anything they are holding. If the target moves more than five feet, they must save or fall prone. Each bag of dust is found with 1d10 + 2 pinches available; newly crafted dusts have a full 12 pinches.

CONSTRUCTION

Requirements Craft Wondrous Item, *slow*; **Cost** 6,000 gp; **Rarity:** Very Rare
Alchemical Formula: Earth (any), Agility, Body

DUST OF CLOUD DISPERSAL

Aura moderate evocation [air]; **CL** 5th
Slot none; **Price** 4,500 gp; **Weight** —

DESCRIPTION

When thrown into any cloud, smoke, dust, or mist, this dust instantly disperses it. This affects magical clouds such as *obscuring mist, cloud kill,* and *stinking cloud.* This leaves the air clean and breathable, though it smells of ozone. Each bag of dust is found with 1d6 pinches available; newly crafted dusts have a full six pinches.

CONSTRUCTION

Requirements Craft Wondrous Item, *dispel magic, gust of wind*; **Cost** 2,250 gp; **Rarity:** Rare
Alchemical Formula: Air (any), Earth (any), Purity

DUST OF CLOUDS

Aura moderate conjuration (creation) [earth]; **CL** 9th
Slot none; **Price** 22,500 gp; **Weight** —

DESCRIPTION

When tossed in the air, this produces a billowing, swirling, cloud of dust. It fills an area of 16 10-foot cubes. This can be a wall 10 feet wide and 160 feet long, a wall 20 feet wide and 80 feet long, or a 40-foot-by-40-foot cloud. Those within the cloud are totally blind, and the cloud completely blocks line of sight. The dust swirls around for an hour before it settles to the ground. When found, there are between 1d8 + 2 pinches of the dust; a newly crafted dust has a full 10 pinches.

CONSTRUCTION

Requirements Craft Wondrous Item, *wall of stone, gust of wind*; **Cost** 11,250 gp; **Rarity:** Rare
Alchemical Formula: Air (any), Earth (any), Mercury (any), Stealth

DUST OF CONFUSION

Aura strong enchantment (compulsion) [mind-affecting]; **CL** 7th
Slot none; **Price** 14,000 gp; **Weight** —

DESCRIPTION

This dust causes any targets nearby to become confused, listless, and indecisive. It is only 10% likely that they take any action in a round. This confusing haze lasts for 2d6 rounds. There is no initial save. After the first round, each target must succeed at a DC 18 Will save to continue to act. Each bag of dust is found with 1d6 + 4 pinches available; newly crafted dusts have a full 10 pinches.

CONSTRUCTION

Requirements Craft Wondrous Item, *confusion*; **Cost** 7,000 gp; **Rarity:** Rare
Alchemical Formula: Earth (any) (2 from different sources), Mind

DUST OF CONSUMPTION

Aura faint transmutation; **CL** 1st
Slot none; **Price** 500 gp; **Weight** —

DESCRIPTION

This dust makes any substance edible. When sprinkled over some organic substance, it breaks it down and allows it to be chewed as if it were tough, tasteless, boiled leather. Substances often have a nasty bitter taste, but they do provide basic nutrition. Each bag of dust is found with 1d12 + 8 pinches available; newly crafted dusts have a full 20 pinches.

CONSTRUCTION

Requirements Craft Wondrous Item, *allfood*; **Cost** 250 gp; **Rarity:** Rare
Alchemical Formula: Earth (any), Plant

DUST OF DECAY

Aura strong necromancy; **CL** 5th
Slot none; **Price** 15,000 gp; **Weight** —

DESCRIPTION

This dust causes non-living material to age and decay. When a pinch is applied, it affects up to three cubic feet of material. This non-living material then rapidly ages approximately 300 years. If two pinches are used, objects age up to 1,000 years. Each bag of dust is found with 1d12 + 8 pinches available; newly crafted dusts have a full 20 doses.
This causes stone to weather, crack, and weaken and, in most cases, dissolves wooden and less-sturdy supports. A full bag affects 600 cubic feet of a building for 300 years, or half for a millennium. Specific effects are left to the adjudication of the GM; a safe damage range for a collapsing building is 10d6 points of damage. The dust is difficult to store, requiring metal containers.
This also rusts and destroys armor, rope, rations, iron spikes, doors, and other equipment. Note that this has no effect on any sort of living organism such as a tree, grass, animals, a human being, or fungi. It causes no damage to undead, but naked vampires are usually not very happy.

CONSTRUCTION

Requirements Craft Wondrous Item, *haste*; **Cost** 7,500 gp; **Rarity:** Very Rare
Alchemical Formula: Earth (any), Decay (x2 from different sources), Speed

DUST OF DEFORMITY

Aura strong necromancy; **CL** 15th
Slot none; **Price** 6,000 gp; **Weight** —

DESCRIPTION

When this dust is used, the target becomes hideously deformed. Their Charisma is reduced to 3 as they are covered in welts, bruises, warts, horn flesh, twisted cysts, and pores oozing multicolored pus. Those viewing the targets must succeed at a DC 18 Will save or be repulsed and unable to bear the appearance of the target.
A *remove curse* or better is required to reverse the effect.

CONSTRUCTION

Requirements Craft Wondrous Item, *horrid wilting*; **Cost** 3,000 gp; **Rarity:** Rare
Alchemical Formula: Earth (any), Disease, Transmutation

DUST OF DELIQUESCENCE

Aura moderate transmutation; **CL** 11th
Slot none; **Price** 33,000 gp; **Weight** —

DESCRIPTION

When spread over once-living material that is no longer alive, this dust produces a thick, dark mist for several moments. This mist contains streams and wisps of sparkling silver smoke, and a soft ominous hissing sound can be heard. Several moments later, the dust clears, and the corpse disappears. This dust has no effect on any living creature and does not affect plant life — only animal. It destroys dead bodies, leather armor, and other dead organic matter in one round, leaving no trace. Most undead are unaffected by this dust, though it does 3d6 damage to corporeal undead that have fewer than 3 hit dice. Each bag of dust is found with 1d6 + 4 pinches available; newly crafted dusts have a full 10 pinches.

CONSTRUCTION

Requirements Craft Wondrous Item, *disintegrate*; **Cost** 16,500 gp; **Rarity:** Rare
Alchemical Formula: Earth (any), Decay

DUST OF DETECT ILLUSION

Aura moderate divination; **CL** 6th
Slot none; **Price** 3,300 gp; **Weight** —

DESCRIPTION

When sprinkled with this dust, illusionary objects and creatures, optical illusions, figments, glamors, patterns, phantasms, and shadows glow faintly and shimmer as if unreal. After this use, all will be immediately detected as such.
This allows characters to see an illusionary pit or wall for an illusion, but it will not penetrate the illusion to reveal what is behind it. It negates a creature's displacement ability or reveals a shadow as such, though it will not prevent the shadow (which is partially real) from causing damage.

CONSTRUCTION

Requirements Craft Wondrous Item, *true seeing*; **Cost** 1,650 gp; **Rarity:** Rare
Alchemical Formula: Earth (any), Sulfur (any)

DUST OF DISPELLING

Aura moderate abjuration; **CL** 15th
Slot none; **Price** 13,500 gp; **Weight** —

DESCRIPTION

Spreading this dust breaks all magical effects that are occurring where the dust is spread. All magical effects are dispelled as if affected by a *dispel magic* cast by a 15th-level caster.
It can be dusted over the caster, a magical trap, or over an item. If dusted over an item, it simply suppresses the magic for a short while. Each bag of dust is found with 1d4 + 2 pinches available; newly crafted dusts have a full six pinches.

CONSTRUCTION

Requirements Craft Wondrous Item, *dispel magic*,; **Cost** 6,750 gp; **Rarity:** Rare
Alchemical Formula: Diamond, Azoth (any), Mercury (any), Sulfur (any)

DUST OF DEPRIVATION

Aura moderate necromancy; **CL** 3rd
Slot none; **Price** 1,500 gp; **Weight** —

DESCRIPTION

This dust contains 1d4 + 1 uses for humanoids or other man-sized creatures. It affects the senses of all living creatures. Roll 1d6 when used; this indicates the severity of damage the dust manages to inflict. Reference **Table 4–5** below for specifics. Every effect is applied up to the number shown on the die. Roll 2d6 to determine the duration of the effect in hours.

TABLE 4–5: DUST OF DEPRIVATION EFFECTS

1d6	Sense	Effect
1	Sight	Vision is blurred, causing a –5 alchemical penalty to hit, one-half alchemical penalty to movement, and removes the targets Dexterity bonus to AC.
2	Taste	Sense of taste is lost
3	Hearing	Deafness. Gain the deafened condition. –4 on initiative checks, fail Perception checks based on sound, –4 penalty on opposed Perception checks, and 20% chance of spell failure.
4	Touch	Tactile sense is lost. One-half movement and running results in falling prone. Dexterity has a –4 alchemical penalty to Dexterity, and there is a 30% chance of dropping anything held in any round in which it is used.
5	Smell	Olfactory sense lost.
6	Sixth Sense	No spells, or spell-like abilities, or supernatural abilities function.

CONSTRUCTION

Requirements Craft Wondrous Item, *blindness/deafness*; **Cost** 750 gp; **Rarity:** Very Rare
Alchemical Formula: Earth (any), Mercury (2 from 2 different sources), Body, Mind

DUST OF DISTRACTION

Aura moderate illusion; **CL** 7th
Slot none; **Price** 8,400 gp; **Weight** —

DESCRIPTION

When thrown on the ground, this dust creates the shape of a rat, snake, or fox depending on the bones used. It then lashes out, looking as if it is attacking anyone within 15 feet of where the dust was thrown.
However, it is just made from dust and cannot actually harm anyone. It thrashes and lashes out in an attempt to draw attention to itself. Weapon and claw attacks pass harmlessly through the dust and do no damage. Creatures of low and greater intelligence can make a DC 14 Will save to recognize the dust as harmless after their first attack.
However, if someone attempts a bite attack versus the dust creature, the attack automatically hits and a DC 18 Fortitude save must be made or the attacker dies in one round, choking to death on the dust. Each bag of dust is found with 1d4 + 2 pinches available; newly crafted dusts have a full six pinches.

CONSTRUCTION

Requirements Craft Wondrous Item, *shadow conjuration*; **Cost** 4,200 gp; **Rarity:** Rare
Alchemical Formula: Air (any), Earth (any), Mercury (any)

DUST OF ECHOES

Aura faint illusion; **CL** 7th
Slot none; **Price** 11,200 gp; **Weight** —

DESCRIPTION

Those affected by this dust have their sensitivity to sound increased so that even the quietest noise sounds like a deafening echo. The target is driven to reduce the amount of noise they make, whispering and moving slowly and quietly. Even hearing sounds at a normal conversational volume is exceedingly painful.
The target has a –2 circumstance penalty to attack rolls, armor class, and saving throws. If this is used on a creature with sensitive hearing, they may become violent or flee.
This dust is found with 2d4 pinches; newly crafted dusts have a full eight pinches. The effect lasts (1d6 + 2) x 10 minutes.

CONSTRUCTION

Requirements Craft Wondrous Item, *phantasmal killer*; **Cost** 5,600 gp; **Rarity:** Rare
Alchemical Formula: Earth (any), Mercury (any), Body, Perception

DUST OF FERTILE GROWTH

Aura faint transmutation; **CL** 5th
Slot none; **Price** 750 gp; **Weight** —

DESCRIPTION

When this dust is spread across any soil in which plants dwell, it has an amazing effect on their growth. It causes one year's worth of growth in a week. It should be noted that this dust has no effect on magical, sentient, or mobile plants. This dust covers up to 1,000 square feet of land.

CONSTRUCTION

Requirements Craft Wondrous Item, *plant growth*; **Cost** 375 gp; **Rarity:** Rare
Alchemical Formula: Earth (any) (x2), Plant, Transmutation

DUST OF FURY

Aura strong enchantment (compulsion) [mind-affecting]; **CL** 9th
Slot none; **Price** 13,500 gp; **Weight** —

DESCRIPTION

When this dust strikes an intelligent creature actively hostile to the wielder, they must succeed at a DC 20 Will save or become enraged. Anyone succeeding at the save may act normally; enraged opponents fly into a berserk fury and attack the nearest creature (even their own friends and comrades) with a +4 moral bonus to Strength and Constitution and a +2 morale bonus to Will saves, but suffers a –2 circumstance penalty to AC. Creatures friendly to the wielder are unaffected. This rage lasts for 1d6 + 6 rounds, during which the enraged creatures attack continually without reason or fear, moving on to attack other creatures if the ones nearest them are slain. Each bag of dust is found with 1d4 + 2 pinches available; newly crafted dusts have a full six pinches.

CONSTRUCTION

Requirements Craft Wondrous Item, *rage, dominate person*; **Cost** 6,750 gp; **Rarity:** Rare
Alchemical Formula: Earth (any), Mercury (any), Emotion

DUST OF THE GRAVE

Aura faint necromancy; **CL** 7th
Slot none; **Price** 28,000 gp; **Weight** —

DESCRIPTION

This dust enhances the connection undead have with the Negative Material Plane. When sprinkled with this dust, undead are treated as having hit dice three higher when being subject to turning or control attempts. It also increases the hit points of the undead by 1 per hit die.
This dust only affects undead of less than six hit dice. When found, there is usually enough dust to coat 1d12 + 8 undead; newly created dust can cover up to 20 undead.

CONSTRUCTION

Requirements Craft Wondrous Item, *enervation*; **Cost** 14,000 gp; **Rarity:** Rare
Alchemical Formula: Earth (any), Planar

DUST OF INSTANT ICE

Aura moderate evocation [cold]; **CL** 7th
Slot none; **Price** 1,400 gp; **Weight** —

DESCRIPTION

When this dust is applied to a body of water, it freezes 1,000 cubic feet of water. Fresh water is frozen instantly, but saltwater takes between 1d4 + 1 rounds to freeze. If there is more than 1,000 cubic feet of water, then the frozen shape does not make a perfect cube, but more of a trapezoidal shape depending on how the dust disperses. Creatures made of water and any creature with the water subtype are affected by this dust as if under a *slow* spell and take 1d8 points of damage.

CONSTRUCTION

Requirements Craft Wondrous Item, *wall of ice*; **Cost** 700 gp; **Rarity:** Rare
Alchemical Formula: Earth (any), Water (any), Cold

DUST OF LIGHTNESS

Aura faint transmutation; **CL** 3rd
Slot none; **Price** 1,500 gp; **Weight** —

DESCRIPTION

When this dust is applied to any non-living object, it reduces the weight and bulk of the object by half for 12 hours. The dust can be washed or blown off, so care must be taken if transporting objects in a storm. This coats 10 man-sized objects.

CONSTRUCTION

Requirements Craft Wondrous Item, *feather fall*; **Cost** 750 gp; **Rarity:** Rare
Alchemical Formula: Rare Earth, Air (x2), Earth (any)

DUST OF LOOPING

Aura strong transmutation; **CL** 15th
Slot none; **Price** 12,000 gp; **Weight** —

DESCRIPTION

This bizarre dust forces the creatures targeted to all make a DC 19 Will save. Those who fail their save all repeat the exact same action they made last round.
They don't perform the action anew — they repeat the exact same motions and movements. Attacks are dodged trivially; they have a –4 circumstance penalty to their armor class. Spells are recast, but if not memorized more than once, this has no effect. The targets have no control over their actions — they repeat the same actions even if it puts them into mortal danger. When found, this dust has 1d4 uses; newly created dusts have the full four uses.

CONSTRUCTION

Requirements Craft Wondrous Item, *temporal stasis*; **Cost** 6,000 gp; **Rarity:** Rare
Alchemical Formula: Azoth (any), Earth (any), Mercury (any), Memory

DUST OF MALADWEOMER

Aura strong abjuration; **CL** 13th
Slot none; **Price** 22,750 gp; **Weight** —

DESCRIPTION

When a target is coated in this dust, they must make a DC 18 Will save. If they fail, it causes all their spells, spell-like abilities, magic items, and magical effects to operate at a minimum effectiveness. Spells do minimum damage, have minimum duration, creatures summoned have minimum hit points, and all variable effects are treated as minimum. People affected by magic originating from the target receive a +4 circumstance bonus on their saving throws. This dust is found with 1d4 + 1 pinches; newly crafted dusts have a full five pinches.

CONSTRUCTION

Requirements Craft Wondrous Item, *limited wish, dispel magic*; **Cost** 11,375 gp; **Rarity:** Rare
Alchemical Formula: Azoth (any), Earth (any), Stasis

DUST OF MIND DULLING

Aura faint transmutation; **CL** 9th
Slot none; **Price** 22,500 gp; **Weight** —

DESCRIPTION

This dust clouds the mind and makes it difficult for spellcasters to successfully cast spells. Spellcasters (and monsters with spell-like effects) must make a DC 18 Fortitude saving throw or find their wits dulled. Spells take longer to cast, quickened spells become standard actions, and standard action spells become full round spells. Full-round spells become 10-round spells, taking a full minute to cast. And in order to successfully cast a spell, the spellcaster must succeed at a Concentration check with a DC equal to 10 + twice the spells level.
Those affected by the dust are impaired for 1d4 + 1 minutes. This dust is found with 1d8 + 2 pinches; newly crafted dusts have a full 10 pinches.

CONSTRUCTION

Requirements Craft Wondrous Item, *feeblemind*; **Cost** 11,250 gp; **Rarity:** Rare
Alchemical Formula: Earth (any), Mind (x2)

DUST OF NON-DETECTION
Aura strong abjuration; **CL** 5th
Slot none; **Price** 750 gp; **Weight** —

DESCRIPTION
Hidden objects or traps sprinkled with this dust are undetectable by magical means of any sort. This does not mean that the item is obscured from view; it simply prevents its detection by magical means. The target cannot be detected or perceived through *clairaudience*, *clairvoyance*, *telepathy*, *crystal balls*, or any other scrying devices. The target emits no discernible aura and any predictions of the future neither mention nor account for the target. Note that when this dust is used to obscure magical traps, this makes them all but undetectable. This dust is permanent until sprinkled with *dust of appearance* or *dispel magic* is cast. This dust can also be sprinkled on a living creature, warding the user against all divination and mental or magical location and or detection for 2d6 hours. This dust can cover one medium object or creature.

CONSTRUCTION
Requirements Craft Wondrous Item, *nondetection*; **Cost** 375 gp; **Rarity:** Rare
Alchemical Formula: Earth (any), Stealth (x2)

DUST OF PANIC
Aura moderate necromancy [fear, mind-affecting]; **CL** 11th
Slot none; **Price** 16,500 gp; **Weight** —

DESCRIPTION
Anyone struck by this dust must drop what they are holding and flee unless they succeed at a DC 16 Will save. On a failed Will save, the targets gain the panicked condition. Each round thereafter, the panicked creatures may attempt to save again. Creatures of low intelligence or other extenuating factors (such as an appropriate illusion) can increase the difficulty of the saving throw. This dust is found with 1d4 + 1 pinches; newly crafted dusts have a full five pinches.

CONSTRUCTION
Requirements Craft Wondrous Item, *symbol of fear*; **Cost** 8,250 gp; **Rarity:** Rare
Alchemical Formula: Earth (any), Fear

DUST OF PARALYZATION
Aura enchantment (compulsion) [mind-affecting]; **CL** 9th
Slot none; **Price** 31,500 gp; **Weight** —

DESCRIPTION
This terrifying dust produces paralysis against all who fail a DC 18 Fortitude save. Targets may attempt a DC 20 Fortitude save at the end of every round to end the effect. If the target fails this save three times, they are paralyzed for a full hour. This dust is found with 1d6 + 1d8 pinches; newly crafted dusts have a full 14 pinches.

CONSTRUCTION
Requirements Craft Wondrous Item, *hold monster*; **Cost** 15,750 gp; **Rarity:** Rare
Alchemical Formula: Earth (any), Stasis

DUST OF PLANAR SEVERANCE
Aura strong abjuration; **CL** 15th
Slot none; **Price** 30,000 gp; **Weight** —

DESCRIPTION
This dust blocks planar connections. It has several effects. Targets can avoid the affects by succeeding at a DC 20 Reflex save. On a failed save, wizards and spell-using monsters are unable to cast spells or use spell-like effects for 1d6 + 1 rounds. Mindless undead have their connections severed to their home plane; they de-animate and drop lifelessly to the floor. Planar effects such as *etherealness* and *blink* are suppressed for 1d6 + 1 rounds. Outsiders are affected as if under a *dimensional anchor* spell. This dust is found with 1d4 + 1 pinches; newly created dust has a full five doses.

CONSTRUCTION
Requirements Craft Wondrous Item, *dimensional lock*; **Cost** 15,000 gp; **Rarity:** Rare
Alchemical Formula: Azoth (any), Earth (any), Planar

DUST OF REDIRECTION
Aura strong enchantment (compulsion) [mind-affecting]; **CL** 9th
Slot none; **Price** 11,250 gp; **Weight** —

DESCRIPTION
This powerful dust has an intense effect upon the targets. They must make a DC 20 Will save or be affected. If this save fails, the thing they currently find most important becomes unimportant. If they are fighting, they stop; if eating, people lose their appetite; and whatever task is currently being attempted ends. The targets remember doing those things, but they no longer have any interest in performing or completing the task. This dust is found with 1d4 + 1 pinches; newly crafted dusts have a full five pinches.

CONSTRUCTION
Requirements Craft Wondrous Item, *dominate person*; **Cost** 5,625 gp; **Rarity:** Rare
Alchemical Formula: Earth (any), Mercury (any), Sulfur (any), Memory

DUST OF RENDING PROTECTIONS
Aura strong abjuration; **CL** 11th
Slot none; **Price** 33,000 gp; **Weight** —

DESCRIPTION
When targets are covered by this dust, any magical or supernatural protections and wards are stripped. The target's armor class receives a −2 alchemical penalty and any DR the creature has is removed for an hour. This has no effect on a target's magic resistance or saving throws. It does nothing to remove natural immunities, such as a fire elemental's resistance to fire. This dust is found with 1d8 + 1d12 pinches; newly crafted dusts have a full 20 pinches.

CONSTRUCTION
Requirements Craft Wondrous Item, *disintegrate*, *dispel magic*; **Cost** 16,500 gp; **Rarity:** Rare
Alchemical Formula: Earth (any), Salt (any), Sulfur (any), Decay

DUST OF REVEALING
Aura moderate divination; **CL** 11th
Slot none; **Price** 3,300 gp; **Weight** —

DESCRIPTION
This dust fills an area of about 28,000 cubic feet (28 contiguous 10 foot by 10 foot by 10 foot cubes) or a circle of about a 30-foot radius that is 10 feet high. The whole dust must be expended for the dust to have an effect. Anything within this area is revealed to be what it truly is. Illusions are made transparent, disguises are revealed, shapeshifters change into their true form, and spells that alter appearance are dispelled. Note that this does not reveal planar creatures, nor creatures out of phase. It just reveals things as they are.

CONSTRUCTION
Requirements Craft Wondrous Item, *true seeing*; **Cost** 1,650 gp; **Rarity:** Rare
Alchemical Formula: Rare Earth, Earth (any), Fire (any), Perception

DUST OF ROUGHAGE
Aura faint conjuration (creation); **CL** 5th
Slot none; **Price** 12,750 gp; **Weight** —

DESCRIPTION
A small pinch of this dust added to at least one gallon of water produces an astounding pile of feed. It forms soft spongy chunks of dry pasty vegetable matter suitable for feeding 50 men (Medium-sized creatures) per day. It feeds one-half as many people for every size category increase and feeds twice as many people for each size category decrease (i.e., 100 small creatures or 25 large creatures). The dust is found with 4d4 + 4 pinches available; newly created dusts have the full 20 doses.
In the unfortunate circumstance that a dry pinch is consumed, it results in the messy gruesome death of the imbiber unless they succeed at DC 24 Fortitude save. Even if they survive, they are violently ill and suffer a point of Constitution drain.

CONSTRUCTION
Requirements Craft Wondrous Item, *create food and water*; **Cost** 6,375 gp; **Rarity:** Rare
Alchemical Formula: Earth (any), Mercury (any) (x2), Plant

DUST OF RUST

Aura moderate transmutation; **CL** 7th
Slot none; **Price** 1,400 gp; **Weight** —

DESCRIPTION

This heinous dust destroys metal. When exposed to *dust of rust*, nonmagical ferrous metals such as iron and steel disintegrate, rusting apart in one round. Base metals such as nickel, lead, zinc, and copper rust in one round and disintegrate in two rounds. Rare, precious, or alloy metals such as mithril, adamantine, bronze, tin, and aluminum rust and disintegrate in one minute. Certain noble metals such as gold, platinum, and silver retain an immunity to this dust. Unattended metal items take 8d6 damage. Ferrous metals have their hardness ignored, and base metals use one-half their hardness. "Magical metal" includes such things as golems, rods, and rings, which increase their hardness by 10 after halving or ignoring the base hardness. This covers up to 100 cubic feet or 1,000 square feet of metal.

CONSTRUCTION

Requirements Craft Wondrous Item, *rusting grasp*; **Cost** 700 gp; **Rarity:** Rare
Alchemical Formula: Earth (any), Salt (any) (x2), Decay

DUST OF SLAYERBANE

Aura moderate necromancy; **CL** 15th
Slot none; **Price** 6,000 gp; **Weight** —

DESCRIPTION

This dust is barely detectable when spread in the air, appearing only as a momentary glimmer. Anyone exposed to this dust must make a DC 16 Fortitude save or become terribly allergic to the creature type whose bones were used in the manufacture of the dust.

As soon as the victim comes within 100 feet of the creature, they experience a violent onset of symptoms. It begins with a sneeze that negates any sort of surprise, and then the eyes water and the nose begins to run. The next round, the victim breaks out in hives all over his or her body that itch painfully. The reaction is moderately impairing, causing a –4 alchemical penalty to Strength and Dexterity; you must succeed at a concentration check of 10 + the spells level to successfully cast a spell. This reaction ends 1d6 rounds after moving more than 100 feet away from the target creature, unless they engage the creature in combat, in which case blood, sweat, and dander cause the condition to linger until the victim cleans themselves.

This dust is created from the full skeleton of the creature that the victim(s) are to be made allergic to. Most often, corpses of monsters killed by the monster hunters are used. The reaction is permanent until a *cure disease* spell is cast.

CONSTRUCTION

Requirements Craft Wondrous Item, *horrid wilting*; **Cost** 3,000 gp; **Rarity:** Rare
Alchemical Formula: Onyx, Earth (any), Body, Disease

DUST OF SLEEP

Aura moderate enchantment (compulsion) [mind-affecting]; **CL** 9th
Slot none; **Price** 22,500 gp; **Weight** —

DESCRIPTION

This powerful dust causes the targets to fall into a comatose slumber. Any creature struck by the dust that fails a DC 18 Fortitude save falls into a deep sleep. To awaken a creature affected by this dust requires one full round. This dust is found with 2d4 + 2 pinches; newly crafted dusts have a full 10 pinches.

CONSTRUCTION

Requirements Craft Wondrous Item, *symbol of sleep*; **Cost** 11,250 gp; **Rarity:** Rare
Alchemical Formula: Earth (any), Mercury (any), Stasis

DUST OF SNEEZING

Aura moderate conjuration (creation); **CL** 5th
Slot none; **Price** 15,000 gp; **Weight** —

DESCRIPTION

This dust causes all creatures within its area of effect to make a DC 18 Fortitude save or be struck by a sneezing fit. Victims that fail their save gain the nauseated condition. They can make a saving throw at the beginning of each round to end the effect. This dust is found with 1d8 + 12 pinches; newly crafted dusts have a full 20 pinches.

CONSTRUCTION

Requirements Craft Wondrous Item, *stinking cloud*; **Cost** 7,500 gp; **Rarity:** Rare
Alchemical Formula: Earth (any), Mercury (any), Disease

DUST OF SOLID VAPOR

Aura moderate evocation [force]; **CL** 9th
Slot none; **Price** 13,500 gp; **Weight** —

DESCRIPTION

This powerful dust has unique properties of stasis and solidification. When tossed into the area of effect of any magical or nonmagical mist or cloud, it begins to harden the vapor into a solid substance. For non-obscuring clouds, this causes the area to become thick and gummy, much like a *web* spell. Those moving through the field each round must make a Strength check to move at half speed. A failed check means moving at a quarter speed. Clouds that already have an obscuring quality become even more dense, hardening into an amber-like substance. Those within the area of effect must make a DC 16 Reflex Save or become trapped in the cloud for the duration. This can be used on a gaseous creature, in which case it is treated as the *hold person* spell cast by a 9th-level caster.

Those trapped in the solid cloud can still breathe and are simply held in place. The solid nature of the cloud protects them from external attack or damage, but the solid vapor still has all its natural properties — beings trapped in a solid acid cloud take damage every round they are trapped. This dust has no effect on air or water, only magical and nonmagical mists, clouds, vapors and other gaseous matter.

This dust lasts for 1d4 + 1 rounds. When found, it has between 1d4 + 2 pinches; newly crafted dusts have a full six pinches.

CONSTRUCTION

Requirements Craft Wondrous Item, *wall of force*; **Cost** 6,750 gp; **Rarity:** Rare
Alchemical Formula: Earth (any), Mercury (any), Transmutation

DUST OF THE SPARKLING MIND

Aura moderate divination; **CL** 9th
Slot none; **Price** 45,000 gp; **Weight** —

DESCRIPTION

This bag contains white dust that sparkles like thousands of tiny gems. Anyone who uses this dust by snorting it up their nose can communicate telepathically for 1d6 + 4 hours with any other user with a range of 50 feet. There are 3d4 + 8 uses per bag; newly crafted dusts have a full 20 uses.

CONSTRUCTION

Requirements Craft Wondrous Item, *telepathic bond*; **Cost** 22,500 gp; **Rarity:** Rare
Alchemical Formula: Earth (any), Mercury (any), Telesthetic

DUST OF SPIRIT BINDING
Aura strong abjuration; **CL** 13th
Slot none; **Price** 45,500 gp; **Weight** —

DESCRIPTION

This dust binds ethereal and noncorporeal undead to the Prime Material
Plane. It worsens the armor class of such creatures by five points, making
them easier to hit, and solidifies their insubstantial form, causing the creature
to take full damage from attacks. A downside to this is that it makes attacks
from the creatures more physically damaging. Double hit point damage from
attacks is dealt or, if no physical attack is given, it gains a claw/claw or slam/
slam routine for 1d8/1d8 damage.
If a body is possessed, this dust paralyzes the body for 3d4 minutes and
imprisons the spirit inside the body for the duration. This dust is found with
2d4 + 2 pinches; newly crafted dusts have a full 10 pinches.

CONSTRUCTION

Requirements Craft Wondrous Item, *banishment*; **Cost** 22,750 gp; **Rarity:**
Rare
Alchemical Formula: Earth (any), Planar, Stasis

DUST OF TOXIN ADHERENCE
Aura faint, divination; **CL** 7th
Slot none; **Price** 1,400 gp; **Weight** —

DESCRIPTION

This useful dust is attracted to toxins and poisons as iron is to a magnet.
When sprinkled or dusted over a surface, it identifies contact and surface
poisons, but also poison in needles, darts, and injected poisons in traps. This
allows certain detection of poison traps and gives a +6 circumstance bonus
to Disable Device checks to disarm them. Anyone that actually manages to
fall prey to the revealed poison — such as an incompetent thief that fails to
disarm a trap — receives a +4 circumstance bonus on their saving throw.
This dust can be used to thoroughly test an area that is 10 feet by 10 feet by
10 feet for poison or up to five separate items.

CONSTRUCTION

Requirements Craft Wondrous Item, *detect poison, neutralize poison*; **Cost**
700 gp; **Rarity:** Rare
Alchemical Formula: Earth (any) (x2), Toxin

DUST OF TURN RESISTANCE
Aura strong necromancy; **CL** 17th
Slot none; **Price** 7,650 gp; **Weight** —

DESCRIPTION

When this dust is spread upon undead creatures, energies from the Negative
Material Plane are strengthened. All undead affected by this dust receive a +5
bonus to their Will saves to resist channel energy effects. On a failure, they
take only half damage, and on a successful save, they take one-quarter the
damage. The dust can cover up to 20 Medium-sized creatures.

CONSTRUCTION

Requirements Craft Wondrous Item, *energy drain*; **Cost** 3,675 gp; **Rarity:**
Rare
Alchemical Formula: Earth (any), Salt (x2), Death

ELIXIRS

Elixirs are usually found in vials with one dose. They consist of one ounce of liquid held in a vial. Typically, the vials are glass or ceramic, more rarely metal or crystal. A typical container has AC 13, 1 hit point, hardness 1, and a break DC of 12. Generally, no labels are on elixir bottles, which requires either experimentation or an alchemist to determine what the potion does. In addition to the standard methods of identification, a character may sample from each container to attempt to determine the nature of the liquid inside with a Perception check. The DC of this check is equal to 15 + the caster level of the elixir. Elixirs of the same type, make, and manufacture may be similar in smell, taste, and appearance, but this is no guarantee. In order to encourage experimentation with elixirs, your GM may have elixirs that have not been subject to identifying magics be more powerful (Maximized effects or duration, etc.) than potions identified using traditional magical or alchemical means. You may randomly determine if an elixir is labeled. Roll 1d6. On a 1–2 the potion is labeled; on a 3–5 it is not. On a 6, the potion is labeled incorrectly. Roll a second elixir and that is what the label says the elixir is.

Unless otherwise noted in the description of the individual elixir below, the effects of a potion last for 1d4 + 4 minutes. In many cases, quaffing a half dose causes the effects to last half as long. It takes a standard action to open and drink an elixir. The elixir takes effect immediately. Using an elixir provokes an attack of opportunity. An enemy may direct an attack of opportunity against the elixir container rather than against the character. A successful attack of this sort can destroy the container, preventing the character from drinking the elixir.

A creature must be able to swallow an elixir. Because of this, incorporeal creatures cannot use elixirs. Any corporeal creature can imbibe an elixir.

A character can carefully administer an elixir to an unconscious creature as a full-round action, trickling the liquid down the creature's throat.

Alchemists can compound elixirs at low cost, this being their primary advantage over wands and other items. However, they do require time and certain rare materials.

Any two elixirs (or potions) can be fused into a potion admixture. This is an extremely difficult process where two magical liquids are combined into one elixir. In order to create a potion admixture, you must succeed at a Craft (alchemy) check with a DC equal to 20 + the caster level of the more powerful elixir or potion. If successful, you now have a single elixir that, when quaffed, provides both effects. On a failure, the elixirs (or potions) still combine, but you must roll on **Table 1–5: Potion Miscibility** in **Chapter 1: Alchemy Basics**.

If successful on your Craft (alchemy) check, you may choose to roll on the **Potion Miscibility Table** by choice, adding 5 to your roll. Note that needing to roll this check due to failure does not provide this protection.

Name	Price
Elixir of Absorption	3,300 gp
Elixir of Aging	1,400 gp
Elixir of Anesthesia	750 gp
Elixir of Balance	300 gp
Elixir of Beauty	300 gp
Elixir of Bestial Boon	2,250 gp
Elixir of Bouncing	150 gp
Elixir of Clarity	4,550 gp
Elixir of Cloaking Shadows	750 gp
Elixir of Control, Animal	750 gp
Elixir of Control, Dragon	7,650 gp
Elixir of Control, Elemental	7,650 gp
Elixir of Control, Giant	2,250 gp
Elixir of Control, Human	2,250 gp
Elixir of Control, Plant	750 gp
Elixir of Control, Undead	750 gp
Elixir of Crawling	750 gp
Elixir of Cure Insanity	750 gp
Elixir of Cure Nervous Disorders	750 gp
Elixir of Danger Sense	1,400 gp
Elixir of Defense +1	750 gp
Elixir of Defense +2	2,250 gp
Elixir of Defense +3	4,550 gp
Elixir of Defense +4	7,650 gp
Elixir of Deflation	4,550 gp
Elixir of Diminution	4,550 gp
Elixir of Dispelling	3,300 gp
Elixir of Dragon Attractant	6,000 gp
Elixir of Dream Speech	2,250 gp
Elixir of Dreams	2,250 gp
Elixir of Eldritch Intensity	4,550 gp
Elixir of Emotions	2,250 gp
Elixir of False Divinity	150 gp
Elixir of Forms	7,650 gp
Elixir of Fur Growth	750 gp
Elixir of Good Fortune	4,550 gp
Elixir of Growth 4,550 gp	
Elixir of Heroic Aid	750 gp
Elixir of Heroic Fighting	750 gp
Elixir of Heroic Fighting, Super	2,250 gp
Elixir of Heroic Larceny	750 gp
Elixir of Heroic Spellcasting	750 gp
Elixir of Immunity, Cold	750 gp
Elixir of Immunity, Control	750 gp
Elixir of Immunity, Fire	750 gp
Elixir of Immunity, Metal	1,400 gp
Elixir of Immunity, Petrification	750 gp
Elixir of Immunity, Poison	750 gp
Elixir of Insanity Shield	6,000 gp

Name	Price
Elixir of Invulnerability	1,400 gp
Elixir of Knitted Bones	300 gp
Elixir of Language	4,550 gp
Elixir of Liquidity	4,550 gp
Elixir of Location	1,400 gp
Elixir of Lockpicking	300 gp
Elixir of Longevity	7,650 gp
Elixir of Lucky Fate	4,550 gp
Elixir of Magnetism	4,550 gp
Elixir of Manners	1,400 gp
Elixir of Memory	300 gp
Elixir of Mental Composure	1,400 gp
Elixir of Mind Damp	6,000 gp
Elixir of Mirrored Eyes	1,400 gp
Elixir of Natural Renewal	4,550 gp
Elixir of Nutrition	1,400 gp
Elixir of Perception	1,400 gp
Elixir of Poison Breath	750 gp
Elixir of Poison Flesh 750 gp	
Elixir of Poison Touch 2,250 gp	
Elixir of Protection from Immiscibility	4,550 gp
Elixir of Protection from Lycanthropes	2,250 gp
Elixir of Protection from Magic Missile	50 gp
Elixir of Protection from Magical Weapons	2,250 gp
Elixir of Protection from Noxious Gas	750 gp
Elixir of Protection from Spirits	2,250 gp
Elixir of Protection from Sprites	2,250 gp
Elixir of Protection from Vampires	2,250 gp
Elixir of Psychic Trap	1,400 gp
Elixir of Rainbow Hues	750 gp
Elixir of Rapid Healing	750 gp
Elixir of Recall	1,400 gp
Elixir of Recuperation	300 gp
Elixir of Reflective Form	1,400 gp
Elixir of Reflex	750 gp
Elixir of Revenge	300 gp
Elixir of Revivification	2,250 gp
Elixir of Safe Consumption	300 gp
Elixir of Scent Control	50 gp
Elixir of Sculpture	4,550 gp
Elixir of Shrieking	1,400 gp
Elixir of Shrubbery	4,550 gp
Elixir of Skeletal Visage	1,400 gp
Elixir of Skill	4,500 gp
Elixir of Sleep	2,250 gp
Elixir of Sleep Breath	300 gp
Elixir of Somatic Remedy	2,250 gp
Elixir of Spines	750 gp
Elixir of Strength, Giant	4,550 gp
Elixir of Strength, Ogre	750 gp

Name	Price
Elixir of Strength, Titan	6,000 gp
Elixir of Suspended Animation	6,000 gp
Elixir of Swimming Fish	1,400 gp
Elixir of Tactile Enhancement	50 gp
Elixir of the Acidic Palm	300 gp
Elixir of the Green	4,550 gp
Elixir of the Iron Fist	2,250 gp
Elixir of the Mole	3,300 gp
Elixir of the Rainbow Bridge	4,550 gp
Elixir of the Remorhaz	1,400 gp
Elixir of the Scorpion	750 gp
Elixir of Tiny Feet	750 gp
Elixir of Toad Skin	750 gp
Elixir of Torpidity	750 gp
Elixir of Treasure Finding	1,400 gp
Elixir of Umbral Shadow	3,300 gp
Elixir of Underground Awareness	2,250 gp
Elixir of Unguis	1,400 gp
Elixir of Vanity	300 gp
Elixir of Venus	2,250 gp
Elixir of Vision of the Eagle	300 gp
Elixir of Vitality	1,400 gp
Elixir of Youth	7,650 gp
Elixir of Zorbo	2,250 gp

ELIXIR OF ABSORPTION

Aura moderate abjuration; **CL** 11th
Slot none; **Price** 3,300 gp; **Weight** —

DESCRIPTION

This powerful elixir allows the imbiber to protect themselves from any kind of damage. The imbiber simply spends a swift action choosing the damage type they wish to be immune to and every round after that, they gain DR 10 versus that type of attack. The elixir can absorb a total of 220 points of damage before expiring. The imbiber may change the damage type immunity as a swift action. The potion duration does not begin before a damage type is declared, but the potion expires if no damage type is declared within 24 hours.

CONSTRUCTION

Requirements Craft Wondrous Item, *globe of invulnerability*; **Cost** 1,650 gp; **Rarity:** Rare
Alchemical Formula: Water (any), Body (any) (x2), Protection

ELIXIR OF AGING

Aura moderate necromancy; **CL** 7th
Slot none; **Price** 1,400 gp; **Weight** —

DESCRIPTION

This elixir causes the imbiber to age rapidly. A human subject becomes 2d10 years older. Creatures that drink this elixir with a shorter or longer maximum lifespan than humans age proportionally to their maximum lifespan.

CONSTRUCTION

Requirements Craft Wondrous Item, *bestow curse*; **Cost** 700 gp; **Rarity:** Uncommon
Alchemical Formula: Water (any), Body (any), Decay

ELIXIR OF ANESTHESIA
Aura faint necromancy; **CL** 5th
Slot none; **Price** 750 gp; **Weight** —

DESCRIPTION
This wonderful elixir has many useful properties. The first and most useful is that it grants a +2 alchemical bonus on Constitution checks and Fortitude saves.

The second effect is that while under the influence of this elixir, the user acts as if he has taken half the physical damage he receives. The user takes half his hit point total and adds it to his hit points. At the end of the elixir's duration, these hit points disappear. They are lost last (i.e., a character with 37 hit points drinks this elixir and gains 18 more hit points for the duration, raising her total to 55. Then she takes 41 points of damage, leaving her with 14 hit points. Then the potion expires, and 18 hit points are lost. She then drops to −4 hit points and begins dying.)

The third and final effect is that this elixir affects the user by delaying poison. For the duration of the potion, any effect from poison is delayed until the elixir expires, at which point it takes effect.

CONSTRUCTION
Requirements Craft Wondrous Item, *cure serious wounds*, *slow poison*;
Cost 375 gp; **Rarity:** Rare
Alchemical Formula: Water (any), Body (any), Healing

ELIXIR OF BALANCE
Aura faint transmutation; **CL** 3rd
Slot none; **Price** 300 gp; **Weight** —

DESCRIPTION
This elixir grants the imbiber superb balance. She gains a +20 alchemical bonus to acrobatics checks to balance. She may move at half her speed across precarious or unstable surfaces and retain all her Dexterity bonuses or may move at full speed across such surfaces giving up her Dexterity bonus. For all other purposes of falling or a changing situation, if the user's Dexterity is less than 20, they are considered to have a Dexterity of 20 for Reflex saves or Combat Maneuver Defense values.

CONSTRUCTION
Requirements Craft Wondrous Item, *cat's grace*; **Cost** 150 gp; **Rarity:** Uncommon
Alchemical Formula: Water (any), Agility

ELIXIR OF BEAUTY
Aura moderate transmutation; **CL** 2nd
Slot none; **Price** 300 gp; **Weight** —

DESCRIPTION
When this elixir is imbibed, the user gains a substantial boost to their appearance and demeanor. Any Charisma penalties or damage is nullified for the duration of the potion and the user gets a +10 circumstance bonus on all Bluff, Diplomacy and Intimidation checks. If the effects wear off in the presence of someone manipulated or influenced by this draught, then the creature has a hostile reaction and attacks the individual who drank the elixir.

CONSTRUCTION
Requirements Craft Wondrous Item, *eagle's splendor*; **Cost** 150 gp; **Rarity:** Uncommon
Alchemical Formula: Water (any), Emotion

ELIXIR OF BESTIAL BOON
Aura strong transmutation; **CL** 9th
Slot none; **Price** 2,250 gp; **Weight** —

DESCRIPTION
When this elixir is imbibed, it causes the drinker to express their inner animalistic tendencies. Roll on **Table 4–7** below to determine the imbiber's spiritual animal guide. Their body quickly transforms as they physically express their inner animal nature. This is a visible transformation, and they take on the literal forms, colors, and traits of the animal that is their guide. Once a guide is determined, it never changes. Subsequent uses of this elixir always produce the same results. All of the attacks gained are melee attacks and should have their damage adjusted for the imbiber's Strength.

TABLE 4–7: ELIXIR OF BESTIAL BOON PHYSICAL CHANGES

1d6	Animal	Ability	Physical Change
1	Wolf	The character adds half their level to survival rolls made to track, and they gain the *scent* special quality. They gain a bite attack that does 1d4 + 1 damage. On a successful hit, they may make a combat maneuver check to trip their opponent.	Their snout elongates, and they grow fur over their body.
2	Cat	Gain 2 claw attacks doing 1d4 points of damage each. If both claw attacks hit, do 2d4 points of rake damage if not wearing shoes. Treat the user as having the Weapon Finesse feat with these attacks. The user also gains a +5 circumstance bonus to Stealth.	They grow claws and fur, and their pupils become vertical slits.
3	Bear	Gain 2d12 temporary hit points. Gain 2 claw attacks doing 1d6 points of damage each. If both claw attacks hit, do an additional 1d6 point of damage from rending damage.	They increase one size category, and they grow fur and claws.
4	Hawk	Gain the ability to fly and a +10 circumstance bonus on the fly skill. Gain a bite attack that does 1d4 damage.	Their arms turn into wings, and feathers grow on their body.
5	Spider	Gain a climb speed of 60 feet. Gain a bite attack that does 1 point of damage. Targets must make a Fortitude save with a DC equal to 10 + 1/2 the character's level + their Constitution modifier. On a failed save, they take 2d6 points of Constitution damage and must save again in one minute. A successful save does half that damage.	They grow additional eyes and stiff bristles over their body. Mandibles grow around their mouth.
6	Dragon	Gain a +2 natural armor bonus and a random breath weapon (roll 1d6: 1–2=fire; 3=acid; 4=lightning; 5=ice; 6=sonic) in a cone to 30 feet (fire, ice, sonic) or a line to 60 feet (acid, lightning). This does 4d6 damage and can be used every 1d4 + 1 rounds.	Their body is covered in scales, and their eyes turn golden.

CONSTRUCTION
Requirements Craft Wondrous Item, *beast shape III*; **Cost** 1,125 gp; **Rarity:** Rare
Alchemical Formula: Water (any), Body, Memory

ELIXIR OF BOUNCING
Aura moderate transmutation; **CL** 1st
Slot none; **Price** 150 gp; **Weight** —

DESCRIPTION
The imbiber of this elixir gains a spring in her step. She bounces 1d12 + 2
feet off the ground on every step. This makes the user somewhat resistant to
falling damage, treating distances fallen as half their actual height, with the
side effect that for every foot fallen, the user rises that many feet high in the
air. Collisions with a ceiling damage the user as falling damage. The user can
add 1d12 + 2 feet to any jump check the user makes. Otherwise, this affects
the user as if making a successful jump check with a result of 1d12 + 2 feet
on every movement the user attempts.

CONSTRUCTION
Requirements Craft Wondrous Item, *jump*; **Cost** 75 gp; **Rarity:** Rare
Alchemical Formula: Water (any), Body

ELIXIR OF CLARITY
Aura moderate divination; **CL** 13th
Slot none; **Price** 4,550 gp; **Weight** —

DESCRIPTION
When this elixir is consumed, a refreshing clarity overcomes the imbiber.
Their mind becomes clear, dispelling any mind-affecting effects such as
feeblemind or *confusion*. The imbiber's vision also clarifies as they are
granted *true seeing* for the duration of the elixir.

CONSTRUCTION
Requirements Craft Wondrous Item, *true seeing, greater restoration*; **Cost**
2,275 gp; **Rarity:** Rare
Alchemical Formula: Water (any), Mind

ELIXIR OF CLOAKING SHADOWS
Aura faint illusion; **CL** 5th
Slot none; **Price** 750 gp; **Weight** —

DESCRIPTION
Once imbibed, this elixir cloaks the imbiber in an ever-shifting, roiling web
of umbral limbs. The imbiber's face, location, and appearance are hidden.
The square the imbiber is in is considered to be in dim light regardless of the
prevailing light level. Darkvision does not pierce this dim light. The imbiber
can see through these shadows with no drawback. As normal, dim light
grants concealment and allows creatures to make Stealth checks to conceal
themselves.

CONSTRUCTION
Requirements Craft Wondrous Item, *displacement*; **Cost** 375 gp; **Rarity:**
Very Rare
Alchemical Formula: Water (any), Stealth

ELIXIR OF CONTROL, ANIMAL
Aura faint enchantment (compulsion) [mind-affecting]; **CL** 5th
Slot none; **Price** 750 gp; **Weight** —

DESCRIPTION
This allows the imbiber to empathize and control the emotions and behavior
of one type of animal (cats, dogs, horses, etc.). The number controlled is
dependent on the size of the animal. It can control up to 5d4 Tiny animals,
4d4 Small animals, 3d4 Medium animals, 2d4 Large animals, or 1d4 Huge
animals. Roll 1d20 on **Table 4–8** below to determine the type of animal that
can be controlled in a found potion:

TABLE 4–8: ELIXIR OF ANIMAL CONTROL

1d20	Animal Type
1–8	Mammal
9–12	Avian
13–16	Reptile/Amphibian/Fish
17–19	Mammal/Avian
20	All

Animals that are well-trained or that have good reason to fear or hate the
imbiber are allowed a DC 16 Will saving throw to avoid the effect. On a
failed save, the animal is inclined to view the imbiber in a favorable light for
the duration of the elixir. It acts in reasonable ways to meet the needs of the
imbiber.
However, without a way to communicate with the animal, there is no way for
the animal to understand the intent of the imbiber. The animal does its best
to meet the needs of the imbiber as it understands them. The animal will not
harm itself or members of its own kind, though it may threaten them. At the
end of the duration of the elixir, the animal is 90% likely to flee in confusion;
otherwise, it attacks.
This elixir doesn't affect humans, monsters, or magical beasts. It affects
creatures only with the animal type.

CONSTRUCTION
Requirements Craft Wondrous Item, *dominate animal*; **Cost** 375 gp; **Rarity:**
Rare
Alchemical Formula: Water (any), Control

ELIXIR OF CONTROL, DRAGON
Aura strong enchantment (compulsion) [mind-affecting]; **CL** 17th
Slot none; **Price** 7,650 gp; **Weight** —

DESCRIPTION
This philter allows the imbiber to charm and control a dragon within 60 feet.
The dragon receives a DC 24 Will save to avoid the effect. Once under the
imbiber's control, they must willingly follow the commands of the imbiber
as a *dominate monster* spell for the duration of the elixir, which lasts for 1d4
+ 1 hours. Roll 1d20 on **Table 4–9** below to determine the type of dragon
controlled if a potion is found:

TABLE 4–9: ELIXIR OF DRAGON CONTROL TYPES

1d20	Color
1–2	White
3–4	Black
5–7	Green
8–9	Blue
10	Red
11–12	Brass
13–14	Copper
15	Bronze
16	Silver
17	Gold
18–19	Evil
20	Good

After the controlled period ends, the dragon is 90% likely to be hostile.

CONSTRUCTION
Requirements Craft Wondrous Item, *dominate monster*; **Cost** 3,825 gp;
Rarity: Very Rare
Alchemical Formula: Water (any), Control, Prowess

ELIXIR OF CONTROL, ELEMENTAL

Aura strong enchantment (compulsion) [mind-affecting]; **CL** 17th
Slot none; **Price** 7,650 gp; **Weight** —

DESCRIPTION

This elixir allows the imbiber to influence up to four elementals as if they are under the effect of a *dominate monster* spell. It has a range of 60 feet and allows a saving throw. If you are influencing just one elemental, the saving throw is a DC 24 Will save. If you are influencing more than a single elemental, the elementals must succeed at a DC 18 Will save. If the desired elemental is under the control of another creature, the elemental receives a +2 circumstance bonus on its saving throw. Roll 1d20 on **Table 4–10** below to determine the type of elemental the potion controls:

TABLE 4–10: ELIXIR OF ELEMENTAL CONTROL TYPES

1d20	Type
1–3	Elemental, Air
4–6	Elemental, Earth
7–9	Elemental, Fire
10–12	Elemental, Water
13	Elemental, Ice
14	Elemental, Lightning
15	Elemental, Magma
16	Elemental, Mud
17–20	All

CONSTRUCTION

Requirements Craft Wondrous Item, *dominate monster*; **Cost** 3,825 gp; **Rarity:** Rare
Alchemical Formula: Azoth (any), Air (any), Earth (any), Fire (any), Water (any), Control

ELIXIR OF CONTROL, GIANT

Aura strong enchantment (compulsion) [mind-affecting]; **CL** 9th
Slot none; **Price** 2,250 gp; **Weight** —

DESCRIPTION

This elixir allows the imbiber to charm and control giants. She can control one or two giants. If one is controlled, it must succeed at a DC 22 Will saving throw to avoid the effect. If attempting to control two giants, they must succeed at a DC 16 Will saving throw to avoid the effect. While under the imbiber's control, they do her bidding, treating her as their master in complete obedience. After the control ends, the giant(s) are 90% likely to be hostile. Roll 1d20 on **Table 4–11** below to determine the type of giant the elixir controls:

TABLE 4–11: ELIXIR OF GIANT CONTROL TYPES

1d20	Type
1–5	Hill
6–9	Stone
10–13	Frost
14–17	Fire
18–19	Cloud
20	Storm

CONSTRUCTION

Requirements Craft Wondrous Item, *dominate person*, *command*, *greater*; **Cost** 1,125 gp; **Rarity:** Rare
Alchemical Formula: Water (any), Body, Control

ELIXIR OF CONTROL, HUMAN

Aura strong enchantment (compulsion) [mind-affecting]; **CL** 9th
Slot none; **Price** 2,250 gp; **Weight** —

DESCRIPTION

This elixir allows the imbiber to control up to 32 hit dice or levels or humans and humanoids as if they were under the effect of a *dominate person* spell. All targets receive a DC 22 Will saving throw. Roll 1d20 on **Table 4–12** below to determine what kind of humanoids can be controlled if a potion is found:

TABLE 4–12: ELIXIR OF HUMAN CONTROL TYPES

1d20	Type
1–2	Dwarves
3–4	Elves/Half-Elves
5–6	Gnomes
7–8	Halflings
9–10	Half-Orcs
11–16	Humans
17–19	Goblinoids
20	Any Humanoid

CONSTRUCTION

Requirements Craft Wondrous Item, *dominate person*, *command*, *greater*; **Cost** 1,125 gp; **Rarity:** Very Rare
Alchemical Formula: Onyx, Water (any), Control

ELIXIR OF CONTROL, PLANT

Aura faint transmutation; **CL** 3rd
Slot none; **Price** 750 gp; **Weight** —

DESCRIPTION

This elixir allows the imbiber to influence the behavior of vegetable lifeforms — including fungi, molds, and monstrous plants such as shambling mounds. The controller can cause them to remain still or active at her whim, according to their natural limits. Vegetable monsters with an intelligence score are entitled to a DC 16 Will saving throw to avoid the effect. All plants within a 20-foot cube can be controlled for the duration of the elixir. The effect has a range of 180 feet.

CONSTRUCTION

Requirements Craft Wondrous Item, *command plants*; **Cost** 375 gp; **Rarity:** Uncommon
Alchemical Formula: Water (any), Control, Plant

ELIXIR OF CONTROL, UNDEAD

Aura faint necromancy; **CL** 5th
Slot none; **Price** 750 gp; **Weight** —

DESCRIPTION

This necromantic elixir allows the imbiber a temporary influence over undead. The effect acts as a *command undead* spell affecting the specific type of undead controlled by the elixir. You can influence up to 16 hit dice of undead creatures. Any intelligent undead receive a DC 22 Will saving throw versus the effect due to the strength of the elixir. Roll 1d10 on **Table 4–13** below to determine the type of undead affected:

1d10	Type
1	Ghasts
2	Ghosts
3	Ghouls
4	Shadows
5	Skeletons
6	Spectres
7	Wights
8	Wraiths
9	Vampires
10	Zombies

CONSTRUCTION

Requirements Craft Wondrous Item, *command undead*; **Cost** 375 gp; **Rarity:** Uncommon
Alchemical Formula: Azoth (any), Salt (any), Water (any), Control

ELIXIR OF CRAWLING

Aura faint transmutation; **CL** 5th
Slot none; **Price** 750 gp; **Weight** —

DESCRIPTION

This elixir grants the imbiber the ability to crawl like a snake. This allows the user to take their full walking movement even while prone or restrained. They may climb over or up any obstacle that is up to twice their height with no movement penalty. This does not prevent them from walking normally or using their limbs.

CONSTRUCTION

Requirements Craft Wondrous Item, *beast shape I*; **Cost** 375 gp; **Rarity:** Rare
Alchemical Formula: Water (any), Agility, Body

ELIXIR OF CURE INSANITY

Aura faint necromancy; **CL** 5th
Slot none; **Price** 750 gp; **Weight** —

DESCRIPTION

When this elixir is imbibed, it cures nervous disorders, madness, and other forms of insanity such as mania, depression, schizophrenia, and obsessive compulsive disorder. Depending on the cause of illness, the cure may be permanent or last only for a few weeks. It does not ward against any future occurrences of insanity.

CONSTRUCTION

Requirements Craft Wondrous Item, *remove disease*; **Cost** 375 gp; **Rarity:** Uncommon
Alchemical Formula: Mercury (any), Water (any), Mind

ELIXIR OF CURE NERVOUS DISORDERS

Aura faint necromancy; **CL** 5th
Slot none; **Price** 750 gp; **Weight** —

DESCRIPTION

When imbibed, this elixir cures common nervous disorders such as generalized anxiety disorder, panic attacks, hysteria, and fear. The imbiber is calm and relaxed within one round. They are cured of any fear and receive a +4 alchemical bonus on fear saves and a +1 circumstance bonus on any morale-type checks for the duration of the elixir. The elixir may be habit forming. Depending on the cause of the nervous disorder, the effect may not be permanent.

CONSTRUCTION

Requirements Craft Wondrous Item, *remove disease*; **Cost** 375 gp; **Rarity:** Uncommon
Alchemical Formula: Mercury (any), Water (any), Stasis

ELIXIR OF DANGER SENSE

Aura moderate divination; **CL** 7th
Slot none; **Price** 1,400 gp; **Weight** —

DESCRIPTION

This elixir allows the imbiber to detect threats to their life and limb. Any hostile potential or immediate danger within 50 feet is detected — the user is alerted by a tingling sensation on the back of their neck or head. The general direction and distance as well as a broad type of danger is indicated, such as if it is a hazard, trap, or monster, but specifics of what the danger is and exactly where it is located cannot be determined.

CONSTRUCTION

Requirements Craft Wondrous Item, *locate creature*; **Cost** 700 gp; **Rarity:** Very Rare
Alchemical Formula: Water (any), Perception

ELIXIR OF DEFENSE

Aura moderate abjuration; **CL** 3rd
Slot none; **Price** 750 gp (+1), 2,250 gp (+2), 4,550 gp (+3), 7,650 gp (+4); **Weight** —

DESCRIPTION

This potion lasts for one minute and provides a +1 alchemical bonus to armor class. The potion toughens the skin near attacks, damage, and other wounds, making it more difficult to damage the opponent. More powerful versions of this potion exist, but they are more expensive to craft. Roll 1d8 on **Table 4–14** below to determine the type of elixir found:

TABLE 4–14: ELIXIR OF DEFENSE BONUSES

1d8	AC Bonus	Price
1–4	+1	750 gp
5–6	+2	2,250 gp
7	+3	4,550 gp
8	+4	7,650 gp

CONSTRUCTION

Requirements Craft Wondrous Item, *mage armor*, *shield*; **Cost** 375 gp (+1), 1,125 gp (+2), 2,275 gp (+3), 3,825 gp (+4); **Rarity:** Very Rare
Alchemical Formula: Water (any), Armor, Protection

ELIXIR OF DEFLATION

Aura strong transmutation; **CL** 13th
Slot none; **Price** 4,550 gp; **Weight** —

DESCRIPTION

When this elixir is consumed, the user changes shape, becoming more and more thin, until all that remains is a paper-thin two-dimensional representation of the character. The character may use this to hide or slip through cracks and narrow spaces that have appropriate vertical or horizontal clearance such as a space under a door.
When quaffed, the imbiber must note which direction the character is facing. Any target directly to either side of the imbiber cannot see the imbiber. Any target within a 90-degree arc of either side of the imbiber, but not directly to the side, treats the imbiber as if they had concealment. Targets to the front and back in a 90-degree arc of the imbiber can see the creature normally. The character can change orientation as a free action during their turn, or as an immediate action outside of their turn.
The user's weight (and encumbrance) are reduced to 0 or very nearly such. This means the user gains a glide speed equal to 150% of their walk speed. Glide is like flying, only the target has the option of moving horizontally without losing altitude. The imbiber can use its natural ability to jump, of course. This also means that they take no damage when falling any distances, heading to the ground very much like a piece of paper.
There is some risk from using this elixir. The final effect of the elixir is that the imbiber takes triple damage from any type of attack due to their paper-thin nature.

CONSTRUCTION

Requirements Craft Wondrous Item, *polymorph, greater*; **Cost** 2,275 gp; **Rarity:** Very Rare
Alchemical Formula: Salt (any), Water (any), Body, Planar

ELIXIR OF DIMINUTION
Aura strong transmutation; **CL** 13th
Slot none; **Price** 4,550 gp; **Weight** —

DESCRIPTION
This magical potion reduces the imbiber and all of their gear to a fraction of their normal size. The imbiber reduces two size categories. Half of the potion may be consumed to reduce the imbiber by one size category. This potion lasts for 60 minutes + (1d6 x 10) minutes.

CONSTRUCTION
Requirements Craft Wondrous Item, *reduce person*, *polymorph*, *greater*; **Cost** 2,275 gp; **Rarity:** Rare
Alchemical Formula: Water (any), Body

ELIXIR OF DISPELLING
Aura strong abjuration; **CL** 11th
Slot none; **Price** 3,300 gp; **Weight** —

DESCRIPTION
Upon consuming this potion, all magical effects on the imbiber are dispelled as if affected by a *dispel magic* cast by a 15th-level caster. This attempts to break all magical effects, positive and negative. Make a separate check for each effect.

CONSTRUCTION
Requirements Craft Wondrous Item, *dispel magic*, *greater*; **Cost** 1,650 gp; **Rarity:** Uncommon
Alchemical Formula: Azoth (any) (x2, each from different sources), Mercury (any), Water (any)

ELIXIR OF DRAGON ATTRACTANT
Aura strong enchantment (compulsion) [mind-affecting]; **CL** 15th
Slot none; **Price** 6,000 gp; **Weight** —

DESCRIPTION
When poured on the ground, this elixir attracts all dragons within one mile. They arrive attracted by the sweet scent of food. It wakes dragons from their slumber. All awake dragons arrive within five minutes. Sleeping dragons arrive within 10 minutes. Dragons that wish to resist the odor must succeed at a DC 26 Will saving throw.
If imbibed, the target becomes a delectable, irresistible morsel to dragons for one hour. The radius of attraction increases to two miles. The imbiber becomes the primary target of any dragons attracted. To attack another target, the dragon must succeed at a DC 20 Will save.

CONSTRUCTION
Requirements Craft Wondrous Item, *form of the dragon III*; **Cost** 3,000 gp; **Rarity:** Rare
Alchemical Formula: Diamond, Water (any), Control, Emotion, Mind, Prowess

ELIXIR OF DREAM SPEECH
Aura moderate illusion (phantasm) [mind-affecting]; **CL** 9th
Slot none; **Price** 2,250 gp; **Weight** —

DESCRIPTION
This strange elixir allows the imbiber to ask a question of any being with an Intelligence score that is asleep or held. The sleeping creature hears and begins moving their mouth silently as if in reply. The response appears in the interrogator's mind directly. The user understands the response, no matter what language the target speaks. This does not affect dead or undead creatures. The potion lasts for only a minute and allows the interrogation of one target.

CONSTRUCTION
Requirements Craft Wondrous Item, *dream*; **Cost** 1,125 gp; **Rarity:** Uncommon
Alchemical Formula: Water (any), Dream

ELIXIR OF DREAMS
Aura faint divination; **CL** 9th
Slot none; **Price** 2,250 gp; **Weight** —

DESCRIPTION
Taken before bed, this elixir gives the imbiber a vivid dream of what they desire most in the world. During this dream, the dreamer gets some information about the desired item. This may be clues to its location, what it is guarded by, nearby landmarks, etc. Only one thing is revealed per dream. The dream does not fade upon awakening, and the dreamer remembers all the details of the dream.
The GM determines the nature of the clue. If there is nothing unknown, or if the object is magically warded or perhaps does not exist, the dreamer suffers a terrible and vivid nightmare.

CONSTRUCTION
Requirements Craft Wondrous Item, *dream*; **Cost** 1,125 gp; **Rarity:** Rare
Alchemical Formula: Water (any), Dream, Prophecy

ELIXIR OF ELDRITCH INTENSITY
Aura strong transmutation; **CL** 13th
Slot none; **Price** 4,550 gp; **Weight** —

DESCRIPTION
This elixir improves the connection of a spellcaster with the elemental power source of spells, so that any spell cast by the imbiber takes full effect. Any spell cast by the imbiber during the duration of this potion is affected as if it were modified by the maximize spell metamagic feat. The caster's saving throw DC gains a +1 alchemical bonus for the duration of the potion. After this elixir expires, there is a short period of 20 minutes where spellcasting is impossible. There is a small chance that overuse of this elixir can burn out the ability to channel magical energy permanently.

CONSTRUCTION
Requirements Craft Wondrous Item, *mage's lucubration*, *limited wish*; **Cost** 2,275 gp; **Rarity:** Very Rare
Alchemical Formula: Azoth (any) (x2 from 2 different sources), Water (any), Mind

ELIXIR OF EMOTIONS
Aura faint enchantment (compulsion) [mind-affecting]; **CL** 9th
Slot none; **Price** 2,250 gp; **Weight** —

DESCRIPTION
When this elixir is consumed, it allows the imbiber to broadcast a strong mental resonance causing emotions in all selected target creatures within a 20-foot radius. Creatures with minds are affected if they fail a DC 20 Will saving throw.
The emotions generated are selected by the imbiber. There are two emotional spectrums that can be manipulated. The imbiber can us a full-round action to alter one of the spectrums for a selection of targets within range. She may take a second full-round action to maximize one of the spectrums for additional effects. This maximization allows a second saving throw to resist. Note that different targets can be affected within the area. The target can affect anyone in sight, as long as all targets affected during a round are within the same 20-foot radius. Creatures can be manipulated to have different simultaneous emotions. The spectrums available to be manipulated are:
Fear/Courage: Creatures can be given the shaken condition. If fear is maximized, they are given the frightened condition. Creatures can be given a +4 morale bonus against fear. If courage is maximized, they are granted a +2 morale bonus on attack rolls, skill checks, and saving throws.
Hate/Friendship: Targets made to hate have a +5 DC on Diplomacy checks made to alter their mood. If hate is maximized, they become enraged, gaining a +2 circumstance bonus to Strength and Constitution and they must immediately attack an opponent, or lacking that, the nearest target. Friendship causes all targets to act as if charmed by the imbiber as if influenced by the spell *charm person*. Maximizing friendship causes the targets to be susceptible to instructions from the imbiber as if they were *suggestions* as the spell.

CONSTRUCTION
Requirements Craft Wondrous Item, *dominate person*; **Cost** 1,125 gp; **Rarity:** Rare
Alchemical Formula: Mercury (any) (x2), Water (any), Emotion (x2)

ELIXIR OF FALSE DIVINITY
Aura faint evocation; **CL** 1st
Slot none; **Price** 150 gp; **Weight** —

DESCRIPTION
This grants the imbiber golden hair, surrounded by a halo. The imbiber's hair turns golden and sheds light in a five-foot radius. It is visible as a glowing ring surrounding the head of the imbiber. The effect lasts for 1d8 + 1 days. This is either used to impersonate a holy figure or to mark a personage.

CONSTRUCTION
Requirements Craft Wondrous Item, *light*, *bless*; **Cost** 75 gp; **Rarity:** Rare
Alchemical Formula: Water (any), Light

ELIXIR OF FORMS
Aura strong transmutation; **CL** 17th
Slot none; **Price** varies; **Weight** —

DESCRIPTION
Once consumed, this rare and complex elixir changes the imbiber's pure form. He or she becomes a being made from a different material for the duration of the elixir. Several different types of *potions of forms* exist, and each has a different effect and requires different materials. During the duration of this potion, the imbiber remains solid, can speak, and any equipment also transforms. Some examples are provided below:
Fire: The imbiber turns into solid flame. Their touch causes 2d6 points of fire damage and sets anything flammable aflame. They are immune to all forms of normal fire and has resist fire 20 for magical and intense heat and flame. They can walk on the surface of lava and magma. **Cost:** 6,832 gp.
Lightning: The imbiber turns into living lightning and may do 2d8 points of electrical damage to any and every target wearing metal armor within 30 feet as a standard action. They may also choose to move 40 feet instantly as a swift action during their turn. They are immune to electrical damage. If exposed to water, they take 4d10 points of damage each round. **Cost:** 6,832 gp.
Stone: The imbiber turns into mobile stone. Their hand-to-hand attacks do a base 1d6 points of damage. If the imbiber's base damage is already higher, increase the die size by one category. They do not need to breathe for the duration of the potion. Their form is resistant to most types of damage, and they gain DR 5 / Bludgeoning. Their weight triples. **Cost:** 6,832 gp.
Undead: The imbiber's body becomes undead for the duration of the elixir. They gain darkvision out to 120 feet and become immune to all mind-affecting spells, death magic, bleeding, disease, exhaustion, fatigue, paralysis, poison, sleep, and stunning. They cannot be subdued or take nonlethal damage and do not need to breathe. However, they are unable to be affected by healing magic for the duration. **Cost:** 6,982 gp.
Other types of *elixirs of forms* are said to exist. You may discuss with your GM what other types there might be.

CONSTRUCTION
Requirements Craft Wondrous Item, *wish*; **Cost** varies (see text); **Rarity:** Very Rare
Alchemical Formula:
Fire: Fire (any) (x3), Water (any), Transmutation
Lightning: Fire (any), Water (any), Electricity (x2), Transmutation
Stone: Earth (any) (x3), Fire (any), Water (any), Transmutation
Undead: Azoth (any) (x2), Fire (any), Water (any), Transmutation

ELIXIR OF FUR GROWTH
Aura moderate transmutation; **CL** 5th
Slot none; **Price** 750 gp; **Weight** —

DESCRIPTION
When consumed, this elixir causes imbibers to grow thick fur over their bodies for 9 + 1d4 hours. It protects the character from cold weather, and they gain resist cold 5. The hair makes it difficult to wear armor, reducing the maximum Dexterity bonus allowed by 1, and increasing the armor check penalty by 2.

CONSTRUCTION
Requirements Craft Wondrous Item, *endure elements*, *beast shape I*; **Cost** 375 gp; **Rarity:** Uncommon
Alchemical Formula: Water (any), Body, Transmutation

ELIXIR OF GOOD FORTUNE
Aura strong divination; **CL** 13th
Slot none; **Price** 4,550 gp; **Weight** —

DESCRIPTION
This elixir blesses the imbiber with astounding luck. For one minute, every time the player rolls any dice, he or she rolls twice as many as normal and picks the desired result. For example, the player would roll two 20-sided dice to hit and select the one he or she wished to use. When rolling damage for a *fireball*, the total damage is rolled twice and the imbiber selects which result to use.

CONSTRUCTION
Requirements Craft Wondrous Item, *limited wish*, *heroism*, *greater*; **Cost** 2,275 gp; **Rarity:** Very Rare
Alchemical Formula: Water (any), Body, Luck

ELIXIR OF GROWTH
Aura strong transmutation; **CL** 13th
Slot none; **Price** 4,550 gp; **Weight** —

DESCRIPTION
When quaffed, this elixir causes the imbiber to increase in size. Garments and other worn and held gear likewise increase in size for the duration of the potion. There are four drafts in the potion; for each one consumed, the imbiber increases one size category. These drafts may be taken separately or together in any quantity.

CONSTRUCTION
Requirements Craft Wondrous Item, *enlarge person*, *polymorph*, *greater*; **Cost** 2,275 gp; **Rarity:** Uncommon
Alchemical Formula: Water (any), Body, Transmutation

ELIXIR OF HEROIC AID
Aura moderate transmutation; **CL** 3rd
Slot none; **Price** 750 gp; **Weight** —

DESCRIPTION
This elixir allows anyone to take heroic action in combat for 1d6 + 2 rounds. For the duration they receive 5d8 + 10 temporary hit points that are lost first or vanish at the end of the duration. The imbiber is also immune to fear effects and gets a +4 alchemical bonus to Will saving throws.

CONSTRUCTION
Requirements Craft Wondrous Item, *aid*, *heroism*; **Cost** 375 gp; **Rarity:** Very Rare
Alchemical Formula: Water (any), Mind, Prowess

ELIXIR OF HEROIC FIGHTING
Aura moderate transmutation; **CL** 3rd
Slot none; **Price** 750 gp; **Weight** —

DESCRIPTION
This increases the fighting power of the imbiber. The improvement is based on the level of the imbiber. The user's Strength and Base Attack Bonus are increased. Consult **Table 4–15** below:

TABLE 4–15: ELIXIR OF HEROIC FIGHTING BONUSES

Level	Temporary Hit Points	BAB Increase	Strength Increase
1–4	4d10	+5	+4
5–9	3d10	+4	+4
10–14	2d10	+3	+2
15–20	1d10	+2	+2

CONSTRUCTION
Requirements Craft Wondrous Item, *heroism*; **Cost** 375 gp; **Rarity:** Uncommon
Alchemical Formula: Water (any), Strength

ELIXIR OF HEROIC FIGHTING, SUPER

Aura moderate transmutation; **CL** 9th
Slot none; **Price** 2,250 gp; **Weight** —

DESCRIPTION

This increases the fighting power of the imbiber as an *elixir of heroic fighting*, but to a more extreme degree. The improvement is based on the level of the imbiber. The user's Strength and Base Attack Bonus are increased. Consult **Table 4–16** below:

TABLE 4–16: ELIXIR OF SUPER HEROIC FIGHTING BONUSES

Level	Temporary Hit Points	BAB Increase	Strength Increase
1–4	6d10	+10	+6
5–9	5d10	+8	+6
10–14	4d10	+6	+4
15–20	3d10	+4	+4

The user also gets access to these feats for the duration of the elixir, regardless of whether or not they meet the prerequisites: Combat Reflexes, Cleave, Great Cleave, Power Attack, Improved Bull Rush, Improved Sunder, Quick Draw, Dodge, Mobility, Spring Attack, Critical Focus, and Whirlwind Attack.

CONSTRUCTION

Requirements Craft Wondrous Item, *greater heroism*; **Cost** 1,125 gp; **Rarity:** Uncommon
Alchemical Formula: Water (any), Agility, Body, Prowess, Strength

ELIXIR OF HEROIC LARCENY

Aura faint transmutation; **CL** 3rd
Slot none; **Price** 750 gp; **Weight** —

DESCRIPTION

This increases the thieving power of the imbiber. The improvement gained is based on the level of the imbiber. In addition, for the duration of the potion, the user gains the sneak attack feature using the listed number of dice. If the character has the sneak attack feature, the listed number of dice are added to the imbiber's sneak attack damage. The user also gets a flat circumstance bonus to all skill checks made for the duration of the elixir.

TABLE 4–17: ELIXIR OF HEROIC LARCENY BONUSES

Level	Temporary Hit Points	Sneak Attack	Dexterity Bonus	Skill competence
1–4	4d8	+4d6	+4	+10
5–9	3d8	+3d6	+4	+5
10–14	2d8	+2d6	+2	+5
15–20	1d8	+1d6	+2	+2

CONSTRUCTION

Requirements Craft Wondrous Item, *heroism*, *cat's grace*; **Cost** 375 gp; **Rarity:** Rare
Alchemical Formula: Water (any), Agility, Body, Prowess, Speed

ELIXIR OF HEROIC SPELLCASTING

Aura faint transmutation; **CL** 3rd
Slot none; **Price** 750 gp; **Weight** —

DESCRIPTION

This increases the spellcasting power of the imbiber. Any spellcaster consuming this potion treats their level as five higher for determining effects of the spell. A 2nd-level character casting *magic missile* would be considered 7th level, meaning they would fire four magic missiles dealing 4d4 + 4 damage. Also, the spell save DC of the caster increases by 2.

CONSTRUCTION

Requirements Craft Wondrous Item, *heroism*, *fox's cunning*; **Cost** 375 gp; **Rarity:** Rare
Alchemical Formula: Azoth (any), Water (any), Mind, Prowess

ELIXIR OF IMMUNITY, COLD

Aura moderate abjuration; **CL** 5th
Slot none; **Price** 750 gp; **Weight** —

DESCRIPTION

This elixir grants the imbiber complete invulnerability to all forms of normal cold such as ice, snow, and arctic winds, as well as complete protection and immunity from magical cold and cold attacks such as *ice storm* and white dragon's breath. However, for the duration of the elixir, the imbiber's skin turns a frosty blue, and she gains vulnerability to fire and electrical damage and receives no saving throw versus such effects. This potion lasts for 5d4 rounds.

CONSTRUCTION

Requirements Craft Wondrous Item, *protection from energy*; **Cost** 375 gp; **Rarity:** Rare
Alchemical Formula: Fire (any), Water (any), Cold, Protection

ELIXIR OF IMMUNITY, CONTROL

Aura moderate abjuration; **CL** 5th
Slot none; **Price** 750 gp; **Weight** —

DESCRIPTION

This elixir grants the imbiber complete invulnerability to all forms of mental or magical control or influence. They are immune to any enchantments, compulsions, or mind-affecting spells. However, for the duration of the potion, the imbiber's skin turns translucent and they become sluggish. They gain a –4 penalty to their natural armor as their skin becomes delicate and quite easy to damage. This potion lasts for 5d4 rounds.

CONSTRUCTION

Requirements Craft Wondrous Item, *nondetection*; **Cost** 375 gp; **Rarity:** Rare
Alchemical Formula: Azoth (any), Water (any), Mind, Protection

ELIXIR OF IMMUNITY, FIRE

Aura moderate abjuration; **CL** 5th
Slot none; **Price** 750 gp; **Weight** —

DESCRIPTION

This elixir grants the imbiber invulnerability to all forms of normal heat and fire such as fire, desert heat, and flaming oil, as well as complete protection and immunity from magical fire and fire attacks such as *fireball* and red dragon's breath. However, for the duration of the elixir, the imbiber's skin turns bright red and they gain a vulnerability to all ice- and water-based attacks and receives no saving throw versus such effects. The elixir lasts for 5d4 rounds.

CONSTRUCTION

Requirements Craft Wondrous Item, *protection from energy*; **Cost** 375 gp; **Rarity:** Rare
Alchemical Formula: Fire (any) (x2), Water (any), Protection

ELIXIR OF IMMUNITY, METAL

Aura moderate abjuration; **CL** 7th
Slot none; **Price** 1,400 gp; **Weight** —

DESCRIPTION

This elixir grants the imbiber complete immunity to metal. Metal weapons pass harmlessly through the body and metal armor falls off. The imbiber can even walk through pure metal doors and walls. However, for the duration of the potion, the imbiber's skin turns green and pulpy and they become physically weakened. All damage taken during the duration of this elixir is increased by 2 points per die. This elixir lasts for 5d4 rounds.

CONSTRUCTION

Requirements Craft Wondrous Item, *dimension door*; **Cost** 700 gp; **Rarity:** Rare
Alchemical Formula: Diamond, Earth (any) (x2), Water (any), Body, Protection

ELIXIR OF IMMUNITY, PETRIFICATION

Aura moderate abjuration; **CL** 5th
Slot none; **Price** 750 gp; **Weight** —

DESCRIPTION

This elixir grants the imbiber complete immunity to petrification from magical effects such as a basilisk's gaze or gorgon's breath. However, for the duration of the potion, the imbiber's skin turns metallic and shiny and they become spiritually weakened. They take a –4 circumstance penalty to all other saves. The potion lasts for 5d4 rounds.

CONSTRUCTION

Requirements Craft Wondrous Item, *remove disease*; **Cost** 375 gp; **Rarity:** Rare
Alchemical Formula: Diamond, Water (any), Body, Protection

ELIXIR OF IMMUNITY, POISON

Aura moderate abjuration; **CL** 5th
Slot none; **Price** 750 gp; **Weight** —

DESCRIPTION

This elixir grants the imbiber complete immunity to all poisons. However, for the duration of the elixir, the imbiber's skin turns bright red and they become physically drained. For the duration of the potion, treat the imbiber as if they had the exhausted condition. This condition vanishes at the end of the duration. This potion lasts for 5d4 rounds.

CONSTRUCTION

Requirements Craft Wondrous Item, *neutralize poison*; **Cost** 375 gp; **Rarity:** Rare
Alchemical Formula: Diamond, Water (any), Protection, Toxin

ELIXIR OF INSANITY SHIELD

Aura strong abjuration; **CL** 15th
Slot none; **Price** 6,000 gp; **Weight** —

DESCRIPTION

This protects the user's mind from psionics and magical and mental attacks by activating a wild insanity on the surface of the brain. This protects the user from psionic attack and psionic disciplines that directly affect the mind like *dominate* and mind-affecting spells such as *charm person*, *command*, and *phantasmal killer*, etc.
While shielded, the imbiber cannot use psionic abilities or magic spells or they are struck dumb as if under the effects of a *feeblemind* spell for one hour. When the elixir expires, there is a 1-in-6 chance that the user is confused for one minute as the spell.

CONSTRUCTION

Requirements Craft Wondrous Item, *mind blank*; **Cost** 3,000 gp; **Rarity:** Rare
Alchemical Formula: Water (any), Control, Protection

ELIXIR OF INVULNERABILITY

Aura moderate abjuration; **CL** 7th
Slot none; **Price** 1,400 gp; **Weight** —

DESCRIPTION

This potion grants the imbiber protection from harm. They gain DR 20/—, and they gain a +2 deflection bonus to armor class and a +2 luck bonus on all saving throws.

CONSTRUCTION

Requirements Craft Wondrous Item, *stoneskin*; **Cost** 700 gp; **Rarity:** Very Rare
Alchemical Formula: Earth (any), Water (any), Healing, Protection

ELIXIR OF KNITTED BONES

Aura faint necromancy; **CL** 3rd
Slot none; **Price** 300 gp; **Weight** —

DESCRIPTION

This elixir heals fractures and broken bones. It also heals damage to chitin, teeth, exoskeletons, shells, and bony carapaces. The healing is not instant, but the bones heal correctly. Most fractures heal in a day, but a more serious injury like a broken back could take up to a week to heal.

CONSTRUCTION

Requirements Craft Wondrous Item, *cure serious wounds*; **Cost** 150 gp; **Rarity:** Uncommon
Alchemical Formula: Water (any), Healing

ELIXIR OF LANGUAGE

Aura faint divination; **CL** 13th
Slot none; **Price** 4,550 gp; **Weight** —

DESCRIPTION

Once imbibed, this elixir allows the drinker to learn a single language very quickly. They must be exposed to the language for the duration of the elixir. At the end of the duration of the potion, they learn the language permanently.

CONSTRUCTION

Requirements Craft Wondrous Item, *tongues*, *limited wish*; **Cost** 2,275 gp; **Rarity:** Very Rare
Alchemical Formula: Moonstone, Azoth (any), Fire (any), Water (any), Mind (x2)

ELIXIR OF LIQUIDITY

Aura strong transmutation; **CL** 13th
Slot none; **Price** 4,550 gp; **Weight** —

DESCRIPTION

When this elixir is consumed, the imbiber and all of his or her equipment splash to the ground, falling into an eight-gallon puddle of liquid. This allows the character to have a movement speed of 30 feet per round, and allows them to traverse small spaces, hide in bodies of water, and travel unnoticed. The user is protected from physical attacks, gaining a +4 circumstance bonus to armor class and suffering half damage from all attacks except cold and ice attacks, which do double damage.

CONSTRUCTION

Requirements Craft Wondrous Item, *polymorph*, *greater*; **Cost** 2,275 gp; **Rarity:** Very Rare
Alchemical Formula: Water (any), Transmutation

ELIXIR OF LOCATION

Aura strong divination; **CL** 7th
Slot none; **Price** 1,400 gp; **Weight** —

DESCRIPTION

This elixir amplifies the user's natural sense of direction and allows them to retrace their steps over any distance. This also renders the imbiber immune to *maze* spells and other enchantments that attempt to bewilder the user's sense of direction, but once protected in this manner, the potion is neutralized. The user can also sense true north and depth underground up to five feet. The potion lasts for 1d12 + 12 hours.

CONSTRUCTION

Requirements Craft Wondrous Item, *divination*; **Cost** 700 gp; **Rarity:** Rare
Alchemical Formula: Water (any), Memory, Mind

ELIXIR OF LOCKPICKING

Aura faint transmutation; **CL** 3rd
Slot none; **Price** 300 gp; **Weight** —

DESCRIPTION

When consumed, this elixir greatly increases the mechanical aptitude of the imbiber, granting preternatural senses and insight. This provides a random +2d10 bonus on any disable device skill check for the duration of the potion. If the imbiber has no natural ability to open locks, detect or disable traps, this potion grants trapfinding for the duration. Note that thieves' tools are still required to pick locks.

CONSTRUCTION

Requirements Craft Wondrous Item, *cat's grace*; **Cost** 150 gp; **Rarity:** Very Rare
Alchemical Formula: Water (any), Agility, Perception

ELIXIR OF LONGEVITY

Aura faint transmutation; **CL** 9th
Slot none; **Price** 7,650 gp; **Weight** —

DESCRIPTION

This elixir reduces the imbiber's age by 1d12 years, restoring youth and vigor. The entire elixir must be consumed to achieve the desired results. It is also useful as a counter to monster-based aging attacks. Each time this elixir is drunk after the first, there is a 1% cumulative chance that the effect is reversed and all aging removed from previous elixirs is restored in the next 2d4 rounds.

CONSTRUCTION

Requirements Craft Wondrous Item, *temporal stasis, wish*; **Cost** 3,825 gp; **Rarity:** Very Rare
Alchemical Formula: Earth (any), Mercury (any), Water (any), Body, Healing

ELIXIR OF LUCKY FATE

Aura strong abjuration; **CL** 13th
Slot none; **Price** 4,550 gp; **Weight** —

DESCRIPTION

This elixir makes the imbiber especially lucky. Anytime during the next hour when a player is required to roll, they may choose the result of any one roll rather than rolling a random result. This effect lasts for one hour or until the luck is used.

CONSTRUCTION

Requirements Craft Wondrous Item, *limited wish, heroism, greater*; **Cost** 2,275 gp; **Rarity:** Rare
Alchemical Formula: Water (any), Luck

ELIXIR OF MAGNETISM

Aura strong transmutation; **CL** 13th
Slot none; **Price** 4,550 gp; **Weight** —

DESCRIPTION

Once consumed, this elixir causes the imbiber to become magnetic. They exude a strong magnetic field out to 30 feet in every direction. Ferrous objects weighing less than 30 pounds are drawn to the imbiber. Objects that are pointed or edged, like weapons, have a 2-in-6 chance of impaling the imbiber as they fly toward them. These are treated as missile attacks. This also allows the imbiber to walk across, hang from, and climb metal surfaces as easily as walking. This elixir lasts only for a short while, expiring after 6d4 rounds.

CONSTRUCTION

Requirements Craft Wondrous Item, *reverse gravity*; **Cost** 2,275 gp; **Rarity:** Rare
Alchemical Formula: Earth (any), Water (any), Body, Transmutation

ELIXIR OF MANNERS

Aura faint enchantment (compulsion) [mind-affecting]; **CL** 7th
Slot none; **Price** 1,400 gp; **Weight** —

DESCRIPTION

This powerful elixir was developed by a totalitarian society to cure inappropriate behavior. After drinking this, the imbiber must be polite, respectful, and caring for an entire year. They will not say negative things, and someone under the influence of this potion will not initiate a fight. Unwilling and aware targets receive a DC 20 Will save to resist the effect when the potion is administered.

CONSTRUCTION

Requirements Craft Wondrous Item, *charm person, daze, lesser geas*; **Cost** 700 gp; **Rarity:** Rare
Alchemical Formula: Mercury (any), Water (any), Control, Mind

ELIXIR OF MEMORY

Aura faint divination; **CL** 3rd
Slot none; **Price** 300 gp; **Weight** —

DESCRIPTION

This elixir allows the alchemist to take a single memory and infuse it into the liquid. They do not lose the memory. Anyone who consumes the potion gains access to the memory as if it were their own. They know it is someone else's memory, but when recalling the memory, they see themselves in the place of the alchemist.

CONSTRUCTION

Requirements Craft Wondrous Item, *detect thoughts*; **Cost** 150 gp; **Rarity:** Rare
Alchemical Formula: Water (any), Memory

ELIXIR OF MENTAL COMPOSURE

Aura moderate enchantment (compulsion) [mind-affecting]; **CL** 7th
Slot none; **Price** 1,400 gp; **Weight** —

DESCRIPTION

This elixir allows the user to maintain an emotional stability of mind where they are not affected by pain, phobias, or minor distractions. They are immune to effects such as itching, dizziness, and confusion. Against spells that cause mind-affecting effects such as *scare, fear, hideous laughter*, and others, the imbiber receives a +4 alchemical bonus to the saving throw.

CONSTRUCTION

Requirements Craft Wondrous Item, *modify memory*; **Cost** 700 gp; **Rarity:** Uncommon
Alchemical Formula: Water (any), Emotion

ELIXIR OF MIND DAMP

Aura strong abjuration; **CL** 15th
Slot none; **Price** 6,000 gp; **Weight** —

DESCRIPTION

This elixir renders the imbiber immune to psionic or magical detection and psionic or mental attack for one week. The includes effects such as *detect thoughts, clairvoyance, divination*, or *crystal balls*, as well as spells and effects that directly affect the mind of the imbiber such as *confusion* and *feeblemind*. This also prevents the imbiber from activating magical or psionic abilities for the duration.

CONSTRUCTION

Requirements Craft Wondrous Item, *nondetection, mind blank*; **Cost** 3,000 gp; **Rarity:** Rare
Alchemical Formula: Water (any), Mind, Stealth

ELIXIR OF MIRRORED EYES
Aura moderate abjuration; **CL** 7th
Slot none; **Price** 1,400 gp; **Weight** —

DESCRIPTION
This elixir changes the eyes of the imbiber to be silver orbs lacking pupils. This does not affect the imbiber's ability to see. However, light is reflected off their eyes, which prevents them from being subject to gaze attacks. Targets performing gaze attacks against the target have a 20% chance to be affected by their own gaze attack (as concealment). The imbiber also has a –4 circumstance penalty to Stealth unless they close their eyes.

CONSTRUCTION
Requirements Craft Wondrous Item, *spell immunity*; **Cost** 700 gp; **Rarity:** Very Rare
Alchemical Formula: Silver, Water (any), Transmutation

ELIXIR OF NATURAL RENEWAL
Aura strong conjuration (healing); **CL** 13th
Slot none; **Price** 4,550 gp; **Weight** —

DESCRIPTION
When consumed, this potion lasts for a full week. During that time, the user gains Fast Healing 1. If it is instead applied to a being that died within the last week, life is restored. After 24 hours, the risen body must make a DC 15 Fortitude save in order to stay alive. Furthermore, if used as a salve, this potion can be used over the period of two weeks to regenerate a lost member of the body. Any one use precludes the others.

CONSTRUCTION
Requirements Craft Wondrous Item, *regenerate*; **Cost** 2,275 gp; **Rarity:** Rare
Alchemical Formula: Water (any), Healing, Life

ELIXIR OF NUTRITION
Aura minor conjuration (creation); **CL** 7th
Slot none; **Price** 1,400 gp; **Weight** —

DESCRIPTION
This potion feeds the imbiber, protecting them from hunger for one week. This potion also protects against items and effects that cause ravenous hunger, allowing the imbiber an additional chance to save versus the effect each time a save is required.

CONSTRUCTION
Requirements Craft Wondrous Item, *minor creation*; **Cost** 700 gp; **Rarity:** Uncommon
Alchemical Formula: Water (any), Body

ELIXIR OF PERCEPTION
Aura faint divination; **CL** 7th
Slot none; **Price** 1,400 gp; **Weight** —

DESCRIPTION
This elixir affects the imbiber in several ways. It provides a +4 bonus on Disable Device checks, a +8 bonus on Perception checks, the target is never considered flatfooted due to not having acted yet in combat, and the imbiber has an automatic 25% chance to be able to see invisible creatures or illusions that is checked when the illusion or creature is first encountered.

CONSTRUCTION
Requirements Craft Wondrous Item, *true seeing*; **Cost** 700 gp; **Rarity:** Rare
Alchemical Formula: Water (any), Mind, Perception

ELIXIR OF POISON BREATH
Aura faint necromancy; **CL** 5th
Slot none; **Price** 750 gp; **Weight** —

DESCRIPTION
This allows the imbiber to spit a terrible poison at a nearby target. Once imbibed, the poison can be held for one minute before it affects the imbiber. The venom can be spat up to 30 feet. The user sprays out the poison in a line. On a successful touch attack with a +4 circumstance bonus for the volume of poison, the target must make a DC 20 Fortitude save. On a failed save, the target takes 3d8 + 3 damage. A successful save reduces the damage by half. This save must be repeated for two more rounds after the initial hit with the same effects.

CONSTRUCTION
Requirements Craft Wondrous Item, *poison*; **Cost** 375 gp; **Rarity:** Very Rare
Alchemical Formula: Water (any), Toxin

ELIXIR OF POISON FLESH
Aura faint necromancy [poison]; **CL** 5th
Slot none; **Price** 750 gp; **Weight** —

DESCRIPTION
This powerful elixir turns your flesh to poison. When consumed, you make a DC 14 Fortitude save. Failure means you feel ill for the duration of the elixir and gain the sickened condition.
If you are bitten or attacked and swallowed, the attacker is affected by the poison that flows within your flesh. They must make a DC 10 + 1/2 your level + your Constitution modifier Fortitude saving throw against poison. If they fail, they become nauseated for one minute, unable to attack or cast spells while retching, after which they die. If they succeed at the save, they are nauseated for 1d6 + 1 rounds.

CONSTRUCTION
Requirements Craft Wondrous Item, *toxic gift*; **Cost** 375 gp; **Rarity:** Very Rare
Alchemical Formula: Water (any), Body, Toxin

ELIXIR OF POISON TOUCH
Aura moderate necromancy; **CL** 9th
Slot none; **Price** 2,250 gp; **Weight** —

DESCRIPTION
When imbibed, if the user immediately swallows a poison, it allows them to poison creatures by touch.
Once the potion and poison are ingested, the imbiber must make a save versus the poison. On a success, the imbiber is not affected by the poison at all. On a failure, the poison affects the imbiber normally.
In either case, your touch gains the ability to poison targets with the poison you ingested. Anyone touched or struck by your bare hands is dosed with the poison. As a move action, you may spread the poison your skin exudes on a melee weapon.

CONSTRUCTION
Requirements Craft Wondrous Item, *plague carrier*; **Cost** 1,125 gp; **Rarity:** Very Rare
Alchemical Formula: Water (any), Body, Toxin (2 from different sources)

ELIXIR OF PROTECTION FROM IMMISCIBILITY
Aura strong abjuration; **CL** 13th
Slot none; **Price** 4,550 gp; **Weight** —

DESCRIPTION
This elixir protects the imbiber from potion immiscibility if those rules are in play. For one minute, the user can drink multiple potions without penalty or risk of disaster.

CONSTRUCTION
Requirements Craft Wondrous Item, *limited wish*; **Cost** 2,275 gp; **Rarity:** Rare
Alchemical Formula: Azoth (any), Water (any), Stasis

ELIXIR OF PROTECTION FROM LYCANTHROPES

Aura moderate abjuration; **CL** 9th
Slot none; **Price** 2,250 gp; **Weight** —

DESCRIPTION

This elixir protects the imbiber from the touch of lycanthropes for the duration. Any lycanthrope wishing to attack the imbiber with natural attacks (claws, et. al.) must succeed at a DC 18 Will saving throw. Once they save, the lycanthrope can attack freely, but the imbiber receives a +4 deflection bonus to their armor class versus these attacks. The imbiber is immune to lycanthropy and any saves versus supernatural, spell-like effects, or spells cast by a lycanthrope are granted a +4 alchemical bonus to the saving throw.

CONSTRUCTION

Requirements Craft Wondrous Item, *dispel chaos*; **Cost** 1,125 gp; **Rarity:** Rare
Alchemical Formula: Water (any), Body, Protection

ELIXIR OF PROTECTION FROM MAGIC MISSILE

Aura faint, abjuration; **CL** 1st
Slot none; **Price** 50 gp; **Weight** —

DESCRIPTION

This potion protects the imbiber from strikes made by *magic missiles* for the duration. Each *magic missile* striking the imbiber allows the character to make a DC 16 Fortitude save. On a success, no damage is taken from the missile. On a failure, the user takes 1 point of damage.

CONSTRUCTION

Requirements Craft Wondrous Item, *shield*; **Cost** 25 gp; **Rarity:** Rare
Alchemical Formula: Azoth (any), Water (any)

ELIXIR OF PROTECTION FROM MAGICAL WEAPONS

Aura moderate abjuration; **CL** 9th
Slot none; **Price** 2,250 gp; **Weight** —

DESCRIPTION

This elixir protects the imbiber from strikes made by magical weapons for the duration. Any attempt to hit the imbiber with a magical weapon grants the imbiber a +4 deflection bonus to their armor class, and magic weapons are denied their magical bonuses and effects when rolling to hit and damage.

CONSTRUCTION

Requirements Craft Wondrous Item, *stoneskin*, *spell immunity*; **Cost** 1,125 gp; **Rarity:** Rare
Alchemical Formula: Diamond, Azoth (any), Mercury (any), Water (any), Body, Protection

ELIXIR OF PROTECTION FROM NOXIOUS GAS

Aura faint abjuration; **CL** 5th
Slot none; **Price** 750 gp; **Weight** —

DESCRIPTION

This potion protects the imbiber from noxious and poisonous gases and odors. This also provides protection from strong gaseous attacks. Any spell over 5th level such as *cloudkill*, gaseous dragon breaths, or poison gas traps receives a +4 alchemical bonus to their saving throw, or grants a saving throw if they otherwise would not.

CONSTRUCTION

Requirements Craft Wondrous Item, *gust of wind*; **Cost** 375 gp; **Rarity:** Rare
Alchemical Formula: Air (any), Water (any), Protection, Toxin

ELIXIR OF PROTECTION FROM SPIRITS

Aura moderate abjuration; **CL** 9th
Slot none; **Price** 2,250 gp; **Weight** —

DESCRIPTION

This elixir protects the imbiber from spirits for the duration. She is protected from the touch of spirits, and any spirit wishing to attack the imbiber with natural attacks (touch, et. al.) must succeed at a DC 18 Will saving throw. Once they successfully save, the spirits may attack freely; however, the imbiber receives a +4 deflection bonus on their armor class versus these attacks. The imbiber is immune to possession or other mental attacks from spirits and any attacks, supernatural abilities, spell-like effects, or spells that require a save are made with a +4 alchemical bonus. Spirits are any fey, outsiders, or undead that are incorporeal.

CONSTRUCTION

Requirements Craft Wondrous Item, *dispel chaos*; **Cost** 1,125 gp; **Rarity:** Rare
Alchemical Formula: Azoth (any), Air (any), Water (any), Protection

ELIXIR OF PROTECTION FROM SPRITES

Aura moderate abjuration; **CL** 9th
Slot none; **Price** 2,250 gp; **Weight** —

DESCRIPTION

This elixir protects the imbiber from sprites and other creatures of the fey creature type for the duration. She is protected from the touch of fey, and any fey wishing to strike the imbiber with natural attacks (claws, et. al.) must succeed at a DC 18 Will save. If they make this save, then they may attack freely, but the imbiber receives a +4 deflection bonus against these attacks. She is immune to fey illusions and glamour, e.g., the user is not affected by a nymph's blinding or deadly beauty and a pixie remains visible to the imbiber while invisible. Any saves made versus spells, supernatural abilities, or spell-like effects coming from a creature of the fey type are made with a +4 alchemical bonus to the saving throw.

CONSTRUCTION

Requirements Craft Wondrous Item, *dispel chaos*; **Cost** 1,125 gp; **Rarity:** Rare
Alchemical Formula: Azoth (any), Air (any), Mercury (any), Water (any), Plant, Protection

ELIXIR OF PROTECTION FROM VAMPIRES

Aura strong abjuration; **CL** 9th
Slot none; **Price** 2,250 gp; **Weight** —

DESCRIPTION

This elixir protects the imbiber from vampires for the duration. She is protected from the touch of vampires. Any vampire wishing to attack the imbiber with natural attacks (slam, et. al.) must succeed at a DC 20 Will save. Once they save, the vampires may attack freely, although the imbiber receives a +4 deflection bonus to their armor class in this case. She is immune to the vampire's energy drain and are not susceptible to the vampire's mental influence. Any attacks, spells, supernatural abilities, or spell-like effects from a vampire that require a save grant the imbiber a +4 alchemical bonus to that saving throw.

CONSTRUCTION

Requirements Craft Wondrous Item, *dispel evil*; **Cost** 1,1252 gp; **Rarity:** Rare
Alchemical Formula: Azoth (any), Water (any), Protection, Prowess

ELIXIR OF PSYCHIC TRAP
Aura moderate abjuration; **CL** 7th
Slot none; **Price** 1,400 gp; **Weight** —

DESCRIPTION
This elixir sets a trap in the mind of the imbiber. Any mental contact or mind-affecting spell such as *telepathy* causes 4d8 + 4 points of damage to the initiator of the contact, attack, or spell and cancels the attack. Note that this effects only spells where the imbiber is targeted at the time of casting. Entering a pre-existing spell effect discharges the trap harmlessly and negates the effect.

CONSTRUCTION
Requirements Craft Wondrous Item, *confusion*; **Cost** 700 gp; **Rarity:** Uncommon
Alchemical Formula: Water (any), Mind

ELIXIR OF RAINBOW HUES
Aura faint transmutation; **CL** 5th
Slot none; **Price** 750 gp; **Weight** —

DESCRIPTION
This thick and syrupy elixir is always found in a metal container. The imbiber gains the ability to turn into any hue or combination of hues desired at will. Any color or combination is possible for as long as the user can hold the thought in their mind until the color is affected. One potion contains seven draughts that can be used independently of each other. A draught of the elixir lasts for 1d12 + 12 hours.

CONSTRUCTION
Requirements Craft Wondrous Item, *rainbow pattern*; **Cost** 375 gp; **Rarity:** Rare
Alchemical Formula: Water (any), Body, Transmutation

ELIXIR OF RAPID HEALING
Aura faint necromancy; **CL** 5th
Slot none; **Price** 750 gp; **Weight** —

DESCRIPTION
This elixir grants the user a superhuman degree of healing. The imbiber gains Fast Healing 3. This lasts for the normal duration of the potion. The user does not grow back any limbs, it does not knit bones, and it does not have any effect on scars and more permanent injuries. This elixir immediately ceases to function if the user's hit point total falls below zero.

CONSTRUCTION
Requirements Craft Wondrous Item, *cure serious wounds*; **Cost** 375 gp; **Rarity:** Rare
Alchemical Formula: Water (any), Healing

ELIXIR OF RECALL
Aura faint divination; **CL** 7th
Slot none; **Price** 1,400 gp; **Weight** —

DESCRIPTION
This elixir provides the imbiber with an eidetic memory for 2d6 hours. Everything they see and hear can be recalled with perfect clarity.

CONSTRUCTION
Requirements Craft Wondrous Item, *mnemonic enhancer*; **Cost** 700 gp; **Rarity:** Uncommon
Alchemical Formula: Water (any), Mind

ELIXIR OF RECUPERATION
Aura faint necromancy; **CL** 3rd
Slot none; **Price** 300 gp; **Weight** —

DESCRIPTION
This elixir completely removes all effects of exhaustion and fatigue, and the user is refreshed as if they had rested a full eight hours, allowing them to continue as if they had just received a full night of sleep. This is effectively eight full hours of sleep for all purposes except for the purpose of spell preparation.

CONSTRUCTION
Requirements Craft Wondrous Item, *restoration, lesser*; **Cost** 150 gp; **Rarity:** Uncommon
Alchemical Formula: Water (any), Body (x2)

ELIXIR OF REFLECTIVE FORM
Aura moderate transmutation; **CL** 7th
Slot none; **Price** 1,400 gp; **Weight** —

DESCRIPTION
When consumed, this elixir changes the clothing, skin, and armor of the imbiber to become highly reflective. This is so distracting that the imbiber or anyone standing adjacent to the imbiber are granted a +2 circumstance bonus to armor class. The imbiber is unable to hide or use stealth. The imbiber is not affected by this distraction and may attack adjacent targets without penalty.

CONSTRUCTION
Requirements Craft Wondrous Item, *spell immunity*; **Cost** 700 gp; **Rarity:** Very Rare
Alchemical Formula: Water (any), Illusion

ELIXIR OF REFLEX
Aura moderate transmutation; **CL** 5th
Slot none; **Price** 750 gp; **Weight** —

DESCRIPTION
This grants the imbiber enhanced reflexes. For the duration of the elixir, they gain a +4 alchemical bonus to Dexterity, a +4 alchemical bonus to initiative, granting them a sum total of +6 to initiative. They also gain access to the Weapon Finesse, Deflect Arrows, and Quick Draw feats, whether they meet the requirements for such feats or not.

CONSTRUCTION
Requirements Craft Wondrous Item, *cat's grace, heroism*; **Cost** 375 gp; **Rarity:** Rare
Alchemical Formula: Water (any), Agility, Body

ELIXIR OF REVENGE
Aura faint evocation; **CL** 3rd
Slot none; **Price** 300 gp; **Weight** —

DESCRIPTION
If wounded while under the influence of this elixir, it extracts revenge from those around you. When your skin is broken and your blood comes into contact with air, it turns a bright viridian and surges forth in a hemisphere, sizzling like oil in a pan out to a radius of 10 feet. All those within the area not being touched by the imbiber take 5d4 + 5 points of acid damage. They may make a DC 18 Reflex save for half damage.

CONSTRUCTION
Requirements Craft Wondrous Item, *acid arrow*; **Cost** 150 gp; **Rarity:** Rare
Alchemical Formula: Iron, Water (any), Acid

ELIXIR OF REVIVIFICATION
Aura moderate conjuration (healing); **CL** 9th
Slot none; **Price** 2,250 gp; **Weight** —

DESCRIPTION
This initially appears as a crystal-clear liquid that has no outstanding qualities. When consumed, it tastes like water. However, if one drop of a person's blood is added, the liquid turns a brilliant red. Afterward, the administration of this liquid restores the user to life. It affects only the person whose blood is mixed with the elixir. As long as the body exists and can be found, it restores life to the user. Any permanent damage to the body (lost limbs, etc.) is not healed, but a long-desiccated corpse can be revived to life.

CONSTRUCTION
Requirements Craft Wondrous Item, *breath of life*; **Cost** 1,125 gp; **Rarity:** Rare
Alchemical Formula: Water (any), Healing, Life (x2)

ELIXIR OF SAFE CONSUMPTION
Aura faint evocation; **CL** 3rd
Slot none; **Price** 300 gp; **Weight** —

DESCRIPTION
This elixir renders the imbiber immune to all harm and danger from nonmagical food and drink. This protects the imbiber from ingested poison and allows them to drink tainted water and eat rotten food or poorly cooked meals, without gagging or showing signs of distress.
It does not change the taste of the food.

CONSTRUCTION
Requirements Craft Wondrous Item, *purify food and drink*, *consecrate*; **Cost** 150 gp; **Rarity:** Uncommon
Alchemical Formula: Water (any), Protection

ELIXIR OF SCENT CONTROL
Aura faint transmutation; **CL** 1st
Slot none; **Price** 50 gp; **Weight** —

DESCRIPTION
This potion allows the imbiber to control the aroma his body exudes. He or she may choose to smell of anything desired for the duration of the potion. This potion is fairly cheap to produce, but highly prized by nobility.

CONSTRUCTION
Requirements Craft Wondrous Item, *pass without trace*; **Cost** 25 gp; **Rarity:** Very Rare
Alchemical Formula: Water (any)

ELIXIR OF SCULPTURE
Aura strong transmutation; **CL** 7th
Slot none; **Price** 4,550 gp; **Weight** —

DESCRIPTION
When consumed, this elixir is an alchemical wonder that transforms the imbiber into a living statue made from clay. This is a temporary condition that lasts only 30 minutes. During this time, anyone may alter or sculpt the living clay statue, altering its appearance or items.
When the elixir ends, any changes left remain and are permanent. Only another draught of this elixir or a *wish* spell may alter the results. Note that the imbiber cannot be killed or destroyed while clay and returns to some semblance of life no matter the final outcome or form. An imbiber who is smashed down into a pulp lives at least for a short while after changing form. True masters of sculpture may even be able to alter raw ability and not just appearance.

CONSTRUCTION
Requirements Craft Wondrous Item, *limited wish*; **Cost** 2,275 gp; **Rarity:** Very Rare
Alchemical Formula: Earth (any), Mercury (any), Water (any), Body, Transmutation

ELIXIR OF SHRIEKING
Aura moderate evocation [sonic]; **CL** 7th
Slot none; **Price** 1,400 gp; **Weight** —

DESCRIPTION
Once consumed, this elixir has two separate effects that may be used. This potion can be used three times before the duration expires. Ether ability may be used as a standard action up to a total of three times in any combination. First, the imbiber may shout in a cone that goes out to 30 feet in front of the imbiber with a width of 30 feet. All targets take 3d6 sonic damage and may make a DC 16 Fortitude save for half. Targets that fail their save are deafened for one minute.
The other ability is a piercing yell. This affects a 20-foot radius. All targets must make a DC 16 Will save versus a sonic mind-affecting effect. On a failed save, targets are stunned for one round. On a successful save, they are only dazed.
Note that the elixir is indiscriminate and affects all creatures within the area.

CONSTRUCTION
Requirements Craft Wondrous Item, *shout*; **Cost** 700 gp; **Rarity:** Rare
Alchemical Formula: Mercury (any), Water (any), Transmutation

ELIXIR OF SHRUBBERY
Aura moderate transmutation (polymorph); **CL** 13th
Slot none; **Price** 4,550 gp; **Weight** —

DESCRIPTION
This transformative elixir allows the user to change into a green leafy bush as a standard action and back at will. The type and shape of bush can vary, from small to large according to the will of the user. This protects the user, providing DR 15 / slashing. The potion grants this ability for 2d6 + 2 days. Every time the imbiber changes into a shrubbery, there is a 1% chance that he or she becomes rooted to the spot, unable to change form until the elixir expires. Otherwise, the imbiber has access to all their senses in plant form and can move at a speed of 10 feet per round while polymorphed.

CONSTRUCTION
Requirements Craft Wondrous Item, *polymorph, greater*; **Cost** 2,275 gp; **Rarity:** Uncommon
Alchemical Formula: Water (any), Plant

ELIXIR OF SKELETAL VISAGE
Aura faint necromancy; **CL** 7th
Slot none; **Price** 1,400 gp; **Weight** —

DESCRIPTION
Originally designed for medical use, this potion turns the skin, muscles, organs, and other viscera of a person transparent, leaving only the bones visible. It effectively gives the imbiber the visage of a skeleton. The skin and flesh of the imbiber remains, turned transparent by the potion. A particularly astute character may notice that this doesn't appear to be an actual undead skeleton by noting that the feet do not touch the floor and through other subtle clues by succeeding at a DC 25 Perception check.
If killed while under the effect of this elixir, the effect does not end, but instead becomes permanent.

CONSTRUCTION
Requirements Craft Wondrous Item, *greater invisibility*; **Cost** 700 gp; **Rarity:** Common
Alchemical Formula: Water (any), Transmutation

ELIXIR OF SKILL
Aura moderate transmutation; **CL** 13th
Slot none; **Price** 4,550 gp; **Weight** —

DESCRIPTION
This rare elixir makes a character skilled at whatever they turn their mind to. They simply think of any craft, profession, or performance talent and then they become exceedingly skilled at that ability. If they are untrained in that ability, having no ranks, they add a +20 enhancement bonus to the skill. If they already have ranks and training in that skill, they add a +10 enhancement bonus to the skill. This works only for one skill per potion. Each potion lasts for 2d4 + 1 days.

CONSTRUCTION
Requirements Craft Wondrous Item, *limited wish*; **Cost** 2,275 gp; **Rarity:** Very Rare
Alchemical Formula: Water (any), Prowess

ELIXIR OF SLEEP
Aura moderate enchantment (compulsion) [mind-affecting]; **CL** 9th
Slot none; **Price** 2,250 gp; **Weight** —

DESCRIPTION
After drinking this tart, apple-flavored liquid, the imbiber sinks into deep, restful sleep for 2d6 x 10 minutes. They experience the effects of normal sleep combined with a feeling of well-being and peace. This means hit points are recovered as with a full night of rest, and spellcasters can prepare spells. Unwilling victims are entitled to a DC 14 Will save to avoid the effect. Anyone under the effects of this potion awakens instantly if attacked. If awakened before the period of rest naturally ends, all benefit is lost.

CONSTRUCTION
Requirements Craft Wondrous Item, *symbol of sleep*; **Cost** 1,125 gp;
Rarity: Very Rare
Alchemical Formula: Water (any), Mind, Stasis

ELIXIR OF SLEEP BREATH
Aura faint enchantment; **CL** 3rd
Slot none; **Price** 300 gp; **Weight** —

DESCRIPTION
This allows the imbiber to put people to sleep with his or her breath. For one hour after consuming the potion, the imbiber has the ability to breathe a cloud of sleep gas that covers a 20-foot square up to 10 feet high up to three separate times. Each use of the cloud requires a full-round action. All within this cloud are affected as if by the wizard spell *sleep*.
If the breath is not used at least once before the duration expires, the imbiber must succeed at a DC 16 Fortitude save or fall into a deep sleep for 2d6 + 2 hours.

CONSTRUCTION
Requirements Craft Wondrous Item, *sleep*; **Cost** 150 gp; **Rarity:** Very Rare
Alchemical Formula: Air (any), Water (any), Stasis

ELIXIR OF SOMATIC REMEDY
Aura moderate abjuration; **CL** 9th
Slot none; **Price** 2,250 gp; **Weight** —

DESCRIPTION
This elixir renders a creature immune to slumber. Natural or magical effects causing sleep fail. This effect lasts for a month. This has no effect on the body's normal, natural need for sleep.

CONSTRUCTION
Requirements Craft Wondrous Item, *spell resistance*; **Cost** 1,125 gp;
Rarity: Very Rare
Alchemical Formula: Azoth (any), Water (any), Mind, Stasis

ELIXIR OF SPINES
Aura faint transmutation; **CL** 5th
Slot none; **Price** 750 gp; **Weight** —

DESCRIPTION
When imbibed, this elixir causes a startling transformation. The skin toughens and turns a dark color, and spikes extend out from the body in all directions. This grants a +1 enhancement bonus to natural armor, and all who attack the user must make a DC 16 Reflex save or take 2d4 damage from being impaled on spines. The user may also automatically do 2d4 + 2 damage to any target stupid enough to grapple or swallow them. The spikes will not grow past any armor heavier than chain. If wearing or donning heavier armor, the potion ceases to function.

CONSTRUCTION
Requirements Craft Wondrous Item, *alter self, beast shape I*; **Cost** 375 gp;
Rarity: Rare
Alchemical Formula: Water (any), Body, Transmutation

ELIXIR OF STRENGTH, GIANT
Aura moderate transmutation; **CL** 13th
Slot none; **Price** 4,550 gp; **Weight** —

DESCRIPTION
This elixir gives you the strength of a mighty giant. The actual effects of the elixir vary depending on the type of giant you become. Roll randomly on **Table 4–18** to determine the type of elixir:

TABLE 4–18: ELIXIR OF GIANT STRENGTH TYPE

Roll	Type	Strength Equivalent
1–6	Hill	25 (+7)
7–10	Stone	27 (+8)
11–14	Frost	29 (+9)
15–17	Fire	31 (+10)
18–19	Cloud	35 (+12)
20	Storm	39 (+14)

The imbiber also gains the rock-throwing ability (range 60 feet, 2d6 damage). Note that the listed Strength score replaces the Strength score of the imbiber for the duration of the potion.

CONSTRUCTION
Requirements Craft Wondrous Item, *giant form I, heroism*; **Cost** 2,275 gp;
Rarity: Rare
Alchemical Formula: Water (any), Body, Strength (x2 from 2 different sources)

ELIXIR OF STRENGTH, OGRE

Aura faint transmutation; **CL** 3rd
Slot none; **Price** 750 gp; **Weight** —

DESCRIPTION

The imbiber of this elixir gains the great strength of a mighty ogre. For the duration of the elixir, the imbiber's Strength is set to 21, regardless of their original score. Note that for some characters, this may lower their strength.

CONSTRUCTION

Requirements Craft Wondrous Item, *bull's strength*; **Cost** 375 gp; **Rarity:** Uncommon
Alchemical Formula: Water (any), Strength

ELIXIR OF STRENGTH, TITAN

Aura strong transmutation; **CL** 15th
Slot none; **Price** 6,000 gp; **Weight** —

DESCRIPTION

This elixir gives the imbiber the strength of a mighty titan. After quaffing this elixir, the imbiber's size increases one category to a maximum of colossal. Their Strength score becomes 45 (+17). They gain a slam attack that deals 2d8 damage, and they gain access to the feats Awesome Blow, Power Attack and Staggering Critical regardless of whether or not they meet the feat prerequisites.

CONSTRUCTION

Requirements Craft Wondrous Item, *giant form II*, *greater heroism*; **Cost** 3,000 gp; **Rarity:** Very Rare
Alchemical Formula: Water (any), Body, Prowess, Strength (x2 from 3 different sources)

ELIXIR OF SUSPENDED ANIMATION

Aura strong transmutation; **CL** 15th
Slot none; **Price** 6,000 gp; **Weight** —

DESCRIPTION

The imbiber of this elixir enters a deep permanent sleep. It can be broken only by an *alter reality* or a *wish*, or the occurrence of a single condition uttered by the imbiber. While sleeping, the imbiber is in stasis. They do not age, their life functions cease, and they cannot be harmed.

CONSTRUCTION

Requirements Craft Wondrous Item, *temporal stasis*; **Cost** 3,000 gp; **Rarity:** Very Rare
Alchemical Formula: Diamond, Moonstone, Rare Earth, Azoth (any), Water (any), Mind, Control, Stasis

ELIXIR OF SWIMMING FISH

Aura moderate abjuration; **CL** 7th
Slot none; **Price** 1,400 gp; **Weight** —

DESCRIPTION

This potion grants the imbiber a swim speed of 90 feet and a +20 alchemical bonus on Swim checks. Although this potion allows powerful swimming, it does not allow the imbiber to swim in medium or heavy armor, nor does it allow water breathing or free movement.

CONSTRUCTION

Requirements Craft Wondrous Item, *water breathing*, *freedom of movement*; **Cost** 700 gp; **Rarity:** Uncommon
Alchemical Formula: Water (any), Agility, Strength

ELIXIR OF TACTILE ENHANCEMENT

Aura faint divination; **CL** 1st
Slot none; **Price** 50 gp; **Weight** —

DESCRIPTION

When this elixir is imbibed, the user's sensation is enhanced to a high degree. This provides several effects. Any surface that is touched when searched increases the Appraisal and Perception skills by +20. It also makes the imbiber more sensitive to damage, taking an additional point of damage per die done due to pain.

CONSTRUCTION

Requirements Craft Wondrous Item, *detect secret doors*; **Cost** 25 gp; **Rarity:** Rare
Alchemical Formula: Water (any), Perception

ELIXIR OF THE ACIDIC PALM

Aura faint conjuration (creation) [acid]; **CL** 3rd
Slot none; **Price** 300 gp; **Weight** —

DESCRIPTION

This elixir causes the imbiber's hands to secrete a powerful acid. This allows bare-handed melee attacks to do an additional 1d8 points of acid damage, but also allows the user to do 2d8 points of damage to soft object per round, ignoring hardness.
Materials such as stone, metal, glass, and gemstones resist better; they take the same 2d8 points of acid damage but apply their hardness to reduce the damage.

CONSTRUCTION

Requirements Craft Wondrous Item, *acid arrow*; **Cost** 150 gp; **Rarity:** Very Rare
Alchemical Formula: Rare Earth, Water (any), Acid (x2)

ELIXIR OF THE GREEN

Aura strong transmutation; **CL** 13th
Slot none; **Price** 4,550 gp; **Weight** —

DESCRIPTION

The bizarre and powerful elixir permanently affects the imbiber, turning him or her into a plant-like being that forgoes eating, acquiring his energy from the sun as plants do.
After imbibing the potion, the drinker suffers severe convulsions for 1d10 rounds and then falls unconscious for 1d4 days. They must make a DC 5 Fortitude save to survive this process. If they fail, they die.
If the imbiber survives, their skin becomes a deep vibrant green and they no longer require food to live. They can process the energy of the sun directly. If denied water, the imbiber becomes dehydrated as normal. If the user does not receive 4+ hours of sunlight per day, they begin to starve. This transformation is one way, permanent, and breeds true.

CONSTRUCTION

Requirements Craft Wondrous Item, *plant growth*, *limited wish*; **Cost** 2,275 gp; **Rarity:** Very Rare
Alchemical Formula: Azoth (any), Water (any), Plant, Transmutation

ELIXIR OF THE IRON FIST

Aura moderate transmutation; **CL** 9th
Slot none; **Price** 2,250 gp; **Weight** —

DESCRIPTION

This elixir turns the hands and arms of the imbiber into solid iron. The iron hands hit as powerful weapons, and the wearer's Strength is increased to compensate. The imbiber gains a melee attack that does 1d10 points of damage, and they gain a +4 alchemical bonus to Strength. If the imbiber is a monk, it increases the monk's bare hand attack up one step or to 1d10, whichever is higher. The imbiber's hands are treated as +3 magical weapons for the purposes of bypassing damage reduction.

CONSTRUCTION

Requirements Craft Wondrous Item, *polymorph*; **Cost** 1,125 gp; **Rarity:** Rare
Alchemical Formula: Earth (any), Water (any), Body

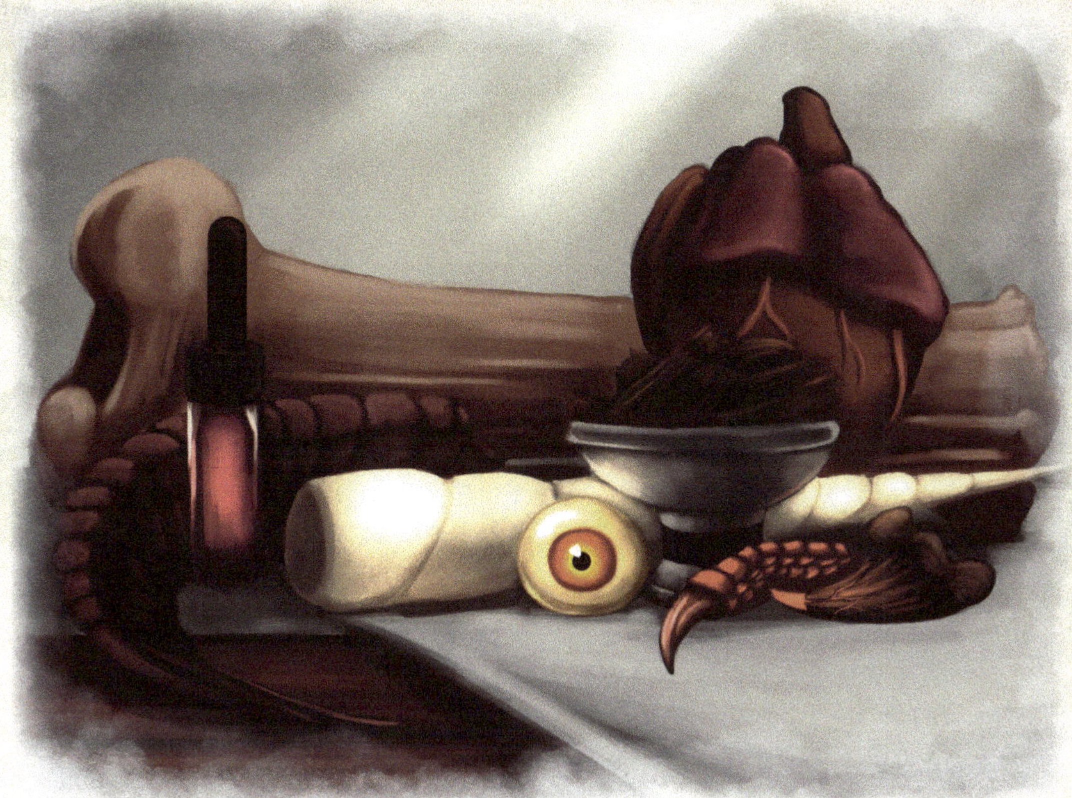

ELIXIR OF THE MOLE

Aura faint transmutation; **CL** 11th
Slot none; **Price** 3,300 gp; **Weight** —

DESCRIPTION

This elixir allows the imbiber to dig through earth at her normal movement rate. The imbiber's hands and arms change, the skin toughens, and nails lengthen, becoming black and gnarled.

The user can tunnel through dirt and earth at their normal movement rate or though solid stone at half their movement rate. While traveling underground, it is 80% likely that the tunnel collapses behind the user. It is possible for others to travel with the digger as long as everyone traveling stays within 10 feet of the digger.

As long as the digger keeps moving, the air stays fresh. If the digger stops for any reason, the air only remains fresh for one minute. This length of time is halved for every additional person.

The strength, claws, and toughness allow the imbiber to make two claw attacks, doing 1d4 damage each.

CONSTRUCTION

Requirements Craft Wondrous Item, *move earth*, *beast form II*; **Cost** 1,650 gp; **Rarity:** Rare
Alchemical Formula: Earth (any), Water (any), Body, Transmutation

ELIXIR OF THE RAINBOW BRIDGE

Aura moderate conjuration (creation) [light]; **CL** 13th
Slot none; **Price** 4,550 gp; **Weight** —

DESCRIPTION

Once quaffed, this elixir does nothing unless the user concentrates on a bridge. Sometime within the next minute, a bridge slowly forms at a location of the imbiber's choosing. It is up to 20 feet wide and up to 200 feet long. The bridge is made of colored force in a rainbow pattern and is indestructible unless it is weighed down with more than 50,000 pounds or is subject to *dispel magic*, in which case it dissipates instantly.

CONSTRUCTION

Requirements Craft Wondrous Item, *limited wish*; **Cost** 2,275 gp; **Rarity:** Rare
Alchemical Formula: Azoth (any), Water (any), Mind

ELIXIR OF THE REMORHAZ

Aura moderate transformation; **CL** 7th
Slot none; **Price** 1,400 gp; **Weight** —

DESCRIPTION

Once imbibed, this elixir raises the heat of the owner's skin. Anyone attacking the imbiber in melee takes 2d4 points of fire damage from the burning heat of the imbiber's skin during the duration of the elixir. The imbiber also gains Resist Fire 2.

CONSTRUCTION

Requirements Craft Wondrous Item, *fire shield*; **Cost** 700 gp; **Rarity:** Very Rare
Alchemical Formula: Fire (any), Water (any), Body, Transmutation

ELIXIR OF THE SCORPION

Aura faint transmutation; **CL** 5th
Slot none; **Price** 750 gp; **Weight** —

DESCRIPTION

Once quaffed, the user grows a large scorpion tail from their lower back. This transformation is stopped if the user is wearing any armor heavier then chain. The tail has a reach of five feet. It does 1d4 points of damage, and on a successful strike that does damage, the target must make a DC 16 Fortitude save versus poison. On a failed save, the target takes an amount of damage equal to Xd6, where X is equal to one-half the imbiber's level. The user may attack with the tail as a swift action. The user is considered to have the feat Weapon Finesse with the tail.

The tail takes one full round to grow. It is not usable until fully grown, and the duration does not begin until the tail is fully grown.

CONSTRUCTION

Requirements Craft Wondrous Item, *beast shape I*; **Cost** 375 gp; **Rarity:** Rare
Alchemical Formula: Water (any), Body, Toxin, Transmutation

ELIXIR OF TINY FEET
Aura faint, conjuration (summoning); **CL** 3rd
Slot none; **Price** 750 gp; **Weight** —

DESCRIPTION
This is a liquid that appears to be made of thousands of tiny, tiny feet. Upon imbibing the liquid, the drinker feels nauseous. For one minute they gain the sickened condition. At the end of the minute, they vomit up 3d10 diminutive inhuman servants (use **homunculus** statistics) about six inches tall. These follow the commands of the imbiber to the best of their ability for one hour. They have access to simple tools as needed. Each is able to perform the labor of one-half man. They may be commanded to fight but they do not come with any weapons or armor.

CONSTRUCTION
Requirements Craft Wondrous Item, *summon swarm*; **Cost** 375 gp; **Rarity:** Very Rare
Alchemical Formula: Water (any), Body, Dream

ELIXIR OF TOAD SKIN
Aura faint transmutation; **CL** 5th
Slot none; **Price** 750 gp; **Weight** —

DESCRIPTION
This elixir covers the imbiber in leaking warts and boils filled with caustic fluid. On a successful unarmed or natural attack, any living target takes 1d4 points of acid damage. The target must succeed at a DC 14 Fortitude save or become nauseated. If they are nauseated, they may repeat this save each round at the start of their turn.

CONSTRUCTION
Requirements Craft Wondrous Item, *stinking cloud*; **Cost** 375 gp; **Rarity:** Very Rare
Alchemical Formula: Water (any), Acid, Body

ELIXIR OF TORPIDITY
Aura faint enchantment (compulsion) [mind-affecting]; **CL** 5th
Slot none; **Price** 750 gp; **Weight** —

DESCRIPTION
Those that take this potion gain a potent ability to talk others to sleep. The potion has a short duration of 10 minutes, during which time the imbiber can speak in sonorous, sobering monotones about any topic at all and cause sleep in listeners. Speaking requires all of the imbiber's attention, disallowing any other actions. All those in earshot must make a save to take any action other than listen while the imbiber speaks. This is a DC 24 Will saving throw if they speak the language the imbiber is speaking. If they are language-using creatures, this is a DC 20 Will save, and non-language using creatures must make a DC 14 Will save. If successful, they can continue to act without issue. At the end of the first round, all who stopped to listen to the imbiber must make a DC 16 Will save to stay awake. They must repeat this save every round until the speaker ceases speaking.
This sleep lasts for four hours. This affects all who can hear the tone of the speaker's voice, regardless of allegiance. Anyone attacked while listening or sleeping instantly snaps out of the effect and is immune. The effect ends if the speaker takes damage.

CONSTRUCTION
Requirements Craft Wondrous Item, *sleep*, *suggestion*; **Cost** 375 gp; **Rarity:** Rare
Alchemical Formula: Water (any), Control, Stasis

ELIXIR OF TREASURE FINDING
Aura moderate divination; **CL** 7th
Slot none; **Price** 1,400 gp; **Weight** —

DESCRIPTION
This elixir grants the imbiber a magical location sense that allows them to locate the nearest mass of treasure within a great distance. If the user is within one mile of treasure equal to one-tenth their wealth by level, the imbiber can sense the direction of the treasure. Once within 400 feet, the user can detect the exact location of the treasure and gain a general sense of how to reach it. Note that this detects only valuable metals such as gold, copper, silver, platinum, gems, and jewelry, not magic items or equipment. Worthless metals and magic items not containing precious metals or gems are ignored. Only lead more than one-inch thick or magical wards can block the effect — other intervening material is irrelevant. This potion lasts for 5d4 minutes. When this elixir is combined with any other elixir, it produces a lethal poison.

CONSTRUCTION
Requirements Craft Wondrous Item, *divination*; **Cost** 700 gp; **Rarity:** Very Rare
Alchemical Formula: Gold, Platinum, Water (any), Mind

ELIXIR OF UMBRAL SHADOW
Aura moderate illusion (shadow); **CL** 11th
Slot none; **Price** 3,300 gp; **Weight** —

DESCRIPTION
This fantastic elixir turns the imbiber's whole person, including any armor and items, into shadow, where they remain against the wall or floor where the elixir was imbibed. They remain there until their path is crossed. Once this occurs, they may choose to become the shadow of the person that crossed them. They move with the person and can take no action or move themselves until the elixir expires in 3d8 minutes. Once the elixir ends, the imbiber silently appears behind or next to their target that they were following.

CONSTRUCTION
Requirements Craft Wondrous Item, *shadow walk*; **Cost** 1,650 gp; **Rarity:** Very Rare
Alchemical Formula: Water (any), Body, Light, Transmutation

ELIXIR OF UNDERGROUND AWARENESS
Aura moderate transmutation; **CL** 9th
Slot none; **Price** 2,250 gp; **Weight** —

DESCRIPTION
This elixir grants a +10 bonus on Perception checks to notice unusual stonework such as traps and hidden doors located in stone walls or floors. The imbiber receives a check to notice such features whenever they pass within 10 feet of them, regardless if they are actually looking. They also gain darkvision and can determine slopes and depth underground on a successful DC 15 Perception check.

CONSTRUCTION
Requirements Craft Wondrous Item, *passwall*, *detect secret doors*; **Cost** 1,125 gp; **Rarity:** Very Rare
Alchemical Formula: Water (any), Perception

ELIXIR OF UNGUIS
Aura moderate transmutation; **CL** 7th
Slot none; **Price** 1,400 gp; **Weight** —

DESCRIPTION
This elixir causes the imbiber to grow terrifying and powerful talons in place of their nails. Their fingers lengthen, and sharp hard claws extend from the tips of their fingers. For the duration of the potion, they may make two claw attacks each round at their full attack bonus doing 1d6 + Strength points of damage. They are considered armed. The imbiber also gains a +4 enhancement bonus to strength.

CONSTRUCTION
Requirements Craft Wondrous Item, *beast shape II*; **Cost** 700 gp; **Rarity:** Very Rare
Alchemical Formula: Water (any), Plant, Transmutation

ELIXIR OF VANITY
Aura faint transmutation; **CL** 3rd
Slot none; **Price** 300 gp; **Weight** —

DESCRIPTION
This elixir enhances one physical quality of the imbiber. A woman may want perfect skin, a man a full head of hair, a gnome a large nose, or a dwarf may desire a luxurious beard. The imbiber imagines the change when consuming the elixir. The change lasts for 1d4 + 1 weeks.

CONSTRUCTION
Requirements Craft Wondrous Item, *eagle's splendor*; **Cost** 150 gp; **Rarity:** Rare
Alchemical Formula: Water (any), Body

ELIXIR OF VENUS
Aura strong enchantment (compulsion) [mind-affecting]; **CL** 9th
Slot none; **Price** 2,250 gp; **Weight** —

DESCRIPTION
This elixir works much like an *elixir of love*, except it produces undying devotion for the first creature seen after imbibing the elixir. This devotion is complete and stronger than a mere charm spell. It may be resisted with a DC 20 Will save, but if a part of the target is used in the formula, such as a piece of hair or a nail clipping, the save is DC 30. A *remove curse* breaks the effect. The devotion is total, as the imbiber now lives life for the purpose of the creature he or she is devoted to. They are aware of their former lives and state and don't care, thankful that they are now devoted to the person viewed. Individuals who give this elixir to the object of their affection often come to view the final results as a curse.

CONSTRUCTION
Requirements Craft Wondrous Item, *dominate person*; **Cost** 1,125 gp; **Rarity:** Very Rare
Alchemical Formula: Water (any), Control, Emotion, Purity

ELIXIR OF VISION OF THE EAGLE
Aura faint transmutation; **CL** 3rd
Slot none; **Price** 300 gp; **Weight** —

DESCRIPTION
This elixir enhances and improves nonmagical sight. It allows you to see clearly and distinguish objects up to a mile away. You can observe details as if these objects were 10 times closer than they actually are. Your penalties to hit due to range with ranged weapons are halved.

CONSTRUCTION
Requirements Craft Wondrous Item, *darkvision*; **Cost** 150 gp; **Rarity:** Uncommon
Alchemical Formula: Water (any), Perception

ELIXIR OF VITALITY
Aura faint transmutation; **CL** 7th
Slot none; **Price** 1,400 gp; **Weight** —

DESCRIPTION
This elixir restores health and vitality to the imbiber for a week. During this week, the drinker is immune to sleep deprivation, suffocation, starvation, and dehydration. This elixir also protects completely versus poison and disease, and the drinker recovers 1 hit point every four hours.

CONSTRUCTION
Requirements Craft Wondrous Item, *restoration*; **Cost** 700 gp; **Rarity:** Rare
Alchemical Formula: Sulfur (any), Water (any), Healing, Protection, Stasis

ELIXIR OF YOUTH
Aura strong transmutation; **CL** 17th
Slot none; **Price** 7,650 gp; **Weight** —

DESCRIPTION
This potent and scarce elixir reverses aging. Drinking the entire elixir reduces the drinkers age by 1d4 + 1 years. Taking a sip first, instead of drinking the entire elixir, reduces the potency and restores only 1d3 years of aging.

CONSTRUCTION
Requirements Craft Wondrous Item, *wish*, *temporal stasis*; **Cost** 3,825 gp; **Rarity:** Very Rare
Alchemical Formula: Diamond, Azoth (any), Water (any), Body, Healing, Mind

ELIXIR OF ZORBO
Aura strong transmutation; **CL** 9th
Slot none; **Price** 2,250 gp; **Weight** —

DESCRIPTION
This elixir allows the imbiber to take on the qualities near the imbiber for two minutes. It must be an external substance that the user touches that is at least as large as the imbiber. You can also meld with any nearby substance as *meld with stone* as well as move within large surfaces such as earth and sand at 20 feet per round. If you take the form of dirt and earth, you gain DR 2/—, a +2 natural armor class, and fast healing 2 as long as you are in contact with earth. Sand grants you DR 10/— and fast healing 10 as long as you are in contact with sand. Stone grants you DR 8/— and a +7 natural armor bonus. Wood grants you DR 5/— and a +5 natural armor bonus. Metal grants you DR 10/— and a +10 natural armor bonus. The substance you touch must at least equal your mass. Energy types may not be absorbed. Confer with your GM about other materials.

CONSTRUCTION
Requirements Craft Wondrous Item, *polymorph*, *meld with stone*; **Cost** 1,125 gp; **Rarity:** Rare
Alchemical Formula: Diamond, Azoth (any), Earth (any), Water (any), Body

SALVES

Salves are substances that are smeared over a surface for an effect. Within a short period of time, they are absorbed or dry on the item and their effect occurs. They take one standard action to apply, and then their effects occur immediately. As with elixirs, salves have a default duration of 1d4 + 4 minutes. If you desire to have a salve's effect end before the duration expires, most oils are removed easily enough with an appropriate solvent. A mild alcohol wash (i.e., something like wine) works well, as does turpentine.

TABLE 4–19: SALVES

Name	Price		Name	Price
Salve of Acceleration	750 gp		Salve of Making	2,250 gp
Salve of Agelessness	4,550 gp		Salve of Monster Repulsion	3,300 gp
Salve of Animal Sanctuary	300 gp		Salve of Pacification	300 gp
Salve of Animation	3,300 gp		Salve of Pilfering	300 gp
Salve of Arcane Scent 1,400 gp			Salve of Power	750 gp
Salve of Armor	300 gp		Salve of Protection, Insect	750 gp
Salve of Basic Blade Enhancement	750 gp		Salve of Protection, Rust	750 gp
Salve of Black Grave	7,650 gp		Salve of Protoplast	7,650 gp
Salve of Blasting	750 gp		Salve of Reanimation	2,250 gp
Salve of Camouflage	300 gp		Salve of Resistance, Acid	750 gp
Salve of Clarity	3,300 gp		Salve of Resistance, Fire	750 gp
Salve of Disenchantment	3,300 gp		Salve of Scentlessness	300 gp
Salve of Elasticity	2,250 gp		Salve of Scribe	3,300 gp
Salve of Elemental Invulnerability	4,550 gp		Salve of Scrying	4,550 gp
Salve of Etherealness	6,000 gp		Salve of Shadows	300 gp
Salve of Eternal Flame	300 gp		Salve of Sharpness	750 gp
Salve of Expert Blade Enhancement	4,550 gp		Salve of Stasis	6,000 gp
Salve of Fiery Burning	750 gp		Salve of Steel	3,300 gp
Salve of Fortifying	1,400 gp		Salve of Stonewalking	2,250 gp
Salve of Illumination	300 gp		Salve of the Green 3,300 gp	
Salve of Immobility	750 gp		Salve of the Marionette	2,250 gp
Salve of Impact	750 gp		Salve of the Threshold	2,250 gp
Salve of Iniquity	1.400 gp		Salve of Timelessness	6,000 gp
Salve of Insectile Barrier	2,250 gp		Salve of Transcendent Filth	3,300 gp
Salve of Iron Flesh	1,400 gp		Salve of Transparency	750 gp
Salve of Loosening	300 gp		Salve of Turning	300 gp
Salve of Magical Backlash	1,400 gp		Salve of Warding 750 gp	

SALVE OF ACCELERATION
Aura moderate transmutation; **CL** 5th
Slot none; **Price** 750 gp; **Weight** —

DESCRIPTION
This oil grants the user increased speed. Air seems to flow around them, armor moves with less resistance, and the user becomes much faster than normal. One application of this oil increases the user's speed by 50%. A human with a movement speed of 30 feet has a movement speed of 45 feet. This oil bypasses restrictions to speed from armor, the armor restriction of weight and bulk is applied, and the resulting movement value is increased by half. Moving at this speed is as tiring as moving at the unmodified rate. This oil tends to dry out quickly due to the extreme speeds the user moves at, cutting its duration in half.

CONSTRUCTION
Requirements Craft Wondrous Item, *haste*; **Cost** 375 gp; **Rarity:** Very Rare
Alchemical Formula: Rare Earth, Salt (any), Speed

SALVE OF AGELESSNESS
Aura strong transmutation; **CL** 13th
Slot none; **Price** 4,550 gp; **Weight** —

DESCRIPTION
This powerful magic salve is a potent preservative. When applied to the skin of a living being, it halts all decay and aging for the span of a year. The aging process stops and resumes at the end of this period. There are no limits to the length of time this oil can be used, though repeated applications dry and yellow the skin. When crafted, enough is made to cover five Medium-sized creatures (or one Medium-sized creature five times). When found, it has 1d4 + 1 doses left.

CONSTRUCTION
Requirements Craft Wondrous Item, *limited wish*; **Cost** 2,275 gp; **Rarity:** Very Rare
Alchemical Formula: Azoth (any), Salt (any), Decay, Life

SALVE OF ANIMAL SANCTUARY
Aura faint abjuration; **CL** 3rd
Slot none; **Price** 300 gp; **Weight** —

DESCRIPTION
This oil is spread over an animal to create a magical ward that protects the creature from harm. Anyone wishing to attack the animal must succeed at a DC 16 Will save in order to attack. Even if able to successfully attack the animal, the animal gains DR 5/— and has a +4 deflection bonus to armor class.

An animal choosing to attack ends this effect instantly. This oil affects only animals, and requires that they have a 3 Intelligence or less. Magical beasts, monsters, and animals with Intelligence scores of 4 or greater are not affected.

CONSTRUCTION
Requirements Craft Wondrous Item, *sanctuary, animal friendship*; **Cost** 150 gp; **Rarity:** Rare
Alchemical Formula: Salt (any), Protection (x2)

SALVE OF ANIMATION
Aura strong transmutation; **CL** 11th
Slot none; **Price** 3,300 gp; **Weight** —

DESCRIPTION
This strange oil has the wonderful ability to animate objects. One vial animates a single man-sized object, which then becomes subservient to the animator's commands. It is important that these commands are simple, consisting of no more than five or six basic words.

Once animated, the items are treated as constructs and can complete basic tasks. Stools can walk, suits of armor can pummel and dance, and musical instruments can play themselves, but no special forms of movement or other abilities are imbued.

CONSTRUCTION
Requirements Craft Wondrous Item, *animate objects*; **Cost** 1,650 gp; **Rarity:** Rare
Alchemical Formula: Azoth (any), Mercury (any), Salt (any), Agility, Body

SALVE OF ARCANE SCENT
Aura moderate divination; **CL** 7th
Slot none; **Price** 1,400 gp; **Weight** —

DESCRIPTION
This salve is applied under the nose. It allows a trained caster to "smell" spells prepared by other casters. It does not detect auras from devices or items.

The person sensing the magical energy can determine with a range of 2d4 levels how many spells or spell-like abilities the target caster has prepared or is able to cast. It also allows the caster to determine the schools of various abilities prepared or used. A vial has 6d4 doses and is created with a full 24 doses. This requires the caster to be within 10 feet of his target. This knowledge can be gained as a free action.

CONSTRUCTION
Requirements Craft Wondrous Item, *scrying*; **Cost** 700 gp; **Rarity:** Very Rare
Alchemical Formula: Azoth (any), Mercury (any), Salt (any), Perception

SALVE OF ARMOR
Aura faint abjuration; **CL** 3rd
Slot none; **Price** 300 gp; **Weight** —

DESCRIPTION
This salve is thin and watery. When applied over a creature's skin, it quickly hardens and acts like armor. The oil lasts for 2d4 + 6 hours. It grants a +6 armor bonus to armor class. It allows up to a +4 Dexterity bonus, has a –2 armor penalty, and has a 10% chance of spell failure.

CONSTRUCTION
Requirements Craft Wondrous Item, *mage armor*; **Cost** 150 gp; **Rarity:** Very Rare
Alchemical Formula: Mercury (any), Salt (any), Armor

SALVE OF BASIC BLADE ENHANCEMENT
Aura faint transmutation; **CL** 5th
Slot none; **Price** 750 gp; **Weight** —

DESCRIPTION
When applied to a weapon, this salve grants the weapon a temporary magical effect. A variety of effects can be applied, and each requires four drams of a different kind of essence. Once applied, this salve lasts the normal duration unless a character rolls a one on an attack. In that case, the salve is scraped off or ruined somehow and no longer has its effect. In spite of the name blade enhancement, these salves can enhance any item that can be used as a weapon, including unarmed attacks (e.g. coating gloves, etc.). Consult **Table 4–20** below.

TABLE 4–20: SALVE OF BASIC BLADE ENHANCEMENT FORMULAS

Weapon Quality	Alchemical Formula
Flaming	Salt (any), Fire (any) (x4)
Frost	Salt (any), Cold (x4)
Shock	Salt (any), Electricity (x4)
Corrosive	Salt (any), Acid (x4)
Keen	Salt (any), Purity (x3)

CONSTRUCTION
Requirements Craft Wondrous Item, *magic weapon, greater*; **Cost** 375 gp; **Rarity:** Rare
Alchemical Formula: See **Table 4–20**.

SALVE OF THE BLACK GRAVE
Aura strong enchantment (compulsion) [death]; **CL** 17th
Slot none; **Price** 7,650 gp; **Weight** —

DESCRIPTION
This demonic oil burns the very soul out of a body. When sprinkled on a surface in the form of an X, the next living thing to cross past that X within 24 hours must make a DC 22 Fortitude save or die. Regardless of the results of the save, the oil works only against the first person across the threshold. The oil is treated as a magical trap with a DC 35 Perception check required to locate it.

CONSTRUCTION
Requirements Craft Wondrous Item, *power word kill*; **Cost** 3,825 gp; **Rarity:** Very Rare
Alchemical Formula: Salt (any), Death (x3)

SALVE OF BLASTING
Aura faint evocation; **CL** 5th
Slot none; **Price** 750 gp; **Weight** —

DESCRIPTION
Any non-living, inanimate object coated in this oil loses its natural properties and becomes a bomb. When thrown, this object detonates and does damage in a 15-foot radius, allowing a DC 16 Reflex save for half damage. Soft materials such as cloth or cotton cause 1d4 points of damage; leather, rope or other tough materials do 1d6 points of damage; glass, ceramic, or bone do 2d6 points of damage; stone does 4d6 points of damage, and metal does 6d6 points of damage. If you use this oil to coat a gemstone, it does 6d6 points of damage plus an additional 1 point per die per 1,000 gp of value, e.g. coating a 1,000-gp gem does 6d6 + 6 damage, whereas coating a 5,000-gp gem does 6d6 + 30 points of damage.

CONSTRUCTION
Requirements Craft Wondrous Item, *fireball*; **Cost** 375 gp; **Rarity:** Rare
Alchemical Formula: Earth (any), Fire (any), Salt (any), Transmutation

SALVE OF CAMOUFLAGE
Aura faint illusion; **CL** 3rd
Slot none; **Price** 300 gp; **Weight** —

DESCRIPTION
When this oil is sprinkled over a target, its coloration changes to closely match the environment. This provides a +15 bonus on Stealth checks when still, and a +5 bonus when moving. If in combat, this oil provides partial concealment.

CONSTRUCTION
Requirements Craft Wondrous Item, *invisibility*; **Cost** 150 gp; **Rarity:** Rare
Alchemical Formula: Mercury (any), Salt (any), Stealth

SALVE OF CLARITY
Aura strong divination ; **CL** 11th
Slot none; **Price** 3,300 gp; **Weight** —

DESCRIPTION
When this salve is applied to the character's eyes, her vision improves. They can detect illusions, as well as good, evil, law, chaos, and magic as the spells. The user can also tell if someone is shapeshifted or under the influence of any mind-affecting effect.

CONSTRUCTION
Requirements Craft Wondrous Item, *true seeing*; **Cost** 1,650 gp; **Rarity:** Rare
Alchemical Formula: Mercury (any), Salt (any), Perception

SALVE OF DISENCHANTMENT
Aura strong abjuration; **CL** 11th
Slot none; **Price** 3,300 gp; **Weight** —

DESCRIPTION
This salve removes and suppresses all enchantment and charms on living creatures and objects. Any living creature has all non-permanent enchantments and charms removed. Any object has its magic suppressed for 1d4 + 4 hours. The salve does not detect as magical, and any item that has its magic suppressed does not detect as magical either, generating no aura at all.

CONSTRUCTION
Requirements Craft Wondrous Item, *dispel magic, greater*; **Cost** 1,650 gp; **Rarity:** Rare
Alchemical Formula: Diamond, Azoth (any), Mercury (any), Salt (any), Decay

SALVE OF ELASTICITY
Aura moderate transmutation (polymorph); **CL** 9th
Slot none; **Price** 2,250 gp; **Weight** —

DESCRIPTION
This powerful salve causes those anointed with it to be able to shift and shape their body and gear as if it were a singular gelatinous mass. They could flatten a limb or stretch it up to three times its normal length. The person anointed with this oil could pour their body through a keyhole or slide beneath a door. They gain a +5 circumstance bonus on Combat Maneuver Checks. They may make melee attacks against any targets within 30 feet, although they threaten only the same number of squares they normally would. They may not extend a limb more than 10 times its natural length.

CONSTRUCTION
Requirements Craft Wondrous Item, *polymorph*; **Cost** 1,125 gp; **Rarity:** Rare
Alchemical Formula: Mercury (any), Salt (any), Agility, Transmutation

SALVE OF ELEMENTAL INVULNERABILITY
Aura moderate abjuration; **CL** 13th
Slot none; **Price** 4,550 gp; **Weight** —

DESCRIPTION
This salve provides protection and total invulnerability from one type of elemental force. Fire invulnerability protects you from lava flows and forest fires. Water protects you from floods, hurricanes, avalanches, and tsunamis. Earth protects you from mudslides, rockslides, and earthquakes. Air protects you from winds, storms, and tornados. You and the square you are in are completely protected from the elemental effect. Difficult terrain of the appropriate type is ignored as the elements part and do not affect you. This also protects you from elemental attacks of the specific elemental type you are invulnerable to. Although they are still effective, you gain the appropriate resistance 10 until the salve expires. There are eight Medium-sized doses inside a flask. If found, randomly determine the elemental type that the salve protects against.

CONSTRUCTION
Requirements Craft Wondrous Item, *protection from energy*, *limited wish*; **Cost** 2,275 gp; **Rarity:** Rare
Alchemical Formula: Air *or* Fire *or* Earth *or* Water (depending on type, x3 from different essences), Salt (any), Body, Protection

SALVE OF ETERNAL FLAME
Aura moderate evocation; **CL** 3rd
Slot none; **Price** 300 gp; **Weight** —

DESCRIPTION
When a torch is soaked in this salve and lit, it burns eternally. Furthermore, the torch burns cool. It does emit heat, but not enough to burn or set things aflame. You could grasp the lit end of this torch, and it would be no hotter than a shield left in the sun.
After one round, the salve soaks into objects and then if lit aflame, will burn forever. It does not really last for all time, but for several years at a minimum. It burns underwater, and if snuffed, will relight. Note that the burning items do decay but at a greatly reduced rate.

CONSTRUCTION
Requirements Craft Wondrous Item, *continual flame*; **Cost** 150 gp; **Rarity:** Uncommon
Alchemical Formula: Fire (any), Salt (any)

SALVE OF ETHEREALNESS
Aura strong transmutation; **CL** 15th
Slot none; **Price** 6,000 gp; **Weight** —

DESCRIPTION
This salve seems to absorb light rather than be illuminated by it. Once used, it makes the target ethereal (as the *ethereal jaunt* spell). The user can end the effect at any time during the duration and re-enter the ethereal at will. Each vial contains enough for one Medium-sized creature.

CONSTRUCTION
Requirements Craft Wondrous Item, *ethereal jaunt*; **Cost** 3,000 gp; **Rarity:** Rare
Alchemical Formula: Salt (any), Light, Planar, Stealth

SALVE OF EXPERT BLADE ENHANCEMENT
Aura faint transmutation; **CL** 13th
Slot none; **Price** 4,550 gp; **Weight** —

DESCRIPTION
If applied to a weapon, this salve grants the weapon a temporary magical effect. A variety of effects can be applied, and each requires four drams of a different kind of essence. Once applied, this salve lasts the normal duration unless a character rolls a one on an attack. In that case, the salve has been scraped off or ruined somehow and no longer has its effect. In spite of the name blade enhancement, these enhance any item that can be used as a weapon, including unarmed attacks (e.g. coating gloves, etc.) Consult **Table 4–21** below:

TABLE 4–21: SALVE OF EXPERT BLADE ENHANCEMENT FORMULAS

Weapon Quality	Alchemical Formula
Flaming + Flaming Burst	Salt, Fire (any)(x8)
Frost + Icy Burst	Salt (any), Cold (x6)
Shock + Shocking Burst	Salt (any), Electricity (x6)
Corrosive + Corrosive Burst	Salt (any), Acid (x6)
Speed	Salt (any), Speed (x6)

CONSTRUCTION

Requirements Craft Wondrous Item, *magic weapon, greater, limited wish*;
Cost 2,275 gp; **Rarity:** Very Rare
Alchemical Formula: See **Table 4–21**

SALVE OF FIERY BURNING

Aura moderate evocation; **CL** 5th
Slot none; **Price** 750 gp; **Weight** —

DESCRIPTION

This salve immediately bursts into flame if it comes into contact with air.
This causes 5d6 points of fire damage within a 10-foot radius, with a DC 16
Reflex save for half damage. Opening the flask does 1d4 points of damage
and requires a DC 12 Reflex save to stopper the flask before it explodes.

CONSTRUCTION

Requirements Craft Wondrous Item, *fireball*; **Cost** 375 gp; **Rarity:**
Uncommon
Alchemical Formula: Fire (any) (x4), Salt (any), Body

SALVE OF FORTIFYING

Aura moderate abjuration; **CL** 7th
Slot none; **Price** 1,400 gp; **Weight** —

DESCRIPTION

When applied, this salve hardens the skin of the owner, granting DR 10/
Magic.

CONSTRUCTION

Requirements Craft Wondrous Item, *stoneskin*; **Cost** 700 gp; **Rarity:** Very
Rare
Alchemical Formula: Salt (any), Body, Transmutation

SALVE OF ILLUMINATION

Aura faint evocation; **CL** 3rd
Slot none; **Price** 300 gp; **Weight** —

DESCRIPTION

This salve is usually found inside a dark, opaque, oddly shaped flask. Once
opened, the flask turns transparent and the salve sheds light as a torch out
to 100 feet. The flask counters magical *darkness* and *deeper darkness* and
works underwater. The oil can be poured out and used to coat objects to
cause them to glow. The oil lasts for 2d6 + 12 hours.

CONSTRUCTION

Requirements Craft Wondrous Item, *continual flame*; **Cost** 150 gp; **Rarity:**
Rare
Alchemical Formula: Fire (any), Salt (any), Light

SALVE OF IMMOBILITY

Aura faint transmutation; **CL** 5th
Slot none; **Price** 750 gp; **Weight** —

DESCRIPTION

This salve has the consistency of thick goop that resists movement, affixing
or locking into place whatever it is applied to. The legs of a stool could be
affixed to the floor. Hinges covered in this paste will not swing. This goop
affects only the part coated and does not increase the hardness of objects.
A door with immobile hinges could be broken through, though the hinges
would not swing; they become as solid as a single iron piece. Each flask can
coat 25 square feet of material, and the application need not be contiguous.
An attempt to force the part to move requires a successful DC 26 Strength
check.

CONSTRUCTION

Requirements Craft Wondrous Item, *hold portal, slow*; **Cost** 375 gp;
Rarity: Rare
Alchemical Formula: Salt (any), Body, Stasis, Strength

SALVE OF IMPACT

Aura faint transmutation; **CL** 5th
Slot none; **Price** 750 gp; **Weight** —

DESCRIPTION

This salve has a powerful effect on any blunt weapon or missile on which it
is spread. It makes no difference if the item is magical or not.
If applied to a bludgeoning weapon such as a hammer, club, or mace, it
gives a +3 bonus to hit and a +6 bonus to damage. The bonus remains with
the weapon for 3d4 + 1 rounds. These rounds are consecutive, as the salve
evaporates in this time regardless of precautions taken.
If applied to a blunt missile such as a thrown hammer, sling stone, or
bullet, it gives a +3 bonus to hit and damage. This lasts until the missile is
fired. Each application of oil treats five rounds of ammunition, two thrown
weapons, or one melee weapon. A flask of *salve of impact* contains 1d4 + 1
applications. The number of applications created when crafting the salve is
five.

CONSTRUCTION

Requirements Craft Wondrous Item, *magic weapon, greater*; **Cost** 375 gp;
Rarity: Very Rare
Alchemical Formula: Azoth (any), Rare Earth, Earth (any), Salt (any),
Strength

SALVE OF INIQUITY

Aura moderate evocation [evil]; **CL** 7th
Slot none; **Price** 1,400 gp; **Weight** —

DESCRIPTION

This unholy salve does 3d8 points of damage to creatures with good
alignments on a direct hit and 1d6 points of damage on a splash. It can also
be used to coat a 10-foot-square surface to cause 2d4 points of damage to any
characters that enter that square as well as 1d4 + 1 to any who end their turn
in that area.
It is fairly sweet smelling and appears to be a healing potion. A successful
DC 30 Perception check is required to discover its true properties. If
consumed internally, good characters must succeed at a DC 18 Fortitude save
or take 6d8 + 6 points of damage. If the saving throw is successful, they take
half. Creatures with a neutral alignment get an upset stomach, and those with
evil alignments treat it as a *potion of cure critical wounds*.

CONSTRUCTION

Requirements Craft Wondrous Item, *unholy blight*; **Cost** 700 gp; **Rarity:**
Uncommon
Alchemical Formula: Azoth (any), Salt (any), Death (x3)

SALVE OF INSECTILE BARRIER
Aura faint abjuration; **CL** 9th
Slot none; **Price** 2,250 gp; **Weight** —

DESCRIPTION
This works as the *salve of protection, insects* except for two crucial changes:
The duration is 1d4 + 1 hours, and the salve is a powerful insect attractant
calling insects from up to three miles away.
These insects surround and travel with the protected character, unable to
reach them, surrounding the character in a sphere five feet in diameter. They
are harmless to the user and disperse at the end of the duration, but anyone
crossing the ward to attack the warded creature is attacked for 2d8 + 2 points
of damage. Any insect control or summoning spells give a GM-determined
bonus to damage for the large number of insects present. Any intelligent
insects receive a DC 16 Will save to resist the attraction.

CONSTRUCTION
Requirements Craft Wondrous Item, *insect plague*; **Cost** 1,125 gp; **Rarity:**
Very Rare
Alchemical Formula: Salt (any), Emotion, Transmutation

SALVE OF IRON FLESH
Aura strong transmutation; **CL** 7th
Slot none; **Price** 1,400 gp; **Weight** —

DESCRIPTION
This salve toughens the skin when it is applied, providing a +6 natural armor
bonus and granting DR 2/—.

CONSTRUCTION
Requirements Craft Wondrous Item, *stoneskin*; **Cost** 700 gp; **Rarity:** Very
Rare
Alchemical Formula: Salt (any), Body, Transmutation (x2)

SALVE OF LOOSENING
Aura faint transmutation; **CL** 3rd
Slot none; **Price** 300 gp; **Weight** —

DESCRIPTION
Once applied to objects, this salve has a variety of effects. It can cover a 10-
foot square area. Webs dissolve, melting away, and cannot find purchase on
any surface coated. Knots are untied; chains, straps, and other restraints fall
off. Spells and terrain are unable to entangle or restrain creatures in the area
of effect, and doors are unlocked.

CONSTRUCTION
Requirements Craft Wondrous Item, *knock*; **Cost** 150 gp; **Rarity:** Rare
Alchemical Formula: Rare Earth, Mercury (any) (x2), Salt (any) Sulfur
(any), Body, Transmutation

SALVE OF MAGICAL BACKLASH
Aura strong abjuration; **CL** 7th
Slot none; **Price** 1,400 gp; **Weight** —

DESCRIPTION
This salve coats a person for up to a full month or an item for up to a full
year. During this time, if any attempt is made to break or disjunct magic,
the attempt is resisted. Spells of 4th level or lower such as *dispel magic* fail
outright, or in the case of stronger effects such as *mage's disjunction*, they
receive a +5 circumstance bonus to their saving throw.

CONSTRUCTION
Requirements Craft Wondrous Item, *globe of invulnerability, lesser*; **Cost**
700 gp; **Rarity:** Very Rare
Alchemical Formula: Azoth (any) (3 from different sources), Air (any), Fire
(any), Mercury (any), Water (any), Salt (any), Sulfur (any), Transmutation

SALVE OF MAKING
Aura faint conjuration; **CL** 9th
Slot none; **Price** 2,250 gp; **Weight** —

DESCRIPTION
This salve is a very fluid liquid, approximately three ounces in size. To use it,
the bottle is upended, and the liquid is dumped out on the ground. The liquid
forms the item that the salve contains. The item created is determined by the
item decided during the salve creation process. The bottle is generally labeled
with a picture of the item. Drinking or ingesting the salve has few harmful
effects, a bit of indigestion, and a few interesting trips to the privy.

CONSTRUCTION
Requirements Craft Wondrous Item, *fabricate*; **Cost** 1,125 gp; **Rarity:** Very
Rare
Alchemical Formula: Mercury (any), Salt (any), Transmutation

SALVE OF MONSTER REPULSION
Aura strong abjuration; **CL** 11th
Slot none; **Price** 3,300 gp; **Weight** —

DESCRIPTION
This salve repels monsters and affects any aberration, magical beast,
monstrous humanoid, ooze, or undead. It can cover up to five Medium
creatures. Any monster type listed above within 80 feet of these creatures
has a −1 circumstance penalty on all attacks, skill checks, and saves. Within
40 feet, this penalty doubles to −2. Any creature within 20 feet receives a −3
penalty, and any creature in melee with a coated target has a −4 circumstance
penalty on attacks, skill checks, and saves.

CONSTRUCTION
Requirements Craft Wondrous Item, *antilife shell*; **Cost** 1,650 gp; **Rarity:**
Rare
Alchemical Formula: Mercury (any), Salt (any), Emotion (x4)

SALVE OF PACIFICATION
Aura moderate enchantment (compulsion) [mind-affecting]; **CL** 3rd
Slot none; **Price** 300 gp; **Weight** —

DESCRIPTION
This salve induces a powerful calm in the user for eight hours. Barbarians
and berserkers find themselves unable to enter rage or battle lust in combat.
To engage in combat requires a successful DC 16 Will save, although if
attacked, the character receives a bonus equal to the damage dealt on this
save. Once made, the character may fight for up to a minute, at which point
the saving throw must be repeated. In addition, stressful situations do not
trigger a lycanthropic change in lycanthropes.

CONSTRUCTION
Requirements Craft Wondrous Item, *calm emotions*; **Cost** 150 gp; **Rarity:**
Uncommon
Alchemical Formula: Salt (any), Stasis

SALVE OF PILFERING
Aura faint transmutation; **CL** 3rd
Slot none; **Price** 300 gp; **Weight** —

DESCRIPTION
This salve increases manual dexterity, allowing an untrained character to
use the skills Disable Device and Sleight of Hand with a +10 competence
bonus. If you are already trained in the skills, the bonus is not as significant,
providing a +5 competence bonus to your skill checks.

CONSTRUCTION
Requirements Craft Wondrous Item, *spell, spell*; **Cost** 150 gp; **Rarity:** Rare
Alchemical Formula: Salt (any), Agility

SALVE OF POWER
Aura faint enchantment (compulsion) [mind-affecting]; **CL** 5th
Slot none; **Price** 750 gp; **Weight** —

DESCRIPTION
Anyone anointed with this salve gains a +6 alchemical bonus to Strength for one minute, but afterword the user is fatigued and they have an additional −10 alchemical penalty for strength for two minutes. After the two minutes, their strength returns to normal, but they remain fatigued.

CONSTRUCTION
Requirements Craft Wondrous Item, *rage*; **Cost** 375 gp; **Rarity:** Rare
Alchemical Formula: Salt (any), Strength

SALVE OF PROTECTION, INSECT
Aura faint abjuration; **CL** 5th
Slot none; **Price** 750 gp; **Weight** —

DESCRIPTION
When covered in this salve, the user is affected as if they have a magical suit of armor against insects. Any insect or bug, such as spiders, scorpions, ants, beetles, centipedes, and flies, cannot touch the user.
Giant-sized creatures can overcome this effect by succeeding at a DC 16 Will saving throw. If successful, the creature can attack, but the user receives a +4 deflection bonus to their armor class and a +4 bonus on all saving throws versus attacks, supernatural abilities, spells, and spell-like effects used by insects. If the Will saving throw fails, the insect is hedged out by the salve and cannot attack. Attacking the insect allows it to automatically succeed at this saving throw.

CONSTRUCTION
Requirements Craft Wondrous Item, *magic circle against evil*; **Cost** 375 gp; **Rarity:** Rare
Alchemical Formula: Salt (any), Emotion

SALVE OF PROTECTION, RUST
Aura faint abjuration; **CL** 5th
Slot none; **Price** 750 gp; **Weight** —

DESCRIPTION
This magical salve protects metal from the effects of natural rust and rust monsters, and liquids and effects that magically destroy, rust, or degrade metal. Spells that affect the metal without damage function normally.

CONSTRUCTION
Requirements Craft Wondrous Item, *protection from energy*; **Cost** 375 gp; **Rarity:** Uncommon
Alchemical Formula: Salt (any), Decay

SALVE OF PROTOPLAST
Aura strong abjuration; **CL** 17th
Slot none; **Price** 7,650 gp; **Weight** —

DESCRIPTION
When this salve is sprinkled over a target, they are forced to return to their natural form. Were-creatures shift into human form, polymorphed or shapechanged creatures return to their natural shape, and beings turned to stone revert to flesh. For the duration of the salve, any natural immunities or resistances (such as a lycanthropes resistance to non-silvered weapons) are removed. Targets receive a DC 24 Will saving throw to avoid the effect if they are unwilling. The potion contains six doses when created. Using it offensively against a target requires a touch attack against the target.

CONSTRUCTION
Requirements Craft Wondrous Item, *mage's disjunction*; **Cost** 3,875 gp; **Rarity:** Rare
Alchemical Formula: Azoth (any), Mercury (any), Salt (any), Body, Stasis, Transmutation

SALVE OF REANIMATION
Aura moderate necromancy; **CL** 9th
Slot none; **Price** 2,250 gp; **Weight** —

DESCRIPTION
This strange and bizarre salve "animates" a dead body. It does not turn the body into a zombie or create any connection between the original spirit and the body. It simply renders a single corpse ambulatory. The corpse must be recently dead, within the last five days. The corpse continues to rot. It can move at half the movement rate it had while alive but takes no other action outside of following the person who anointed the corpse with the salve. It cannot be commanded and can take no other actions. It has the same hit point total and armor class it had while alive. This effect does not prevent the target from being raised at a later time. The target is obviously dead, but a well-preserved corpse in a hat and dark glasses can fool a beach house full of people or an assassin.

CONSTRUCTION
Requirements Craft Wondrous Item, *raise dead*; **Cost** 1,125 gp; **Rarity:** Uncommon
Alchemical Formula: Salt (any), Body

SALVE OF RESISTANCE, ACID
Aura faint abjuration; **CL** 5th
Slot none; **Price** 750 gp; **Weight** —

DESCRIPTION
This salve provides virtual invulnerability to acids. The salve wears off slowly, lasting for a full 24 hours on one Medium-sized creature. It may be spread on more creatures or creatures of a larger size and protect for a proportionally shorter duration.
When the salve is applied, roll 10d10 and add it to 100. This is the total amount of points of acid damage the salve absorbs before becoming useless. This value is divided among the number of targets the salve is used on. Damage is completely absorbed until this limit is reached.

CONSTRUCTION
Requirements Craft Wondrous Item, *protection from energy*; **Cost** 375 gp; **Rarity:** Uncommon
Alchemical Formula: Salt (any), Acid, Protection

SALVE OF RESISTANCE, FIRE
Aura faint abjuration; **CL** 5th
Slot none; **Price** 750 gp; **Weight** —

DESCRIPTION
This salve provides virtual invulnerability to fire. The salve wears off slowly, lasting for a full 24 hours on one Medium-sized creature. It may be spread on more creatures or creatures of a larger size and protect for a proportionally shorter duration.
When the salve is applied, roll 10d10 and add it to 100. This is the total amount of points of fire damage the salve absorbs before becoming useless. This value is divided among the number of targets the salve is used on. Damage is completely absorbed until this limit is reached.

CONSTRUCTION
Requirements Craft Wondrous Item, *protection from energy*; **Cost** 375 gp; **Rarity:** Uncommon
Alchemical Formula: Fire (any), Salt (any), Protection

SALVE OF SCENTLESSNESS

Aura faint transmutation; **CL** 3rd
Slot none; **Price** 300 gp; **Weight** —

DESCRIPTION

This salve neutralizes all scent. Once applied, the user becomes odorless. This eliminates the ability of monsters and animal to track the person. It applies a –10 alchemical penalty to all creatures who attempt to track using scent. When in combat with any monster highly dependent on their sense of smell (such as creatures with the scent special quality), those creatures take a –1 alchemical penalty on attack and damage rolls.

CONSTRUCTION

Requirements Craft Wondrous Item, *pass without trace*; **Cost** 150 gp; **Rarity:** Uncommon
Alchemical Formula: Salt (any), Stealth

SALVE OF SCRIBE

Aura moderate divination; **CL** 11th
Slot none; **Price** 3,300 gp; **Weight** —

DESCRIPTION

This salve has several effects when applied to any surface. Any text is rendered comprehensible as a *comprehend languages* spell, and magic spells are made clear so that spells can be trivially identified. *Arcane marks* are revealed, and *secret pages* and *illusionary scripts* are made clear. One vial covers 200 pages.

CONSTRUCTION

Requirements Craft Wondrous Item, *true seeing*; **Cost** 1,650 gp; **Rarity:** Rare
Alchemical Formula: Azoth (any), Salt (any), Mind

SALVE OF SCRYING

Aura moderate divination; **CL** 13th
Slot none; **Price** 4,550 gp; **Weight** —

DESCRIPTION

This salve acts as a *crystal ball* when poured into standing water, like that which collects in a basin. For the duration of the salve, anyone may use the reflecting surface as a basic *crystal ball*. Some GMs may allow additional material components and essences to be used in the crafting of the item to allow the character to simulate a more advanced *crystal ball*. The connection is lost if the water is disturbed, and the water must be calm before trying again.

CONSTRUCTION

Requirements Craft Wondrous Item, *true seeing*; **Cost** 2,275 gp; **Rarity:** Rare
Alchemical Formula: Azoth (any), Air (any), Salt (any), Sulfur (any), Mind, Perception (x2 from different sources)

SALVE OF SHADOWS

Aura faint illusion [darkness]; **CL** 3rd
Slot none; **Price** 300 gp; **Weight** —

DESCRIPTION

When this salve is used, it coats the user like a shadow, absorbing light. This grants a +10 bonus on Stealth checks.

CONSTRUCTION

Requirements Craft Wondrous Item, *darkness*; **Cost** 150 gp; **Rarity:** Rare
Alchemical Formula: Salt (any), Stealth

SALVE OF SHARPNESS

Aura moderate transmutation; **CL** 5th
Slot none; **Price** 750 gp (+1), 1,500 gp (+2), 2,250 gp (+3), 3,000 gp (+4), 3,750 gp (+5), 4,500 gp (+6); **Weight** —

DESCRIPTION

This salve appears to be the sort that is used to clean and care for weapons. When applied to the blade of any sharp or edged weapon, this salve causes the weapon to be treated as a magical weapon for 3d4 + 1 rounds. The bonus that the weapon provides is determined randomly when found. The materials and gold values are for creating +1 magical weapons. Multiply these amounts to determine the price of more powerful salves. A *salve of sharpness +2* is worth 1,500 gp.

A found flask of *salve of sharpness* has 1d4 + 1 applications. Use **Table 4–22** below to determine the strength of the oil:

TABLE 4–22: SALVE OF SHARPNESS STRENGTH TABLE

1d20	Bonus	Character Level	Cost
1–2	+1	5th	750
3–5	+2	9th	1,500
6–11	+3	13th	2,250
12–16	+4	17th	3,000
17–19	+5	20th	3,750
20	+6	24th	4,500

CONSTRUCTION

Requirements Craft Wondrous Item, *magic weapon, greater*; **Cost** 375 gp (+1), 750 gp (+2), 1,125 gp (+3), 1,500 gp (+4), 1,875 gp (+5), 2,250 gp (+6); **Rarity:** Very Rare
Alchemical Formula: Salt (any), Prowess

SALVE OF STASIS

Aura strong transmutation; **CL** 15th
Slot none; **Price** 6,000 gp; **Weight** —

DESCRIPTION

There is enough of this salve to coat one small object. An object coated by this salve is removed from the effects of time and space. It is unaffected by any force or energy short of a *disintegrate* spell. The effect can be dispelled as any magical ward, but the object itself is immune to harm. The coated object exudes a dim rose glow and can be moved, but it cannot be touched or manipulated (for example, a chest could not be opened, a potion could not be drunk, or a book cannot be read).

The salve does not work on living creatures; however, a living creature in a container would be affected by the temporal stasis.

CONSTRUCTION

Requirements Craft Wondrous Item, *temporal stasis*; **Cost** 3,000 gp; **Rarity:** Rare
Alchemical Formula: Azoth (any), Salt (any), Planar, Stasis

SALVE OF STEEL

Aura faint transmutation; **CL** 11th
Slot none; **Price** 3,300 gp; **Weight** —

DESCRIPTION

When this salve is used to coat a Medium-sized object, it changes the properties of the object to steel. The object visually and tactually remains unchanged (ropes remain flexible and glass remains clear), but it is treated as steel for all in-game mechanical purposes such as hardness, breakage, hit points, and resistance to elements. Weight, coloration, texture, and all other object properties are unchanged. It is effective only against objects and must set for a minute before it takes effect. It cannot be applied to creatures, even plant ones. There are five doses when crafted and 1d4 + 1 when found.

CONSTRUCTION

Requirements Craft Wondrous Item, *ironwood*; **Cost** 1,650 gp; **Rarity:** Very Rare
Alchemical Formula: Iron, Earth (any), Salt (any), Body, Strength, Transmutation

SALVE OF STONEWALKING

Aura moderate transmutation; **CL** 9th
Slot none; **Price** 2,250 gp; **Weight** —

DESCRIPTION

This thick salve allows items and characters to pass through stone. An object coated in this salve can be lightly pushed through solid rock as if into pudding. The duration of this salve on objects is permanent and lasts until the salve is washed off. The objects stay where they are placed and may be retrieved by reaching into the stone to retrieve them.

When applied to living creatures, the effect lasts for 3d6 minutes and grants them the ability to swim through solid rock and stone at half their movement speed. This is treated as burrowing but without disturbing the surrounding materials. Your senses are enhanced in no applicable way, so you move blindly through the rock. If you are within solid rock when the duration expires, you are slain instantly on a failed DC 22 Fortitude save. A successful save shunts you 20 feet toward open space and does 8d6 damage. If the 20 feet isn't far enough to move you to open space, the saving throw is made again with identical effect until you are expelled to the surface.

CONSTRUCTION

Requirements Craft Wondrous Item, *passwall*; **Cost** 1,125 gp; **Rarity:** Very Rare
Alchemical Formula: Iron, Earth (any), Salt (any), Agility, Body, Planar, Transmutation

SALVE OF THE GREEN

Aura faint conjuration; **CL** 11th
Slot none; **Price** 3,300 gp; **Weight** —

DESCRIPTION

This thick green oil allows anyone anointed with it to pass through any vegetation, no matter how dense, at full speed while leaving no trace. It also allows the user to enter any plant as *transport via plants* and exit from another tree within 100 feet.

CONSTRUCTION

Requirements Craft Wondrous Item, *transport via plants*; **Cost** 1,650 gp; **Rarity:** Rare
Alchemical Formula: Earth (any), Salt (any), Planar, Plant

SALVE OF THE MARIONETTE

Aura moderate transmutation; **CL** 9th
Slot none; **Price** 2,250 gp; **Weight** —

DESCRIPTION

When this salve is sprinkled on any Medium-sized or smaller object, it gives the user the ability to telekinetically control the object with their hand. It gives the user full control over the item, which is treated as an appropriate-sized animated object. It takes a move action to command the object.

CONSTRUCTION

Requirements Craft Wondrous Item, *telekinesis*; **Cost** 1,125 gp; **Rarity:** Rare
Alchemical Formula: Earth (any), Salt (any), Telesthetic

SALVE OF THE THRESHOLD

Aura moderate necromancy; **CL** 9th
Slot none; **Price** 2,250 gp; **Weight** —

DESCRIPTION

When this oil is carefully applied to a threshold, it damages anyone who attempts to cross. It takes a full minute to apply. Victims must make a DC 16 Will save when they cross the threshold or enter the square where the salve is applied or they take 3d6 damage. A successful save does no damage. You can be affected only once by the salve. The salve retains its potency for one week. It is treated as a magical trap with a DC 22 Perception check to discover it.

CONSTRUCTION

Requirements Craft Wondrous Item, *symbol of pain*; **Cost** 1,125 gp; **Rarity:** Rare
Alchemical Formula: Agate, Rare Earth, Earth, Salt (any), Pain

SALVE OF TIMELESSNESS

Aura strong transmutation; **CL** 15th
Slot none; **Price** 6,000 gp; **Weight** —

DESCRIPTION

This salve causes material — particularly organic material, but also stone and metal — to resist the passage of time. Each object is affected as if the passage of a year were only a period of 24 hours and they receive an untyped bonus of +2 on all saving throws the item must make.

Enough salve is contained in each flask to coat eight Medium-sized objects or a 20-square-foot area. Under normal circumstances, this oil never wears off, though it can be removed. It is edible and tasteless, allowing the storage of food or items for very long-term situations. It does not affect living or animate creatures besides keeping them looking fresh.

CONSTRUCTION

Requirements Craft Wondrous Item, *temporal stasis*; **Cost** 3,000 gp; **Rarity:** Uncommon
Alchemical Formula: Salt (any), Decay, Stasis

SALVE OF TRANSCENDENT FILTH

Aura moderate transmutation; **CL** 11th
Slot none; **Price** 3,300 gp; **Weight** —

DESCRIPTION

When poured on the ground, this salve creates a pile of pure filth. This dirt is so disgusting that anyone who even so much as looks at it becomes covered in dirt and filth.

A DC 20 Will save is required to avoid the effects if not averting their eyes. If this save is failed, they become covered in filth. They must immediately make a DC 18 Fortitude save or become nauseated. They have a −2 alchemical penalty to hit and damage regardless of the result of the saving throw. People react to the target as if their Charisma score were 10 lower than it actually is. This affects everyone who can see the filth, which decays at the end of a minute.

CONSTRUCTION

Requirements Craft Wondrous Item, *move earth*; **Cost** 1,650 gp; **Rarity:** Very Rare
Alchemical Formula: Salt (any), Body, Decay, Disease, Plant

SALVE OF TRANSPARENCY
Aura faint transmutation; **CL** 5th
Slot none; **Price** 750 gp; **Weight** —

DESCRIPTION
When applied to a surface, this salve renders a material transparent like
glass. If polished, the substance can be made almost invisible, making
it more difficult to find, but the primary purpose of this salve is to turn
objects transparent temporarily. Much like rubbing a greasy object on paper,
this transparency takes a minute to take effect and lasts for the standard
duration of the salve. It works on surfaces up to 10 feet thick, turning them
transparent.
The transparency is two-way but does nothing to the structural integrity of
the material.

CONSTRUCTION
Requirements Craft Wondrous Item, *clairvoyance*; **Cost** 375 gp; **Rarity:**
Very Rare
Alchemical Formula: Air (any), Salt (any), Body, Transmutation

SALVE OF TURNING
Aura faint abjuration; **CL** 3rd
Slot none; **Price** 300 gp; **Weight** —

DESCRIPTION
When this salve is applied to a holy symbol, it increases the priest's ability
to channel energy against the undead (or whatever creature type the cleric
channels energy against). It provides a +2 divine bonus to the Will saving
throw DC.

CONSTRUCTION
Requirements Craft Wondrous Item, *disrupt undead*, *divine favor*; **Cost** 150
gp; **Rarity:** Rare
Alchemical Formula: Salt (any), Purity

SALVE OF WARDING
Aura faint abjuration; **CL** 5th
Slot none; **Price** 750 gp; **Weight** —

DESCRIPTION
This thaumaturgic salve provides protection against all dangers and risks. For
24 hours, any creature that has this paste applied gains a +2 alchemical bonus
on all their saving throws.

CONSTRUCTION
Requirements Craft Wondrous Item, *magic circle against evil*; **Cost** 375 gp;
Rarity: Rare
Alchemical Formula: Salt (any), Body, Protection

OTHER

Various other wondrous items fall outside the strictures above but have proven themselves useful for alchemy. These are listed below.

TABLE 4–23: WONDROUS ITEMS

Name	Price
Alchemical Jug	12,000 gp
Alchemical Mine	2,500 gp
Alchemical Retort	50,000 gp
Automated Alchemist	50,000 gp
Beaker of Plentiful Potions	12,500 gp
Bedroll of Rest	1,500 gp
Bottle, Brazen	45,000 gp
Bottle of Heckling	1,800 gp
Bottle of Holding	20,000 gp
Bottle of Pleasing Odors	350 gp
Bottle of Preservation	500 gp
Bottle, Reinforced	2,000 gp
Box, Cooling	4,000 gp
Box, Heating	6,000 gp
Caltrops, Walking	250 gp
Carafe of Steeds	16,000 gp
Case of Freshness	1,000 gp
Cauldron of Potions	5,000 gp
Censer of Incense Burning	3,000 gp
Cloak, Aegis	12,000 gp
Cloak of Eyestalks	38,000 gp
Cloak of Light	1,500 gp
Cloak of Rigidity	10,000 gp
Cloak of Wilderness Comfort	1,400 gp
Copper Flask	1,000 gp
Crown of Ails	13,000 gp
Fabric, Air	2,000 gp
Fabric, Chameleon	2,500 gp
Globe, Banishment	3,000 gp
Globe, Cosmetic	2,000 gp
Globe of Ooze, Slimes, and Jellies	5,000 gp
Globe, War Shroud	7,500 gp
Gloves, Energy Bolt	20,000 gp
Goblet of Purity	8,000 gp
Ink, Toxic	1,000 gp
Liquid Iron	10,000 gp
Liquid Road	1,000 gp
Medusa Wig	11,000 gp
Monster Teeth	2,000+ gp
Mortar and Pestle of Force	6,000 gp
Portable Valise of Frugality	30,000 gp
Rope, Endless	1,400 gp
Rope, Extension	500 gp
Rope of Iron	1,200 gp
Shroud of Smoke	12,000 gp
Skeleton Key	1,800 gp
Split-Second Sphere	9,000 gp
Waterskin, Endless	1,000 gp

ALCHEMICAL JUG

Aura strong transmutation; **CL** 13th
Slot none; **Price** 12,000 gp; **Weight** 3 lbs.

DESCRIPTION

This alchemical device is extremely useful for the working alchemist, as it produces liquid upon command. How much of the liquid is produced depends on what liquid is being produced. The jug has the ability to produce only one liquid each day. The liquid selected can be poured from the jug up to seven times.

TABLE 4–24: PRODUCTION OF ALCHEMICAL JUG

Name	Volume
Alcohol	1 gill (4 oz.)
Ale/Beer	4 Gallons
Ammonia	1 Quart
Aqua Regia	2 gills (8 oz.)
Chlorine	8 Drams (1 oz.)
Cyanide	4 Drams (1/2 oz.)
Oil	1 Pint
Vinegar	2 Gallons
Water, Fresh	8 Gallons
Water, Salt	16 Gallons
Wine	1 Gallon

CONSTRUCTION

Requirements Craft Wondrous Item, *limited wish*; **Cost** 6,000 gp; **Rarity:** Rare
Alchemical Formula: Not applicable

ALCHEMICAL MINE

Aura faint evocation; **CL** 3rd
Slot none; **Price** 2,500 gp; **Weight** 1 lb.

DESCRIPTION

This causes the selected grenade to be converted into a mine. When "set" by the user, the mine turns invisible and is triggered by the next creature to walk within 10 feet of it. The purchase price does not include the price of the grenade that is converted. An alchemist can use a bomb in place of the grenade to convert to an alchemical mine.

CONSTRUCTION

Requirements Craft Wondrous Item, *invisibility*; **Cost** 1,250 gp + the cost of the grenade; **Rarity:** Very Rare
Alchemical Formula: Not applicable

ALCHEMICAL RETORT

Aura overwhelming transmutation; **CL** 17th
Slot none; **Price** 50,000 gp; **Weight** 3 lbs.

DESCRIPTION

When added to an alchemist's lab, this magical retort cuts the crafting time of any crafted or enchanted alchemical item by one half. The final calculated time is divided by two, and that is the length of time it takes to craft the item.

CONSTRUCTION

Requirements Craft Wondrous Item, *wish*; **Cost** 25,000 gp; **Rarity:** Very Rare
Alchemical Formula: Not applicable

AUTOMATED ALCHEMIST

Aura strong conjuration; **CL** 13th
Slot none; **Price** 50,000 gp; **Weight** 1 lb.

DESCRIPTION

There are three gems on the vial, which produces a magical liquid (potion, philter, or elixir) once per day. The order in which the three buttons are pushed determines which potion is created. Once the gems are depressed three times, the vial fills with a potion and deactivates for 24 hours. If the liquid is poured out of the vial, it becomes nonmagical water. The potion produced is randomly selected, but once a specific combination of gems produces a potion, it always produces that potion. When created, there is no way to control or select which potions the device can create. This produces 27 different kinds of magical liquids.

CONSTRUCTION

Requirements Craft Wondrous Item, *limited wish*; **Cost** 25,000 gp; **Rarity:** Very Rare
Alchemical Formula: Not applicable

BEAKER OF PLENTIFUL POTIONS

Aura strong conjuration; **CL** 13th
Slot none; **Price** 12,500 gp; **Weight** 1 lb.

DESCRIPTION

This wondrous magical beaker of alchemy creates random potions! Roll 1d4 + 1 random elixirs or salves. These are the number of potions the beaker holds — cursed potions are certainly possible. The potions rolled are layered, in order, within the beaker. Potions are produced with varying frequency. The frequency of potion production is determined by the number of potions within the beaker. Four or five different potions produce two doses of each potion, once per week. Three potions produce three doses of each potion, twice per week. Two potions produce four doses of each potion three times per week.

The doses must be consumed or poured out in order. For example, if *potion of invisibility* and *elixir of fire breath* are rolled, four doses of *invisibility* must be consumed before getting access to *fire breath*. Beakers have a full complement of five potions when created and lose the ability to generate one random potion per month until they are generating only two different potions.

CONSTRUCTION

Requirements Craft Wondrous Item, *limited wish*; **Cost** 6,250 gp; **Rarity:** Very Rare
Alchemical Formula: Not applicable

BEDROLL OF REST

Aura moderate abjuration; **CL** 3rd
Slot none; **Price** 1,500 gp; **Weight** 5 lbs.

DESCRIPTION

This alchemically enchanted bedroll provides warm comfort. The person sleeping on this is always at a comfortable temperature, never too warm or too cold. It also protects the sleeper from insects, rain, snow, and other minor disturbances. The person wakes alert and refreshed after six hours of rest if they wish, although this does not shorten the rest needed to cast spells. This does not protect against temperatures lower than −40⁰ Fahrenheit or higher than 113⁰ Fahrenheit.

CONSTRUCTION

Requirements Craft Wondrous Item, *sleep*; **Cost** 750 gp; **Rarity:** Rare
Alchemical Formula: Not applicable

BOTTLE, BRAZEN

Aura faint enchantment; **CL** 15th
Slot none; **Price** 45,000 gp; **Weight** 1 lb.

DESCRIPTION

This appears to be a highly burnished bottle. The bottle is corked, and both the cork and the bottle are covered with arcane warding runes.

When opened, this bottle can be used to trap extraplanar creatures in the bottle. If one target is affected, they must make a DC 24 Will save to resist. For two creatures to be affected, their save is a DC 21 Will save. If more than two creatures are affected, it is a DC 16 Will save. It affects all extra-dimensional creatures in a 30-foot radius of the bottle. If they stay within that radius, those creatures must save every round to avoid getting sucked into the bottle.

Creatures trapped in the bottle are released when the bottle is next opened. They are certain to be in a foul mood. If trapped in the bottle for a millennium or more, they may be so thankful for being released that they may offer to provide service.

CONSTRUCTION

Requirements Craft Wondrous Item, *binding*; **Cost** 22,500 gp; **Rarity:** Uncommon
Alchemical Formula: Not applicable

BOTTLE OF HECKLING

Aura faint illusion; **CL** 5th
Slot none; **Price** 1,800 gp; **Weight** 1 lb.

DESCRIPTION

This bottle contains a marbled crimson liquid. When uncapped for a round, the bottle unleashes a chorus of boos, hisses, and insults. Everyone within 60 feet must make DC 16 Will save. Those who fail receive a −2 morale penalty to attack and damage rolls for six minutes. Each time this item is used, there is less liquid contained in the bottle. After three uses, the bottle is empty.

CONSTRUCTION

Requirements Craft Wondrous Item, *heroism*; **Cost** 900 gp; **Rarity:** Rare
Alchemical Formula: Not applicable

BOTTLE OF HOLDING

Aura moderate conjuration; **CL** 9th
Slot none; **Price** 20,000 gp; **Weight** 1 lb.

DESCRIPTION

This useful bottle can hold and organize a vast amount of liquid. It can contain up to 30 units of fluid. A unit is a gallon of normal nonmagical liquid (oil, water, ink) or one dose of a magical or alchemical liquid. The bottle maintains separation between all it contains, and a simple verbal command is required to access the appropriate fluid. The bottle always appears empty. The liquid must be poured out to be used; one cannot drink from the jug as it were. If broken, all the contained liquids vanish. The bottle is made of crystal.

CONSTRUCTION

Requirements Craft Wondrous Item, *secret chest*; **Cost** 10,000 gp; **Rarity:** Uncommon
Alchemical Formula: Not applicable

BOTTLE OF PLEASING ODORS

Aura faint illusion; **CL** 3rd
Slot none; **Price** 350 gp; **Weight** 1 lb.

DESCRIPTION

When uncorked, this bottle produces a pleasing smell as it removes offensive odors from the air.

CONSTRUCTION

Requirements Craft Wondrous Item, *purify food and drink*; **Cost** 175 gp; **Rarity:** Uncommon
Alchemical Formula: Not applicable

BOTTLE OF PRESERVATION

Aura moderate abjuration; **CL** 15th
Slot none; **Price** 500 gp; **Weight** 1 lb.

DESCRIPTION

These bottles appear to be normal and indistinguishable from other bottles. However, when non-living substances are placed within the bottle, their contents are preserved. Things placed within the bottles do not spoil or rot.

CONSTRUCTION

Requirements Craft Wondrous Item, *temporal stasis*; **Cost** 250 gp; **Rarity:** Uncommon
Alchemical Formula: Not applicable

BOTTLE, REINFORCED

Aura strong abjuration; **CL** 9th
Slot none; **Price** 2,000 gp; **Weight** 1 lb.

DESCRIPTION

These bottles are virtually indestructible, gaining +10 hardness, +10 hit points, and +4 to their break DC.

CONSTRUCTION

Requirements Craft Wondrous Item, *fabricate*; **Cost** 1,000 gp; **Rarity:** Rare
Alchemical Formula: Not applicable

BOX, COOLING

Aura faint transmutation; **CL** 7th
Slot none; **Price** 4,000 gp; **Weight** 150 lbs.

DESCRIPTION

This nondescript steel box can cool a medium-sized room to 59⁰ Fahrenheit. It can also cool any object placed inside to a temperature of −40⁰ Fahrenheit. This box provides a +1 circumstance bonus to alchemical checks if installed in an alchemical lab. The interior temperature is adjustable.

CONSTRUCTION

Requirements Craft Wondrous Item, *ice storm*; **Cost** 2,000 gp; **Rarity:** Uncommon
Alchemical Formula: Not applicable

BOX, HEATING

Aura faint evocation; **CL** 5th
Slot none; **Price** 6,000 gp; **Weight** 150 lbs.

DESCRIPTION

This nondescript steel box has the capacity to heat a medium-sized room to 95⁰ Fahrenheit or to heat an object inside the box to a temperature up to 464⁰ Fahrenheit. This box provides a +1 circumstance bonus to alchemical checks if installed in an alchemical lab. The interior temperature is adjustable.

CONSTRUCTION

Requirements Craft Wondrous Item, *fireball*; **Cost** 3,000 gp; **Rarity:** Uncommon
Alchemical Formula: Not applicable

CALTROPS, WALKING

Aura faint transmutation; **CL** 11th
Slot none; **Price** 250 gp; **Weight** 2 lbs.

DESCRIPTION

These work exactly like normal caltrops, except every round they move toward the nearest living creature. As soon as they enter an area with a target, that target must save as well as anyone who enters that area this round. They act this way for one minute. After use, they may be collected and reused. They may be used only once per day.

CONSTRUCTION

Requirements Craft Wondrous Item, *animate object*; **Cost** 125 gp; **Rarity:** Uncommon
Alchemical Formula: Not applicable

CARAFE OF STEEDS

Aura strong conjuration; **CL** 13th
Slot none; **Price** 16,000 gp; **Weight** 1 lb.

DESCRIPTION

This marvelous device contains a violent roiling liquid. When poured on the ground, this contains enough liquid to produce 1d8 mounts. Roll on **Table 4–25** below to determine the type of chimerical beasts summoned:

TABLE 4–25: CARAFE OF STEEDS RANDOM MOUNTS

1d20	Mount
1–2	Riding Dog
3	Trained Axebeak
4	Riding Ape
5	Giant Ant
6	Crocodile
7	Pony
8–12	Light Riding Horse
13–14	Heavy Riding Horse
15–16	Warhorse
17	Bear
18	Rhinoceros Beetle
19	Mammoth
20	Griffon

Note that the creature is nonaggressive and may not be commanded to attack. However, the creatures defend themselves if attacked. The energy in the carafe is unstable, and the type of mount must be checked every time they are poured out. These mounts last for eight hours before they must return to the carafe. They are colorless constructs, not real animals. These mounts dissipate if they are more than 300 feet from the carafe. When crafted, there is enough liquid for eight mounts. When the mounts die or are too distant from the carafe, the number of mounts the carafe can produce is reduced permanently.

CONSTRUCTION

Requirements Craft Wondrous Item, *mount, greater polymorph*; **Cost** 8,000 gp; **Rarity:** Rare
Alchemical Formula: Not applicable

CASE OF FRESHNESS

Aura faint abjuration; **CL** 3rd
Slot none; **Price** 1,000 gp; **Weight** 5 lbs.

DESCRIPTION

This marvelous case is useful in alchemical labs and kitchens. If stored in this case overnight with one dram of sugar, salt, and 10 carats of pearl, any herb, plant, fruit, or vegetable is restored to freshness. This reduces an alchemist's monthly upkeep costs by 10%.

CONSTRUCTION

Requirements Craft Wondrous Item, *purify food and water*; **Cost** 500 gp; **Rarity:** Uncommon
Alchemical Formula: Not applicable

CAULDRON OF POTIONS
Aura strong conjuration; **CL** 17th
Slot none; **Price** 5,000 gp; **Weight** 35 lbs.

DESCRIPTION
This marvelous cauldron produces a single dose of any magical or nonmagical liquid per day. The user simply thinks of the liquid he or she desires, and the cauldron produces it. There is a 10% chance that any potion produced is cursed, though there is no way to tell ahead of time if this occurred. Not enough of the material or potion is produced to allow an alchemist to learn how to produce a potion from the sample. The potion provided lasts until used or until the cauldron produces another potion.

CONSTRUCTION
Requirements Craft Wondrous Item, *wish*; **Cost** 2,500 gp; **Rarity:** Very Rare
Alchemical Formula: Not applicable

CENSER OF INCENSE OF BURNING
Aura moderate transmutation; **CL** 5th
Slot none; **Price** 3,000 gp; **Weight** 3 lbs.

DESCRIPTION
When incense is burnt in this portable censer, it adds an additional 10 feet to the radius of the incense. In order for this power to function, the censer must be wielded.

CONSTRUCTION
Requirements Craft Wondrous Item, *gust of wind*; **Cost** 1,500 gp; **Rarity:** Uncommon
Alchemical Formula: Not applicable

CLOAK, AEGIS
Aura moderate abjuration; **CL** 5th
Slot shoulders; **Price** 12,000 gp; **Weight** 3 lbs.

DESCRIPTION
This rare cloak is designed to protect the alchemist while also being a useful weapon.
When worn, any attack that misses may be entangled. The wearer rolls a d20. If the number on the die is higher than the attacker's adjusted attack roll, the weapon is hopelessly entangled in the cloak for 1d4 + 1 rounds. It may be freed only with a successful DC 21 Strength check. If the cloak is removed and the user spends a round rolling it up, it becomes a cudgel. It strikes as a +1 weapon and does 1d4 + 1 points of damage. It can parry attacks, as entanglement above, but for any attack, not just those that miss. If the unmodified d20 roll is higher than the attacker's modified to-hit roll, the attack is parried. The cloak is destroyed if it parries a magical weapon six times.

CONSTRUCTION
Requirements Craft Wondrous Item, *entropic shield*, *mage armor*; **Cost** 6,000 gp; **Rarity:** Rare
Alchemical Formula: Not applicable

CLOAK OF EYESTALKS
Aura strong evocation; **CL** 13th
Slot shoulders; **Price** 38,000 gp; **Weight** 3 lbs.

DESCRIPTION
Eyestalks sprout from plates attached at various places on this cloak. These eyestalks grant the wearer all-around vision. They cannot be flanked or attacked from the rear. They also receive a penalty of –4 versus any gaze attacks or attacks that can cause blindness or that impair the eyesight. Also, the user reacts to all other people as if their charisma were 4 points higher and receives a +2 enhancement bonus to non-vision affecting saving throws. Once per minute, the user can activate the second power of the cloak. The user draws the cloak around them, and a power, determined randomly from the following list, is activated, affecting everyone within 30 feet, friend or foe.

TABLE 4–26: CLOAK OF EYESTALKS EFFECTS

1d8	Power
1	*Dominate monster*
2	*Sleep*
3	*Flesh to stone*
4	*Disintegrate*
5	*Slow*
6	*Fear*
7	*Inflict serious wounds*
8	*Death ray*

A successful DC 18 Reflex saving throw will negate the effects. Note that the effect must be selected randomly.

CONSTRUCTION

Requirements Craft Wondrous Item, *cause fear, clairvoyance, disintegrate, dominate monster, inflict serious wounds, limited wish, power word kill, sleep, slow*; **Cost** 19,000 gp; **Rarity:** Very Rare
Alchemical Formula: Not applicable

CLOAK OF LIGHT

Aura faint evocation; **CL** 3rd
Slot shoulders; **Price** 1,500 gp; **Weight** 3 lbs.

DESCRIPTION

This cloak is a dark color on the outside, but the inner lining glows. When commanded, the cloak flares out, shedding light as a torch in a hemisphere. Anyone aiming missile attacks at the wearer from the front receives a −1 penalty to hit.

CONSTRUCTION

Requirements Craft Wondrous Item, *continual flame*; **Cost** 750 gp; **Rarity:** Rare
Alchemical Formula: Not applicable

CLOAK OF RIGIDITY

Aura moderate abjuration; **CL** 3rd
Slot shoulders; **Price** 10,000 gp; **Weight** 3 lbs.

DESCRIPTION

This cloak hardens when struck by any melee attack, preventing up to 2 points of physical damage per attack. It grants DR / 2 to the wearer. It also provides total protection from nonmagical missiles. However, it does this by means of a flexible metal mesh. This mesh acts as an attractant for electricity. This negates any opportunity for a saving throw versus electrical damage and causes the wearer to take maximum damage from electrical attacks.

CONSTRUCTION

Requirements Craft Wondrous Item, *protection from arrows*; **Cost** 5,000 gp; **Rarity:** Very Rare
Alchemical Formula: Not applicable

CLOAK, WILDERNESS COMFORT

Aura moderate abjuration; **CL** 11th
Slot shoulders; **Price** 1,400 gp; **Weight** 3 lbs.

DESCRIPTION

This marvelous cloak has several special features to help people who wander through the wilderness. It produces rations that are enough to feed a single adult male three times a day. It also produces two gallons of clear cool water or hot spiced tea. It protects the wearer from inclement weather and temperatures down to −40° Fahrenheit. At night, it can be used as a one-person tent and bedroll.

CONSTRUCTION

Requirements Craft Wondrous Item, *hallow*; **Cost** 700 gp; **Rarity:** Rare
Alchemical Formula: Not applicable

COPPER FLASK

Aura faint conjuration; **CL** 3rd
Slot none; **Price** 1,000 gp; **Weight** 1 lb.

DESCRIPTION

This flask produces 10 gallons of green-tinged, foul-smelling water. It is otherwise untainted and safe to drink.

CONSTRUCTION

Requirements Craft Wondrous Item, *create water*; **Cost** 500 gp; **Rarity:** Rare
Alchemical Formula: Not applicable

CROWN OF AILS

Aura moderate necromancy; **CL** 7th
Slot head; **Price** 13,000 gp; **Weight** 3 lbs.

DESCRIPTION

This crown is decorated with nine cabochon gemstones. This crown allows the wearer to touch any nearby creature to discover any ailments that affect the creature touched. The crown has a second and more deadly purpose that occurs if the wearer removes any of the stones. Do so infects the wearer with a horrible plague or disease. The wearer will not die of this disease as long as he or she possesses the gemstone. If the stone is replaced in the crown, the possessor of the crown becomes highly contagious, becoming 75% likely to infect anyone within a 10-foot radius with the disease.

CONSTRUCTION

Requirements Craft Wondrous Item, *contagion*; **Cost** 6,500 gp; **Rarity:** Very Rare
Alchemical Formula: Not applicable

FABRIC, AIR

Aura faint abjuration; **CL** 3rd
Slot none; **Price** 2,000 gp; **Weight** 5 lbs.

DESCRIPTION

This fabric weighs nothing and can be used to construct armor that has no Armor Check penalty and has a −15% spell failure chance. This material is literally without weight. It hangs where it is placed. If wearing a suit of this armor, it reduces falling damage by 1 point per die with no minimum.
The price listed is for one 40-yard bolt of air fabric. One bolt is needed for light armor, two bolts for medium armor, and four bolts for heavy armor. Only armors traditionally made of cloth or leather can be made out of this fabric.

CONSTRUCTION

Requirements Craft Wondrous Item, *feather fall*; **Cost** 1,000 gp; **Rarity:** Very Rare
Alchemical Formula: Rare Earth, Air (any) (x3), Mercury (any), Transmutation

FABRIC, CHAMELEON

Aura faint illusion; **CL** 3rd
Slot none; **Price** 2,500 gp; **Weight** 10 lbs.

DESCRIPTION

This fabric blends in with the background. A cloak made of this material provides a +2 circumstance bonus to Stealth. A full suit of clothing (including the cloak) provides a +5 circumstance bonus to Stealth.
The price listed is for one 40-yard bolt of chameleon fabric.

CONSTRUCTION

Requirements Craft Wondrous Item, *invisibility*; **Cost** 1,250 gp; **Rarity:** Rare
Alchemical Formula: Rare Earth, Air (any), Mercury (any), Plant, Transmutation

GLOBE, BANISHMENT

Aura strong abjuration; **CL** 13th
Slot none; **Price** 3,000 gp; **Weight** 1 lb.

DESCRIPTION

When this globe is thrown at an extra-dimensional creature, it banishes them to their home dimension as the wizard spell *banishment*.

CONSTRUCTION

Requirements Craft Wondrous Item, *banishment*; **Cost** 1,500 gp; **Rarity:** Very Rare
Alchemical Formula: Not applicable

GLOBE, COSMETIC

Aura faint illusion; **CL** 3rd
Slot none; **Price** 2,000 gp; **Weight** 1 lb.

DESCRIPTION

This globe is placed in a small bowl of water, which quickly dissolves. The water becomes brightly colored. Anyone placing their hands, feet, or face within the bowl is subject to whatever cosmetic procedure they wish, e.g. haircut/color, manicure, makeup, exfoliating scrub, etc.

CONSTRUCTION

Requirements Craft Wondrous Item, *eagle's splendor*; **Cost** 1,000 gp; **Rarity:** Uncommon
Alchemical Formula: Not applicable

GLOBE OF OOZE, SLIMES, AND JELLIES

Aura strong conjuration; **CL** 13th
Slot none; **Price** 5,000 gp; **Weight** 1 lb.

DESCRIPTION

When you throw this globe against a hard surface, an ooze, slime, or jelly bursts out, affecting everyone with five feet as if they had suffered an attack from the creature. It then becomes a fully grown, uncontrolled ooze, slime, or jelly of its type. If the user falls or is subject to sonic damage while carrying these, the orb has 1 hardness, 3 hit points, and a break DC 5. The contents will be released affecting the carrier if the globe is broken. The type of ooze slime or jelly contained within is determined at the time of crafting and can be any creature with the Ooze subtype that is CR 5 or less.

CONSTRUCTION

Requirements Craft Wondrous Item, *limited wish*; **Cost** 2,500 gp; **Rarity:** Rare
Alchemical Formula: Azoth (any), Earth (any), Water (any), Body, Transmutation, any 2 essences from the type of ooze to be contained in the globe

GLOBE, WAR SHROUD

Aura moderate evocation; **CL** 9th
Slot none; **Price** 7,500 gp; **Weight** 1 lb.

DESCRIPTION

This cloak can rapidly fill a 40-foot radius with thick, clinging, opaque purple smoke. This smoke blocks all vision, obscuring everything. It provides total concealment to *true seeing*, low-light vision, and darkvision. The cloud follows anyone exposed to it, clinging around them in a 10-foot radius. Everyone within the smoke must make a DC 16 Will save. If they fail this save, they are affected as if by the magic-user spell *slow*.

CONSTRUCTION

Requirements Craft Wondrous Item, *cloudkill*, *slow*; **Cost** 3,750 gp; **Rarity:** Very Rare
Alchemical Formula: Air (any), Water (any), Stealth

GLOVES, ENERGY BOLT

Aura moderate evocation; **CL** 5th
Slot gloves; **Price** 20,000 gp; **Weight** 1 lb.

DESCRIPTION

These gloves allow the wearer to fling a bolt of energy for 8d6 points of damage at a single target. On a successful DC 16 Reflex save, the target takes half damage. These gloves are activated once per round as a standard action. Nothing may be held in either hand, as both hands are necessary to fling the bolt. They may be activated once every three rounds to a maximum of three times a day.

Each type of bolt requires different materials. Materials and effects are listed below:

TABLE 4–27: ENERGY BOLT GLOVE REQUIREMENTS

Type	Vital Essence	Gemstone	Effect
Fire	Fire (any) (x15)	Powdered Ruby	Set objects aflame
Acid	Acid (x10)	Powdered Turquoise	Damage Objects on a failed save
Ice	Cold (x10)	Powdered Moonstone	Makes items save at −2 (Reduce Break DC by 2)
Electricity	Electricity (x10)	Powdered Sapphire	Stuns target for one round on a failed save
Sonic	Pain (x10)	Powdered Agate	Target deafened for 1d4 rounds on a failed save.

CONSTRUCTION

Requirements Craft Wondrous Item, a spell with the element descriptor of the appropriate type over 3rd level; **Cost** 9,000 gp + gemstones and essences; **Rarity:** Rare
Alchemical Formula: Each type of glove requires a gemstone and a vital essence; see **Table 4–27**.

GOBLET OF PURITY

Aura moderate abjuration; **CL** 5th
Slot none; **Price** 8,000 gp; **Weight** 1 lb.

DESCRIPTION

This goblet neutralizes any poisons or venoms contained within it.

CONSTRUCTION

Requirements Craft Wondrous Item, *neutralize poison*; **Cost** 4,000 gp; **Rarity:** Very Rare
Alchemical Formula: Not applicable

INK, TOXIC

Aura moderate necromancy; **CL** 9th
Slot none; **Price** 1,000 gp; **Weight** 0.1 lb.

DESCRIPTION

This ink is toxic. Anyone perusing a book for more than a round must make a DC 16 Fortitude save in 24 hours or die. For every minute they read the book, the DC increases by 1.

CONSTRUCTION

Requirements Craft Wondrous Item, *poison*; **Cost** 500 gp; **Rarity:** Very Rare
Alchemical Formula: Rare Earth, Water (any), Death, Stasis, Toxin

LIQUID IRON

Aura strong transmutation; **CL** 15th
Slot none; **Price** 10,000 gp; **Weight** 1 lb.

DESCRIPTION

This small vial contains a flat, gray liquid. It can coat or create up to four Medium-sized objects. It then bonds with the item completely. This causes the item to be treated as iron for all purposes. If a magical item is coated in this substance, it ceases to function. If tossed on a creature, it stiffens quickly. The target must make a DC 16 Reflex save. If it fails, its movement is inhibited by 50% and it receives a –2 circumstance penalty on all rolls. If successful, it only receives a –2 circumstance penalty on all rolls. The creature can take three minutes to clean off the substance to remove the penalty.

CONSTRUCTION

Requirements Craft Wondrous Item, *iron body*; **Cost** 5,000 gp; **Rarity:** Rare
Alchemical Formula: Iron, Rare Earth, Earth (any), Mercury (any), Water (any), Transmutation

LIQUID ROAD

Aura strong transmutation; **CL** 9th
Slot none; **Price** 1,000 gp; **Weight** 1 lb.

DESCRIPTION

This small vial contains a gray liquid. When poured, it creates a firm, solid surface in a five-foot-square area. Each vial contains enough liquid to coat 400 square feet. This can cover a path five feet wide and 80 feet long, a 20-foot-by-20-foot square, or any other option of 16 five-foot squares. This is used to create passable surfaces over a swamp, in a pool or river, or even in a magma flow.

CONSTRUCTION

Requirements Craft Wondrous Item, *fabricate*; **Cost** 500 gp; **Rarity:** Rare
Alchemical Formula: Not applicable

MEDUSA WIG

Aura strong conjuration; **CL** 9th
Slot head; **Price** 11,000 gp; **Weight** 5 lbs.

DESCRIPTION

This creates a helm covered in metal coils that writhe and hiss, each a small replica of a snake. The helm is aggressive and attacks anyone nearby the wielder. If anyone attempts to grapple the wearer, the helm attacks at the wielder's full attack bonus, or with a +8, whichever is better. Alternately, the wearer can attack with their head in lieu of other attacks at the same bonus. Or the wearer can attack with this helm at the end of their normal sequence of attacks with a –5 penalty on their normal chances to hit.
The *medusa wig* does 1d4 points of damage per bite and injects the target with a stored poison, which the creature must save at a DC 2 higher than normal. The wig may hold up to 10 doses of poison. Each dose may be from a different poison, but if more than one poison is stored in the helm, then the poison used is determined randomly.

CONSTRUCTION

Requirements Craft Wondrous Item, *poison, snake staff*; **Cost** 5,500 gp; **Rarity:** Rare
Alchemical Formula: Not applicable

MONSTER TEETH

Aura strong conjuration; **CL** varies
Slot none; **Price** 2,000 gp x monster HD; **Weight** 0.1 lb.

DESCRIPTION

Alchemists have discovered a wondrous ancient secret — the entire record of a being is recorded in its teeth. When these teeth are thrown on the ground, they grow into a creature from which they were taken in one full round. These creatures are under the full command of the alchemist that created them.
They remain in this form for one minute, at the end of which, if they are still alive, they revert to teeth. They can then be collected and reused again after 24 hours pass. Each time they are used, they are created at full health. No other essences can be taken from the creature used, the body must be whole and without major injury (decapitation, etc.), and the body is destroyed in the process of making the teeth. The alchemist can raise the difficulty by 5 while crafting in order to have them follow the person who utters a command word instead of himself. The number of hit dice divided by 2 and rounded up indicates the level of the summon monster spell you must use if you create these magically.

CONSTRUCTION

Requirements Craft Wondrous Item, *summon monster I–IX*; **Cost** 1,000 gp / monster HD; **Rarity:** Rare
Alchemical Formula: Rare Earth, Air (any), Earth (any), Mercury (any), Body, Memory, Transmutation

> *Monster teeth* are one of the strongest and most iconic items alchemists can create. It ties into them collecting items from monsters in order to concoct their mystic substances, gives the alchemist an interesting and unique ability to use in combat, and creates interesting game choices for the players. *Monster teeth* are an item too important to be overlooked.

MORTAR AND PESTLE OF FORCE

Aura strong transmutation; **CL** 17th
Slot none; **Price** 6,000 gp; **Weight** 1 lb.

DESCRIPTION

This powerful mortar and pestle allows you to grind the hardest of materials to dust. It can also be used to destroy magic items, but the pestle must beat the item's break DC. The pestle makes a check of the user's Strength +8. Note that this cannot be used in combat. This decreases the time it takes to craft alchemical items and magic items by 10%.

CONSTRUCTION

Requirements Craft Wondrous Item, *crushing hand*; **Cost** 3,000 gp; **Rarity:** Very Rare
Alchemical Formula: Not applicable

PORTABLE VALISE OF FRUGALITY

Aura strong transmutation; **CL** 13th
Slot none; **Price** 30,000 gp; **Weight** 20 lbs.

DESCRIPTION

This marvelous device concentrates the power of consumable alchemical items. You may attempt to produce a third dose of any basic alchemical item such as potions, dusts, powders, and liquids if you already have two doses. It requires eight hours and two doses of an alchemical item. On a successful DC 25 Craft (alchemy) skill roll, a third dose of the substance is produced. This uses special reagents in order to accomplish this process. There are enough of these reagents to use this device 5d10 + 20 times. A new *valise of frugality* has 70 uses. For the expenditure of one charge, this also functions as an alchemy lab for 24 hours.

CONSTRUCTION

Requirements Craft Wondrous Item, *limited wish*; **Cost** 15,000 gp; **Rarity:** Very Rare
Alchemical Formula: Not applicable

ROPE, ENDLESS

Aura moderate transmutation; **CL** 9th
Slot none; **Price** 1,400- gp; **Weight** 5 lbs.

DESCRIPTION

This is a small spool of one-quarter-inch silk rope. The user can extend up to 500 feet of rope at once. To rewind the rope, you simply press your hand against the side of the spool, and it rewinds on its own at the rate of 100 feet per round. If the rope is cut, it dissipates into smoke. This does not limit or remove the amount of rope available. The spool can always be unwound to a maximum length of 500 feet.

CONSTRUCTION

Requirements Craft Wondrous Item, *secret chest*; **Cost** 700 gp; **Rarity:** Rare
Alchemical Formula: Not applicable

ROPE, EXTENSION

Aura moderate transmutation; **CL** 7th
Slot none; **Price** 500 gp; **Weight** 10 lbs.

DESCRIPTION

At the user's command, this 50-foot rope extends 300 feet in length. It then shortens upon command. If the command is not given, the extra length rots away after four hours. The rope extends only from one end. The other end is knotted. Untying the knot destroys the rope.

CONSTRUCTION

Requirements Craft Wondrous Item, *minor creation*; **Cost** 250 gp; **Rarity:** Rare
Alchemical Formula: Not applicable

ROPE OF IRON

Aura moderate transmutation; **CL** 9th
Slot none; **Price** 1,200 gp; **Weight** 5 lb.

DESCRIPTION

This 100-foot-long silk rope has the ability to turn into rigid iron if the command word is given. When it does, it saves as metal with a +2 bonus. It has hit points and the hardness of iron. If it is broken in either iron or rope form, then the magic is broken and it becomes nonmagical silk rope.

CONSTRUCTION

Requirements Craft Wondrous Item, *wall of iron*; **Cost** 600 gp; **Rarity:** Rare
Alchemical Formula: Not applicable

SHROUD OF SMOKE

Aura moderate illusion; **CL** 5th
Slot shoulder; **Price** 12,000 gp; **Weight** 2 lbs.

DESCRIPTION

This cloak appears as a roiling mist or smoke descending from the wearer's collar. It has several functions. It can be drawn around the wearer to increase the chances of moving unseen by providing a +2 circumstance bonus to Stealth checks.

It can expand to obscure the nearby area as the spell *obscuring mist* three times a day. This cloud lasts for one minute. The wearer can also use it to defend themselves in combat by using the total defense option, which allows the cloak to grant an additional +2 dodge bonus to armor class on top of the bonus for total defense.

CONSTRUCTION

Requirements Craft Wondrous Item, *obscuring mist*; **Cost** 6,000 gp; **Rarity:** Rare
Alchemical Formula: Not applicable

SKELETON KEY

Aura strong abjuration; **CL** 3rd
Slot none; **Price** 1,800 gp; **Weight** 0.1 lb.

DESCRIPTION

When used, this key allows you an attempt to open a lock using the Disable Device skill with 0 ranks and a +3 circumstance bonus. On any roll of a 1, the key breaks. You may not take 10. If you are trained in the Disable Device skill, it adds a +5 enhancement bonus to your attempt to unlock locks instead.

CONSTRUCTION

Requirements Craft Wondrous Item, *knock*; **Cost** 900 gp; **Rarity:** Rare
Alchemical Formula: Not applicable

SPHERE, SPLIT-SECOND

Aura strong transmutation; **CL** 17th
Slot none; **Price** 9,000 gp; **Weight** 1 lb.

DESCRIPTION

This globe is used like a grenade. Every target within 10 feet of the place where this strikes the ground must make a DC 16 Fortitude save. If they fail this save, they are shunted 1d4 + 1 rounds into the future, after which they reappear in the exact same spot. If only one target is in range, the DC is 22. For two targets, the DC of the saving throw is 20. Three or four targets have a DC of 18. Five or more creatures receive no modifier to their saving throws.

There is a 5% chance that a target is instead sent back in time. If this occurs, the previous rounds must be replayed.

CONSTRUCTION

Requirements Craft Wondrous Item, *time stop*; **Cost** 4,500 gp; **Rarity:** Very Rare
Alchemical Formula: Not applicable

WATERSKIN, ENDLESS

Aura faint conjuration; **CL** 3rd
Slot none; **Price** 1,000 gp; **Weight** 4 lbs.

DESCRIPTION

This waterskin holds a half gallon of water. It refills one cup of water per hour until full.

CONSTRUCTION

Requirements Craft Wondrous Item, *create water*; **Cost** 500 gp; **Rarity:** Rare
Alchemical Formula: Not applicable

CURSED

Sometimes when crafting items, the process goes awry. Any time a crafting roll for an item fails by 5 or more, there is a chance that the item is cursed. These are examples of specific cursed alchemical items that can result from the failures:

ELIXIR OF AMNESIA

Aura faint enchantment [mind-affecting]; **CL** 3rd
Slot none; **Weight** —

DESCRIPTION

This appears to be a beneficial elixir for all purposes of examination. The imbiber of this elixir suffers complete memory loss for 1d8 + 6 hours. She does not forget how to walk, speak, or use any of her other skills, class abilities, or talents, though she may be unaware that she has them. There is a 5% chance that the condition is permanent, requiring a *remove curse* or *limited wish* to restore lost memory

CONSTRUCTION

Magic Items any elixir
Alchemical Formula: Not applicable

ELIXIR OF BUBBLES

Aura moderate transmutation; **CL** 3rd
Slot none; **Weight** —

DESCRIPTION

This appears to be a beneficial elixir for all purposes of examination. However, upon drinking the elixir, a terrible curse befalls the imbiber. Each time they open their mouths to speak, a stream of bubbles erupts from their mouth. If the imbiber refuses to open their mouths, bubbles stream from their ears and nose.

This usually lasts a full eight days and in rare cases (1% of the time) is permanent. While cursed with the bubble breath, the user is considered to have the shaken condition.

CONSTRUCTION

Magic Items any elixir
Alchemical Formula: Not applicable

ELIXIR OF BLINDNESS

Aura moderate transmutation; **CL** 3rd
Slot none; **Weight** —

DESCRIPTION

This appears to be a beneficial elixir for all purposes of examination. However, upon drinking the elixir, the imbiber is struck blind, permanently.

CONSTRUCTION

Magic Items any elixir
Alchemical Formula: Not applicable

ELIXIR OF COWARDICE

Aura moderate enchantment (compulsion) [mind-affecting]; **CL** 3rd
Slot none; **Weight** —

DESCRIPTION

This appears to be a beneficial elixir for all purposes of examination. However, upon imbibing the elixir, the imbiber gains 3 negative levels, or gains enough negative levels to drop the character to level 1, whichever is higher. These negative levels vanish after 24 hours.

CONSTRUCTION

Magic Items *elixir of heroism*
Alchemical Formula: Not applicable

ELIXIR OF DEAFNESS

Aura moderate transmutation; **CL** 3rd
Slot none; **Weight** —

DESCRIPTION

This appears to be a beneficial elixir for all purposes of examination. However, upon drinking the elixir, the imbiber is struck deaf, permanently.

CONSTRUCTION

Magic Items any elixir
Alchemical Formula: Not applicable

ELIXIR OF DRUNKENNESS

Aura moderate enchantment (compulsion) [mind-affecting]; **CL** 3rd
Slot none; **Weight** —

DESCRIPTION

This appears to be a beneficial elixir for all purposes of examination. However, upon imbibing the elixir, the imbiber is rendered drunk, gaining a –4 on attacks and skill checks. In order to cast spells, the imbiber must succeed at a Concentration check of DC 10 + spell level and opponents get a +2 circumstance bonus to their save versus spells.

This lasts for six hours and causes the imbiber to have a splitting headache after it wears off, leaving them unable to attack or defend themselves or take any action other than movement for three hours.

CONSTRUCTION

Magic Items any elixir
Alchemical Formula: Not applicable

ELIXIR OF GLUTTONY

Aura faint enchantment (compulsion) [mind-affecting]; **CL** 3rd
Slot none; **Weight** —

DESCRIPTION

This appears to be a beneficial elixir for all purposes of examination. However, upon drinking the elixir, the imbiber is overcome with insatiable hunger and stops whatever he is involved in, including combat, in order to eat, consuming everything in sight for 1d10 + 2 rounds.

CONSTRUCTION

Magic Items any elixir
Alchemical Formula: Not applicable

ELIXIR OF INSOMNIA

Aura faint enchantment; **CL** 9th
Slot none; **Weight** —

DESCRIPTION

This appears to be a beneficial elixir for all purposes of examination. A sip of this elixir tastes wonderful and makes the user feel fantastic. Once they finish the draught, they feel sharp for a bit. As time wears on, they become more weary. When night comes, a startling discovery is made as the imbiber is unable to fall asleep. This condition is permanent. Fatigue and exhaustion eventually accumulate. A *remove curse* cast by a 14th-level or higher cleric ends the effect.

CONSTRUCTION

Magic Items any elixir
Alchemical Formula: Not applicable

ELIXIR OF LETHARGY

Aura moderate transmutation; **CL** 3rd
Slot none; **Weight** —

DESCRIPTION

This appears to be a beneficial elixir and appears so for all purposes of examination. Anyone drinking this elixir is affected by the wizard spell *slow*.

CONSTRUCTION

Magic Items *potion of haste*
Alchemical Formula: Not applicable

ELIXIR OF MADNESS

Aura faint enchantment (compulsion) [mind-affecting]; **CL** 3rd
Slot none; **Weight** —

DESCRIPTION

This appears to be a beneficial elixir for all purposes of examination. A single sip of this elixir causes the imbiber to go insane and act as if affected by *confusion* as the wizard spell until a *heal*, *restoration*, or *limited wish* spell is used to remove the madness. Once a creature is affected, the remaining draught loses all magical properties and becomes a foul liquid.

CONSTRUCTION

Magic Items any elixir
Alchemical Formula: Not applicable

ELIXIR OF PESTILENCE

Aura moderate necromancy; **CL** 3rd
Slot none; **Weight** —

DESCRIPTION

This appears to be a beneficial healing elixir for all purposes of examination. However, upon drinking the elixir, the imbiber is cured for 4 points of damage but is infected with a debilitating disease. The disease affects the imbiber in 1d4 + 1 days. During that time, the imbiber is a carrier and infects anyone she comes into contact with that fails a DC 12 Fortitude save. The imbiber then acquires the disease (selected randomly) after the incubation period ends. These effects are removed or negated by a *cure disease* or better.

CONSTRUCTION

Magic Items any *cure wounds* potion or *healing* elixir.
Alchemical Formula: Not applicable

ELIXIR OF PETRIFICATION

Aura moderate transmutation; **CL** 3rd
Slot none; **Weight** —

DESCRIPTION

This appears to be a beneficial elixir for all purposes of examination. A single sip of this elixir turns the imbiber to stone. Only a *stone to flesh* spell or better restores the imbiber to mobility and life.

CONSTRUCTION

Magic Items any elixir
Alchemical Formula: Not applicable

ELIXIR OF POX

Aura faint necromancy; **CL** 3rd
Slot none; **Weight** —

DESCRIPTION

This appears to be a beneficial elixir for all purposes of examination. Anyone drinking this potion is affected as if they had consumed nothing. One hour after ingestion, boils and pus-filled pustules accompanied by a rash cover the user. The imbiber's temperature goes up, and they become feverish. Blisters and sores appear where there is friction, and hives cover any remaining skin. This is not a disease but a magical curse, and it is not contagious.
Every hour after the elixir's consumption, the pox gets worse. All the user's physical stats drop 1 point every hour unless a DC 16 Fortitude save is succeeded. Each time a save is succeeded, a permanent +1 bonus is applied to the DC of the save. The only cures are a vial of *sweet water* or *dispel magic* followed by *remove curse* followed by *remove disease*.

CONSTRUCTION

Magic Items any elixir
Alchemical Formula: Not applicable

ELIXIR OF RAGE

Aura faint enchantment (compulsion) [mind-affecting]; **CL** 3rd
Slot none; **Weight** —

DESCRIPTION

This appears to be a beneficial healing elixir for all purposes of examination. When quaffed, it heals 1d4 + 4 points of damage. However, the elixir has a hidden effect. The next time the imbiber is threatened, angered, attacked, stressed, or provoked, he or she flies into a berserker rage and attacks every person in sight until subdued or killed. They receive a +4 enhancement bonus to strength, and the rage lasts for 3d6 + 3 rounds

CONSTRUCTION

Magic Items any *cure* wounds potion or *healing* elixir
Alchemical Formula: Not applicable

ELIXIR OF REDUCTION

Aura moderate transformation; **CL** 3rd
Slot none; **Weight** —

DESCRIPTION

This appears to be a beneficial elixir for all purposes of examination. This potion permanently reduces the size of the imbiber to diminutive over the course of five rounds. Only the imbiber is affected, not his gear or equipment. *Remove curse* removes the affliction, and potions and magic items causing growth have a 1-in-4 chance of breaking the curse.

CONSTRUCTION

Magic Items *elixir of growth* or *potion of enlarge person* or *potion of reduce person*
Alchemical Formula: Not applicable

ELIXIR OF REGRESSION

Aura faint transmutation; **CL** 3rd
Slot none; **Weight** —

DESCRIPTION

This appears to be a beneficial elixir for all purposes of examination. Once this elixir is imbibed, the user's body regresses to the physical state of 5 years of age. The user's physical stats are reduced. Her Strength and Constitution are reduced to 25% of its current value, reaching 50% at age 10, and 75% at age 13, and back to its normal value at age 16. The user has a –2 age penalty to Strength until age 14. Her mind is unchanged, and all her equipment is adult-sized. This change is permanent, requiring a *remove curse* within 48 hours or better to cure.

CONSTRUCTION

Magic Items any elixir
Alchemical Formula: Not applicable

ELIXIR OF TRAGIC HEROISM

Aura moderate enchantment; **CL** 3rd
Slot none; **Weight** —

DESCRIPTION

This appears to be a beneficial elixir for all purposes of examination. Drinking this elixir grants the imbiber the benefits of an *elixir of heroism*, but also enrages every monster within 100 feet and causes them to attack the imbiber. The monsters are so furious that they get a +4 alchemical bonus to strength and a +2 alchemical bonus to saving throws for the duration. The monsters attack the imbiber until death.

CONSTRUCTION

Magic Items *elixir of heroism* or *elixir of super-heroism*
Alchemical Formula: Not applicable

ELIXIR OF VENTRILOQUISM, REVERSAL

Aura faint enchantment; **CL** 3rd
Slot none; **Weight** —

DESCRIPTION

This appears to be a beneficial elixir for all purposes of examination. After consuming this elixir, a random target within 50 feet is selected and that person can make their voice come from the imbiber's mouth. The random target is instantly made aware of the character and their ability to make their voice come from his or her mouth.

CONSTRUCTION

Magic Items *potion of ventriloquism, reversal*
Alchemical Formula: Not applicable

ELIXIR OF VULNERABILITY, FIRE

Aura faint abjuration; **CL** 3rd
Slot none; **Weight** —

DESCRIPTION

This appears to be a beneficial elixir for all purposes of examination. When imbibed, the drinker suffers double damage from heat and fire attacks. If the fire is particularly hot or magical — such as lava, dragon's breath, or a spell — the damage is increased by 1 point per die before doubling.

CONSTRUCTION

Magic Items any protection elixir or a *potion of resist energy*
Alchemical Formula: Not applicable

ELIXIR OF WEAKNESS
Aura faint transmutation; **CL** 3rd
Slot none; **Weight** —

DESCRIPTION
This appears to be a beneficial elixir for all purposes of examination. Upon drinking this elixir, the imbiber is wracked by pain and becomes dazed for a minute, and his or her Strength is reduced to a score of 5 for 2d10 + 4 rounds.

CONSTRUCTION
Magic Items *potion of bull's strength*
Alchemical Formula: Not applicable

ELIXIR OF WORM CALLING
Aura faint conjuration; **CL** 3rd
Slot none; **Weight** —

DESCRIPTION
This appears to be a beneficial elixir for all purposes of examination. When this elixir is consumed, the imbiber becomes a target for vermin of all types, crawling insects, rats, bees, hornets, wasps, snakes, worms, and even carrion crawlers, purple worms, and linnorms (1d12 creatures or swarms are called for every minute of the potion's operation).

CONSTRUCTION
Magic Items any elixir
Alchemical Formula: Not applicable

ELIXIR OF YELLOW MOLD
Aura faint necromancy ; **CL** 3rd
Slot none; **Weight** —

DESCRIPTION
This appears to be a beneficial elixir for all purposes of examination. What it actually is are condensed yellow mold spores extracted into fluid paste. It is a murky yellow in color with milky white clumps. When quaffed, the imbiber's flesh and organs are turned into yellow mold, irrevocably slaying the imbiber and exploding into a 10-foot cloud of spores. Anyone within range must succeed at a DC 18 Fortitude save or die.
Some liches use this offensively, turning their regenerating organs and skin into yellow mold.

CONSTRUCTION
Magic Items any elixir or potion exposed to yellow mold
Alchemical Formula: Not applicable

SALVE OF FUMBLING
Aura faint transmutation; **CL** 3rd
Slot none; **Weight** —

DESCRIPTION
This appears to be a beneficial salve for all purposes of examination. However, when the character is subject to some stressful situation (combat, conversation with the in-laws, going outside in a major city, going into work, leaving the house), it immediately causes a 50% chance to drop whatever is held in the hands each round. If nothing is held in the hands and the character is attempting to do anything other than move at half speed, they must succeed at a DC 15 Acrobatics check or fall prone. This salve wears of in 2d6 days.

CONSTRUCTION
Magic Items any salve
Alchemical Formula: Not applicable

SALVE OF LIGHTNING
Aura faint invocation; **CL** 3rd
Slot none; **Weight** —

DESCRIPTION
This appears to be a beneficial salve for all purposes of examination. However, if spread upon a surface, that surface becomes highly charged and attracts lightning bolts for the next 1d4 hours.
If outside, storm clouds gather, heavy rains start, and 1d12 bolts per hour strike the target, doing 8d6 points of electrical damage each, allowing a DC 16 Reflex saving throw for half.
Indoors, each contact with metal surfaces such as doorknobs and hinges produce a bolt doing 2d6 damage. Contact is any interaction within five feet of a metal object. The user may make a DC 16 Reflex saving throw for half damage.

CONSTRUCTION
Magic Items any salve
Alchemical Formula: Not applicable

SALVE OF PHOSPHORESCENCE
Aura faint invocation; **CL** 3rd
Slot none; **Weight** —

DESCRIPTION
This appears to be a beneficial salve for all purposes of examination. When this is applied, it causes any living creature to glow as if it were aflame. This is permanent and sheds orange-yellow light, making the individual highly visible as they shed dim light out to a radius of five feet. The effect can be removed only by *remove curse* or a similar spell.

CONSTRUCTION
Magic Items any salve applied to the skin
Alchemical Formula: Not applicable

SALVE OF POISON
Aura faint necromancy; **CL** 3rd
Slot none; **Weight** —

DESCRIPTION
This appears to be a beneficial salve and appears so for all purposes of examination. When they character applies the salve, they must succeed at a DC 18 Fortitude save or die.

CONSTRUCTION
Magic Items any salve applied to the skin
Alchemical Formula: Not applicable

SALVE OF SCENTS
Aura faint transmutation; **CL** 3rd
Slot none; **Weight** —

DESCRIPTION
This appears to be a beneficial salve for all purposes of examination. However, when applied to the skin, the salve causes a hideous stench for 1d8 hours. The chances for encountering random and wandering monsters are doubled. The stench can be removed with *dispel magic* or greater.

CONSTRUCTION
Magic Items any salve applied to the body
Alchemical Formula: Not applicable

SALVE OF SULFUR
Aura faint evocation; **CL** 3rd
Slot none; **Weight** —

DESCRIPTION
This appears to be a beneficial salve for all purposes of examination. When the character comes under stress or attempts to use the ability he believes the salve provides, instead of the expected effect, the salve bursts into flame and causes 3d8 + 2 points of damage per round until the salve can be washed off.

CONSTRUCTION
Magic Items any salve applied to the skin
Alchemical Formula: Not applicable

CHAPTER FIVE: ALCHEMICAL MAGECRAFT

Some items blend magical crafting and alchemy so closely that they become indistinguishable. These items are a new category of magic item called alchemical magecraft and require Craft (alchemy) instead of Spellcraft to craft, as well as only being able to be crafted, and in some cases used, by someone with the Craft Alchemical Magecraft feat.

The primary types of alchemical magecraft are mineral alchemy, mineral apotheosis, sigils, and talismans. Each of these categories is outlined in this chapter with individual explanations as to how those items work and who can use them.

NEW FEAT

Craft Alchemical Magecraft (Item Creation)
You have discovered the processes required to blend alchemy and magic seamlessly, granting you the ability to craft alchemical magecraft items.

Prerequisites: Caster level 3rd, 3 ranks in Craft (alchemy)

Benefit: You can create a variety of alchemical magecraft items. Crafting an alchemical magecraft item takes one day for each 1,000 gp in its price. To create an alchemical magecraft item, you must use up raw materials costing half of its base price.

You can also mend a broken alchemical magecraft item if it is one that you could make. Doing so costs half the raw materials and half the time it would take to craft that item. See magic item creation rules and the specific category of alchemical magecraft item for more information.

Special: An alchemist can craft any alchemical magecraft items he is able to, using his alchemist level as his caster level. The alchemist does not need to meet the caster level prerequisites for this feat.

NEW ALCHEMIST DISCOVERIES

Alchemical Magientist
You have discovered enough about alchemy to make it indistinguishable from magic.

Benefit: An alchemist who takes this discovery gains the Craft Alchemical Magecraft feat, ignoring prerequisites.

Crafty Magientist
Prerequisite: Alchemical Magientist discovery
You have bridged the gap between magic and alchemy, learning the secrets of magic item creation.

Benefit: An alchemist who takes this feat treats their alchemist level as their caster level for all item creation feats.

MINERAL ALCHEMY

Gemstones contain power. Alchemists have developed specialized techniques developed to extract the magical energy inherent in gemstones. Each type of gemstone has certain abilities and powers over which it has influence, and anyone can take a Craft Alchemical Magecraft feat to allow them to activate those abilities. The types of effects are limited based on the energies in the gemstone. It is different from other types of item crafting, because it requires nothing beyond the material component of the gemstone of an appropriate value to create it. The value of the gem is a representation of its true value, not an indicator of its market value. A 10-gp agate gemstone refers to the actual quality of the gemstone. Due to demand, location, or other factors, the price for a gemstone of that quality on the market may be higher or lower. For instance, inland landlocked countries usually have much higher prices for coral gemstones. You must have a gemstone of the appropriate value in order to craft an alchemical mineral; no substitutes are possible. Gem rarity and availability are factors that must be kept in mind when attempting to craft these items.

Once enchanted, gemstones can express their inner energies in five different forms. They are as follows: lozenges which are swallowed; catagemmas which are applied to the skin; fulminating charges, which are thrown as grenades; flowers, which are possessed and produce a magical scent; and lenses, which are held to the eyes.

A person can only use or be under the effect of a single type of mineral alchemy at a time. An attempt to use or activate more than one type of mineral alchemy causes all active and inactive alchemical gemstones to turn to gray dust due to the conflict of magical resonances.

Lozenges are gemstones and jewels treated in such a way to dissolve in liquids and saliva. It is a swift action to use one, and it takes one full round once consumed before it takes effect. If not otherwise noted, the duration of a lozenge is one hour. Once used, the gemstone is destroyed.

Catagemma (lit. against the gem) are gemstones or jewels treated in such a way that when rubbed against the skin, they dissolve, being absorbed in the flesh. It takes a standard action to do so. If not otherwise noted, catagemma gemstones last for one hour. Once applied and absorbed into the skin, the gem is destroyed

Fulminating charges are gemstones or jewels that have been treated to explode when thrown. They are thrown as a grenade-like weapon. Once they explode, the gem is destroyed.

Flowers are gemstones or jewels that have been treated to release a magical odor. Once prepared, these are activated by squeezing them in your hand as a standard action. After that, they provide their function or benefit only if the person who activated the flower is within 10 feet or is in possession of the gem. It provides no function for anyone else. If not otherwise noted, flowers have a duration of 24 hours.

Lenses are gemstones or jewels that have been treated to use as a sighting device. They amplify alchemical and arcane energies to allow auras and other normally invisible weaves and patterns to be seen. They are activated as flowers, by gently squeezing them in your hand. Afterward, they must simply be looked through to function. If not otherwise noted, the duration of these effects are an hour, which need not be contiguous, being used up in one-minute activations. After the gemstone's energy resonance is expended, the gem turns into worthless gray glass.

TABLE 5–1: MINERAL ALCHEMY PRICE LIST

Name	Price	Name	Price
Agate Catagemma of Warding	200 gp	Diamond Lens of Electricity Control	2,000 gp
Agate Flower of Rapport	20 gp	Diamond Lozenge of Deliquescence	10,000 gp
Agate Lozenge of Hydration	20 gp	Emerald Lens of Sight	2,000 gp
Alexandrite Flower of Fortune	100 gp	Emerald Lozenge of Recall	2,000 gp
Amber Catagemma of Sense Restoration	1,000 gp	Fire Opal Catagemma of Fame	2,000 gp
Amber Fulminating Charge of Lightning	200 gp	Fire Opal Fulminating Charge of Flame	2,000 gp
Amber Lozenge of Health	200 gp	Garnet Flower of Health	200 gp
Amethyst Catagemma of Arcane Shield	200 gp	Garnet Lens of Darkvision	200 gp
Aquamarine Flower of Concord	1,000 gp	Hematite Catagemma of Sealing	20 gp
Aquamarine Lozenge of Wealth	2,000 gp	Hematite Lozenge of the Warrior	100 gp
Bloodstone Catagemma of Invisibility	1,000 gp	Jacinth Catagemma of the Heart	10,000 gp
Bloodstone Fulminating Charge of Smoke	100 gp	Jacinth Flower of Teleportation Stability	10,000 gp
Carnelian Catagemma of Healing	50 gp	Jacinth Lens of Spirituality	2,000 gp
Carnelian Flower of Courage	200 gp	Jacinth Lozenge of Sleep	10,000 gp
Carnelian Fulminating Charge of Calm	100 gp	Jade Catagemma of Preservation	200 gp
Carnelian Lozenge of Neutralize Poison	400 gp	Jade Lozenge of Resuscitation	2,000 gp
Chalcedony Flower of Undead Ward	200 gp	Jasper Catagemma of Aegis	2,000 gp
Chalcedony Fulminating Charge of Undead Torment	200 gp	Jet Lozenge of Death Ward	200 gp
Chalcedony Lozenge of Strength	100 gp	Lapis Lazuli Flower of Morale	100 gp
Chrysoberyl Flower of Luck	100 gp	Malachite Lozenge of Feather Fall	100 gp
Chrysoberyl Fulminating Charge of Banishing	1,000 gp	Onyx Fulminating Charge of Chaos	200 gp
Chrysoberyl Lozenge of Fate	100 gp	Peridot Flower of Warding	1,000 gp
Chrysoprase Flower of Non-Detection	100 gp	Peridot Lozenge of Wit	1,000 gp
Chrysoprase Lozenge of Oratory	100 gp	Rock Crystal Flower of Shade	100 gp
Coral Catagemma of Warding	1,000 gp	Ruby Catagemma of the Burning Touch	2,000 gp
Coral Flower of the Mind	200 gp	Ruby Flower of Warmth	100 gp
Coral Lozenge of the Sea	200 gp	Ruby Lozenge of Fire Breath	2,000 gp
Diamond Catagemma of Fate	10,000 gp	Sapphire Lozenge of Escape	10,000 gp
Diamond Flower of Undead Warding	10,000 gp	Violet Garnet Lens of Ultravision	1,000 gp
Diamond Fulminating Charge of Blasting	2,000 gp	Violet Garnet of Health	1,000 gp

AGATE CATAGEMMA OF WARDING
Aura faint abjuration
Slot none; **Price** 200 gp; **Weight** —

DESCRIPTION
This catagemma provides two bonuses when applied. First, it provides a +2 alchemical bonus to saves versus poison and electricity. Second, it also provides *protection from evil* as the spell for one hour.

CONSTRUCTION
Requirements Craft Alchemical Magecraft; **Rarity:** Uncommon
Alchemical Formula: Agate Gemstone (100 gp), Protection

AGATE FLOWER OF RAPPORT
Aura faint transmutation
Slot none; **Price** 20 gp; **Weight** —

DESCRIPTION
Once activated, this stone releases a pleasant fragrance in a 10-foot radius. The holder of the stone is granted a +4 enhancement bonus to Charisma. Once someone spends one minute in the presence of the bearer, under the effect of the stone, the bearer may make a *suggestion* as the spell once per person affected.

CONSTRUCTION
Requirements Craft Alchemical Magecraft; **Rarity:** Uncommon
Alchemical Formula: Agate Gemstone (10 gp), Emotion

AGATE LOZENGE OF HYDRATION
Aura faint abjuration
Slot none; **Price** 20 gp; **Weight** —

DESCRIPTION
Once the lozenge is dissolved, the target is provided with hydration in the most extreme conditions for 48 hours. Also, if exposed to any disease or illness during this time, they receive a +1 alchemical bonus on their saving throw to resist the disease.

CONSTRUCTION
Requirements Craft Alchemical Magecraft; **Rarity:** Uncommon
Alchemical Formula: Agate Gemstone (10 gp), Water (any)

ALEXANDRITE FLOWER OF FORTUNE
Aura faint enchantment
Slot none; **Price** 100 gp; **Weight** —

DESCRIPTION
This scent provides good fortune to the holder. It lasts for 24 hours. Once during this period, the bearer may add 1d6 to the result of any die rolled for an attack, skill check, saving throw, or damage roll after the result is known. When this occurs, the scent is expended and the gem crumbles to dust.

CONSTRUCTION
Requirements Craft Alchemical Magecraft; **Rarity:** Uncommon
Alchemical Formula: Alexandrite Gemstone (50 gp), Luck

AMBER CATAGEMMA OF SENSE RESTORATION
Aura faint necromancy
Slot none; **Price** 1,000 gp; **Weight** —

DESCRIPTION
Applying this catagemma restores hearing and sight when applied to the skin.

CONSTRUCTION
Requirements Craft Alchemical Magecraft; **Rarity:** Uncommon
Alchemical Formula: Amber Gemstone (500 gp), Healing

AMBER FULMINATING CHARGE OF LIGHTNING
Aura faint evocation
Slot none; **Price** 200 gp; **Weight** —

DESCRIPTION
This charge when thrown explodes in a shocking sphere of electricity. It has a radius of five feet and does 1d4 + 1 points of electrical damage. You may use a more valuable stone to increase the effect, as per **Table 5–2** below. Targets may make a DC 20 reflex save for half damage. Every doubling of the stone's value increases the radius by five, the save DC by 2, and the damage by 1d4 + 1.

TABLE 5–2: AMBER FULMINATING CHARGE POWER INCREASE

Gemstone value	Price	Radius	Save DC	Damage
200 gp	400 gp	10 feet	22	2d4 + 2
400 gp	800 gp	15 feet	24	3d4 + 3
800 gp	1,600 gp	20 feet	26	4d4 + 4
1,600 gp	3,200 gp	25 feet	28	5d4 + 5
3,200 gp	6,400 gp	30 feet	30	6d4 + 6
6,400 gp	12,800 gp	35 feet	32	7d4 + 7

CONSTRUCTION
Requirements Craft Alchemical Magecraft; **Rarity:** Uncommon
Alchemical Formula: Amber Gemstones (100 gp or more, see above)

AMBER LOZENGE OF HEALTH
Aura faint abjuration
Slot none; **Price** 200 gp; **Weight** —

DESCRIPTION
Once the lozenge is dissolved, the consumer is provided with a +4 bonus on any saving throws against disease for the next 48 hours.

CONSTRUCTION
Requirements Craft Alchemical Magecraft; **Rarity:** Uncommon
Alchemical Formula: Amber Gemstone (100 gp), Healing

AMETHYST CATAGEMMA OF ARCANE SHIELD
Aura faint abjuration
Slot none; **Price** 200 gp; **Weight** —

DESCRIPTION
An amethyst combined with some baboon hair and a swallow feather provides protection versus sorcery. This provides a +1 alchemical bonus against all spells and spell-like effects for the next 24 hours when used.

CONSTRUCTION
Requirements Craft Alchemical Magecraft; **Rarity:** Uncommon
Alchemical Formula: Amethyst Gemstone (100 gp), Protection

AQUAMARINE FLOWER OF CONCORD
Aura faint enchantment
Slot none; **Price** 1,000 gp; **Weight** —

DESCRIPTION
This fragrance clears your head and improves the attitude of people near you. You receive a +4 alchemical bonus to Intelligence and Charisma for 24 hours.

CONSTRUCTION
Requirements Craft Alchemical Magecraft; **Rarity:** Uncommon
Alchemical Formula: Aquamarine (500 gp), Emotion

AQUAMARINE LOZENGE OF WEALTH
Aura faint divination
Slot none; **Price** 2,000 gp; **Weight** —

DESCRIPTION
Once this lozenge is dissolved, the consumer gains the ability to detect precious metals for one hour. The imbiber concentrates and senses the distance and direction to the largest concentration of precious metals such as gold, platinum, and silver within one mile.

CONSTRUCTION
Requirements Craft Alchemical Magecraft; **Rarity:** Very Rare
Alchemical Formula: Aquamarine Gemstone (1,000 gp), Perception

BLOODSTONE CATAGEMMA OF INVISIBILITY
Aura faint illusion
Slot none; **Price** 1,000 gp; **Weight** —

DESCRIPTION
Combining a bloodstone with the essence of sunflower seeds produces this catagemma, which allows the user to fade from view. It treats the wearer as if they were under the effects of a *greater invisibility* spell for one minute.

CONSTRUCTION
Requirements Craft Alchemical Magecraft; **Rarity:** Rare
Alchemical Formula: Bloodstone (500 gp), Illusion

BLOODSTONE FULMINATING CHARGE OF SMOKE
Aura faint evocation
Slot none; **Price** 100 gp; **Weight** —

DESCRIPTION
When this charge is dashed on the floor, it produces a thick black cloud of smoke that completely blocks all vision to anyone contained within it. Anyone who stays in the cloud must make a DC 16 Fortitude save or become nauseas. The cloud is 20 feet high and 40 feet long and wide.

CONSTRUCTION
Requirements Craft Alchemical Magecraft; **Rarity:** Uncommon
Alchemical Formula: Bloodstone (50 gp), Toxin

CARNELIAN CATAGEMMA OF HEALING
Aura faint necromancy
Slot none; **Price** 50 gp; **Weight** —

DESCRIPTION
This catagemma when applied heals the target for 1d4 + 1 points of damage. You may use a more valuable stone to increase the effect. For every doubling of the gem's value, the healing is increased by 1d4 + 1 points of damage.

TABLE 5–3: CARNELIAN CATAGEMMA POWER INCREASE

Gemstone value	Sale price	Healing value
100 gp	200 gp	2d4 + 2
200 gp	400 gp	3d4 + 3
400 gp	800 gp	4d4 + 4
800 gp	1,600 gp	5d4 + 5
1,600 gp	3,200gp	6d4 + 6
3,200 gp	6,400 gp	7d4 + 7
6,400 gp	12,800 gp	8d4 + 8

CONSTRUCTION
Requirements Craft Alchemical Magecraft; **Rarity:** Uncommon
Alchemical Formula: Carnelian Gemstone, Healing

CARNELIAN FLOWER OF COURAGE
Aura faint abjuration
Slot none; **Price** 200 gp; **Weight** —

DESCRIPTION
This flower's scent reassures the possessor and provides a +4 alchemical bonus versus fear saves and charms for 24 hours once activated.

CONSTRUCTION
Requirements Craft Alchemical Magecraft; **Rarity:** Uncommon
Alchemical Formula: Carnelian Gemstone (100 gp), Protection

CARNELIAN FULMINATING CHARGE OF CALM
Aura faint enchantment (compulsion) [mind-affecting]
Slot none; **Price** 100 gp; **Weight** —

DESCRIPTION
This charge explodes in a cloud of dust covering a 15-foot radius. All within this radius have their emotions calmed. It stops rage, fighting, and revelry. Note that although it temporarily makes creatures sedate and non-hostile for one minute, they are not under any compulsion to remain calm and strike back at those that attack them.
If the targets are under the effect of spells that affect their fighting abilities — such as *bless*, *heroism*, *rage*, or other mind-affecting compulsions — the bonuses from those spells are suppressed for 2d6 rounds.

CONSTRUCTION
Requirements Craft Alchemical Magecraft; **Rarity:** Uncommon
Alchemical Formula: Carnelian Gemstone (50 gp), Emotion

CARNELIAN LOZENGE OF NEUTRALIZE POISON
Aura faint conjuration (healing)
Slot none; **Price** 400 gp; **Weight** —

DESCRIPTION
Once this lozenge is dissolved, it instantly neutralizes poison in the user. It provides no further protection against future incidences of poisoning.

CONSTRUCTION
Requirements Craft Alchemical Magecraft; **Rarity:** Uncommon
Alchemical Formula: Carnelian Gemstone (200 gp), Body

CHALCEDONY FLOWER OF UNDEAD WARD
Aura faint abjuration;
Slot none; **Price** 200 gp; **Weight** —

DESCRIPTION
The scent this gemstone exudes is not detectable by living creatures, but it confuses and confounds those of the living dead that attempt to assault the wearer. The person with this flower in their possession gains a +2 circumstance bonus to their armor class versus any attack launched by an undead creature. This scent lasts for 24 hours.

CONSTRUCTION
Requirements Craft Alchemical Magecraft; **Rarity:** Uncommon
Alchemical Formula: Chalcedony Gemstone (100 gp), Life

CHALCEDONY FULMINATING CHARGE OF UNDEAD TORMENT
Aura faint evocation
Slot none; **Price** 200 gp; **Weight** —

DESCRIPTION
This charge when thrown explodes in radiating waves of glowing warmth that lasts for one round. These waves are painful and damaging to the undead and all those who have a connection to the Negative Material Plane. The waves have a radius of five feet and do 1d4 + 1 points of radiant damage to the undead. The undead can make a DC 20 Reflex save for half damage. You may use a more valuable stone to increase the effect. Every doubling of the stone's value increases the saving throw DC by 2, the radius by five feet, and the damage by 1d4 + 1 points of radiant damage.

TABLE 5–4: CHALCEDONY FULMINATING CHARGE POWER INCREASE

Gemstone value	Price	Radius	Save DC	Damage
200 gp	400 gp	10 feet	22	2d4 + 2
400 gp	800 gp	15 feet	24	3d4 + 3
800 gp	1,600 gp	20 feet	26	4d4 + 4
1,600 gp	3,200 gp	25 feet	28	5d4 + 5
3,200 gp	6,400 gp	30 feet	30	6d4 + 6
6,400 gp	12,800 gp	35 feet	32	7d4 + 7

CONSTRUCTION
Requirements Craft Alchemical Magecraft; **Rarity:** Uncommon
Alchemical Formula: Chalcedony Gemstone (half the crafting cost), Light

CHALCEDONY LOZENGE OF STRENGTH
Aura faint enchantment
Slot none; **Price** 100 gp; **Weight** —

DESCRIPTION
Once dissolved, this lozenge blesses the consumer with increased strength, providing a +2 alchemical bonus to Strength for one hour.

CONSTRUCTION
Requirements Craft Alchemical Magecraft; **Rarity:** Uncommon
Alchemical Formula: Chalcedony Gemstone (50 gp), Strength

CHRYSOBERYL FLOWER OF LUCK
Aura faint abjuration
Slot none; **Price** 100 gp; **Weight** —

DESCRIPTION
The odor this stone produces smells mildly of mint. The user appears blessed, with harm never quite befalling them. They are granted a +1 circumstance bonus to saving throws.

CONSTRUCTION
Requirements Craft Alchemical Magecraft; **Rarity:** Common
Alchemical Formula: Chrysoberyl Gemstone (50 gp), Luck

CHRYSOBERYL FULMINATING CHARGE OF BANISHING
Aura faint abjuration
Slot none; **Price** 1,000 gp; **Weight** —

DESCRIPTION
This powerful charge has two effects. If thrown on the ground, it works as a banishment or exorcism. The offending outsiders must succeed at a DC 16 saving throw or be banished back to their home plane or cast out from the body they inhabit. This DC is increased by 1 per 500 gp of the gem's value over its base value. A 5,000-gp chrysoberyl has a DC 26 saving throw. It has a second use. If this gem is carried and the possessor is subject to an attack against their spirit attempting possession of the body, the attacker's soul is instead contained within the gem, trapping them until they can find a way free.

CONSTRUCTION
Requirements Craft Alchemical Magecraft; **Rarity:** Very Rare
Alchemical Formula: Chrysoberyl Gemstone (500 gp), Azoth (any), Planar

CHRYSOBERYL LOZENGE OF FATE
Aura faint enchantment
Slot none; **Price** 100 gp; **Weight** —

DESCRIPTION
Once dissolved, this lozenge aligns the user with destiny, providing a +1 alchemical bonus to attack and damage rolls for one hour.

CONSTRUCTION
Requirements Craft Alchemical Magecraft; **Rarity:** Uncommon
Alchemical Formula: Chrysoberyl Gemstone (50 gp), Luck

CHRYSOPRASE FLOWER OF NON-DETECTION
Aura faint abjuration;
Slot none; **Price** 100 gp; **Weight** —

DESCRIPTION
This powerful scent extends around you and affects the minds of those nearby. Even though their eyes may see you, their minds refuse to notice your presence. It gives a +5 alchemical bonus to disguise and Stealth for 24 hours.

CONSTRUCTION
Requirements Craft Alchemical Magecraft; **Rarity:** Uncommon
Alchemical Formula: Chrysoprase Gemstone (50 gp), Mind

CHRYSOPRASE LOZENGE OF ORATORY
Aura faint enchantment
Slot none; **Price** 100 gp; **Weight** —

DESCRIPTION
Once dissolved, this lozenge causes the throat to relax and the tongue to become loose, slivered, and nimble. It provides a +5 alchemical bonus to the Bluff, Use Magical Device, and any Performance skill that uses the voice. The effect lasts for an hour.

CONSTRUCTION
Requirements Craft Alchemical Magecraft; **Rarity:** Uncommon
Alchemical Formula: Chrysoprase Gemstone (50 gp), Emotion

CORAL CATAGEMMA OF WARDING
Aura faint abjuration
Slot none; **Price** 1,000 gp; **Weight** —

DESCRIPTION
Once this sparkling catagemma is spread across the skin, the user is protected from witchcraft. The user receives a +4 alchemical bonus against any charms, enchantment, compulsion, or fear spells or effects. This bonus lasts for 24 hours.

CONSTRUCTION
Requirements Craft Alchemical Magecraft; **Rarity:** Uncommon
Alchemical Formula: Coral Gemstone (500 gp), Protection

CORAL FLOWER OF THE MIND
Aura faint abjuration
Slot none; **Price** 200 gp; **Weight** —

DESCRIPTION
This scent is a marvelous restorative to the mind. When possessed, the user is cured of any magically induced insanity and gains a +2 alchemical bonus to saves versus mind-affecting spells. It also provides some measure of mental defense, preventing the first 5 points of damage from psionic, illusionary, and mental attacks.

CONSTRUCTION
Requirements Craft Alchemical Magecraft; **Rarity:** Uncommon
Alchemical Formula: Coral Gemstone (100 gp), Mind

CORAL LOZENGE OF THE SEA
Aura faint transmutation
Slot none; **Price** 200 gp; **Weight** —

DESCRIPTION
Once dissolved, this coats the lungs, allowing them to extract breathable air from the water. The user gains the ability to breathe water as the spell *water breathing* for an hour.

CONSTRUCTION
Requirements Craft Alchemical Magecraft; **Rarity:** Uncommon
Alchemical Formula: Coral Gemstone (100 gp), Water (any)

DIAMOND CATAGEMMA OF FATE
Aura faint enchantment
Slot none; **Price** 10,000 gp; **Weight** —

DESCRIPTION
This extremely power catagemma gives the wearer victory over those who oppose him. The user receives a +5 inherent bonus in their base attack bonus. The character also receives a +4 enhancement bonus to Strength. Any weapons the character attacks with are more powerful, being treated as if its size category (and damage die) were one size larger than it is. The user also gains DR 5/—. Finally, they gain an additional 1d8 + 1 temporary hit points for each 2,000 gp value of the gem, up to a maximum of 5d8 + 5 for a 10,000-gp diamond gemstone. This catagemma lasts for one hour.

CONSTRUCTION
Requirements Craft Alchemical Magecraft; **Rarity:** Uncommon
Alchemical Formula: Diamond Gemstone (5,000 gp), Prowess

DIAMOND FLOWER OF UNDEAD WARDING
Aura strong abjuration
Slot none; **Price** 10,000 gp; **Weight** —

DESCRIPTION
This rarified scent protects the wearer from undead. When they encounter this smell, they are unable to approach easily, with the undead needing to succeed at a DC 14 Will save to approach within 10 feet of the scent. Once they do, they must succeed at a DC 18 Fortitude save or be unable to attack. Even if they are able to attack, the possessor receives a +4 circumstance bonus to their armor class, and they gain DR 5/— versus attacks from undead. The wearer is also immune to energy drain and cannot acquire negative levels, though the gem has no effect on current negative levels. The scent lasts for 24 hours.

CONSTRUCTION
Requirements Craft Alchemical Magecraft; **Rarity:** Uncommon
Alchemical Formula: Diamond Gemstone (5,000 gp), Life

DIAMOND FULMINATING CHARGE OF BLASTING
Aura faint evocation
Slot none; **Price** 2,000 gp; **Weight** —

DESCRIPTION
When thrown, this charge explodes with terrible blasting force. The effect has a radius of five feet and does 1d10 + 1 points of force damage in addition to causing targets to fall prone and be stunned. A DC 16 Reflex save allows half damage and prevents the target from being stunned. Roll a 1d20 and add the damage dealt to see if it overcomes any of the target's CMD to see if they are knocked prone. You may use a more valuable stone to increase the effect. For every doubling of the stone's value, increase the saving throw DC by 2, the radius by five feet, and the damage by 1d10 + 1.

TABLE 5–5: DIAMOND FULMINATING CHARGE POWER INCREASE

Gemstone value	Price	Radius	Save DC	Damage
2,000 gp	4,000 gp	10 feet	18	2d10 + 2
4,000 gp	8,000 gp	15 feet	20	3d10 + 3
8,000 gp	16,000 gp	20 feet	22	4d10 + 4
16,000 gp	32,000 gp	25 feet	24	5d10 + 5
32,000 gp	64,000 gp	30 feet	26	6d10 + 6
64,000 gp	128,000 gp	35 feet	28	7d10 + 7

CONSTRUCTION
Requirements Craft Alchemical Magecraft; **Rarity:** Uncommon
Alchemical Formula: Diamond Gemstone (see **Table 5–5** for price), Prowess

DIAMOND LENS OF ELECTRICITY CONTROL
Aura faint evocation
Slot none; **Price** 2,000 gp; **Weight** —

DESCRIPTION
While looking through this lens, the perceiver can see the electrical charge, the strength of the connection to the Elemental Plane of Electricity and the electric potential of all objects in sight.
Any lightning bolt in view of the perceiver is under their complete control. They are able to direct it to any target or targets they wish. A 12d6 lightning bolt may be directed across 12 kobolds in a circle or other non-linear formation.
As a full-round action, the user may open a gate to the Elemental Plane of Electricity and use it to alter the electrical potential between any two targets. They both take 4d6 points of damage, with a DC 18 Reflex saving throw for half.
The lens must be held to the eyes. It allows control of electricity for up to one hour. If the user is somehow subjected to electrical damage during the use of this lens (perhaps if they are standing in water), they get a +4 circumstance bonus on their saving throw, taking no damage on a successful save and half damage on a failure, and have Resist Electricity 10.

CONSTRUCTION
Requirements Craft Alchemical Magecraft; **Rarity:** Uncommon
Alchemical Formula: Diamond Gemstone (1,000 gp), Electricity, Planar

DIAMOND LOZENGE OF DELIQUESCENCE
Aura moderate illusion
Slot none; **Price** 10,000 gp; **Weight** —

DESCRIPTION
This diamond does indeed have the power to render a being invisible, but not in the way most think. When this lozenge dissolves, the user may freely shift between the Ethereal and Prime Material planes at will.
This means they can remain hidden from sight, getting a +20 alchemical bonus to Stealth and if they do shift into the Prime Material Plane to attack, they are treated as incorporeal creatures taking only half damage from attacks that don't extend into the other plane. People attacking the user take a –4 circumstance penalty to their attacks as if they were fighting an invisible opponent, unless they can see into the Ethereal Plane.
This lasts for 60 rounds which do not need to be consecutive or until 24 hours pass, whichever comes first.

CONSTRUCTION
Requirements Craft Alchemical Magecraft; **Rarity:** Rare
Alchemical Formula: Diamond Gemstone (5,000 gp), Azoth (any), Planar

EMERALD LENS OF SIGHT
Aura faint divination
Slot none; **Price** 2,000 gp; **Weight** —

DESCRIPTION

This causes anyone who activates it and uses the lens to gain a substantial bonus to their ability to notice fine detail. They gain a +10 alchemical bonus to Perception. The lens is usable for a full hour, which does not have to be consecutive.

CONSTRUCTION

Requirements Craft Alchemical Magecraft; **Rarity:** Uncommon
Alchemical Formula: Emerald Gemstone (1,000 gp), Perception

EMERALD LOZENGE OF RECALL
Aura faint divination
Slot none; **Price** 2,000 gp; **Weight** —

DESCRIPTION

When this lozenge is dissolved, the user can recover a 1st-level spell they have already cast. They must have prepared the spell and cast it within the last 24 hours. You may use a more valuable stone to increase the effect. The gem allows you to recall a number of levels of spells equal to its price in thousands of gold pieces. A 4,000-gp emerald allows you to recover four spell levels in any combination. For instance, the user may recover one 4th-level spell, four 1st-level spells, two 2nd-level spells, a 3rd-level spell and a 1st-level spell, or two 1st-level spells and a 2nd-level spell.

CONSTRUCTION

Requirements Craft Alchemical Magecraft; **Rarity:** Uncommon
Alchemical Formula: Emerald Gemstone (1,000 gp), Memory

FIRE OPAL CATAGEMMA OF FAME
Aura faint abjuration
Slot none; **Price** 2,000 gp; **Weight** —

DESCRIPTION

When used, this catagemma gives the user invulnerability to normal fires such as torches, bonfires, and hot coals, as well as granting Resist Fire 10. Saving throws versus attacks that use heat, fire, or flame gain a +4 circumstance bonus to the saving throw.

CONSTRUCTION

Requirements Craft Alchemical Magecraft; **Rarity:** Rare
Alchemical Formula: Fire Opal (1,000 gp), Protection

FIRE OPAL FULMINATING CHARGE OF FLAME
Aura faint evocation
Slot none; **Price** 2,000 gp; **Weight** —

DESCRIPTION

When thrown, this charge explodes in a burning flame. The flame has a radius of five feet and does 1d8 + 2 points of fire damage. You may make a DC 16 Reflex save for half damage. You may use a more valuable stone to increase the effect. Every doubling of the stone's value increases the saving throw DC by 2, the radius by five feet, and the damage by 1d8 + 2 points of fire damage.

TABLE 5–6: FIRE OPAL FULMINATING CHARGE POWER INCREASE

Gemstone value	Price	Radius	Save DC	Damage
2,000 gp	4,000 gp	10 feet	18	2d8 + 4
4,000 gp	8,000 gp	15 feet	20	3d8 + 6
8,000 gp	16,000 gp	20 feet	22	4d8 + 8
16,000 gp	32,000 gp	25 feet	24	5d8 + 10
32,000 gp	64,000 gp	30 feet	26	6d8 + 12
64,000 gp	128,000 gp	35 feet	28	7d8 + 14

CONSTRUCTION

Requirements Craft Alchemical Magecraft; **Rarity:** Uncommon
Alchemical Formula: Fire Opal (price varies; see **Table 5–6**), Fire (any)

GARNET FLOWER OF HEALTH
Aura faint enchantment
Slot none; **Price** 200 gp; **Weight** —

DESCRIPTION

This scent provides a robust constitution to the bearer, granting a +2 alchemical bonus to Constitution for 24 hours.

CONSTRUCTION

Requirements Craft Alchemical Magecraft; **Rarity:** Uncommon
Alchemical Formula: Garnet Gemstone (100 gp), Body

GARNET LENS OF DARKVISION
Aura faint divination
Slot none; **Price** 200 gp; **Weight** —

DESCRIPTION

When this lens is applied to the eye, the viewer gains darkvision 60 feet for the duration. This lens functions for an hour of use, which does not need to be consecutive.

CONSTRUCTION

Requirements Craft Alchemical Magecraft; **Rarity:** Uncommon
Alchemical Formula: Garnet Gemstone (100 gp), Perception

HEMATITE CATAGEMMA OF SEALING
Aura faint conjuration (healing)
Slot none; **Price** 20 gp; **Weight** —

DESCRIPTION

Applying this catagemma to your skin protects against bleeding attacks for the next 24 hours. Anytime you are subject to a bleeding effect, the wounds seal quickly and the bleeding stops. If lowered to below 0 hit points, you automatically stabilize.

CONSTRUCTION

Requirements Craft Alchemical Magecraft; **Rarity:** Uncommon
Alchemical Formula: Hematite Gemstone (10 gp), Body

HEMATITE LOZENGE OF THE WARRIOR
Aura faint enchantment
Slot none; **Price** 100 gp; **Weight** —

DESCRIPTION

When this is consumed, it provides the user with a +1 alchemical bonus to damage for an hour.

CONSTRUCTION

Requirements Craft Alchemical Magecraft; **Rarity:** Uncommon;
Alchemical Formula: Hematite (50 gp), Strength

JACINTH CATAGEMMA OF THE HEART
Aura strong enchantment
Slot none; **Price** 10,000 gp; **Weight** —

DESCRIPTION

Once applied, this hardens and grants the user 10d6 + 10 temporary hit points. You may use a more powerful gem to increase the effect. For every additional 1,000 gp of value in the gem beyond the base value of 5,000 gp, you gain an additional 2d6 + 2 temporary hit points, up to a maximum gem size of 10,000 gp (and 20d6 + 20 hit points).

CONSTRUCTION

Requirements Craft Alchemical Magecraft; **Rarity:** Uncommon
Alchemical Formula: Jacinth Gemstone (5,000 and up), Body

JACINTH FLOWER OF TELEPORTATION STABILITY
Aura faint abjuration
Slot none; **Price** 10,000 gp; **Weight** —

DESCRIPTION
This flower's scent makes teleportation easier. Roll 2d6 + 1 to determine the number of percentage points you may alter your roll when attempting to teleport on target. For instance, if you roll a 3 and a 2, you may alter your final percentile roll by 6. If you are teleporting somewhere you've been only once and you roll an 82 causing you to be off target, you can reduce six points to a 76, putting you back on target. The flower lasts until a teleportation roll is not on target, at which point the 2d6 are rolled and the flower turns to dust.

CONSTRUCTION
Requirements Craft Alchemical Magecraft; **Rarity:** Rare
Alchemical Formula: Jacinth Gemstone (5,000 gp), Transportation

JACINTH LENS OF SPIRITUALITY
Aura faint divination
Slot none; **Price** 2,000 gp; **Weight** —

DESCRIPTION
Once applied, these lenses, unlike other lenses, fasten to the eyes of the wearer and allow her to see into the Astral and Ethereal planes. They receive a +2 circumstance bonus to hit all astral and ethereal creatures. When striking these creatures, any weapon the user is wielding does full damage. These lenses function for an hour, which does not need to be consecutive.

CONSTRUCTION
Requirements Craft Alchemical Magecraft; **Rarity:** Uncommon
Alchemical Formula: Jacinth Gemstone (1,000 gp), Perception

JACINTH LOZENGE OF SLEEP
Aura strong enchantment (compulsion) [mind-affecting]
Slot none; **Price** 10,000 gp; **Weight** —

DESCRIPTION
This lozenge has different effects. First, the user can rest for 1d4 + 1 minutes and recover as if they had spent a full night resting. This includes the ability to prepare and cast a new allotment of spells.
The user may touch a single living target up to 8 hit dice and cause them to fall asleep with no saving throw.
The user can breathe out a 30-foot cloud of sleep smoke. All creatures subject to sleep must succeed at a DC 20 Fortitude save or fall into a restful slumber as the spell *sleep*.
The lozenge functions until six uses of any combination of its three abilities are used.

CONSTRUCTION
Requirements Craft Alchemical Magecraft; **Rarity:** Rare
Alchemical Formula: Jacinth Gemstone (5,000 gp), Stasis (x3)

JADE CATAGEMMA OF PRESERVATION
Aura faint abjuration
Slot none; **Price** 200 gp; **Weight** —

DESCRIPTION
When this catagemma is applied, the body is protected from aging for a short while. Any magical aging effect is nullified for one hour.

CONSTRUCTION
Requirements Craft Alchemical Magecraft; **Rarity:** Uncommon
Alchemical Formula: Jade Gemstone (100 gp), Stasis

JADE LOZENGE OF RESUSCITATION

Aura faint conjuration (healing)
Slot none; **Price** 2,000 gp; **Weight** —

DESCRIPTION

When inserted into the mouth of a dying or recently dead person, this pill temporarily restores some semblance of life. They may speak and take a standard action every round, though they may not take any full round actions and their movement is limited to five feet each round. If they engage in any strenuous activity — say, attempting to break up a wedding, steal a princess, kill a count, and make an escape — then there is a strong possibility of death. For every minute that contains any strenuous activity, they must succeed at a DC 5 Constitution check or die. After an hour, if the person taking the pill is still alive, then they are alive for good but gain the exhausted condition.

CONSTRUCTION

Requirements Craft Alchemical Magecraft; **Rarity:** Very Rare
Alchemical Formula: Jade Gemstone (1,000 gp), Life

JASPER CATAGEMMA OF AEGIS

Aura faint abjuration
Slot none; **Price** 2,000 gp; **Weight** —

DESCRIPTION

When this catagemma is rubbed into the skin, it acts as a shield that absorbs damage. It grants DR 5/— to a maximum of 80 points of damage. If it reaches that total or if 24 hours pass, it ceases to function.

CONSTRUCTION

Requirements Craft Alchemical Magecraft; **Rarity:** Rare
Alchemical Formula: Jasper Gemstone (1,000 gp), Protection

JET LOZENGE OF DEATH WARD

Aura faint abjuration
Slot none; **Price** 200 gp; **Weight** —

DESCRIPTION

When this is used, it provides a +4 alchemical bonus to saving throws versus all death effects. This lasts 24 hours.

CONSTRUCTION

Requirements Craft Alchemical Magecraft; **Rarity:** Uncommon
Alchemical Formula: Jet Gemstone (100 gp), Life

LAPIS LAZULI FLOWER OF MORALE

Aura faint enchantment
Slot none; **Price** 100 gp; **Weight** —

DESCRIPTION

The user of this flower has a temporary increase in their leadership ability. They gain a +2 alchemical bonus to their Charisma and an additional +1 bonus to their leadership score. Any of their followers are granted a +1 morale bonus to attacks, armor class, or saves. The user decides.

CONSTRUCTION

Requirements Craft Alchemical Magecraft; **Rarity:** Uncommon
Alchemical Formula: Lapis Lazuli Gemstone (50 gp), Emotion

MALACHITE LOZENGE OF FEATHER FALL

Aura faint abjuration
Slot none; **Price** 100 gp; **Weight** —

DESCRIPTION

Once dissolved, this lozenge remains active for up to 24 hours. It can be triggered by a thought to cause the user to float as gently as a feather if falling for the next minute.

CONSTRUCTION

Requirements Craft Alchemical Magecraft; **Rarity:** Uncommon
Alchemical Formula: Malachite Gemstone (50 gp), Flight

ONYX FULMINATING CHARGE OF CHAOS

Aura faint evocation (chaos)
Slot none; **Price** 200 gp; **Weight** —

DESCRIPTION

When thrown, this charge explodes in the terrible flames of chaos. The effect has a radius of five feet and does 1d4 + 1 points of anarchic damage in addition to causing *confusion* as the spell. You may make a DC 16 Will save for half damage and to avoid the confusion effect. You may use a more valuable stone to increase the effect. Every doubling of the stones value increases the DC by 2, the radius by five feet, and the damage by 1d4 + 1.

TABLE 5–7: ONYX FULMINATING CHARGE POWER INCREASE

Gemstone value	Price	Radius	Save DC	Damage
200 gp	400 gp	10 feet	22	2d4 + 2
400 gp	800 gp	15 feet	24	3d4 + 3
800 gp	1,600 gp	20 feet	26	4d4 + 4
1,600 gp	3,200 gp	25 feet	28	5d4 + 5
3,200 gp	6,400 gp	30 feet	30	6d4 + 6
6,400 gp	12,800 gp	35 feet	32	7d4 + 7

CONSTRUCTION

Requirements Craft Alchemical Magecraft; **Rarity:** Uncommon
Alchemical Formula: Onyx Gemstone (see **Table 5–7** for price), Death

PERIDOT FLOWER OF WARDING

Aura faint abjuration
Slot none; **Price** 1,000 gp; **Weight** —

DESCRIPTION

This scent is of fragrant oils and petals. It wards the user against all magic and sorcery, granting a +4 alchemical bonus against all spells and spell-like effects for 24 hours.

CONSTRUCTION

Requirements Craft Alchemical Magecraft; **Rarity:** Uncommon
Alchemical Formula: Peridot Gemstone (500 gp), Protection

PERIDOT LOZENGE OF WIT

Aura faint enchantment
Slot none; **Price** 1,000 gp; **Weight** —

DESCRIPTION

This increases the user's wit, granting them a silvered razor-sharp tongue that allows them to taunt opponents (figuratively). Taunting is an extraordinary ability that allows you to use your voice as a swift action to enrage your opponent. First, you roll to affect them, rolling a d20 and adding your Charisma modifier and a +5 alchemical bonus for using the lozenge. You must hit a target number equal to 10 + their Wisdom modifier. If you do, they must succeed on a DC 10 + 1/2 the value of your attack Will save or become enraged. This is an enchantment (compulsion) [mind-affecting] effect. While enraged, they cease any activity they are engaged in and attack the person taunting them. This lasts until they are victorious or die or succeed at a DC 20 Will save that they may attempt at the end of their turn. You may continue to taunt them each turn; this raises the DC of the Will save to 30.
You may also taunt a group of indifferent creatures to turn them hostile; they must succeed at a DC 14 Will save to avoid attacking.

CONSTRUCTION

Requirements Craft Alchemical Magecraft; **Rarity:** Uncommon
Alchemical Formula: Peridot Gemstone (500 gp), Mind

ROCK CRYSTAL FLOWER OF SHADE

Aura faint abjuration
Slot none; **Price** 100 gp; **Weight** —

DESCRIPTION

This scent cools and refreshes the wearer, maintaining the temperature of 68° Fahrenheit. If the temperature rises above 160° Fahrenheit, the user feels the temperature rise by 1 degree for each degree it is over 160°. The bearer is protected from heat stroke and exhaustion and other high temperature influences, including superheated air from magma or lava. Anyone standing nearby experiences a cool breeze of fresh air and the scent of freshly turned soil. Once activated, the scent lasts for 24 hours. The effect is not strong enough to resist elemental fire or heat. A *fireball* still does normal damage.

CONSTRUCTION

Requirements Craft Alchemical Magecraft; **Rarity:** Uncommon
Alchemical Formula: Rock Crystal Gemstone (50 gp), Cold

RUBY CATAGEMMA OF THE BURNING TOUCH

Aura faint evocation
Slot none; **Price** 2,000 gp; **Weight** —

DESCRIPTION

Once applied, the user is able to cause her touch to leave searing wounds on opponents. The user must succeed at a touch attack on the target to do 1d6 + 1 points of fire damage. You may use a more valuable stone to increase the effect. Every doubling of the stone's value increases the damage by 1d6 + 1. The catagemma lasts for one hour.

TABLE 5–8: RUBY CATAGEMMA POWER INCREASE

Gemstone value	Price	Damage
2,000 gp	4,000 gp	2d6 + 2
4,000 gp	8,000 gp	3d6 + 3
8,000 gp	16,000 gp	4d6 + 4
16,000 gp	32,000 gp	5d6 + 5
32,000 gp	64,000 gp	6d6 + 6
64,000 gp	128,000 gp	7d6 + 7

CONSTRUCTION

Requirements Craft Alchemical Magecraft; **Rarity:** Uncommon
Alchemical Formula: Ruby Gemstone (1,000 gp and up), Fire (any)

RUBY FLOWER OF WARMTH

Aura faint abjuration
Slot none; **Price** 100 gp; **Weight** —

DESCRIPTION

This scent warms and comforts the wearer, maintaining a temperature of 74° Fahrenheit. Once the temperature reaches −60° Fahrenheit, the temperature lowers 1 degree for every degree lower than −60° that the temperature falls. The bearer is protected from frostbite and hypothermia and other low temperature influences such as freezing shock. Anyone standing nearby experiences a warm breeze of fresh air and the scent of burning wood. Once activated, the scent is produced for 24 hours. This effect is not strong enough to resist elemental cold or ice. An *ice storm* still does normal damage.

CONSTRUCTION

Requirements Craft Alchemical Magecraft; **Rarity:** Uncommon
Alchemical Formula: Ruby Gemstone (50 gp), Fire (any)

RUBY LOZENGE OF FIRE BREATH

Aura faint evocation
Slot none; **Price** 2,000 gp; **Weight** —

DESCRIPTION

Once dissolved, this lozenge lets the user breathe a gout of flame in an arc 20 feet long and 10 feet wide at the far end. The flames do 1d10 + 2 points of fire damage, and targets may make a DC 20 Reflex save for half damage. This can be used every 1d4 rounds for up to an hour.
You may use a more valuable stone to increase the effect. A stone worth at least 5,000 gp in value does 2d10 + 4 points of fire damage and have an arc 40 feet long and 15 feet wide at the far end. A 10,000-gp ruby does 5d10 + 10 points of fire damage and has a gout up to 80 feet long and 20 feet wide at the far end.

CONSTRUCTION

Requirements Craft Alchemical Magecraft; **Rarity:** Uncommon
Alchemical Formula: Ruby Gemstone (1,000 gp and up), Fire (any)

SAPPHIRE LOZENGE OF ESCAPE

Aura faint conjuration (teleportation)
Slot none; **Price** 10,000 gp; **Weight** —

DESCRIPTION

Once this lozenge dissolves, the user has no conscious control over it. The next time the user is grappled, bound, or otherwise physically restrained, he or she immediately teleports to a safe place within 400 feet of his or her choosing.
If the consumer is subject to a magical imprisonment effect such as *maze*, *imprisonment*, or *force cage*, they find themselves teleported to a user-determined safe place that exists on the same plane as the user. The lozenge is active for a full month, and after one use it is no longer effective.

CONSTRUCTION

Requirements Craft Alchemical Magecraft; **Rarity:** Uncommon
Alchemical Formula: Sapphire Gemstone (5,000 gp), Agility

VIOLET GARNET OF HEALTH

Aura moderate transmutation
Slot none; **Price** 1,000 gp; **Weight** —

DESCRIPTION

This scent provides a superior constitution to the bearer, granting a +4 alchemical bonus to Constitution and 2d8 + 2 temporary hit points. It has a duration of 25 hours.

CONSTRUCTION

Requirements Craft Alchemical Magecraft; **Rarity:** Uncommon
Alchemical Formula: Violet Garnet Gemstone (500 gp), Healing

VIOLET GARNET LENS OF ULTRAVISION

Aura moderate transmutation
Slot none; **Price** 1,000 gp; **Weight** —

DESCRIPTION

When applied to the eye, this lens grants darkvision and a +5 competence bonus to Perception checks. These lenses function for a period of up to an hour, which need not be contiguous.

CONSTRUCTION

Requirements Craft Alchemical Magecraft; **Rarity:** Uncommon; **Special Reagents**: Violet Garnet Gemstone (500 gp)
Alchemical Formula: Violet Garnet Gemstone (500 gp), Perception

MATERIAL APOTHEOSIS

Alchemy is not just the creation of items to get you high and melt your opponents' faces. It is the pursuit of purity. The entire endeavor is about taking materials and transforming them into pure substances. And the pursuit of alchemy for some is about reflecting that physical process of material purity into a spiritual one. Material apotheosis is the culmination of that pursuit. Once a material is made so pure that it is no longer the material, but the idea of that material, it can be combined with the soul.

This study is the foundation for all higher levels of alchemy. The materials are removed of all physical, magical, and psionic properties. The purely platonic ideal that remains takes on a powerful resonance. Some of these substances are used as ingredients in the most powerful alchemical creations. Others can be used to transcend reality. These substances straddle the border of reality, existing with physical mass and subjective philosophical spirituality.

Most appear to be an unreal liquid or solid. Some hum or sing or even pulse, sending off mystical energies. All require special containers as part of the crafting cost — vials made of diamond or woven sacks of translucent ether or other fantastic restraints. These containers cannot be reused. Universal solvents are used in the makeup of these items, see **Chapter Three: Alchemical Items** for more information on crafting universal solvents and their costs and properties.

Even though these are enchanted items, material apotheosis may be accomplished only with alchemy. The crafter must possess the Craft Alchemical Magecraft feat, as well as have the ability to cast *limited wish*, and he or she must be able to succeed at the Craft (Alchemy) skill roll required in order to craft a Material Apotheosis. Due to the mystical and alchemical processes involved, only one of these may be crafted by any individual alchemist during each lunar cycle.

True metals work on any substance or target, but the spirituality of the alchemist is relevant in the creation and use of elemental transubstantiation. These may be created only by a skilled alchemist and may be used only by the alchemist that created them. This is not magic, but material above divinity. Although our understanding of the basic effects is listed below, the spiritual nature of the creator of the substance must be taken into account, for the effects will be modified by the nature of the alchemist. The nature of these modifications is left up to the whims

of the gods (or the imagination of your GM). Any individual item may be affected only by one true metal, and any alchemist may consume only one elemental transubstantiation in their lifetime.

The prices given are for their hypothetical value. No one with access to an apotheosis will sell it (or even can sell it, in the case of elemental transubstantiations), and even if they did, there are plenty of people who would rather just kill the holder rather than hand over the wealth of a kingdom.

APOTHEOSIS OF AIR (ELEMENTAL TRANSUBSTANTIATION)
Aura overwhelming transmutation; **CL** 13th
Slot none; **Price** —; **Weight** —

DESCRIPTION
This creates a handful of light crystalline grains that swirl around in different shapes as if blown by the wind. They are multicolored pastels that leave tiny visible burns behind as they scar the dimensional boundaries with their motion. They require no container, being controlled and contained by the will of the creator. If he or she is killed before the grains are consumed, they fall to the ground as harmless, useless, gray dust.

When they are consumed, the imbiber permanently gains the power of flight. Their flight skill gains a permanent alchemical bonus equal to their level. They gain a flight speed of 100 feet. They also become immune to falling damage and take half damage from bludgeoning attacks. They also gain Darkvision out to 60 feet or have the range of their Darkvision increase by 60 feet if they already possess it.

This requires a successful DC 40 Craft (alchemy) check to create. As with all elemental transubstantiations, only the alchemist who crafted it possesses the spiritual purity to consume it.

CONSTRUCTION
Requirements Craft Alchemical Magecraft, *limited wish*, *overland flight*;
Cost 101,350 gp; **Rarity:** Very Rare
Alchemical Formula: Air (any), Universal Solvent

APOTHEOSIS OF COPPER (TRUE COPPER)

Aura overwhelming transmutation; **CL** 13th
Slot none; **Price** —; **Weight** —

DESCRIPTION

This is contained within a transparent lead vial. It produces a rich copper liquid that is never still and swirls with metallic highlights that glow within the flask. Even after looking away, you can see the highlights in the back of your eyes for hours afterward.

When this substance is added to up to one ton of molten gold, it transforms the substance into Orichalcum.

This requires a successful DC 35 Craft (alchemy) check to create.

CONSTRUCTION

Requirements Craft Alchemical Magecraft, *limited wish*, *wall of iron*; **Cost** 101,550 gp; **Rarity:** Very Rare
Alchemical Formula: Copper, Universal Solvent

APOTHEOSIS OF EARTH (ELEMENTAL TRANSUBSTANTIATION)

Aura overwhelming transmutation; **CL** 13th
Slot none; **Price** —; **Weight** —

DESCRIPTION

This requires a bowl made from platinum and lead filled with thick, heavy, solid, brown grains that always rest as close to the ground as possible. They exude a scent of rich earth.

Once consumed, the alchemist gains a +8 inherent Strength bonus while standing on or in earth or stone. They also gain darkvision out to 60 feet or gain an additional 60 feet of range if they have it already. They gain tremorsense out to 60 feet.

They also gain the ability to earthglide at their base speed.

This requires a successful DC 40 Craft (alchemy) check to create. As with all elemental transubstantiations, only the alchemist who crafted it possesses the spiritual purity to consume it.

CONSTRUCTION

Requirements Craft Alchemical Magecraft, *limited wish*, *move earth*; **Cost** 101,350 gp; **Rarity:** Very Rare
Alchemical Formula: Earth (any), Universal Solvent

APOTHEOSIS OF FIRE (ELEMENTAL TRANSUBSTANTIATION)

Aura overwhelming transmutation; **CL** 13th
Slot none; **Price** —; **Weight** —

DESCRIPTION

This creates a bright sphere an inch in diameter made of white flame. It has a luminous aura that radiates out with blues, reds, and greens shot throughout it in burning electric lines. It is warm to the touch, but not hot.

Once consumed, the alchemist becomes immune to all fire and heat. She could bathe in magma. She may also raise the temperature of her body to catch items on fire. She can do an additional 1d6 + 1 points of fire damage on any melee attack with a bare hand or a weapon. She may also fling fire bolts at targets as ranged touch attacks that do 1d4 + 1 points of fire damage as an attack action, or breathe fire in a 15-foot cone doing 5d6 points of damage to all targets caught in the blast as a standard action. Victims may succeed at a DC 18 Reflex save for half damage. All of these may be done at will. She gains vulnerability to cold and ice, with a −2 alchemical penalty to save on any magical or natural attacks that involve cold or ice.

This requires a successful DC 40 Craft (alchemy) check to create. As with all elemental transubstantiations, only the alchemist who crafted it possesses the spiritual purity to consume it.

CONSTRUCTION

Requirements Craft Alchemical Magecraft, *limited wish*, *delayed blast fireball*; **Cost** 101,350 gp; **Rarity:** Very Rare
Alchemical Formula: Fire (any), Universal Solvent

APOTHEOSIS OF GOLD (TRUE GOLD)

Aura overwhelming transmutation; **CL** 13th
Slot none; **Price** —; **Weight** —

DESCRIPTION

This appears as one ounce of a clear liquid with an iridescent blue tinge. Countless golden flakes float within the liquid, which radiates a shining golden aura that casts light out to 10 feet. When given to any person or used on any corpse, it restores that person to life as *resurrection* regardless of the length of time that person has been deceased.

Whether taken by a living or dead person, all wounds are healed and all limbs regenerated. If taken or used on a living person, the imbiber is restored to the prime of their lives. Humans return to being 25 years old. A DC 2 Constitution check roll must be made to survive. The difficulty increases by +1 DC per decade for the first century of death, and then by +1 DC per century after that. If living, the DC increases by 2 for every 10% of lifespan past your prime.

If this apotheosis is used a second time, the final DC of the first Constitution check is the base DC of the second. For example, humans have a maximum age of 70 + 2d20 years; this puts 10% of their lifespan equal to 11 years (70 + 40 = 110). So a 50-year-old human takes the *apotheosis of gold* and reverts to 25 years of age. This is an age reduction of 25 years (25 divided by 11 is 2.27, which is rounded down to 2). Every 10% increases the DC of the check by 2. In this case, the total DC of the Constitution save of the survival check is increased by 4. This person succeeds at their DC 6 Constitution check. If they wait until they are 50 and take the *apotheosis of gold* again, then their new DC is a DC 10 Constitution check. They use their new base of 6, the difficulty from last time, plus the same increase of 4, for being 20% of your lifespan past your prime. Everyone has to die sometime.

This requires a successful DC 35 Craft (alchemy) check to create.

CONSTRUCTION

Requirements Craft Alchemical Magecraft, *limited wish*, *raise dead*; **Cost** 102,400 gp; **Rarity:** Very Rare
Alchemical Formula: Gold, Universal Solvent

APOTHEOSIS OF IRON (ELEMENTAL TRANSUBSTANTIATION)

Aura overwhelming transmutation; **CL** 13th
Slot none; **Price** —; **Weight** —

DESCRIPTION

This creates one dram of gray, sand-like grains. They are much heavier than they appear. When they shift against each other, they make a sound like grinding stone.

When consumed, this gives the imbiber a perfect body. Their hit points increase as if they had rolled maximum rolls for hit points at each level and their Constitution gains a +6 permanent untyped bonus and their Charisma gains a +2 permanent untyped bonus as they become more attractive.

The alchemist also gains perfect control over his or her body functions, which allows them, for example, to speed up their heart rate, control the flow of their blood, and strengthen and toughen their skin. The alchemist also gains DR 5/—.

They may also generate an electrical charge using their body and can do 1d4 + 1 points of electrical damage with a touch attack and do an additional 1d4 + 1 points of electrical damage on any successful melee strike with a metal weapon or a natural attack.

This requires a successful DC 40 Craft (alchemy) check to create. As with all elemental transubstantiations, only the alchemist who crafted it possesses the spiritual purity to consume it.

CONSTRUCTION

Requirements Craft Alchemical Magecraft, *limited wish*, *stoneskin*; **Cost** 101,550 gp; **Rarity:** Very Rare
Alchemical Formula: Iron, Universal Solvent

APOTHEOSIS OF LEAD (TRUE LEAD)
Aura overwhelming transmutation; **CL** 13th
Slot none; **Price** —; **Weight** —

DESCRIPTION
Once completed this produces one ounce of clear translucent liquid surrounding a smoky gray spider-web like cloud that contracts and expands while emitting dim flashes of orchid and alabaster light.
This substance can mix with paint, mortar, or metal to cover 1,000 square feet or 100 cubic feet of material, providing the material with a spell resistance of 35. It provides this resistance to the armor or surface only.
This requires a successful DC 35 Craft (alchemy) check to create.

CONSTRUCTION
Requirements Craft Alchemical Magecraft, *limited wish*, *globe of invulnerability*; **Cost** 102,150 gp; **Rarity:** Very Rare
Alchemical Formula: Lead, Universal Solvent

APOTHEOSIS OF MERCURY (TRUE MERCURY)
Aura overwhelming transmutation; **CL** 15th
Slot none; **Price** —; **Weight** —

DESCRIPTION
Once completed, this produces one dram of fine metallic reddish grains (60 grains). When the grains slide and run across each other, the grains make soft noises that sound like the ringing of distant brass bells.
When mixed with molten lead, each grain transmutes that lead to purest molten gold. The change is nearly instantaneous. Each grain transmutes approximately 100 pounds of lead. Each pound of lead costs 6 gp, so 6,000 pounds of lead costs 36,000 gp. Each pound of gold is worth 50 gp, so 6,000 pounds of lead converted to gold is equal to 300,000 gp. This provides a net profit of 161,850 gp. This includes the crafting price. Note the results of a failed crafting check, per the standard rules.
This requires a successful DC 35 Craft (alchemy) check to create.

CONSTRUCTION
Requirements Craft Alchemical Magecraft, *limited wish*, *polymorph any object*; **Cost** 102,150 gp; **Rarity:** Very Rare
Alchemical Formula: Mercury (any), Universal Solvent

APOTHEOSIS OF PLATINUM (TRUE PLATINUM)
Aura overwhelming transmutation; **CL** 13th
Slot none; **Price** —; **Weight** —

DESCRIPTION
This creates one ounce of silvery liquid, within which swirls a dark vortex that absorbs all light and color. Small particles of colored light appear outside the vial, before they spiral away into nothingness.
This substance is used to coat one small item. For every application of one ounce, the item can then absorb 1d4 + 1 spell levels of spells cast at the bearer of the item. These spell levels can be discharged as a standard action that automatically hits a single target within 30 feet to do 1d6 + 1 points of damage per stored spell level. All stored spell levels need not be discharged at once. The victim may succeed at a DC 20 Reflex save for half damage. These stored spell levels may also allow the bearer to cast spells, draining the spell levels from the item instead of having the spell leave their brain.
Spell levels absorbed last for one hour before they begin to fade, losing one spell level an hour from the item. If a spell of a higher level is cast than the item can absorb, it does not absorb the spell.
An item may be doused in true platinum more than once, but each attempt past the first carries a cumulative 15% chance of failure. In the event of failure, the item cannot accept any further doses of true platinum.
This requires a successful DC 35 Craft (alchemy) check to create.

CONSTRUCTION
Requirements Craft Alchemical Magecraft, *limited wish*, *spell turning*; **Cost** 121,750 gp; **Rarity:** Very Rare
Alchemical Formula: Platinum, Universal Solvent

APOTHEOSIS OF SILVER (TRUE SILVER)
Aura overwhelming transmutation; **CL** 13th
Slot none; **Price** —gp; **Weight** —

DESCRIPTION
This creates one ounce of dark silver liquid. It appears as if thousands of insubstantial cubes tumble throughout the vial.
A drop mixes with paint, mortar, or metal to cover up to 1,000 square feet or 100 cubic feet of material to provide a +1 bonus on saves. If a drop is mixed with molten metal or applied to armor, it gives a +1 enhancement bonus to armor class or weapon attacks and damages.
This can be applied multiple times, stacking the bonus, each time carrying a cumulative failure chance of 25% for each application past the first. In the event of a failure, no more applications are possible, but the given bonus remains. Because it is applied when molten, the drops must be added in total first, and then the failure chance is checked.
An ounce contains 360 drops.
This requires a successful DC 35 Craft (alchemy) check to create.

CONSTRUCTION
Requirements Craft Alchemical Magecraft, *limited wish*, *magic vestment*; **Cost** 107,800 gp; **Rarity:** Very Rare
Alchemical Formula: Silver, Universal Solvent

APOTHEOSIS OF SULFUR (ELEMENTAL TRANSUBSTANTIATION)
Aura overwhelming transmutation; **CL** 13th
Slot none; **Price** —; **Weight** —

DESCRIPTION
This creates a small transparent sphere. Although it is just the size of a pebble, it weighs approximately one stone (20–25 lbs.). A small gold light smolders within its center.
Anyone who consumes this stone is cursed with immortality. They cease to age and can no longer die. If their body parts are severed or removed, they still continue to live. A heart beats, a head talks, and an arm grasps. The limb reattaches seamlessly if recovered.
It also has the side effect of making the body immune to alteration. Any new tattoos fade in a week, and haircuts regrow in a few hours. The alchemist preserves his body in its current form for eternity.
The subject no longer ages and is no long affected by effects that cause death or damage. They can be hurt or wounded, but this damage heals quickly.
The subject gains Fast Healing 5. Even acid and fire do nothing to stop this healing.

There are only two ways to stop someone who consumes an apotheosis of sulfur. First, you may entomb the body, either together or separately. Entombment can also include banishment to extraplanar prisons. The other way is to destroy every atom of the imbiber's body simultaneously by exposing them to the molten center of a planet, throwing them into a star, or having them be victim to a retributive strike, a *bag of holding* being inserted into a *portable hole*, or some other conflagration of magical power.

Most alchemists who imbibe this elemental transubstantiation regret it. As the centuries pass, their skin turns more ashen and they begin to look less human.

This requires a successful DC 40 Craft (alchemy) check to create. As with all elemental transubstantiations, only the alchemist who crafted it possesses the spiritual purity to consume it.

CONSTRUCTION

Requirements Craft Alchemical Magecraft, *limited wish*, *statue*; **Cost** 113,800 gp; **Rarity:** Very Rare
Alchemical Formula: Sulfur (any), Universal Solvent

APOTHEOSIS OF TIN (TRUE TIN)

Aura overwhelming transmutation; **CL** 17th
Slot none; **Price** —; **Weight** —

DESCRIPTION

This creates one ounce of liquid that burns as a gray flame within the bottle. A drop of this substance animates any small object it is poured on that is less than nine cubic feet. It imparts no will, ego, or mobility not already possessed by the object. A sword cannot float but could unsheathe itself only to fall on the floor. A stool could walk across the room on its legs. The objects follow the alchemist's simple commands. This animation is permanent. There are 360 drops to an ounce. It is said that this can be useful if one wishes to provide true life to a construct, though one would need the entire ounce to succeed at such a procedure.

This requires a successful DC 35 Craft (alchemy) check to create.

CONSTRUCTION

Requirements Craft Alchemical Magecraft, *wish*; **Cost** 103,450 gp; **Rarity:** Very Rare
Alchemical Formula: Tin, Universal Solvent

APOTHEOSIS OF WATER (ELEMENTAL TRANSUBSTANTIATION)

Aura overwhelming transmutation; **CL** 13th
Slot none; **Price** —; **Weight** —

DESCRIPTION

This creates a dark blue liquid that glows with an eerie green light. When imbibed, the alchemist gains the ability to breathe water and to walk upon any non-solid liquid surface (water, clouds). She gains a swim speed double her walking speed and gains an immunity to any magical or natural attacks involving cold or ice. As a standard action, she may breathe a 15-foot cone of freezing wind that does 5d6 points of cold damage. It also covers the terrain in ice for 1d4 + 1 rounds. Victims may succeed at a DC 16 Fortitude save for half damage. A creature traversing slick ice at more than half speed is required to make a DC 15 Acrobatics check at the start of the movement. Failure causes the creature to fall prone at the start of the movement. Running or charging on slick ice increases the DC by 5, with the same effect on a failed skill check. A creature that succeeds at this check by 5 or more can increase its move across the ice by 10 feet but is considered flat-footed until the start of its next turn. Creatures (like those with enough levels of barbarian or rogue) that can't be caught flat-footed at the start of combat are immune to this flat-footed effect as well.

Her health, movement, vision, and mobility are not affected by cold or ice. She gains a fire vulnerability with a −2 alchemical penalty to save against any magical or natural attack that involves heat or flame.

This requires a successful DC 40 Craft (alchemy) check to create. As with all elemental transubstantiations, only the alchemist who crafted it possesses the spiritual purity to consume it.

CONSTRUCTION

Requirements Craft Alchemical Magecraft, *limited wish*, *water breathing*; **Cost** 101,350 gp; **Rarity:** Very Rare
Alchemical Formula: Water (any), Universal Solvent

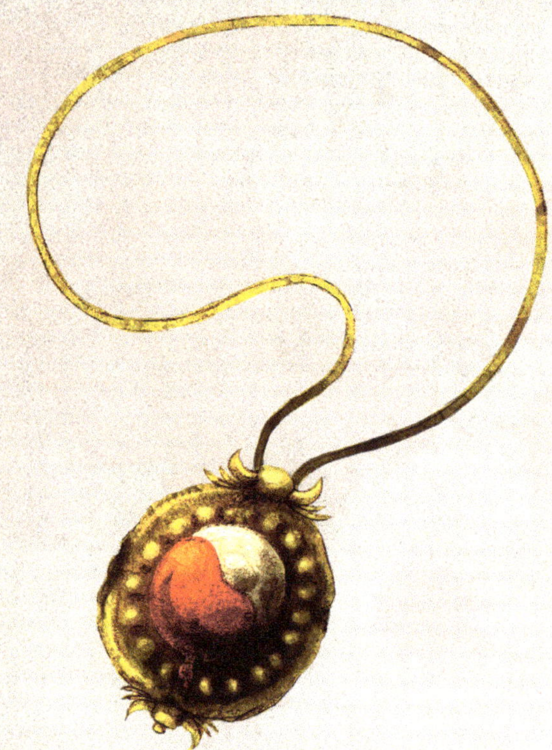

SIGILS

Sigils are magical runes. They are a specialized form of glyph engraved on a metal and worn like an amulet. They are powered and activated by the unconscious energies of the wearer — they work by focusing this energy.

Anyone may use a sigil, but the sigil must be made for the use of a specific person. If anyone besides the person the sigil was made for attempts to use the sigil, it has no effect. Anyone with Craft Alchemical Magecraft may also reassign sigils. Sigils work only for the user they are created for, but the sigil may be reassigned by anyone with this feat using a process that costs 1,000 gp in raw materials and takes one day.

When the sigil is concentrated on, the energy is focused and causes the effect for which this sigil is created. This is a full-round action.

Unless otherwise noted, this effect lasts for one hour. Multiple sigils may be carried and used. Sigils may be activated up to twice daily. Between any two activations of any two sigils, there must be a rest period of at least six hours. Attempts to use sigils more frequently result in unconsciousness lasting between 10–60 minutes and severe headaches, causing the sickened condition for 24 hours due to the unconscious energy of the subject being exhausted. Under no circumstances may the user activate any number of sigils more than twice a day, even if they are of different types. To craft and reassign sigils, the feat Craft Alchemical Magecraft must be taken.

There are three categories of sigils: silver, golden, and platinum. Examples of several types are given below, although other reasonable sigils can be created. Silver sigils usually contain minor personal effects equivalent to 2nd-level spells or less; golden sigils contain more powerful detection and enhancement effects equivalent to 3rd- to 5th-level spells; and platinum sigils contain more damaging and debilitating effects equivalent to 6th- to 8th-level spells in power.

Sigils do *not* directly duplicate spell effects (see potions) but they are a type of enchanted rune crafted specifically for a person to achieve a desired end. They are quite popular charms with merchants and nobility that can afford to have them crafted. Certain occupations and jobs also use sigils as tools in order to accomplish dangerous or distasteful jobs.

Note that actual gemstones are required to create these, not carats of gemstone powder.

TABLE 5–9: SIGILS

Name	Price
Sigil of Allegiance Detection	6,000 gp
Sigil of Curing	2,000 gp
Sigil of Dimensional Jaunts	18,000 gp
Sigil of Extension	6,000 gp
Sigil of Extrasensory Perception	6,000 gp
Sigil of Fear	18,000 gp
Sigil of Fire Resistance	2,000 gp
Sigil of Flame	18,000 gp
Sigil of Fortitude	2,000 gp
Sigil of Gusting Winds	18,000 gp
Sigil of Healing	2,000 gp
Sigil of Holding	18,000 gp
Sigil of Hypnotism	18,000 gp
Sigil of Life Detection	6,000 gp
Sigil of Light	6,000 gp
Sigil of Protection from Evil	6,000 gp
Sigil of Silence	18,000 gp
Sigil of Sprightly Stride	2,000 gp
Sigil of Strength	2,000 gp
Sigil of Swaddling	2,000 gp
Sigil of the Sea	6,000 gp
Sigil of Tongues	6,000 gp

SIGIL OF ALLEGIANCE DETECTION
Aura moderate divination; **CL** 9th
Slot neck; **Price** 6,000 gp; **Weight** —

DESCRIPTION
When activated, this sigil allows the user to examine a creature to determine its alignment with certain universal forces. For one minute, you may examine an area or creatures for law, goodness, chaos, or evil, as the appropriate detection spell.

CONSTRUCTION
Requirements Craft Alchemical Magecraft, *detect law/good/chaos/evil*; **Cost** 3,000 gp; **Rarity:** Rare
Alchemical Formula: Gold, Water (any), Perception

SIGIL OF CURING
Aura moderate conjuration (healing); **CL** 5th
Slot neck; **Price** 2,000 gp; **Weight** —

DESCRIPTION
When activated, this sigil begins to cure disease. It must be activated while resting once a day for six days. If the user engages in other activities besides bedrest, it disrupts the healing process.

CONSTRUCTION
Requirements Craft Alchemical Magecraft, *cure disease*; **Cost** 1,000 gp; **Rarity:** Uncommon
Alchemical Formula: Silver, Water (any), Healing

SIGIL OF DIMENSIONAL JAUNTS

Aura strong conjuration (teleportation); **CL** 15th
Slot neck; **Price** 18,000 gp; **Weight** —

DESCRIPTION

This sigil allows the user to instantly transport themselves to any location within 400 feet. It takes one full-round action to make this journey. Anything held is transported with the user. If your destination is occupied, you take 2d6 points of bludgeoning damage and are shunted to the nearest open space. If there is no open space within 100 feet, you must make a DC 22 Fortitude save or die. On a success you take another 4d6 points of bludgeoning damage and are shunted to the nearest open space. Once activated, you may make one such jump every minute.

It is possible to add an additional reagent to the creation of this sigil that allows you to gain a dimensional step ability, which allows you to transport yourself at will as a swift action from a location of one substance to another within 400 feet. No more than one additional reagent can be applied. If this is found instead of crafted, there is a 25% chance of the sigil being modified.

TABLE 5–10: DIMENSIONAL JAUNT ESSENCES

Dimensional Step Type	Essence
Fire Step	Fire Essence (10)
Shadow Step	Light Essence (20)
Tree Step	Plant Essence (10)

CONSTRUCTION

Requirements Craft Alchemical Magecraft, *dimensional door*, *teleport*; **Cost** 9,000 gp; **Rarity:** Very Rare
Alchemical Formula: Platinum, Air (any), Transportation

SIGIL OF EXTENSION

Aura moderate transmutation; **CL** 9th
Slot neck; **Price** 6,000 gp; **Weight** —

DESCRIPTION

When held aloft while casting a spell, this sigil extends the duration of the spell by 50% (a spell that lasts four rounds will now last six). This functions for one spell.

CONSTRUCTION

Requirements Craft Alchemical Magecraft, *mage's lucubration*; **Cost** 3,000 gp; **Rarity:** Rare
Alchemical Formula: Gold, Azoth (any), Stasis

SIGIL OF EXTRASENSORY PERCEPTION

Aura moderate divination; **CL** 9th
Slot neck; **Price** 6,000 gp; **Weight** —

DESCRIPTION

When activated, this provides a similar effect to detect thoughts. You can detect the thoughts of those nearby and after a period of concentration, sift through them. Each round of concentration produces a more powerful effect. The effects of this sigil last for one minute.

TABLE 5–11: SIGIL OF EXTRASENORY PERCEPTION EFFECTS

Round	Effect
1st	Detect the presence or absence of thinking creatures
2nd	Detects the number and intelligence of each creature
3rd	Detects the surface thoughts of a creature in the area. Targets receive a DC 14 Will save to resist if they wish. A failure allows you to try again for the duration. Each time a target succeeds on this saving throw, the user of the sigil takes 1d4 points of nonlethal damage.
4th	Allows you to scan a mind for the answer for a specific question or to get information on a general topic. This can be used only on a target that has had its surface thoughts detected. The target can succeed at a DC 12 Will save to resist. A failure to scan the target's mind allows you to try again for the duration. Every time a target succeeds on this saving throw, the user of the sigil takes 2d4 points of nonlethal damage.

CONSTRUCTION

Requirements Craft Alchemical Magecraft, *detect thoughts*; **Cost** 3,000 gp; **Rarity:** Rare
Alchemical Formula: Gold, Azoth (any), Perception

SIGIL OF FEAR

Aura strong necromancy; **CL** 15th
Slot neck; **Price** 18,000 gp; **Weight** —

DESCRIPTION

Once activated, this sigil causes all who view the possessor to see her as fearful and terrible. Creatures with less than 4 hit dice flee. Creatures who have 4–10 hit dice must make a DC 20 Will save or gain the frightened condition. Creatures who have more than 10 hit dice must make a DC 20 Will save or become shaken. The sigil may be activated once, affecting all who see it, and the condition lasts for one minute.

CONSTRUCTION

Requirements Craft Alchemical Magecraft, *fear*; **Cost** 9,000 gp; **Rarity:** Very Rare
Alchemical Formula: Platinum, Azoth (any), Fear

SIGIL OF FIRE RESISTANCE

Aura moderate abjuration; **CL** 5th
Slot neck; **Price** 2,000 gp; **Weight** —

DESCRIPTION

This grants the user Resist Fire 5 and a +2 resistance bonus to saving throws made versus fire.

CONSTRUCTION

Requirements Craft Alchemical Magecraft, *resist energy*; **Cost** 1,000 gp; **Rarity:** Uncommon
Alchemical Formula: Silver, Fire (any), Protection

SIGIL OF FLAME

Aura strong evocation [fire]; **CL** 15th
Slot neck; **Price** 18,000 gp; **Weight** —

DESCRIPTION

When activated, this sigil produces a gout of flame. It strikes out in a line that is five feet wide and 15 feet long, affecting all targets in the line. It does 4d6 + 6 points of damage to all targets, who may make a DC 16 Reflex save for half damage. This effect lasts for one minute and allows the user to activate a gout of flame as a standard action for this duration.

CONSTRUCTION

Requirements Craft Alchemical Magecraft, *fireball*; **Cost** 9,000 gp; **Rarity:** Very Rare
Alchemical Formula: Platinum, Fire (any), Body, Transmutation

SIGIL OF FORTITUDE

Aura moderate abjuration; **CL** 5th
Slot neck; **Price** 2,000 gp; **Weight** —

DESCRIPTION

When activated, this sigil prevents sickness and nausea. For the duration, the user is immune to being sickened or nauseated. If activated while ill, this calms the user's stomach and nerves, and all penalties are eliminated. At the end of the duration, the protection ends. If still under effects that cause those conditions, the conditions return.

CONSTRUCTION

Requirements Craft Alchemical Magecraft, *remove sickness*; **Cost** 1,000 gp; **Rarity:** Uncommon
Alchemical Formula: Silver, Body, Protection

SIGIL OF GUSTING WINDS

Aura strong evocation [air]; **CL** 15th
Slot neck; **Price** 18,000 gp; **Weight** —

DESCRIPTION

When held forth and invoked, a mighty gust of wind originates from the sigil and moves in the direction the sigil is displayed. The 30–50 mile per hour winds extinguish light sources and fan larger fires. Small or smaller flying creatures are blown back 1d6 x 10 feet. Medium flying creatures must succeed at a DC 15 flight check in order to move at half-speed toward the wind. Larger flying creatures are not affected. Vapors and gases are dispersed. Medium and smaller creatures on the ground must make DC 15 Acrobatics checks to move without falling prone at full speed. They may move at half-speed in the area with no penalty. Missile and thrown weapon attacks that pass through the area of effect have a −8 penalty to hit. This effect covers an area up to 20 feet wide and 100 feet long. It lasts for one minute and may be aimed as the wielder desires.

CONSTRUCTION

Requirements Craft Alchemical Magecraft, *gust of wind*; **Cost** 9,000 gp; **Rarity:** Very Rare
Alchemical Formula: Platinum, Air (any), Strength (x3)

SIGIL OF HEALING

Aura moderate conjuration (healing); **CL** 5th
Slot neck; **Price** 2,000 gp; **Weight** —

DESCRIPTION

When activated, this heals the user for 1d6 + 1 points of damage.

CONSTRUCTION

Requirements Craft Alchemical Magecraft, *cure light wounds*; **Cost** 1,000 gp; **Rarity:** Uncommon
Alchemical Formula: Silver, Healing

SIGIL OF HOLDING

Aura strong enchantment (compulsion) [mind-affecting]; **CL** 15th
Slot neck; **Price** 18,000 gp; **Weight** —

DESCRIPTION

Once activated, the user can attempt to use the sigil to paralyze creatures. Each round, the user may attempt to hold up to any number of humanoid creatures no more than 30 feet apart, or one or two living creatures that are not humanoids. If holding a group of humanoids, every target must save versus a DC 18 Will save or be paralyzed. They may repeat this save as a full-round action, and the paralysis ends when it is successful. If targeting a single non-humanoid living creature, it must succeed at a DC 20 Will save. Attempting to hold two monstrous creatures requires them to make DC 16 Will saves. Failures on these saves mean the target is paralyzed. They may retry the save as a full-round action.

This effect lasts for one minute, and the user may target a new group of creatures or the same creatures each round as a standard action. Targeting a new group frees the old group. Targeting an existing group requires them to succeed at a save versus the new paralysis attempt, as well as succeeding at their save as a full-round action.

CONSTRUCTION

Requirements Craft Alchemical Magecraft, *hold monster*; **Cost** 9,000 gp; **Rarity:** Very Rare
Alchemical Formula: Platinum, Stasis (x3)

SIGIL OF HYPNOTISM

Aura strong enchantment (compulsion) [mind-affecting; **CL** 15th
Slot neck; **Price** 18,000 gp; **Weight** —

DESCRIPTION

When held aloft, this sigil spins, reflecting interesting pulses of light. All living creatures within 30 feet not allied with the sigil holder must succeed at a DC 18 Will save. If they fail this save, they stop taking actions and stare at the holder of this sigil, becoming fascinated, for as long as he keeps the sigil displayed. During this time, the wielder may make a language-dependent *suggestion* as the spell to the targets who failed their will save. They view that suggestion as reasonable for as long as it doesn't result in harming themselves or others they care about. Taking damage ends this effect. Anyone disturbing the creature (slapping, yelling at it, etc.) grants the creature a new saving throw. Anyone who looks at the sigil within 30 feet must make a saving throw once per round to avoid being fascinated by it.

Creatures in combat, paranoid, or untrusting of the caster have a +2 circumstance bonus on this saving throw. If this is used to affect only a single creature outside of combat, that target must make a DC 20 Will save to avoid the effect. Creatures that have been hypnotized do not recall that it occurred. This effect lasts for up to one minute.

CONSTRUCTION

Requirements Craft Alchemical Magecraft, *dominate person*; **Cost** 9,000 gp; **Rarity:** Very Rare
Alchemical Formula: Platinum, Control, Mind

SIGIL OF LIFE DETECTION

Aura moderate divination; **CL** 9th
Slot neck; **Price** 6,000 gp; **Weight** —

DESCRIPTION

This allows the user to determine the presence of life in all creatures within her vision. The user is able to note connections to either the Positive or Negative Material planes. This allows him to tell how much life a creature has, as well as if it is living, dead, or undead. This vision extends through walls and other obstructions to vision but is blocked by more than 10 feet of stone, one foot of metal, or a thin sheet of lead. When activated, this ability lasts for one minute.

CONSTRUCTION

Requirements Craft Alchemical Magecraft, *detect thoughts*; **Cost** 3,000 gp; **Rarity:** Rare
Alchemical Formula: Gold, Life

SIGIL OF LIGHT

Aura moderate evocation (light); **CL** 9th
Slot neck; **Price** 6,000 gp; **Weight** —

DESCRIPTION

When activated, this causes the sigil to shed light for 60 feet that is visible only to the holder. The illumination in the area is unchanged for all other creatures that are unable to view the light from this sigil.

CONSTRUCTION

Requirements Craft Alchemical Magecraft, *light*; **Cost** 3,000 gp; **Rarity:** Rare
Alchemical Formula: Gold, Light

SIGIL OF PROTECTION FROM EVIL

Aura moderate abjuration; **CL** 9th
Slot neck; **Price** 6,000 gp; **Weight** —

DESCRIPTION

This sigil protects the user from evil, as the spell *protection from evil*.

CONSTRUCTION

Requirements Craft Alchemical Magecraft, *magic circle against evil*; **Cost** 3,000 gp; **Rarity:** Rare
Alchemical Formula: Gold, Protection

SIGIL OF SILENCE

Aura strong transmutation; **CL** 15th
Slot neck; **Price** 18,000 gp; **Weight** —

DESCRIPTION

This sigil silences a single creature. When presented to a target, the target's lips disappear and appear on the sigil itself. The lips still appear to move but no sound comes out, and the target no longer has a mouth. If a target has a bite attack, breath weapon, or other effect, it no longer functions. You must be within 30 feet of the target. There is no saving throw. It may be activated only once, affecting one target.

CONSTRUCTION

Requirements Craft Alchemical Magecraft, *silence*; **Cost** 9,000 gp; **Rarity:** Rare
Alchemical Formula: Platinum, Body, Transmutation

SIGIL OF SPRIGHTLY STRIDE

Aura moderate enchantment; **CL** 5th
Slot neck; **Price** 2,000 gp; **Weight** —

DESCRIPTION

This allows the user to be unimpeded by their environment. They treat difficult terrain as normal terrain. They may pass through underbrush, overgrowth, and briars without leaving a trace. They also gain a +4 to their CMD versus grapples or other effects that impede movement and the Escape Artist skill.

CONSTRUCTION

Requirements Craft Alchemical Magecraft, *feather step*; **Cost** 1,000 gp; **Rarity:** Uncommon
Alchemical Formula: Silver, Agility

SIGIL OF STRENGTH

Aura moderate enchantment; **CL** 5th
Slot neck; **Price** 2,000 gp; **Weight** —

DESCRIPTION

This grants the user a +4 enhancement bonus to strength. This bonus lasts for 1d4 + 4 rounds.

CONSTRUCTION

Requirements Craft Alchemical Magecraft, *bull's strength*; **Cost** 1,000 gp; **Rarity:** Uncommon
Alchemical Formula: Silver, Strength

SIGIL OF SWADDLING

Aura moderate abjuration; **CL** 5th
Slot neck; **Price** 2,000 gp; **Weight** —

DESCRIPTION

When activated, this protects the user in several ways. First you gain DR 5 / piercing. You are also kept warm and protected from nonmagical extremes of cold for the duration. This reduction from damage lasts for one minute, but the warmth lasts for a full six hours.

CONSTRUCTION

Requirements Craft Alchemical Magecraft, *cushioning bands*; **Cost** 1,400 gp; **Rarity:** Uncommon
Alchemical Formula: Silver, Protection

SIGIL OF THE SEA
Aura moderate transmutation; **CL** 9th
Slot neck; **Price** 6,000 gp; **Weight** —

DESCRIPTION
This allowed the user of this sigil extended mobility underwater. Once activated, the user is able to breathe water or other aerated liquids as if they were air. They also grow webbing between their fingers, hair recedes into their body, and their skin becomes thick and rubbery. They gain a swim speed of 30 feet as well as a +10 circumstance bonus on swim checks. In addition, penalties for underwater combat are ignored.

CONSTRUCTION
Requirements Craft Alchemical Magecraft, *water breathing*, *freedom of movement*; **Cost** 3,000 gp; **Rarity:** Rare
Alchemical Formula: Gold, Transmutation

SIGIL OF TONGUES
Aura moderate transmutation; **CL** 9th
Slot neck; **Price** 6,000 gp; **Weight** —

DESCRIPTION
When activated, this sigil allows the user to read and comprehend any languages, as well as hear and speak any languages. Note that this effect just allows the user to translate what is heard or read into something they understand; it does not grant the user any specific knowledge of the language in question. The user cannot speak any words of any language he or she does not know unless he or she is actively seeking to communicate with a creature that does not share a language with the user. In that case, they communicate what they wish to say in a language the target understands.

CONSTRUCTION
Requirements Craft Alchemical Magecraft, *comprehend languages*, *suggestion*; **Cost** 3,000 gp; **Rarity:** Rare
Alchemical Formula: Gold, Perception

Talismans
Talismans are special items that take pure alchemical gemstones and focus their power. There are only 12 different kinds of talismans, one for each type of alchemical gemstone, and each has a different power. In order to create and use talismans, the Craft Alchemical Magecraft feat is required. Though each talisman can be created, only one can be worn at a time. It takes 24 hours before a new talisman takes effect. The talisman takes up the neck slot. Note that talismans are useless and unusable to any character that does not have the Craft Alchemical Magecraft feat, and they are almost never found for sale for this reason.

AGATE TALISMAN
Aura moderate transmutation; **CL** 6th
Slot none; **Price** 40,000 gp; **Weight** —

DESCRIPTION
This allows the user to detect motivations and lies. It grants a +20 alchemical bonus to the user's Sense Motive skill.

CONSTRUCTION
Requirements Craft Alchemical Magecraft; **Cost** 20,000 gp; **Rarity:** Common
Alchemical Formula: Agate, Perception

AMETHYST TALISMAN
Aura moderate enchantment (compulsion) [mind-affecting]; **CL** 6th
Slot none; **Price** 30,000 gp; **Weight** —

DESCRIPTION
This talisman allows the user to influence the emotions of a single target within 20 feet as a spell-like ability three times per day by affecting the target as a *crushing despair*, *good hope*, *calm emotions*, or *cause fear* spell. Once per week, the wearer can influence a single target with a single effect as the spells *sympathy* or *antipathy*.

CONSTRUCTION
Requirements Craft Alchemical Magecraft; **Cost** 15,000 gp; **Rarity:** Common
Alchemical Formula: Amethyst, Mind

DIAMOND TALISMAN
Aura moderate divination; **CL** 6th
Slot none; **Price** 18,000 gp; **Weight** —

DESCRIPTION
This allows the user to see invisible and ethereal creatures within 60 feet.

CONSTRUCTION
Requirements Craft Alchemical Magecraft; **Cost** 9,000 gp; **Rarity:** Common
Alchemical Formula: Diamond, Perception

EMERALD TALISMAN
Aura moderate abjuration; **CL** 6th
Slot none; **Price** 25,000 gp; **Weight** —

DESCRIPTION
This grants a +2 alchemical bonus to armor class and all saving throws.

CONSTRUCTION
Requirements Craft Alchemical Magecraft; **Cost** 12,500 gp; **Rarity:** Common
Alchemical Formula: Emerald, Protection

JADE TALISMAN
Aura moderate abjuration; **CL** 6th
Slot none; **Price** 40,000 gp; **Weight** —

DESCRIPTION
This talisman allows the user to *neutralize poison* as the spell three times per day and provides the wearer with a +4 alchemical saving throw bonus versus poisons.

CONSTRUCTION
Requirements Craft Alchemical Magecraft; **Cost** 20,000 gp; **Rarity:** Common
Alchemical Formula: Jade, Healing

MALACHITE TALISMAN
Aura moderate transmutation; **CL** 6th
Slot none; **Price** 20,000 gp; **Weight** —

DESCRIPTION
This allows the user to breathe aerated liquid as the spell *water breathing*.

CONSTRUCTION
Requirements Craft Alchemical Magecraft; **Cost** 10,000 gp; **Rarity:** Common
Alchemical Formula: Malachite, Transmutation

MOONSTONE TALISMAN
Aura moderate abjuration; **CL** 6th
Slot none; **Price** 40,000 gp; **Weight** —

DESCRIPTION
This grants the wearer Resist Cold 10 and a +4 alchemical bonus to their saving throw versus cold and ice attacks, spells, and effects.

CONSTRUCTION
Requirements Craft Alchemical Magecraft; **Cost** 20,000 gp; **Rarity:** Common
Alchemical Formula: Moonstone, Cold

ONYX TALISMAN
Aura moderate illusion; **CL** 6th
Slot none; **Price** 24,000 gp; **Weight** —

DESCRIPTION
This allows the user to become *invisible* as a standard action, as per the spell of the same name.

CONSTRUCTION
Requirements Craft Alchemical Magecraft; **Cost** 12,000 gp; **Rarity:** Common
Alchemical Formula: Onyx, Stealth

PEARL TALISMAN
Aura moderate conjuration (healing); **CL** 6th
Slot none; **Price** 40,000 gp; **Weight** —

DESCRIPTION
This grants the wearer Fast Healing 1 and allows them to cure 2d4 + 3 hit points by touch three times per day.

CONSTRUCTION
Requirements Craft Alchemical Magecraft; **Cost** 20,000 gp; **Rarity:** Common
Alchemical Formula: Pearl, Healing

RUBY TALISMAN
Aura moderate abjuration; **CL** 6th
Slot none; **Price** 40,000 gp; **Weight** —

DESCRIPTION
This grants the wearer Resist Fire 10 and a +4 alchemical bonus to their saving throw versus fire attacks, spells, and effects.

CONSTRUCTION
Requirements Craft Alchemical Magecraft; **Cost** 20,000 gp; **Rarity:** Common
Alchemical Formula: Ruby, Protection

SAPPHIRE TALISMAN
Aura moderate transmutation; **CL** 6th
Slot none; **Price** 40,000 gp; **Weight** —

DESCRIPTION
This allows the user to fly as the spell *fly* and gain half their level as an alchemical bonus to the fly skill.

CONSTRUCTION
Requirements Craft Alchemical Magecraft; **Cost** 20,000 gp; **Rarity:** Common
Alchemical Formula: Sapphire, Flight

TURQUOISE TALISMAN
Aura moderate transmutation; **CL** 6th
Slot none; **Price** 90,000 gp; **Weight** —

DESCRIPTION
Three times per day, the user can move through wooden, plaster, or stone walls, but not through metal or other harder materials. This allows them to move up to 100 feet of distance through solid rock or stone. The user phases through the rock and gains tremorsense to 60 feet only while phased in the rock. The user can remain within the rock or stone for up to one hour but moving more than 100 feet or staying inside longer than an hour ejects the user to the nearest open area. Upon leaving the solid surface the effect ends.

CONSTRUCTION
Requirements Craft Alchemical Magecraft; **Cost** 45,000 gp; **Rarity:** Common
Alchemical Formula: Turquoise, Planar

CHAPTER SIX: ALCHEMY IN STRUCTURES

ALCHEMICAL MORTARS

Alchemical mortars are special materials used in the construction of keeps, towers, temples, and other permanent stone structures. The walls of ancient buildings were not solid stone or rock. Large 10-foot-thick castle walls often had a mortar type filler between layers. This material was also packed between the bricks or stone used when constructing the walls. A similar coating was used between the outer and inner wooden walls, and indeed is still used today! This binding substance is a mortar that can be enhanced by alchemical processes.

Each mortar creates about a gallon of pebble-sized granules of crystal and stone. These are often multicolored, looking much like small jewels and gems. They are mixed with mortars, varnishes, and fillers during construction. Most can be applied to stone and wooden walls.

Batches are crafted in five-pound increments, with each pound covering one 10-foot cube of space. One batch (five pounds) of alchemical mortar will cover a 10-foot-thick wall that is 10 feet high and 50 feet long. Each section of a wall may be treated by only one shroud and one bulwark type. Any other attempts cause the magical energies to conflict and fail. Sections may be treated with multiple wards and stone types. The types are listed after the name. Shrouds and wards affect one side of the wall only, which must be selected permanently upon use.

These alchemical technologies developed in response to magical environments. The desire to create certain areas safe from scrying and teleportation, or to protect a city from flying foes drove the creation of these items to protect areas. Now when the characters encounter these areas that are warded in certain areas within the game, you can address their existence within the structure of the rules. This also provides options for characters who wish to defend against such techniques being used against them.

Even though these are "nonmagical" alchemical items, their effects are considered magic items for the purposes of *dispel magic*. Each 10-foot-cubic section of wall is considered a single item. Suppressing the effect of a mortar does not affect the entire wall, just the section targeted. Because these are alchemical items and have no caster level, the DC for the *dispel magic* check is equal to the crafting DC for the item. A *greater dispel magic* can temporarily suppress all effects from mortars within the 20-foot-radius burst (keeping lines of effect and sight in mind), and a *mage's disjunction* can permanently turn mortared walls into normal wood or stone. Doing enough damage to the wall to destroy it also terminates the effect.

TABLE 6–I: ALCHEMICAL MORTARS

Name	Price
Acid Shroud	4,000 gp
Arcana Ward	5,000 gp
Blade Shroud	10,000 gp
Clearstone	4,000 gp
Death Ward	1,000 gp
Fire Ward	1,000 gp
Fissurestone	15,000 gp
Flame Shroud	15,000 gp
Flight Ward	10,000 gp
Hypnosis Shroud	5,000 gp
Ice Shroud	5,000 gp
Lightning Shroud	15,000 gp
Mirror Shroud	1,000 gp
Mist Shroud	1,000 gp
Mist Shroud, Acidic	10,000 gp
Mist Shroud, Death	15,000 gp
Mist Shroud, Solid	5,000 gp
Mist Shroud, Stinking	5,000 gp
Phasing Ward	5,000 gp
Repairstone	5,000 gp
Scrying Ward	4,000 gp
Shatter Ward	1,000 gp
Stalwart Bulwark I	1,000 gp
Stalwart Bulwark II	2,000 gp
Stalwart Bulwark III	5,000 gp
Stalwart Bulwark IV	10,000 gp
Stalwart Bulwark V	15,000 gp
Swarm Shroud	15,000 gp
Teleportation Ward	5,000 gp
Terror Shroud	10,000 gp
Time Ward	1,000 gp
Weather Ward	1,000 gp
Web Shroud	2,000 gp
Wind Shroud	5,000 gp

Acid Shroud (Shroud): This mortar causes the wall sections to secrete a powerful acid. It deals 4d6 points of acid damage to items that ignores hardness that touch the wall. This is enough to dissolve boots, gloves, ladders leaning against the wall, and any other non-living item. Ladders as they dissolve have a cumulative 25% chance of sliding off the wall. Living creatures who touch the acid take 1 point of acid damage the first round, 2 points of acid damage the second consecutive round of contact, 4 points of acid damage the third consecutive round of contact, 8 points of acid damage the fourth consecutive round of contact, and finally 16 points of acid damage for the fifth and following rounds of contact. Breaking contact with the wall reverses the process one round at a time. If a character takes four rounds to climb an acid shroud wall, the first round their gloves and shoes dissolve. The second round they take 1 point of acid damage, then 2 points of acid damage, then 4 points of acid damage. The round after that, they break contact and take another 2 points of acid damage, followed by 1 point of acid damage the round after that. The acid can be washed off the skin with an alkaline solution such as wine but cannot be removed from the wall. This mortar may be applied only to stone walls.

DC 20 Craft (alchemy); *Rarity:* Rare; *Price:* 4,000 gp; *Weight:* 5 lbs.; *Alchemical Formula:* Diamond (x10), Turquoise (x100), Salt (any)

Arcana Ward (Ward): This mystical ward protects the wall from magical effects and spells. When the wall is targeted by spells such as *disintegrate*, *rock to mud*, *warp wood*, or other magical effects, it is considered to have a Spell Resistance equal to 26. This ward may be applied to stone and wooden structures.

DC 26 Craft (alchemy); *Rarity:* Rare; *Price:* 5,000 gp; *Weight:* 5 lbs.; *Alchemical Formula:* Diamond (x10), Onyx (x100), Earth (any)

Blade Shroud (Shroud): This shroud covers the wall in constantly shifting razor-sharp piercing stones. Anyone or anything that comes into contact with the wall takes 10d6 points of piercing damage per round they are in contact with the wall as the stones tear through armor and flesh. This mortar may be applied only to stone walls.

DC 30 Craft (alchemy); *Rarity:* Rare; *Price:* 10,000 gp; *Weight:* 5 lbs.; *Alchemical Formula:* Diamond (x10), Ruby (x100), Turquoise (x100), Earth (any)

Clearstone (Stone): When mixed and used to secure a wall, this stone turns the relevant wall sections transparent. This produces a glass-like effect where the contours of the wall are still visible, but it is possible to see through them. The wall is not invisible and still is visible, if transparent. This does not affect the composition of the walls, and their ability to resist and sustain damage remains the same. This mortar may be applied to stone and wooden walls.

DC 22 Craft (alchemy); *Rarity:* Rare; *Price:* 4,000 gp; *Weight:* 5 lbs.; *Alchemical Formula:* Diamond (x10), Sapphire (x100), Air (any), Earth (any)

Death Ward (Ward): This holy ward protects against nefarious hordes of undead. Any undead that approaches within 20 feet takes 1d4 + 1 positive energy damage. They continue to take this damage every round until they remove themselves from the area near the wall. Any undead that actually touch the wall take 3d6 + 3 positive energy damage and must succeed at a DC 18 Will save or gain the frightened condition for 10 rounds.

DC 16 Craft (alchemy); *Rarity:* Uncommon; *Price:* 1,000 gp; *Weight:* 5 lbs.; *Alchemical Formula:* Diamond (x10), Jade (x10), Onyx (x10), Life

Fire Ward (Ward): This ward protects walls from fire. Anytime the wall must make a saving throw versus fire, it gains a +4 alchemical bonus to the saving throw. It also gains Fire Resistance 20. If using the catching fire rules in **Chapter 1: Alchemy Basics**, fires that are used against a wall with this ward diminish on a damage roll of 1, 2, or 3. This mortar may be applied to wooden and stone walls.

DC 16 Craft (alchemy); *Rarity:* Uncommon; *Price:* 1,000 gp; *Weight:* 5 lbs.; *Alchemical Formula:* Diamond (x10), Onyx (x10), Ruby (x10), Fire (any), Protection

Fissurestone (Stone): This marvelous stone allows you to create portals in the stone with your bare hand. When the mortar is applied, a command word or phrase is chosen; alternately, an item or selection of items may be selected. Anyone who says the word or phrase or who possesses one of the items may touch the wall and create openings in any section of the wall. These openings can be up to 100 square feet and can travel through the entire length of *fissurestone*-enhanced walls. This can be used to create portals, footholds, doorways, and passages. If not closed the same way they are opened, these passageways close themselves one minute later. Anyone caught inside is shunted to the nearest open space. This mortar may be applied to wooden and stone walls.

DC 25 Craft (alchemy); *Rarity:* Very Rare; *Price:* 15,000 gp; *Weight:* 5 lbs.; *Alchemical Formula:* Agate (x100), Diamond (x100), Pearl (x100), Planar, Transportation

Flame Shroud (Shroud): This shroud covers a wall in flames. The flame burns eternally, with no visible fuel source. It is actual fire and produces heat, light, and sets other things aflame. The flame is the color desired by the creator. The wall is immune to any damage from this effect. Anyone within five feet of the wall takes 1d4 + 1 points of damage and is at risk of catching fire. Anyone touching the wall takes 2d6 damage and is automatically on fire. This mortar may be applied only to stone walls.

DC 30 Craft (alchemy); *Rarity:* Rare; *Price:* 15,000 gp; *Weight:* 5 lbs.; *Alchemical Formula:* Diamond (x100), Ruby (x100), Fire (any), Pain

Flight Ward (Ward): This ward protects the interior of a wall from flying opponents. Anyone crossing over the wall by flying up to 100 feet above the wall is affected by the spell *gust of wind*. The wind blows them in the direction of the exterior of the wall. This also affects creatures descending from above, over 100 feet. Anyone within 50 feet of either side of this wall that descends from above is affected as well. This mortar may be applied to wooden and stone walls.

DC 20 Craft (alchemy); *Rarity:* Rare; *Price:* 10,000 gp; *Weight:* 5 lbs.; *Alchemical Formula:* Diamond (x100), Sapphire (x100), Air (any), Stasis

Hypnosis Shroud (Shroud): This shroud causes the formation of a fascinating pattern that enraptures anyone who approaches this wall. Anyone within 20 feet of the wall must make a DC 17 Will save. If they fail the save, they are fascinated for 4d4 rounds. Once you save, you are immune to this ability for 24 hours.

DC 28 Craft (alchemy); *Rarity:* Rare; *Price:* 5,000 gp; *Weight:* 5 lbs.; *Alchemical Formula:* Diamond (x10), Pearl (x100), Salt (any), Illusion

Ice Shroud (Shroud): This shroud covers a stone wall with a heavy sheet of ice that never melts. The ice is slick and difficult to climb, adding +10 to the DC of any Climb checks on the wall. If not wearing appropriate cold-weather gear, anyone within 10 feet of the wall takes 1d4 points of nonlethal damage every round. This mortar may be applied only to stone walls.

DC 25 Craft (alchemy); *Rarity:* Very Rare; *Price:* 5,000 gp; *Weight:* 5 lbs.; *Alchemical Formula:* Diamond (x10), Malachite (x100), Salt (any), Cold

Lightning Shroud (Shroud): This shroud coats the wall in arcing electricity. From a distance, the wall seems to sparkle and flash. Anyone within 10 feet of the wall is struck for 4d8 points of electrical damage. Targets may make a DC 17 Reflex save in order to reduce the damage by half. Anyone touching the wall is electrocuted for 9d8 points of electrical damage. There is no save versus this damage.
If multiple targets are in a 10-foot-by-10-foot area, only one is struck per round. Everyone touching the wall at any time takes the damage. This shroud may be applied only to stone walls.

DC 32 Craft (alchemy); *Rarity:* Very Rare; *Price:* 15,000 gp; *Weight:* 5 lbs.; *Alchemical Formula:* Diamond (x100), Onyx (x100), Sapphire (x100), Electricity

Mirror Shroud (Shroud): This shroud causes a defensive wall to become highly reflective. This makes targeting the wall or things behind it more difficult than normal. All ranged attacks made in the direction of the wall have a −2 circumstance penalty to hit. Bright lights or other circumstance modifiers may cause this penalty to increase. All creatures with gaze attacks must avert their gaze or be subject to their own reflection.
This mortar may be applied to wooden and stone walls.

DC 20 Craft (alchemy); *Rarity:* Rare; *Price:* 1,000 gp; *Weight:* 5 lbs.; *Alchemical Formula:* Diamond (x10), Sapphire (10), Salt (any), Illusion

Mist Shroud (Shroud): This shroud covers the wall in mist. This mist obscures the wall and anything within 20 feet. People within this area have partial concealment if five feet from the edge of the cloud or another person, or total concealment if farther away. Different variations of the *mist shroud* exist, but only one may be used on any given wall.
Mist shrouds may be applied to wooden and stone walls.

DC 18 Craft (alchemy); *Rarity:* Uncommon; *Price:* 1,000 gp; *Weight:* 5 lbs.; *Alchemical Formula:* Diamond (x10), Moonstone (x10), Stealth

Mist Shroud, Acidic (Shroud): This works in an identical way to the mist shroud in all ways, except anyone within the mist takes 2d4 points of acid damage each round.

DC 25 Craft (alchemy); *Rarity:* Rare; *Price:* 10,000 gp; *Weight:* 5 lbs.; *Alchemical Formula:* Diamond (x100), Moonstone (x100), Turquoise (x100), Acid, Stealth

Mist Shroud, Death (Shroud): This works in an identical way to the *mist shroud* in all ways, except that people in the mist must succeed at a DC 18 Fortitude save each round or take 5d4 + 5 points of damage each round. Those who fail the save also gain the sickened condition and then fail every save for this effect automatically until one full round after they leave the cloud.

DC 30 Craft (alchemy); *Rarity:* Rare; *Price:* 15,000 gp; *Weight:* 5 lbs.; *Alchemical Formula:* Diamond (x100), Moonstone (x100), Onyx (x100), Stealth, Toxin

Mist Shroud, Solid (Shroud): This works identically to *mist shroud* above in all ways except that the mist is very thick. Anyone attempting to move through the mist treats it as difficult terrain.

DC 25 Craft (alchemy); *Rarity:* Rare; *Price:* 5,000 gp; *Alchemical Formula:* Diamond (x10), Moonstone (x100), Onyx (x10), Earth (any), Transmutation, Stealth

Mist Shroud, Stinking (Shroud): This works in an identical way to the *mist shroud* in all ways, except that the mist causes all those within to become terribly sick. All those within the cloud must make a DC 16 Fortitude save each round or gain the nauseated condition.

DC 25 Craft (alchemy); *Rarity:* Rare; *Price:* 5,000 gp; *Weight:* 5 lbs.; *Alchemical Formula:* Diamond (x10), Malachite (x10), Moonstone (x100), Disease, Stealth

Phasing Ward (Ward): This ward provides protection from planar travelers. This wall is as solid on the Astral, Ethereal, and other planes that coexist with the Prime as it is on the Prime Material Plane. In addition, if the wall is contiguous and encloses an area, the top and bottom are shielded by a dome that is an impenetrable barrier on the Astral and Ethereal planes. This dome is neither visible nor has any presence or effect on the Prime Material Plane, as it is used only to block the passage of planar creatures.
This mortar may be applied to wooden and stone walls.

DC 25 Craft (alchemy); *Rarity:* Rare; *Price:* 5,000 gp; *Weight:* 5 lbs.; *Alchemical Formula:* Diamond (x10), Emerald (x10), Jade (x100), Planar, Protection

Repairstone (Stone): This stone is designed of an alchemical material that repairs itself as it becomes damaged. Every time this wall is damaged, it gains Fast Healing 1 until all the damage is repaired, and then, after the repair is complete, the maximum hit point total of the wall increases by 1. Each time the wall is damaged, it exudes an alchemical substance that fixes the breach and increases the structural integrity of the wall. The maximum hit points of the wall cannot double more than once per decade.
This mortar may be applied to wooden and stone walls.

DC 25 Craft (alchemy); *Rarity:* Rare; *Price:* 5,000 gp; *Weight:* 5 lbs.; *Alchemical Formula:* Diamond (x10), Emerald (x100), Turquoise (x10), Healing

Scrying Ward (Ward): This ward provides mystical protection from scrying attempts. In order for this to work, all the space to be protected must be enclosed by walls fused with this alchemical mortar. Any open side or passage allows a scrying attempt to succeed. Once the ward is in place, the area is protected from scrying as the spell *nondetection*. The caster level check that needs to be beaten in order to scry is equal to the crafting DC.

DC 24 Craft (alchemy); *Rarity:* Rare; *Price:* 4,000 gp; *Weight:* 5 lbs.; *Alchemical Formula:* Diamond (x10), Onyx (x100), Turquoise (x10), Azoth (any), Protection

Shatter Ward (Ward): This mortar provides protection from blunt striking attacks. This is particularly effective at resisting battering rams, catapults, and ballistae. This grants a +5 bonus to the break DC of the material, +1 to its hardness, and an additional 10 hit points per cubic 10-foot section.

DC 16 Craft (alchemy); *Rarity:* Uncommon; *Price:* 1,000 gp; *Weight:* 5 lbs.; *Alchemical Formula:* Diamond (x10), Onyx (x10), Turquoise (x100), Body, Protection

Stalwart Bulwark I (Bulwark): This bulwark increases the strength of the wall with which it is mixed. This increases the hit points of the wall by 1 per foot and increases the hardness of the wall by 1.
This may be applied to wooden and stone walls.

DC 20 Craft (alchemy); *Rarity:* Common; *Price:* 1,000 gp; *Weight:* 5 lbs.; *Alchemical Formula:* Diamond (x10) Turquoise (x10), Strength

Stalwart Bulwark II (Bulwark): This bulwark increases the strength of the wall. This increases the hit points of the wall by 2 per foot (+20 hit points per 10 feet) and increases the hardness of the wall by 3. The break difficulty of the wall increases by 5.
This may be applied to wooden and stone walls.

DC 25 Craft (alchemy); *Rarity:* Uncommon; *Price:* 2,000 gp; *Weight:* 5 lbs.; *Alchemical Formula:* Diamond (x10) Turquoise (x25), Strength (x2)

Stalwart Bulwark III (Bulwark): This bulwark increases the strength of the wall. This increases the hit points of the wall by 5 per foot (+50 hit points per 10 feet) and increases the hardness of the wall by 5. The break difficulty increases by 10.
This may be applied to wooden and stone walls.

DC 30 Craft (alchemy); *Rarity:* Rare; *Price:* 5,000 gp; *Weight:* 5 lbs.; *Alchemical Formula:* Diamond (10), Turquoise (x100), Strength (x4)

Stalwart Bulwark IV (Bulwark): This bulwark increases the strength of the wall. This increases the hit points of the wall by 10 per foot (+100 hit points per 10 feet) and increases the hardness of the wall by 10. This increases the break difficulty by 15.
This may be applied to wooden and stone walls.

DC 35 Craft (alchemy); *Rarity:* Very Rare; *Price:* 10,000 gp; *Weight:* 5 lbs.; *Alchemical Formula:* Diamond (x10) Turquoise (x200), Strength (x8)

Stalwart Bulwark V (Bulwark): This bulwark increases the strength of the wall. It increases the hit points of the wall by 20 per foot (+200 hit points per 10 feet) and increases the hardness of the wall by 20. The break difficulty of the wall increases by 25.
This may be applied to wooden and stone walls.

DC 38 Craft (alchemy); *Rarity:* Very Rare; *Price:* 15,000 gp; *Weight:* 5 lbs.; *Alchemical Formula:* Diamond (x100) Turquoise (x200), Strength (x8)

Swarm Shroud (Shroud): This nefarious shroud creates many tiny porous openings in the wall and exudes a strong attractant to various insects. They live and breed in the wall. Swarms of insects attack anyone approaching within five feet of the wall. Creatures take 1d4 + 1 points of damage for as long as they remain within five feet of the wall. Creatures with one hit die or less must make a DC 16 Will save. On a failure, they gain the frightened condition.

Attempting to kill all the insects is possible but extremely difficult. Consider that each 10-foot cubic section of wall contains 1d4 + 4 swarms of 2d8 HD of vermin or insects. Trying to drive them from the wall can cause them to pour out and attack. Possible basic swarms include ants, centipedes, spiders, rats, and wasps.

This mortar may be applied to stone and wooden walls.

DC 30 Craft (alchemy); *Rarity:* Rare; *Price:* 15,000 gp; *Weight:* 5 lbs.; *Alchemical Formula:* Amethyst (x100), Diamond (x100), Moonstone (x100), Emotion

Teleportation Ward (Ward): This ward acts as a planar barrier to travelers. Anyone attempting to teleport, phase, or otherwise extra-dimensionally travel across this barrier finds themselves teleported 1d100 miles in a random direction.

Note that this works only if the attempted dimensional travel such as *teleport*, *dimensional door*, or *shadow walk* attempts to cross the wall. If the walls are not completely enclosed, teleportation is possible.

This mortar may be applied to wooden and stone walls.

DC 25 Craft (alchemy); *Rarity:* Uncommon; *Price:* 5,000 gp; *Weight:* 5 lbs.; *Alchemical Formula:* Diamond (x10), Emerald (x100), Pearl (x10), Planar, Protection

Terror Shroud (Shroud): This shroud causes terrible fear in all who approach. Anyone who approaches within 20 feet must make a DC 20 Will save or gain the panicked condition. This mortar may be applied to wooden and stone walls.

DC 28 Craft (alchemy); *Rarity:* Rare; *Price:* 10,000 gp; *Weight:* 5 lbs.; *Alchemical Formula:* Diamond (x100), Malachite (x100), Moonstone (x100), Fear

Time Ward (Ward): This useful ward prevents the decay of the wall from age. Wood and stone will not sag, stone will not weather, and the wall remains impervious to decay and damage from normal wear, requiring no upkeep. This also increases the hardness of the wall by 1.

This mortar may be applied to wooden and stone walls.

DC 16 Craft (alchemy); *Rarity:* Uncommon; *Price:* 1,000 gp; *Weight:* 5 lbs.; *Alchemical Formula:* Diamond (x10), Emerald (x10), Onyx (x10), Stasis

Weather Ward (Ward): This useful ward prevents the surface from sustaining damage from weather. Rain, hail, lightning, and other weather effects cause no damage or wear on this wall.

This mortar may be applied to wooden and stone walls.

DC 14 Craft (alchemy); *Rarity:* Uncommon; *Price:* 1,000 gp; *Weight:* 5 lbs.; *Alchemical Formula:* Diamond (x10), Sapphire (x10), Turquoise (x10), Protection

Web Shroud (Shroud): This ward covers the entire surface of the wall with hideous sticky spider webs. This causes anyone climbing the wall to gain the entangled condition.

DC 25 Craft (alchemy); *Rarity:* Uncommon; *Price:* 2,000 gp; *Weight:* 5 lbs.; *Alchemical Formula:* Agate (x25), Diamond (x10), Onyx (x25), Stasis, Transmutation

Wind Shroud (Shroud): This covers the front of the walls with swirling winds. Any missile attacks directed at the wall are blown away. This protects people standing on the parapets from missile fire, providing improved cover, increasing the cover AC bonus against ranged and thrown attacks to +8 and Reflex saves by +4. This also provides the wall an additional 10 points of hardness versus large missile attacks such as ballistae, catapults, and other siege engines.

DC 28 Craft (alchemy); *Rarity:* Very Rare; *Price:* 5,000 gp; *Weight:* 5 lbs.; *Alchemical Formula:* Diamond (x10), Onyx (x10), Sapphire (x100), Air (any), Strength

CHAPTER SEVEN: SPELLS, SPELLCASTING, AND ALCHEMY

ALCHEMICAL ITEMS AS SPELL COMPONENTS

Arcane formulations concocted in a dark laboratory seething with eldritch power is a staple of fantasy. The following systems allow you to use alchemical items and essences to increase the power of spells. But who wants to stop play to cross reference a spell or item to determine the effect an essence or item has on a magic spell?

No one, that's who.

USING CRAFTED ALCHEMICAL ITEMS TO ENHANCE SPELLS

First, there must be some connection between the item and the spell it is designed to affect. A flask of *alchemist's fire* improves spells that deal with fire and warmth but is quite useless when used to try to improve a *cone of cold*. *Slickshell grenades* affect spells that have or create surfaces to affect, while solvents will intensify acids. The general rule is that if an alchemical item shares a damage type with a spell's energy type, or if they share a common school of magic, then that item can be used to enhance the spell, through the GM as final adjudicator. It's important to remember that when doing this, the cost of the component must be burned to enhance the spell, so erring on the side of flexible is encouraged.

Nothing special must be done when preparing your spells for the day. The use of an alchemical item does not add any casting time, nor does it prevent the need for the normal material components of the spell. Normally the item is used up, unless enhancing a cantrip (0-level spell). Crafted items, i.e. items not requiring a feat to craft, may only affect spells of levels 1–4.

For every 50 gp or fraction thereof of the retail cost of a crafted item, your GM will determine which one of the following effects may be added to a spell. Unless noted, each effect may be applied only once.

- The duration may be extended by one round.
- The radius may be increased by five feet.
- It may add 1 point of damage of the energy type of the item to an unrelated spell. For example, adding an alchemical fire to a *burning hands* spell increases the damage to 5d4 + 1 points of fire damage. An *alchemist's inferno* would add +12 points of damage because it is 600 gold (600 gold divided by 50 gold is 12).
- You may cause a single 100-square-foot section of the spell if destroyed to do 1d6 points of damage of the energy type of the spell to anyone who dispels or destroys it. If a segment of a wall of fire is dispelled, the person dispelling it is targeted by a wave of fire that does 1d6 points of fire damage.
- You may apply a related secondary effect of the item to a single target that fails its saving throw versus the spell. For example, you could use an *alchemist's fire* to have a secondary round of burning damage when applied to a *fireball* spell.

- If the spell requires multiple checks versus multiple targets, you may reroll one check per 50 gp of the cost of the item, such as using five *slickshells* on a *black tentacles* spell. You use up the items and then have the option of rerolling one of the CMB checks for the tentacles.
- Increase the difficulty of the saves or checks the spell requires by 1 per 100 gold of the item, to a maximum of 4 for a 400-gp alchemical item.
- You may cause a 10-foot-square area to gain the quality the item provides. A section of a *grease* or *web* spell could be conjured aflame and burning for the duration of the spell with an *alchemist's fire*.
- You may add +2 to any checks that are not attack or damage rolls while casting the spell.
- You may add +1 to your attack roll to hit with the spell, to a maximum of +4. If you only add +1 to hit, the item is not used up for a 200-gp item or greater.
- You may increase the damage by +1 per caster level, to a maximum of +10.
- It is important that a discussion about what items have which effects occur before play. Here are some guidelines for determining how to assign effects:
- Each alchemical item will have only one of the above effects when paired with each spell.
- Only one alchemical modification can be made to each spell.
- The effects of the items must be similar or related in some way.
- Opposite effects cause the spell to fizzle (using a bottle of *alchemist's ice* for a *fireball* will be unimpressive, but using *alchemist's ice* on a *web* spell could add 1 point of cold damage each round to anyone trapped in the web).

USING CONSUMABLE ENCHANTED ITEMS TO ENHANCE SPELLS

For every 500 gp or fraction thereof of the retail cost of a *consumable enchanted* item, such as a potion or scroll, your GM will determine which one of the following effects may be added to a spell. Unless noted, each effect may be applied only once.

- The duration may be increased as if you were one level higher.
- The radius may be increased by five feet.
- It may add 1 point of damage per die of the energy type, to a maximum of +5.
- You may apply the potion's effect as a secondary effect to targets that fail their save.
- You may increase the difficulty of a related save by 1, to a maximum of +4.
- You may increase your damage by caster level by +1, to a maximum of +5.

The same guidelines for crafted items apply to consumable enchanted items. Each item has only one effect when paired with each spell. Only one alchemical modification can be made to each spell. The effects of the items must be similar or related in some way. Opposite effects cause the spell to fizzle.

DISCOVERY

Another variation on this is discovery, where the player announces before the game which items he plans to use to enhance his spells and then the GM determines the effects ahead of time. This way, the player can experiment to discover the effects of alchemical items.

EMPOWERMENT OF A SPELL USING ESSENCES

Essences themselves can increase the power of spells. Simply using a number of essences related to the effects of the spell cause the following effects:

- Related essences are associated in some way with the schools or keywords of the spell. Necromancy spells could use Death Essence, or Mind Essence could be used to enhance enchantment spells.
- Spells enhanced by essences take a full-round action to cast, taking effect before the start of the spellcaster's next turn.
- Certain effects require specific types of essences, while others require essences related to the spell. Instead of the listed effect, you may substitute standardized Metamagic effects at your whim.
- If this system is too powerful for your campaign, increase the number of essences required or require that they come from a creature of HD equal or greater than the spell level it affects. This works best in campaigns where essences are not just freely available for purchase.

Only one set of essences can affect a spell.

TABLE 7–1: ALCHEMICAL ENHANCEMENTS

Effect	Type of Essence	Number of Essences
Admixture	Fire/Acid/Electricity/Cold	2
Amplified	Essence Related to Spell Type	2
Breaching	Prowess	2
Caustic	Acid or Fire	3
Concussive	Pain	5
Discriminatory	Luck	6
Freezing	Cold	6
Glitz	Light	4
Intensified	Purity	2
Indefatigable	Strength	4
Mighty	Prowess	3
Maximum	Prowess	6

Effect	Type of Essence	Number of Essences
Malaise	Toxin	5
Planar	Planar	2
Prolonged	Essence Related to Spell Type	2
Quiet	Emotion	2
Reaching	Transportation	5
Reflecting	Illusion	2
Repetitive	Magic	5
Stagnant	Stasis	3
Subdual	Love	1
Tranquil	Stasis	2
Thundering	Electricity	3

Admixture: For any spell that causes elemental damage, using two essences of a different element causes half the damage of the spell to be of the essence type. A 6th-level caster using two acid essences on a *fireball* does 3d6 points of fire damage and 3d6 points of acid damage.

Amplified: Spells that are cast at range have their range doubled.

Breaching: This adds five to your caster level for purposes of penetrating spell resistance.

Caustic: Spells that cause damage continue to persist and do damage. This works only on spells that cause damage. Anyone who fails the save versus this spell takes an additional amount of damage of the type that the spell causes equal to the level of the spell on the round the spell hits and then again on the next round. For example, a *fireball* does 3 points of damage the first round and another 3 the next.

Concussive: Any damage-causing spell gains a thunderous burst. This blast causes anyone who fails their save versus the spell to be stunned for one round.

Discriminatory: This causes spells with area effects to selectively miss targets selected by the caster. The targets selected by the caster are not affected by the spell.

Freezing: This causes spells with cold damage to freeze their opponents, causing their movement to be impeded. This reduces their speed by half and they receive a −2 penalty to attacks and armor class.

Glitz: Any damage-causing spell gains a brilliant visual effect. Anyone dealt damage by the spell who fails their save versus the spell is dazed for a number of rounds equal to the level of the spell. They may attempt to save versus the original spell every round to end the daze effect.

Indefatigable: This causes the recipient of any spell that requires a save to roll two saves and take the worse result. This has no effect on spells that do not require saves.

Intensified: This spell becomes more difficult to resist. The saving throw DC to resist the spell increases by +2.

Malaise: This causes any spell that causes damage to sicken the targets. This works only on spells that cause damage. Anyone who fails the save versus this spell becomes ill in addition to the normal save. This causes a −2 penalty on all attack rolls, weapon damage, saving throws, ability and skill checks. They are sickened a number of rounds equal to the level of the spell. They may make a saving throw each round to end the effect.

Maximum: This maximizes all variable numeric effects of the spell. A 3rd-level wizard casting a *magic missile* does 10 points of damage, while a 6th-level wizard casting *fireball* does 36 damage. This also affects any other effects modifying the spell.

Mighty: This increases all the variable numeric effects of the spell by half. This doesn't affect saving throws, nor does it affect spells that lack random variable. A 6d6 *fireball* does 9d6 points of damage. A 2d4 + 2 *magic missile* does 3d4 + 3 points of damage. You may instead multiply the final result by 1.5

Planar: This spell affects targets on planes contiguous to the Prime Material Plane. Ethereal and astral creatures are fully affected by the spell.

Reflecting: A reflected spell is one that, if it fails to affect a target in any way, may instead be directed to affect a nearby target by the caster.

Repetitive: This powerful effect causes the spell to repeat itself once cast. The spellcaster unleashes the spell's energy, and the very next round the spell is recast with all the same parameters. New targets are not selected. The spell is cast in exactly the same place the second time. Variable numbers are rerolled.

Prolonged: Spells that have a non-instantaneous duration that do not require concentration can have their duration doubled.

Quiet: This causes spells to be cast successfully without the verbal component. If the spell has only a verbal component, this has no effect.

Reaching: Your touch spells increase in range. A touch spell gains a range of 30 feet. This changes the spell from requiring a melee touch attack to requiring a ranged touch attack.

Stagnant: This slows down the effect of an instantaneous spell. It does no additional damage to targets but persists until the start of the spellcaster's next turn. This means it affects anyone who enters the area of effect. If the spell produces a visual effect, it remains and obscures anyone within the area of the spell. It provides concealment to creatures within five feet of the edge or within the cloud adjacent to each other and total concealment beyond that. A *fireball* hangs in the air and provides concealment, affecting anyone who enters its area during their turn.

Subdual: This causes any damage-dealing spell to deal nonlethal subdual damage. This effect halves all damage versus dragons.

Thundering: Spells that cause damage deafen opponents. This works only on spells that cause damage. Anyone who fails the save versus this spell becomes deaf for a number of rounds equal to the level of the spell.

Tranquil: This causes spells to be cast successfully without the somatic component. If the spell has only a somatic component, this has no effect.

TABLE 7–2: ALCHEMIST SPELL LIST

1st level	Description
Acid Mist	Create a caustic cloud of obscuring mist
Adhesion	Affix two objects to each other
Buoyancy	Cause objects to float in water
Control Vapor	Manipulate gaseous clouds
Gauntlet	Create a gauntlet of force
Liquid Modulation	Transmutes nonmagical, non-alchemical liquids
Liquid Sphere	Create a sphere of nonmagical, non-alchemical liquid
Protection from Nonmagical Gas	Protects the caster from smoke
Smokey Sphere	Create a smoke grenade
Stone Flame	Freeze a small flame
2nd level	
Acid Cloud	Create an acidic grenade
Acid Scourge	Create an acid whip
Augmented Olfaction	The caster gains scent and increased olfactory ability
Boiling Oil	Pour boiling oil over a target
Burning Blood	Cause a wounded target's blood to burn
Corrosive Solvent	Create a powerful acid
Disperse Vapor	Cause a gas cloud to dissipate
Grease Slick	Create a slick of grease more powerful than the *grease* spell
Hold Vapor	Holds a gaseous cloud or creature in place
3rd level	
Acid Bolt	Shoot two bolts of acid doing 6d4 + 6 points of damage
Control Fluid	Allows the caster to manipulate and control fluids
Death Smoke	Create a cloud of blinding poisonous vapors
Rusting Grasp	Rust ferrous metals with a touch
Vitriolic Sphere	Coats a target in bubbling, spraying acid
4th level	
Acid Storm	Create an increasingly damaging storm of acid
Evaporate Fluid	Causes a large amount of water to evaporate instantly
Neutralize Gas	Neutralizes dangerous gases, spores, and attacks
Orb of Containment	Completely contain a small object safely
Physical Invisibility	Turn a single creature completely transparent
Preservation of the Flesh	Put some of your lifeforce into a candle
Property Transference	Trade a single trait between any two objects
5th level	
Abominable Amorphous Amoeba	Loose a horrible creature upon the world
Crystalbrittle	Turn a substance into brittle crystal.
Venom Ward	Protect a creature from poisons and toxins

TABLE 7–3: WIZARD/SORCERER SPELL LIST

2nd level	
Gauntlet	Create a Gauntlet of Force
Liquid Modulation	Transmutes nonmagical, non-alchemical liquids
Protection from Nonmagical Gas	Protects the caster from smoke
Grease Slick	Create a slick of grease more powerful than the *grease* spell
3rd level	
Acid Bolt	Shoot two bolts of acid doing 6d4 + 6 points of damage
Acid Mist	Create a caustic cloud of obscuring mist
Burning Blood	Cause a wounded target's blood to burn
Control Vapor	Manipulate gaseous clouds
Disperse Vapor	Cause a gas cloud to dissipate
Hold Vapor	Holds a gaseous cloud or creature in place
4th level	
Death Smoke	Create a cloud of blinding poisonous vapors

ABOMINABLE AMORPHOUS AMOEBA

School necromancy; **Level** alchemist 5th
Casting Time 1 standard action
Components V, S, M
Range touch
Target a prepared glass orb costing 1,000 gp and taking 1d4 weeks to prepare
Duration instantaneous
Saving Throw none; **Spell Resistance** no

The alchemist must prepare a glass orb for this spell and fill it with an eldritch alchemical fluid. When the spell is cast, the liquid becomes a terrible living single-celled creature. The sphere is then smashed by hurling it against an opponent, at which point the sphere shatters and the uncontrolled beast is released. The beast then begins to feed, fueling its awful growth.

The material component of this spell is a crystal orb filled with a gelatinous alchemical fluid. It takes 1d4 weeks to produce and costs 1,000 gold.

The caster is not in control of the creature.

ABOMINABLE AMORPHOUS AMOEBA

CE ooze
Init −2; **Senses** blindsight 30 ft., tremorsense 60 ft.;
Perception −5
AC 9, touch 9, flat-footed 9 (−2 Dex, +1 size)
hp 28 (3d8 + 15); fast healing 2
Fort +6; **Ref** −1; **Will** −4
Defensive Abilities acid skin; **Immune** electricity, cold,
mind-affecting effects, ooze traits, bludgeoning damage

Speed 20 ft., increases by +5 ft. per size category
Melee slam +4 (2d4 + 1 plus 3d6 acid damage)
Space 5 ft.; **Reach** 5 ft.
Special Attacks acid damage

Str 12, **Dex** 6, **Con** 20, **Int** —, **Wis** 1, **Cha** 1
Base Atk +1; **CMB** +3 **CMD** 10
Skills Climb +14; **Racial Modifiers** +10 to climb
Languages —
SQ consume opponent

Acid Damage (Ex) On a successful melee strike, the amoeba
deals 3d6 points of acid damage to the target.
Acid Skin (Ex) Any person attacking the amoeba with a
melee weapon without reach takes 1d6 + 1 points of acid
damage. Anyone striking or grappling with the amoeba takes
3d6 points of acid damage.
Consume Opponent (Ex) As a standard action or as part of
an attack action that kills or knocks an opponent unconscious,
the amoeba may consume any unconscious or dead opponent.
When it does so, the opponent's body is destroyed and the
amoeba is fully healed. It also permanently gains 1 hit point
per hit die of the creature consumed. For every 8 hit points
gained from this ability and the immunity to electricity
ability, the amoeba gains a hit die and increases to the next
largest size category. It also gains a permanent +2 increase
to Strength and Constitution, in addition to the effects of an
additional hit die and size increase.
Immunity to Cold (Su) The amoeba takes no damage from
cold spells. Any cold spell cast at the amoeba causes it to act
as if affected by the wizard spell *slow* for 1d4 + 1 rounds
Immune Electricity (Su) The amoeba takes no damage
from electricity and is healed for the amount of damage the
electricity would cause. Also, it gains 1 additional hit point per
die of damage. This fuels the creature's growth (see consume
opponent).

ACID BOLT

School evocation; **Level** alchemist 3rd, wizard/sorcerer 3rd
Casting Time 1 standard action
Components V, S, M
Range medium (100 feet + 10 feet per level)
Target one or two creatures
Duration instantaneous
Saving Throw none; **Spell Resistance** yes
This alchemist uses this spell to create two dart-shaped bolts of flesh-
corroding acid. They float near the caster's hand for a moment until rushing
forth to unerringly strike their target(s). The targets must be visible to the
caster, and the bolts seek them out around barriers and obstacles. The bolts
strike the creatures and cannot be aimed at specific parts or equipment.
Each bolt does 6d4 + 6 points of acid damage to the targets. This damage
affects only living targets, constructs and undead remain unharmed.
The material component for this spell is a small arrow dipped into a vial of
acid.

ACID CLOUD

School conjuration [acid, air]; **Level** alchemist 2nd
Casting Time 1 standard action
Components V, S, M (4 Rare Earth)
Range personal
Area 15-foot-radius burst
Target you
Duration 3 rounds
Saving Throw special; **Spell Resistance** no
When this spell is cast, the crystal sphere held in the caster's hand fills with
a yellowish acidic smoke. This can be thrown as a grenade-like weapon with
a range increment of 30 feet. When it strikes a surface, it shatters and fills a
15-foot-radius with yellow acrid fumes.
Friend and foe alike are subject to the effects of an acid bath. All targets take
4d4 points of acid damage with no save. Every round any target is within the
cloud, they take another 1d4 points of acid damage. Gear and objects must
make a saving throw each round or become broken. They are destroyed on a
second failed save.
The crystal stays filled with the acid fumes for only three rounds. If not used
before that time elapses, the fumes become inert and useless. Once thrown,
the cloud lasts for one round per two levels of the caster and affects those
within the radius and no others. If the sphere is shattered before it is thrown,
the effect is centered on the sphere. Any sort of atmospheric disturbance (e.g.
rain, wind, et al.) negates the spell in one round.
The material component is a six-inch crystal sphere and four drams of Rare
Earths.

ACID MIST

School evocation [acid]; **Level** alchemist 1st, wizard 2nd
Casting Time 1 standard action
Components V, S, M
Range personal
Area 20-foot-radius spread
Target none
Duration 2 rounds
Saving Throw negates; **Spell Resistance** yes
This allows the alchemist to cover an area with an acidic mist. When the
spell is cast, mildly obscuring smoke pours out of the caster's hands to fill
a circular area with a 20-foot radius centered on the caster. At the start of
the next round, the smoke turns into translucent acidic green mist, and all
creatures that breathe within the mist may make a saving throw versus spell.
Those who fail their save take 2d4 points of acid damage as the mist causes
internal burns and blisters on the throat, lungs, and mucus membranes. The
next round, any creatures within the mist take 1d4 points of acid damage as it
begins to dissipate. Those within the cloud gain partial concealment.
This mist is immobile and does not affect the caster, who may enter and leave
the area of effect after casting without taking damage. It can be destroyed
or dispelled using a *gust of wind*, *part water*, *dispel magic*, or some other
similar spell.
The material component is half an onion.

School evocation [acid]; **Level** alchemist 2nd
Casting Time 1 standard action
Components V, S, M
Range personal
Target you
Duration 3 rounds + 1 round/level (D)
Saving Throw no; **Spell Resistance** yes

The alchemist brings her hands together over her head and a brilliant viridian green scourge seven feet long forms and reaches the ground. It appears to ooze effulgent violet drops.

The scourge is immaterial; it is cohesive acidic energy. The caster may wield this scourge as a weapon, attempting to strike opponents. The caster is protected from all harm caused by the scourge. If the scourge strikes a solid surface, it rebounds in a random direction.

The corrosive field of the whip does 4d4 points of acid damage. The whip has a reach of 15 feet. The caster attacks with the whip with a base attack bonus equal to her hit die, modified by her Dexterity and relevant bonuses with a whip, and needs only to make a touch attack versus a target to cause damage. Alternately, the caster may attack all targets adjacent to her by waving the whip back and forth. No matter how many times a single individual is hit with the whip, they never take more than 4d4 points of acid damage. Hitting the target three times does the same damage as striking the target once.

This spell only damages creatures, not objects. This spell lasts for three full rounds +1 round per caster level. During this period, the alchemist cannot cast other spells or hold anything in her hands.

The spell can be ended before the duration expires with a simple thought. The material components for this spell are a seven-foot-long string and three drops of acid.

ACID STORM

School evocation [water, acid]; **Level** alchemist 4th
Casting Time 1 standard action
Components V, S, M
Range medium (100 feet + 10 feet per level)
Area 20-foot-radius emanation
Target you, one creature, etc.
Duration 1 round/level
Saving Throw half; **Spell Resistance** yes

This creates a storm of gelatinous acid rain. All targets are coated in corrosive acid. The acid can be neutralized by vinegar, wine, or a successful *dispel magic*.

The acid storm becomes more damaging as time goes on. Targets who enter or are in the cloud the first round take 1d4 points of acid damage, 1d6 points of acid damage for a second round, and 2d8 points of damage thereafter. A successful Fortitude save halves the damage. Once the spell ends, the damage stops. If the target cleanses themselves of the acid, the progression begins again.

ADHESION

School transmutation; **Level** alchemist 1st
Casting Time 1 standard action
Components V, S, M
Range touch
Target any 2 adjacent objects in a 5-foot radius
Duration 10 minutes/level
Saving Throw negates (objects); **Spell Resistance** yes

This alchemical dweomer temporarily affixes two objects to each other for the duration of the effect. The objects must be solid and touching. While casting the spell, the alchemist touches the spot where the two objects meet and then they hold fast. This bond may be severed only by a Strength check, with a DC equal to the caster's spell saving throw, casting a *dispel magic*, or applying massive force of about 500 + 500 pounds per level (with 500 pounds being about equivalent to the force a single horse can exert). If this spell is used on an object in a creature's possession, the creature receives a saving throw.

The material component is powered hooves from a domesticated working animal such as an ox or a horse.

AUGMENTED OLFACTION

School transmutation; **Level** alchemist 2nd
Casting Time 1 standard action
Components V, S, M
Range personal
Target you
Duration 10 minutes/level
Saving Throw no; **Spell Resistance** no

The caster's nose becomes extremely sensitive to odors. This gives the alchemist several benefits. They gain the scent special quality and receive a +2 bonus on all their Perception rolls. In addition, they can locate and identify all liquids or organic materials within 30 feet unless they are hermetically sealed.

This does have the side effect of making the alchemist extremely sensitive to scent-based attacks such as troglodyte stench or a *stinking cloud* spell. The alchemist has a −4 circumstance penalty to save against these effects.

The material component is a piece of dried cabbage and dog dung.

BOILING OIL

School evocation; **Level** alchemist 2nd
Casting Time 1 standard action
Components V, S, M
Range close (25 ft. + 5 ft./2 levels)
Target one creature
Duration instantaneous
Saving Throw half; **Spell Resistance** yes

The alchemist indicates a nearby target and boiling oil pours on top of the target. The target can make a Reflex saving throw to avoid damage from the spell. If the target fails the saving throw, they take 3d8 + 3 points of fire damage from the boiling oil and are blinded. They may repeat the saving throw every round to end the blinded condition. On a success, they take half damage and are not blinded.

The material components are a pinch of sulfur and a few drops of oil.

BUOYANCY

School transmutation [air]; **Level** alchemist 1st
Casting Time 1 standard action
Components V, S, M
Range close (25 ft. + 5 ft./2 levels)
Target objects, weighing less than 100 lbs./level
Duration 10 minutes/level
Saving Throw negates (harmless); **Spell Resistance** yes

This allows the alchemist to select a number of objects that normally do not float within close range that weigh less than 100 pounds per level and cause them to float upon a small layer of bubbles. This allows heavy objects such as gold, lead, stone, or even living creatures to float in water. It can also be used to raise objects that have sunk.

The material component is a small cork and a pinch of bromine salt.

BURNING BLOOD

School necromancy; **Level** alchemist 2nd, wizard/sorcerer 3rd
Casting Time 1 standard action
Components V, S, M
Range close (25 feet + 5 feet per 2 levels)
Target 1 creature
Duration 3 rounds + 1 round per 2 levels
Saving Throw negates; **Spell Resistance** yes

The alchemist selects one living creature. That creature must have exposed wounds. This means that they must have taken damage from an edged or piercing weapon. If this is the case, the exposed blood of the target is turned into burning acid.

The target may make a Fortitude saving throw every round. Any success indicates that they resist the damage for that round.

The burning blood does 2d4 points of damage + 1 per level of the alchemist. The alchemist does not need to touch the target.

The material component for this spell is a pinch of salt and salt peter.

CONTROL FLUID

School transmutation [water]; **Level** alchemist 3rd
Casting Time 1 standard action
Components V, S, M
Range close (25 ft. + 5 ft./2 levels)
Target 6 cubic feet of liquid per level
Duration 1 hour (D)
Saving Throw special; **Spell Resistance** no

Alchemists use this spell to control the movement of liquids. Any liquid or fluid such as oil, water, wine, acid, or blood can be controlled. The caster merely concentrates, and the liquid can be moved or turned into any shape as long as the caster exerts minimal concentration.

The liquid can be moved at a movement rate of 15 feet a round, floating through the air or running along a surface. The caster can affect an amount of liquid only up to his maximum; he can separate out this volume from a larger body of water. The caster can also clear out an area inside a liquid sized equal to the amount of liquid he can affect.

This spell can also be used to attempt to drown targets, but it does not affect their mobility. They can still move out of the area of effect. This spell can also be used against creatures from the Elemental Plane of Water or creatures with the water subtype to control their movements, but they receive a saving throw versus spells each round to ignore the caster's control.

The material components are a small glass tube and a sea sponge.

CONTROL VAPOR

School alteration [air]; **Level** alchemist 1st, wizard/sorcerer 3rd
Casting Time 1 standard action
Components V, S, M
Range medium (100 feet + 10 feet a level)
Area 20-foot radius
Target gas clouds
Duration 10 minutes
Saving Throw special (see text); **Spell Resistance** no

This useful spell has two functions. It can either be used to control the location, direction of movement, and speed of a body of gaseous vapor, or it can be used to create a zone of pure air.

Any gas or vapor contained within the area of effect can be moved with a movement rate of 30 feet. The alchemist only needs to use a move action to control the vapors. Control can be relinquished to cast other spells or to take other actions and then reacquired sometime later during the duration with no penalty.

Alternatively, the spell can expel all natural and magical vapor and gas from the area of effect. This allows only the natural background air in — if the air itself is foul, this spell will not produce fresh oxygen. This spell functions against natural mist or gas, or against spells such as *wall of fog*, *cloudkill*, *incendiary cloud*, or even gas breath weapons and creatures in gaseous form! In the event that the gas cloud is a creature, if it is unwilling, it receives a saving throw versus the effect.

The material component is a small glass tube and miniature bellows.

CORROSIVE SOLVENT

School conjuration [acid]; **Level** alchemist 2nd
Casting Time 1 standard action
Components V, S, M
Range close (25 feet + 5 feet per 2 levels)
Area 1 square foot per level
Target you, one creature, etc.
Duration 3 rounds
Saving Throw half; **Spell Resistance** yes

Alchemists use this spell to conjure a short-lived strong cohesive acid. It has the consistency of a slimy paste and begins eating away at whatever it is conjured against. It eats through six inches of organic material, four inches of stone, or one inch of metal per round. It can be conjured on the ceiling, but if so, it eats through the ceiling at only half the rate as bits drip to the floor. Against living targets, the solvent is less effective. If the target is a construct made from wood, stone, or metal, the solvent does 1d4 points of damage to the target per square foot affected, then half that damage total in the second round, then just 1 point of damage for each square foot affected. Targets receive a saving throw versus spells for half damage. For example, a 7th-level alchemist uses this against a caryatid column. She would affect seven square feet, so the first round she does 7d4 damage, and rolls 20 points of damage. The second round, half that damage is done (10 points), and the

final round the alchemist does 7 points of damage. Each time the damage is done, the target may make a Fortitude save for half damage.

This spell is much less effective against flesh, doing just 1 point of damage per caster level for three rounds. However, if the target is carrying any equipment, the gear must succeed at saves or become broken on the first failed save or destroyed on the second.

The material components of this spell include a drop of black pudding, vinegar, and water.

CRYSTALBRITTLE

School transmutation; **Level** alchemist 5th
Casting Time 1 standard action
Components V, S
Range touch
Area 2 cubic feet/level
Target one object
Duration instantaneous
Saving Throw special; **Spell Resistance** yes

This spell allows the alchemist to turn any metal or stone to fragile crystal. This spell affects weapons, armor, and even creatures made from metal or stone. This change is permanent and cannot be undone by any means short of a *wish* spell. *Dispel magic* does not have any effect.

The item to be affected must be touched. If it is something being worn or used, a melee touch attack must be made. The item to be affected must be a single item. A suit of armor could be affected, but a shield would not. All magical items get one chance to save. Creatures receive a Fortitude saving throw. Relics are unlikely to be affected. This brittle crystal has 1 hit point per inch of thickness and a hardness of 0.

DEATH SMOKE

School evocation; **Level** alchemist 3rd, wizard/sorcerer 4th
Casting Time 1 standard action
Components V, S, M
Range medium (100 feet + 10 feet per level)
Area 20-foot radius spread
Duration 1 round + 1 round per 2 levels
Saving Throw half; **Spell Resistance** yes

The alchemist points his finger at a spot within range and a pellet flies to that spot and strikes the ground. Thick opaque smoke begins to pour out from that point to cover a 20-foot radius from that center.

Those within the cloud are blind. Every round they remain within the cloud, they suffer 5d4 + 5 points of damage. Any targets entering the cloud gain the blinded condition and take the damage. A successful save ends the blind condition if the person is not in the cloud and halves the damage. Creatures immune to poison damage don't take any damage from this cloud. This cloud always forms on the ground and is 15 feet high.

The material component is a crushed spider and a pinch of sand.

DISPERSE VAPOR

School abjuration [air]; **Level** alchemist 2nd, wizard/sorcerer 3rd
Casting Time 1 standard action
Components V, S, M
Range close (25 feet + 5 feet per two levels)
Area 50-foot cube
Target one gas cloud
Duration 2 rounds/level
Saving Throw none; **Spell Resistance** no

This spell dissipates any fog, vapor, gas, or other substance in the air. When this spell is cast, any gas, vapor, fog, breath weapon, or gaseous creature, natural or magical in nature, is dispersed. If the cloud is larger than the area the spell covers, then an area the size of the area of effect is cleared. Nonmagical effects and magical spells of 4th level and below are negated. Higher-level magical effects are treated as if a *dispel magic* were cast. Creatures in gaseous form receive a Fortitude saving throw. If they fail this saving throw, they take 1d6 points of damage per caster level up to a maximum of 10d6 points of damage. Success indicates that they take half damage. In either case, they are forced from the area of effect, to the nearest open space.

The material component for the spell is a small cloth fan and a tiny piece of charcoal.

EVAPORATE FLUID

School transmutation [air]; **Level** alchemist 4th
Casting Time 1 standard action
Components V, S, M
Range close (25 ft. + 5 ft./2 levels)
Target a 10 foot cube of fluid per level
Duration instantaneous
Saving Throw special; **Spell Resistance** no

This spell causes exposed liquid to immediately vaporize. The liquid still exists; it is just sublimated into the atmosphere. This affects water, acid, oil, blood, liquid metals, poisons, potions, liquid rock — any liquid can be vaporized. When changed out of liquid form, the substance is rendered inert and is safe, posing no threat or danger of any kind; toxic and thermal properties are normalized and neutralized. If a portion of a larger body of liquid is vaporized, liquid rushes in to fill the remaining space.

This spell can also be used against creatures from the Elemental Plane of Water or creatures with the water subtype. In that case, the creature may make a Fortitude saving throw. On a successful save, nothing happens. On a failure, the creature takes 1d8 + 1 points of damage per level of the alchemist.

The material component is a pinch of salt.

GAUNTLET

School evocation [force]; **Level** alchemist 1st, wizard/sorcerer 2nd
Casting Time 1 standard action
Components V, S, M
Range personal
Target you
Duration 10 minutes
Saving Throw none (harmless); **Spell Resistance** yes

This spell protects the alchemist's hand. It creates a gauntlet of force that is transparent, silent, resistant, and nonconductive. It is impossible to damage. The alchemist can use the gauntlet to stop a gate or door from closing, removing his hand and leaving the force gauntlet inside. Once his hand is removed, the gauntlet lasts until the duration expires and the alchemist may no longer use it.

It can be used as a weapon to do 1d6 + 1 points of damage. It is considered a magical weapon for purposes of striking protected creatures. Being made of force, it can also damage incorporeal creatures. It can also be used as a shield, raising the alchemist's armor class by 1 versus one opponent as a swift action.

The primary purpose of the gauntlet is to allow the handling of dangerous materials. It can protect against extreme heat, acid, boiling liquids, deadly vapors, and more without damage. It is immune to disease, molds, and mummy rot, and nothing adheres to it. The gauntlet prevents spell casting that requires a somatic component.

The material component is a lump of rock crystal.

GREASE SLICK

School conjuration (creation); **Level** alchemist 2nd, wizard/sorcerer 2nd
Casting Time 1 standard action
Components V, S, M
Range close (25 ft. + 5 ft./2 levels)
Target one object or 15-foot square
Duration 1 minute a level
Saving Throw special (see text); **Spell Resistance** no

This is an improved version of the *grease* spell. The alchemist can create a spray of grease from his fingertips that coats a 15-foot-by-15-foot area. Any creature in the area when the spell is cast must make a successful Reflex save or fall. A creature can walk within or through the area of grease at half normal speed with a DC 15 Acrobatics check. Failure means it can't move that round (and must then make a Reflex save or fall), while failure by 5 or more means it falls (see the Acrobatics skill for details). Creatures that do not move on their turn must still make this saving throw to stay standing and are considered flat-footed

The spell can also be used to create a greasy coating on an item. Material objects not in use are always affected by this spell, while an object wielded or employed by a creature requires its bearer to make a Reflex saving throw to avoid the effect. If the initial saving throw fails, the creature immediately drops the item. A saving throw must be made in each round that the creature attempts to pick up or use the greased item. A creature wearing greased armor or clothing gains a +15 circumstance bonus on Escape Artist checks and Combat Maneuver checks made to escape a grapple, and to their CMD to avoid being grappled.

The material component is a pinch of lard.

HOLD VAPOR

School abjuration [air]; **Level** alchemist 2nd, wizard/sorcerer 3rd
Casting Time 1 standard action
Components V, S, M
Range close (25 ft. + 5 ft./2 levels)
Area 20-foot-radius area + 5 feet/level
Target one gas cloud
Duration special (1 hour maximum)
Saving Throw special (see text); **Spell Resistance** yes

The alchemist can use this spell to hold and stop any fog, vapor, gas, or other substance's movement in the air. When this spell is cast, any gas, vapor, fog, breath weapon, or gaseous creature, natural or magical in nature, is held. It does not prevent the movement of creatures in and out of the area of effect. This works even against magical control and effects such as *gust of wind* that would move the vapor. It even can constrain creatures in gaseous form or of the air subtype. These creatures receive a Fortitude saving throw each round; if they fail, they are held as if subject to *hold person*. While held, creatures able to change or solidify their form are unable to do so.

This spell has a duration of up to an hour and requires the caster to continue concentrating for the duration. It does not allow the caster to control or move vapor, only hold it in place.

The material component for this spell is a small bladder.

LIQUID MODULATION

School transmutation [water]; **Level** alchemist 1st, wizard/sorcerer 2nd
Casting Time 1 standard action
Components V, S, M
Range close (25 ft. + 5 ft./2 levels)
Area 1 cubic foot of liquid a level
Target you, one creature, etc.
Duration instantaneous
Saving Throw special (see text); **Spell Resistance** no

This spell changes one type of liquid into another type of nonmagical, non-alchemical liquid. Examples of the types of liquids that can be produced are oil, water, blood, wine, vinegar, and juice. It is possible to convert magical liquids, but they receive a saving throw. Living creatures are unaffected unless the creature is from the Elemental Plane of Water or has the water subtype. If this is the case, then they receive a Fortitude saving throw. If this saving throw is failed, the creature takes 1d4 points of damage per level of the caster.

This spell is cast by taking a single drop of the substance that will be produced and putting it on the caster's tongue while touching the liquid to be transformed. This means there is some danger when creating foul liquids, poisons, and liquid metals.

Also, the target of the spell must be touched directly. In the case of affecting a creature, a touch attack must successfully be made.

LIQUID SPHERE

School conjuration (summoning) [water]; **Level** alchemist 1st
Casting Time 1 standard action
Components V, S, M
Range personal
Target you
Duration instantaneous
Saving Throw none; **Spell Resistance** no

This spell allows the alchemist to create a sphere of liquid in their hand. It creates one gallon per caster level. The liquid must be of normal temperature (i.e., not boiling or freezing), and it cannot be flammable or acidic enough to cause damage. The sphere rests inertly in the alchemist's hands. It can be released or poured into a container. It can be thrown clumsily with a 10-foot range increment and a −2 to hit. It does no damage. If there is more than a gallon of liquid, it does 1d4 points of damage to creatures with the fire subtype per gallon.

This spell often is used to provide the alchemist with fresh water, ink, dye, juice, cider, soup, and other harmless liquids. Alchemical liquids may not be created with this spell.

The material component for this spell is a small clear glass bead.

MANIFOLD LUBRICATION

School transmutation; **Level** alchemist 3rd
Casting Time 1 standard action
Components V, S, M
Range medium (100 feet + 10 feet per level)
Target special (see text)
Duration 2 rounds/level
Saving Throw special; **Spell Resistance** yes

Alchemists use this spell for three separate functions. It can affect objects, creatures, or surfaces, similar in manner to the way grease functions.

If applied to a creature, it functions identically to *salve of slipperiness*.

When this spell is applied to an object, it makes the object impossible to grasp for the duration. It simply cannot be held, lifted, or otherwise moved or possessed. If this is cast on an object held by a creature, then they may make a Reflex save to negate the effect.

If cast on a surface, it acts as the alchemist spell *grease slick*.

The material component is a pinch of graphite and one dram of pig lard.

NEUTRALIZE GAS

School abjuration [air]; **Level** alchemist 4th
Casting Time 1 immediate action
Components V, S, M
Range medium (100 feet + 10 feet per level)
Area 10-foot-radius area/level
Duration instantaneous
Saving Throw none; **Spell Resistance** no

The alchemist can use this spell to neutralize any harmful gas, cloud, vapor, or fog of any kind. The substance is rendered totally inert and dissipates within the area of effect. It affects *cloudkill*, *stinking cloud*, *solid fog*, *death fog*, *incendiary cloud*, *acid storm*, *acid cloud*, *acid mist*, smoke, or any dangerous gas.

This spell does nothing to heal or reverse the effects of any gases that have already caused damage. This spell can also be used as a counter spell to gaseous breath weapons, spores, mold, and other gaseous attacks. Cast in the same round as one of these attacks, it provides a +4 circumstance bonus to saves made and halves damage. This spell does not affect creatures.

The material component is a small piece of gauze and some charcoal.

ORB OF CONTAINMENT

School evocation; **Level** alchemist 4th
Casting Time 1 standard action
Components V, S, M (1,000-gp diamond)
Range medium (100 feet + 10 feet per level)
Area 6-inch-radius sphere
Target one object or substance
Duration special
Saving Throw none; **Spell Resistance** no

This allows the alchemist to contain dangerous substances. When cast, the alchemist indicates a substances or object that must be contained and the spell creates a crystal sphere up to 12 inches in diameter that surrounds and secures the object.

The spell fails if the object is too large. The sphere is unbreakable and is able to contain any substance no matter how volatile or inimical to life. Time is suspended within the sphere.

The sphere is immune to all physical attacks, though *dispel magic* or *disintegrate* spell can destroy the orb. The duration of the spell is one day, though it can be extended by recasting the spell.

The material components for this spell are a 1,000-gp diamond and a shard of glass. Only the shard is necessary for renewal. The diamond shatters when the sphere is created.

PHYSICAL INVISIBILITY

School transmutation; **Level** alchemist 4th
Casting Time 1 standard action
Components V, S, M
Range touch
Target one creature touched
Duration 5 rounds/level
Saving Throw special; **Spell Resistance** yes

This spell causes *invisibility* as the spell, but the processes used are not magically hiding the object from sight. Instead, the object is literally made transparent.

This means the subject disappears from view and is not detectable by normal vision. The subject can attack without disrupting his invisibility and is immune to magical means of detection such as *detect invisibility*.

This spell can be canceled by *dust of appearance* or by a successful *dispel magic* or *anti-magic field*. *Dispel illusion* or other methods are useless. *True seeing* reveals the subject.

The material components for this spell are a shard of a mirror and a small rock crystal.

PROPERTY TRANSFERENCE

School transmutation; **Level** alchemist 4th
Casting Time 1 standard action
Components V, S, M
Range touch
Target 2 objects
Duration permanent
Saving Throw none; **Spell Resistance** yes

This useful spell allows the alchemist to trade a property between two objects that are no larger than one cubic foot per level of the alchemist. Any single property can be switched between the two objects: strength, color, durability, brittleness, melting points, edibility, weight, etc. Each object retains all other relative properties. For example, the alchemist could cause a suit of plate mail to become transparent with a piece of glass. The suit would function identically in all other ways but have the translucence of glass. Conversely, a vial could be given the strength of steel.

Both objects must be non-living. Both objects must be nonmagical. The material components for this spell are a small mechanical switch and length of wire in addition to the two objects.

PROTECTION FROM NONMAGICAL GAS

School abjuration [air]; **Level** alchemist 1st, wizard/sorcerer 2nd
Casting Time 1 standard action
Components V, S, M
Range personal
Area 20-foot-radius sphere
Target you
Duration 10 minutes/level
Saving Throw none (harmless); **Spell Resistance** yes

This spell creates a 20-foot-radius transparent immaterial sphere centered on the caster. This sphere provides total protection from all nonmagical gases and mists. When they come into contact with the sphere, they are dissipated instantly, leaving nothing but pure, clean air.

The sphere is filled with clean air for the duration of the effect. If the air surrounding the sphere is foul and there is no inlet for fresh air, it allows the caster to continue to breathe safely for the duration of the effect. This spell will not work in a vacuum or underwater.

The spell ends upon contact with magical gases (such as *cloudkill*, *stinking cloud*, *obscuring mist*, etc.) or if the caster moves at a rate of greater than 120 feet per round, such as by riding on a horse or teleporting.

The material components are a silk fan and a two-inch square of thick gauze.

PRESERVATION OF THE FLESH

School necromancy; **Level** alchemist 4th
Casting Time 1 standard action
Components V, M (a 1,000-gp candle)
Range touch
Target you
Duration 8 hours + 4 hours/level
Saving Throw none; **Spell Resistance** no

This allows the caster to create a vessel in which to store lifeforce. The caster creates a candle using 1,000 gp of rare materials. Then, when this spell is cast, 3d4 hit points are drained from the alchemist and transferred to the candle, which then lights. Casters cannot transfer more hit points than they currently have; they are always left with 1 hit point remaining.

The candle burns for the duration of the spell. If extinguished or destroyed, the alchemist is wounded and loses the hit points stored within the candle. They must be recovered normally.

If the caster is mortally wounded before the duration expires, then he or she appears to die. This death appears real to sight, tests, and even divination spells. However, when the candle burns down, the borrowed lifeforce re-enters the caster's body and restores them to life. If the caster is "dead" and the candle is extinguished before the spell ends, then the caster's spirit is set free and experiences its final reward.

Some normal wounds are repaired when the lifeforce flows back into the body, but missing limbs, disease, critical wounds, disintegrated body parts, limbs trapped in stone, petrification, burn wounds, etc., persist. This could mean the caster immediately perishes again. This is also true if the alchemist cannot survive in their new environment. Only one use of this spell can be in effect. The material component is the candle made with 1,000 gp worth of rare materials.

RUSTING GRASP

School transmutation [water]; **Level** alchemist 3rd
Casting Time 1 standard action
Components V, S, M
Range personal
Target you
Duration 1 round/level
Saving Throw special (see text); **Spell Resistance** yes

This allows the alchemist to corrode ferrous metals at her touch. This spell works only on ferrous metals, so iron or iron alloys are affected, but gold, silver, and the like are not. Any item touched receives a saving throw to avoid being destroyed. Magic weapons and armor receive their bonus. This allows the alchemist to make touch attacks against armor or disarm attacks versus weapons to destroy them for the duration of the spell. If facing a creature made from ferrous metal — an iron golem, for instance — then on a successful touch attack this spell does 2d8 + 1 points of damage per alchemist level on a failed Fortitude save.

The material component is a scale or antenna from a rust monster.

SMOKY SPHERE

School conjuration; **Level** alchemist 1st
Casting Time 1 standard action
Components V, S, M
Range personal
Area 10-foot-radius burst
Target you
Duration 1 round/3 rounds, see text;
Saving Throw negates; **Spell Resistance** yes

When this spell is cast, the glass sphere held in the caster's hand fills with a dense, choking smoke. This can be thrown as a grenade-like weapon with a range increment of 30 feet. When it strikes a surface, it shatters and fills a 10-foot-radius with thick, acrid smoke.

Everyone within the radius must succeed at a Fortitude save or cough and gasp for 1d4 + 1 rounds. This causes all who fail their save to gain the sickened condition. Spellcasters attempting to cast that are affected by the smoky sphere have a 30% chance of spell failure. The cloud does not obscure vision.

The sphere stays filled with smoke only for three rounds; if not used before that time elapses, the smoke becomes inert and useless. Once thrown, the cloud lasts only for one round and affects those within the radius and no others. If the sphere is shattered before it is thrown, the effect is centered on the sphere. The material component is a six-inch glass sphere and a charred stick.

STONE FLAME

School enchantment; **Level** alchemist 1st
Casting Time 1 standard action
Components V, S, M
Range touch
Target a small flame
Duration 10 minutes/level
Saving Throw none; **Spell Resistance** no

This spell is cast on a small active flame, like that of a campfire or torch. When cast, the flame freezes into an orange stone keeping the exact same shape it has at the moment of casting. The stone remains stuck at its location, either at the end of a torch or on the ground.

For the duration of the spell the stone gives off light as a fire but is cool to the touch like stone. If the stone is broken, the spell ends and the fire is extinguished. If the spell expires, the stone turns back into flame.

The material component is a dram of fine sand mixed with a dram of raw sugar.

VENOM WARD

School necromancy; **Level** alchemist 5th
Casting Time 1 standard action
Components V, S, M
Range touch
Target one creature
Duration 1 hour/level
Saving Throw none (harmless); **Spell Resistance** yes
This protects one creature touched by the alchemist, including herself,
from all toxins, venoms, and poisons for the duration of the spell. This
spell includes poisonous gases. It produces no visible effect, but the magic
neutralizes any poison the caster comes into contact with.
The material component is a few drops of liquid poison and one nail from
the corpse of a creature who died from poison. They are not consumed in the
casting.

VITRIOLIC SPHERE

School conjuration (creation) [water, acid]; **Level** alchemist 3rd
Casting Time 1 standard action
Components V, S, M
Range close (25 ft. + 5 ft./2 levels)
Area 5-foot-radius spread
Target one creature
Duration special
Saving Throw half; **Spell Resistance** no
This spell conjures a bright green sphere full of corrosive acid. The alchemist
picks a target and the sphere flies unerringly toward the target. Once
slamming into the target, the sphere envelops the target in vivid, emerald
green acid. For the duration of the spell, acid splatters and streams on all
people and objects within five feet of the target.
The target may attempt a Reflex save each round for half damage. A
successful save after the first round ends the spell. If the save is successful on
the first round, the spell continues — a second successful save is necessary
to end the spell. For every level of the alchemist, the target takes 1d4 points
of acid damage. For every following round, two damage dice are subtracted
and a new damage total is rolled. A 10th-level alchemist will do 10d4 points
of acid damage on the first round, 8d4 points of acid damage on the second
round, 6d4 points of acid damage on the third round, and so on until no more
damage is being done.
While the spell continues to function, anyone nearby the target is splashed
with gouts of acid. All those within five feet of the target take 1 point of
damage per level of the alchemist while the spell functions.
The material component for this spell is a drop of stomach acid from a troll.

APPENDIX

100 ALCHEMICAL MISHAPS

You may allow saving throws, or not. Unless noted, all save DCs are equal to item difficulties. Assume all results are permanent. What specifically happens should be the most interesting thing to happen.

TABLE A–1: ALCHEMICAL MISHAPS

1d100	Result
1	Vines entangle the alchemist and his entire lab.
2	Noxious fumes cause the caster to vomit randomly for 1d4 weeks.
3	All metal corrodes and is useless in the lab causing (1d4 + 1) x 100 damage to all metal objects.
4	All magical items are drained of 1d4 charges or suppressed for 24 hours.
5	The item and all materials turn to dust.
6	The item becomes a randomly selected slime.
7	The item becomes a randomly selected ooze.
8	The item becomes a randomly selected fungus.
9	User's hair goes white from fumes. Item is fine.
10	Caster gains a scent.
11	Explosion! 2d6 points of damage.
12	Fire in lab causes 1d6 x 100 gp of damage.
13	All glass shatters in lab, causing 50d10 gp of damage.
14	All leather disintegrates in the lab, causing 10d4 gp of damage.
15	Spill! Lab is coated in vermin attractant.
16	Alchemist's limbs become invisible.
17	Gravity is permanently doubled in the lab.
18	Item created is actually of a different one of a random type.
19	Disaster causes amnesia.
20	Disaster causes insanity.
21	Lab animates as a small or medium construct.
22	Explosion! All flesh in the lab is crystallized.

1d100	Result
23	Lab animates as a large or huge construct.
24	The alchemist changes shape.
25	All metal in the lab becomes plated in gold.
26	All metal in the lab quadruples in weight.
27	All creatures in the lab turned to gas.
28	All creatures have flesh removed from their bodies and become living skeletons.
29	All creatures in the lab age 2d10 years.
30	All magic items are disjuncted as if by a 20th-level caster.
31	Creatures in the lab have a random number of their limbs double in length.
32	Lab teleports 10 feet straight up.
33	Explosion! Lab frozen, doing 6d8 points of damage.
34	Creatures in the lab are paralyzed from the waist down.
35	All objects and creatures in the lab radiate sunlight.
36	All creatures in the lab are struck blind.
37	Alchemist stains his hands, arms, neck, and torso.
38	Experiment bubbles over, leaving 20 gray pills that heal 2d10 points of damage when eaten.
39	Mishap produces a frozen cubic foot of human blood.
40	All dead within one mile are raised.
41	Creatures in lab become permanently drunk or high.
42	Disaster produces 1d10 gems worth 100d4 gp each.
43	Creatures within one mile have a chance of gaining the body parts of animals.
44	Explosion! Choking gas, succeed at a Fortitude DC 18 or die.
45	Smoke damage to the lab causes 10d12 gp of damage.
46	Creatures within one mile grow mysterious new organs.
47	Creatures within one mile become pregnant regardless of gender.
48	Creatures within one mile grow a second face.

1d100	Result
49	Creatures within one mile have their teeth turn into thumbs.
50	Creatures within one mile have a permanently numb extremity.
51	Permanent loss of 1d4 − 1 (minimum 1) hit points.
52	Creatures within one mile gain a permanent scent.
53	Creatures within one mile grow a plant from their body.
54	The lab and everything non-living within it vanishes and reappears in 1d100 minutes.
55	Explosion! Lab shatters like glass, causing 3d10 points of damage.
56	One of the alchemist's extremities doubles in size.
57	Creatures within one mile appear to have skin made from chrome.
58	Laboratory and everything inside it becomes a random solid metal.
59	A dense fog permanently covers the lab, inside and out.
60	The laboratory turns into gingerbread.
61	The laboratory levitates 1d10 meters.
62	The laboratory sinks 2d12 feet into the ground.
63	The laboratory grows bark, repeatedly.
64	The laboratory is packed full of potatoes.
65	The laboratory temperature is raised to 300⁰ Fahrenheit.
66	Explosion! Alchemist has limb or extremity burnt off!
67	An elemental (small) is summoned.
68	An elemental (medium) is summoned.
69	An elemental (large) is summoned.
70	A succubus is summoned.
71	The laboratory and everything inside turns ethereal or astral.
72	The laboratory is coated in save or die contact poison.
73	The laboratory and everything in it vanishes.
74	The laboratory is transported somewhere interesting.
75	The laboratory is wreathed in darkness.
76	. The laboratory collapses.

1d100	Result
77	Explosion! The laboratory is doused in acid that does 8d10 points of damage.
78	The laboratory travels 5d6 weeks into the future.
79	The laboratory becomes invisible.
80	All trees within one-mile animate and become hostile.
81	The laboratory doubles in size.
82	The laboratory becomes transparent.
83	The laboratory turns to sand.
84	Groundwater is rendered toxic in a two-mile radius.
85	The item becomes a nugget of neutronium.
86	The laboratory permanently becomes pleasant smelling.
87	A plague breaks out.
88	Explosion! Sonic blast does 12d12 damage.
89	All food within one mile causes madness.
90	All metal within 500 yards liquefies.
91	Everything within one mile is covered in moss.
92	The laboratory is drained of color.
93	Creatures within one mile are unable to sleep for 2d4 days.
94	The laboratory dissolves into one million insects.
95	The laboratory becomes a gate to another plane.
96	The laboratory is teleported into space.
97	The laboratory is permanently covered in thick webbing.
98	Item created is 10 times more powerful than normal.
99	Explosion! Laboratory disintegrates.
100	Explosion! Everything in a 2,000-foot radius takes 20d8 points of damage.

100 RANDOM POTION EFFECTS

Roll on **Table A–2** below when a random alchemical item effect is needed. Duration is normally 1d4 + 4 minutes, but the effect can be permanent.

TABLE A–2: POTION MISHAPS

1d100	Result
1	User glows like a torch.
2	User inflates like a balloon for 1d6 turns.
3	User's skin changes color.
4	User turns to stone.
5	User enlarges.
6	User shrinks.
7	User bleeds from eyes for 2d10 + 1 rounds, taking 1 point of damage per round.
8	User's gender changes.
9	User is granted a wish.
10	User is enraged and attacks nearest target with a +4 alchemical bonus to Strength.
11	User gains an inherent 1d4 Strength bonus permanently.
12	User is cursed.
13	User ages 1d12 + 24 years.
14	User become 1d6 + 1 years younger.
15	User vomits sawdust.
16	User gains Fire Resistance 40.
17	User gains Fire Vulnerability.
18	User gains Acid Resistance 40.
19	User gains Acid Vulnerability.
20	User gains Ice Resistance 40.
21	User gains Ice Vulnerability.
22	User gains an inherent 1d4 Dexterity bonus permanently.
23	User can *spider climb* as the spell.
24	User can *comprehend language* as the spell.
25	User can *speak with animals* as the spell.
26	A dragon is summoned that is not under the control of the imbiber.
27	User's shape changes into a dragon.
28	User gains *detect thoughts* as the spell.
29	User is subject to *fear* as the spell.
30	User gains 1,000 XP.
31	User gains double experience points for 24 hours.
32	Caster gains 1 pound per round for 1d100 rounds.
33	User permanently gains an inherent 1d4 Constitution bonus.
34	User gains animal affinity, gaining one random animal trait.
35	User is *feebleminded* as the spell.
36	User gains luck and gets +20% (+4) to all rolls.
37	User is put to *sleep* as the spell.
38	User can breathe fire as an *elixir of fire breathing*.
39	User can *fly* as the spell.
40	User gains permanent *invisibility* as the spell.
41	User is blinded.
42	User is deafened.
43	User creaks and pops like a squeaky wheel when moving.
44	User permanently gains an inherent 1d4 Intelligence bonus.
45	User gains *blur* as the spell.
46	User gains *blink* as the spell.
47	User gains *mirror image* as the spell.
48	User changes race.
49	User is slowed as the spell.
50	User is hasted as the spell.
51	User gains +4 to armor class.
52	User gains a magic aura as the spell.
53	User turns into an insect.
54	User is polymorphed into an amphibian.
55	User permanently gains an inherent 1d4 Wisdom bonus.
56	User turns into a tree.
57	User turns into a cloud of wasps.
58	User gains the ability to *command* as the spell.
59	User gains *water breathing* as the spell.
60	User is subject to *cure disease* as the spell.
61	User is subject to *cure serious wounds* as the spell.
62	User gains two tentacles.
63	User's hands double in size.
64	User is *silenced* as the spell.
65	User loses all his hair.
66	User permanently gains an inherent 1d4 Charisma bonus.
67	User's hair turns into precious metals.
68	User becomes gaseous.
69	User turns into a zombie.
70	User is invisible to non-humans.
71	User gains *water walking* as the spell.
72	User grows a prehensile tail.
73	User grows a tail that grants a secondary slap attack and does 1d4 points of damage.
74	User grows a second face on their body.
75	User gains the ability to *wind walk* as the spell.
76	User gains an inherent 1d6 + 1 Strength, Dexterity, and Constitution bonus.
77	User grows a turtle shell.
78	User turns into salt.
79	User is subject to a *statue* spell.
80	User's head grows to double size.
81	User can speak only gibberish.
82	User gains darkvision 1 foot.
83	User gains darkvision 30 feet.
84	User gains darkvision 60 feet.
85	User begins uncontrollably dancing.
86	User attracts vermin.
87	User gains immunity to normal weapons.
88	User gains an inherent 1d6 + 1 Intelligence, Wisdom, and Charisma bonus.
89	User can *speak with dead* as the spell.
90	User gains *duo-dimension* as the spell.
91	User is flatulent.
92	User is subject to *reverse gravity* as the spell.
93	User becomes translucent.
94	User gains *feign death* as the spell.
95	User gains *true seeing* as the spell.
96	User is subject to a *heal* as the spell.
97	User gains an inherent 1d4 + 1 bonus points to all statistics.
98	User gains *fire shield* as the spell.
99	Roll again, result is permanent.
100	Roll two times. If this result occurs again, user dies.

ALCHEMICAL QUIRKS

There is a 25% chance any given beneficial item also has a quirk. These last for the duration of the item.

TABLE A–3: ALCHEMICAL QUIRKS

1d100	Result
1	User glows a color.
2	User's skin changes color.
3	User cannot speak due to swollen tongue for 1d4 hours.
4	User's senses sharpen and they receive a +1 bonus on Perception rolls.
5	User has tinnitus for the duration of the item or for three minutes, whichever is longer.
6	Item works at half power.
7	Item has double duration.
8	User is drunk for 2d12 hours after using item.
9	User loses or gains infravision to 60 feet.
10	This item does not affect humans.
11	This item does not affect demihumans.
12	User experiences disorientation, giving a −2 penalty to hit and AC.
13	User experiences drowsiness
14	User glows in dark
15	The item is sickening to use. Wielder must make a DC 10 Constitution check to use and succeed at a DC 16 Fortitude to avoid being sickened (−2 on all rolls).
16	User has a random statistic lowered by 2
17	Item becomes useless if exposed to air for more than one round; it evaporates or congeals.
18	The item has an unpredictable effect. Roll 1d10: 1–5 indicates normal effects; 6–8 indicates nothing happens; and a 9–10 indicates nothing occurs and the user becomes ill.
19	Explosive! The item has a 75% chance to explode and be ruined.
20	User gets logorrhea.
21	Item is addictive.
22	User's skin acquires a pattern for 24 hours. Roll 1d6: 1–3 is spots; 4–6 is stripes.
23	User is slowed and covered in ice.
24	User appears wreathed in phantasmal fire.
25	User's hair grows two inches per minute.
26	User's voice sounds robotic, like grinding metal.
27	User's eyes glow.
28	Smoke pours from the user's ears and eyes, filling a 10-square cube per round.
29	All the user's hair falls out (permanently).
30	All water that comes within 10 feet of the user turns to blood.
31	User is *confused* as the spell.
32	Item causes 1d4 + 1 rounds of vomiting after use.
33	The item's effect is reversed.
34	User gains a disease.
35	User's hair changes color.
36	User becomes terribly thirsty.
37	User develops a migraine.
38	User's hair turns to snakes.
39	User's hands twist and become useless.
40	User hiccups uncontrollably.
41	User's skin becomes transparent.
42	User levitates one inch off the ground.
43	User's footprints glow.
44	User is covered in scales.
45	User appears to be made of ice.
46	User oozes sweet-smelling oil.
47	User has an illusionary double that appears five feet away.
48	User looks like a nearby creature.
49	User becomes starving.
50	User becomes dehydrated.
51	User vomits up a random potion at the end of the duration.
52	User experiences a seizure that lasts for 1d3 rounds.
53	User can read the thoughts of any visible creature within 10 feet.
54	User's thinking is stunted; −5 to Intelligence and Wisdom.
55	Noise is made when the user moves, such as humming, squeaking, etc.
56	User's skin oozes oil filled with soot.
57	User gains a rash, giving −1 penalty to hit and AC.
58	User takes 2d8 points of damage.
59	User has blurry vision for the duration (−1 circumstance penalty to hit).
60	User exudes stench that causes −2 penalty to hit and −4 damage on a failed DC 14 Fortitude save for all within 10 feet.
61	User gains tremors that cause −1 circumstance penalty to hit and damage.
62	User is subject to falls. Succeed at a DC 10 Acrobatics check when moving or fall prone.
63	Temperature drops 1d4 x 10 degrees in 30-foot radius.
64	Temperature rises 1d4 x 10 degrees in 30-foot radius.
65	User shrinks proportionate to lost hit points.
66	User is unable to move his or her face while speaking, causing −2 penalty to Charisma-based skills.
67	User's eyes turn insectile.
68	Item does not affect men.
69	Item does not affect women.
70	User suffers exhaustion.
71	User is panicked.
72	User is *hasted* as the spell.
73	User's hair turns to wire.
74	User is blinded or deafened for the duration.
75	User develops a stutter.
76	User sprouts feathers.
77	User suffers vertigo.
78	Non-humans become invisible to the user.
79	User's fingernails fall out.
80	User's skin acquires a brick-like texture.
81	User may speak only in tongues.
82	User grows antennae.
83	User's eyes turn black.
84	User grows nonfunctional wings.
85	User stinks of dirty socks.
86	User forgets only his name and his friends.
87	User's natural armor class improves by 2.
88	User hears voices.
89	User sees visions and hallucinations.
90	Runes cover user.
91	User grows a new extremity or limb.
92	User grows mandibles.
93	User's skin oozes honey.
94	User's skin becomes bloodstained.
95	User cannot speak
96	User gains 4d10 pounds.
97	User grows claws, granting two primary attacks that do 1d6 points of damage each.
98	User can see into the ethereal.
99	User is allergic to item and must a DC 20 Fortitude save or die.
100	Effect of item becomes permanent.

This isn't just a book with lists of treasure. Each item in this book can be used to start a story or add a twist to a story. Below are 100 examples you can expand upon.

TABLE A–4: STORY IDEAS

1d100	Result
1	Local children have been stealing *alchemist's befuddlement* grenades and drinking them to get high. The long-term effects of drinking these grenades are terrible and already one child has died.
2	A nearby ogre kidnapped a group of kobolds and is forcing them to craft *alchemist's fire* to fuel his new war machine.
3	A nearby tribe of wererats has been dumping *alchemist's terror* into the water supply. How will the characters respond to a city of madmen?
4	An alchemist has discovered a way to make *black-light* permanent. She is slowly expanding a permanent globe of darkness from her tower.
5	An angel of retribution has attacked a local church. The priest is being punished for killing good creatures to create *blessed spheres*.
6	People in town are seen with bright stains on their skin. When questioned, they say nothing. They are engaged in a secret underground gaming ring involving *dye bombs* to mark the losers.
7	Firewood in town keeps exploding in searing bursts of flame. A nearby dryad alchemist is seeding trees with *fireburst pellets* to protect her forest.
8	Thieves are using *flash pellets* to stage dramatic robberies. They appear to be immune to the pellets' effects.
9	A popular fashion among youth is using *frost sap* to scar themselves. One youth was seriously injured.
10	A nearby lighthouse suddenly begins shining a dim blue-green light. The town suspects it is haunted, but secretly an alchemist with a vendetta is playing a prank on the lighthouse maintainer by replacing all her oil with *shadow oil*.
11	An earthquake opened a crevice near an important natural resource. The crevice releases a gas that functions as *sleepsmoke*.
12	A new entertainment venue has opened: a skating rink on large blocks of granite covered in *slickshell*. However, the proprietor has been stealing local livestock in order to get enough animal fat to keep his supply current.
13	An alchemist's shop has been closed for weeks and the city wonders why. The god of fungus and slime turned the alchemist into a spellcasting slime in retribution for producing *slime bane*.
14	An alchemist producing *alchemist's kindness* is being harangued by teetotalers. The situation is ready to erupt into violence.
15	Explosions in the cemetery have occurred, leaving shattered remains. A local prankster under the influence of a necromancer has been sneaking into the cemetery and covering bones in *bone bomb* solution. How's he sneaking into the cemetery? He's a vampire.
16	Several adventurers have gone missing. It turns out the *potions of healing* they are buying aren't actually curing anything. They are just extremely alcoholic.
17	A necro-alchemist is coating undead in *death flames*. This scourge must be stopped.
18	The king is dead! But a cloaked figure approaches the party and claims that he has been given *false slumber*. They must rescue him before it is too late.
19	A brave knight disappeared and she is needed for a quest. The knight is a coward who has been using *carnelian flower of courage* to get up the gumption to do quests. Now she's too drunk to do anyone any good.
20	A village seems preternaturally calm in the face of disaster. The mayor is an alchemist and has everyone in the village addicted to a substance of some kind.
21	An alchemical stimulant has been outlawed! Yet citizens are still using it. Who's making it?
22	A wandering alchemist recently sold a number of defective potions in town, and then headed for the hills. Is he a nefarious anarchist working alone, or was this part of a sinister plot?
23	A harmless old lady is selling *black candles* in her candle shop. A curious wizard hires the characters to discover where she is getting her materials to craft such an item.
24	The water in town has suddenly become diseased, and it does not appear to be a normal matter.
25	A thief who uses his ethereal ability to commit crimes hires the party to replace a museum's *phasebound incense* with normal incense.
26	Rats are overrunning the city. That strange smell at night is *stinkstuff incense*. A naga is calling the rats to the city!
27	A merchants' guild is wildly profitable. The characters are hired to find out why. They are using amounts of *buoyancy ointment* to overload their ships.
28	An area has been scoured for a scrying mage causing trouble, and he can't be found. He's using *clarity ointment* to extend the range of his influence.
29	A sorcerer arrived, and the king has taken a liking to her. She's using an ointment of some kind to influence the king. How can she be stopped without drawing the wrath of her new best friend?
30	*Insect repellent* is killing bees, and the beekeeper is hopping mad.
31	The characters are sold fake magic items covered in a paste that creates a false magic aura. Who is at fault? The seller or the merchant he buys from?
32	The characters are approached by some disgruntled townsfolk. A mountebank came into town to sell them *salve of protection, rust*. It worked when he showed it off, but what they bought ruined all the metal they used it on. They want the characters to track down the seller who happens to be a leprechaun.
33	One of the characters' henchmen is using cologne that causes a wild reaction in all those who encounter the party.
34	A thief in plate armor has been committing heists. She's treated the armor with *armor malleability* and *quieting paste* until it's as comfortable as normal clothing. She does it to hide the fact that she's either the queen, a character's mother, or the demure wife of a political figure.

35	Someone used *absorption powder* to turn a moat into paste. The culprit? A traitor who did so for the army that plan to attack in the morning.
36	Healthy people are dying of mysterious heart attacks! No sign of magic is detected. The murderer is injecting a powder into their veins that causes blood clots.
37	Denizens of the forest come to ask the party to track down the alchemist who's seeding their forest with *defoliant powder*. The alchemist is a bitter mountain ogre mage.
38	A well-known public figure begins acting strangely but no enchantment is detected. Who is dosing him with *contrariness powder* and can they be stopped before it becomes permanent?
39	A cult of secrets is dosing its members with *delirium powder*. Several prominent council members joined or are considering joining the cult. Those who are as risk of having their secrets exposed are panicking.
40	An alchemist posts a reward for anyone who can produce a container capable of holding an *alkahest*.
41	A woman asks for help seeking an alchemist who can produce *tincture of wolfsbane*. However, as you travel, you appear to be stalked by a wolf …
42	Who are the characters? Each has an amazing variety of skills, but none of them even knows their own name. They must discover who dosed them with *dust of amnesia* and attempt to restore their memory.
43	An orc force has been making devastating strikes against nearby elven encampments. No one knows how they created stealthy war machines. The tribe's alchemist has learned to produce *dust of blending*.
44	The characters are poisoned with *dust of blighted bones*! They have seven days to track down who killed them.
45	A huge cloud of dust springs up east of town. The party is sent to investigate. An evil wizard and his minions are using *dust of clouds* to cause a distraction to hide the construction of a tower.
46	Farmers and livestock traders are angry because an alchemist producing *dust of consumption* is making them obsolete, feeding the populace with the novel food of flavored rocks.
47	The woods are filled with a mysterious tribe of deformed ogres, and villagers keep disappearing. An alchemist is secretly kidnapping townsfolk and using *dust of deformity* on them.
48	A forest is growing up near town. At first it seems like a boon, but then it begins to encroach upon the road, and traffic dwindles. Will they be able to stop the centaur alchemist using *dust of fertile growth* before the town is overrun?
49	A local tribe of primitives has begun viciously attacking townsfolk. An alchemist has been addicting them to *dust of fury*.
50	A strange hazy chamber is said to drive anyone mad who enters. They just endlessly repeat the same action again and again. It is actually just a large chamber filled with *dust of looping*.
51	The court wizard suddenly becomes weak and ineffective. Can they find the imp dosing her food with *dust of maladweomer*.
52	A high-level party is asked to retrieve an item. Easy right? Except that it's hidden in a chest filled with *dust of nondetection*.
53	A nearby temple is discovered, but everyone who visits leaves in terror. *Dust of panic* coats the floor of the entrance hall.
54	Strange murders are occurring, and the bodies appear to have exploded from within. They are surrounded by a red, pulpy substance. Will the characters discover the noble alchemist who is poisoning his opponents with *dust of roughage*?
55	A gang of mercenary criminals is known for being totally silent while they work. The party is hired to stop them. Can they survive against a group that coordinates their actions using *dust of the sparkling mind*?
56	A village suddenly becomes old overnight. A night hag visited each villager in their dreams and dosed them with an *elixir of aging*.
57	A band of yeti are attacking a southern town. The yeti are actually bandits who quaff *elixirs of fur growth* to hide their identities.
58	A new pugilist is upsetting all the thieves' guild's carefully planned fights. Turns out he had a 2–11 record before this comeback. The party is hired to investigate. Will they discover his use of the *elixir of the iron fist*?
59	A prophecy occurred, and an ancient hero has not awakened from her *elixir of suspended animation*. No one knows what condition was set.
60	Somebody is selling *elixir of super heroic fighting* — cheap! No way they are free of side effects. Not only that, enemies of the characters seem to be snapping them up.
61	The elven archers always win the kingdom's archery competition — but now they have lost to a squad of dwarven archers! They suspect trickery, and their suspicions are correct: the dwarves consumed *elixirs of vision of the eagle*.
62	Animals are setting traps in the forest! A hag alchemist is dosing the woodland creatures with *philters of the awakened mind*.
63	A good dragon is attacking the town! Why? Ask the alchemist in the woods with a *potion of dragon control*.
64	Psionicists are being killed one by one — even powerful ones. The assassin must be using *philter of insanity shield* to protect themselves.
65	An important political figure has fallen in love with an inappropriate person! Can the characters find out who dosed the leader with an *elixir of Venus*?
66	The enemy seems to know every secret plan and all troop locations. Nothing has gone missing. Can the characters find the spy using an *elixir of recall*?
67	The kingdom mandates the use of an elixir on prisoners that causes them to tell the truth when questioned. Protests are occurring. Which side will the characters choose?
68	A rival thieves' guild is using *potions of clairvoyance* and *potions of clairaudience* to outperform the competition. Now they have decided to solve the problem by destroying the alchemist's guild. Can the alchemist's guild be saved?
69	The kingdom's secrets are escaping! At night, a werebat is using an *elixir of dream speech* to spy on the king.
70	A giant is terrorizing a small hamlet, but it turns out that the "giant" is just a gnome suffering from permanent miscibility of an *elixir of growth*.
71	Cheap *potions of invisibility* cause problems on two fronts: a war over a diamond mine and a rash of invisible crimes. Can the characters stop this masterminded plan of a goblin alchemist?

72	An elixir has gone terribly wrong. Spells being cast by the local wizard take physical form and terrorize those nearby.
73	A metal golem is actually an ogre with a permanent *elixir of reflective form*. The confused party may expect a much tougher fight than it is.
74	A cultist gave his minions an *elixir of revenge* for a nasty surprise.
75	A strange shrubbery is seen in several places around town. Will they discover the halfling thief under the influence of an *elixir of shrubbery*.
76	A strange cult is turning people into living skeletons using an *elixir of skeletal visage*.
77	A murderous tiger is attacking a village, but the villagers seem unable to stop it. It has been warded with an *salve of animal sanctuary*.
78	A nearby wererat mage attempted to animate his furniture with *salve of animation* so it would clean itself. But something went horribly wrong and now they won't stop.
79	A mysterious sprite is performing strange curses in the castle. Will the characters discover that she is using a *salve of the green* to enter through the tree in the throne room?
80	The local contest's first prize turned them into a monstrous beast that now terrorizes the area.
81	A vampire used *salve of immobility* to trap the residents of a castle. Can they be saved?
82	A goblin alchemist has received a permanent effect from an *elixir of emotions*, and it has bred true! The resulting scourge of suddenly-powerful goblins must be stopped.
83	A troll alchemist has mastered the formulas for *salve of acid resistance* and *salve of fire resistance*.
84	A shipment of *salve of stonewalking* is en route to those besieging a city. Can the shipment be stopped before it spells doom for those trapped in the city?
85	A statue in the center of town stands up one day and walks out of town. What orders does the construct have?
86	A magma construct being used as a moat has rebelled, and now no one can enter or leave the castle.
87	An alchemist is selling alchemical potions that have a random effect, sepite the fact that they are being prepared properly. What is happening, and why?
88	A noble purchased a *sigil of silence* to use on his wife, but now he finds he cannot speak. Can the characters do anything to help him fix his subconscious?
89	An alchemist is said to be attempting to create all 13 gem talismans. Since only three can be used at most, what is he planning on doing with them?
90	A fire demon appeared and is causing havoc in a local village. It isn't a demon, but an alchemist who wasn't pure of spirit who attempted to consume an *apotheosis of fire (elemental transubstantiation)*.
91	A character is arrested and dragged before the court. They offer the character freedom if the party can locate the source of the mysterious golden bars devaluing the currency. Can they track down whoever is crafting *apotheosis of mercury*?
92	They characters corner their final opponent. But no matter what they do to kill him, he just laughs and laughs! How can they defeat someone who has consumed a *apotheosis of sulfur*?
93	After a mountebank rolled through town, everyone bought new restful mattresses. Only no one is getting any rest at all, and now there is chaos and fighting in the city. Were they tricked or is there something wrong with the *bedrolls of rest*?
94	What's in that *bottle of holding*?
95	In a large city, there's a huge demand for *heating* and *cooling boxes*. However, there are not enough essences to craft as many as people want. Some unscrupulous people are trying to raise hell hounds and yeti — in the same breeding facility!
96	The *cloak of eyestalks* seemed like a great bargain until the stalks seemed to gain minds of their own.
97	All the party's items disappeared in the night and were replaced with potions and elixirs.
98	A series of pools are springing up nearby. What strange subterranean alchemist is causing this?
99	A rash of poisonings has occurred. Can the characters track down the werewolf gnomes producing this new poison?
100	Several politicians are swaying large numbers of people toward violent acts. Can the characters discover the bugbear alchemist vampires behind the act?

Tables 4
Introduction 5
Why Alchemy? 5
How to Use This Book 5
Chapter One: Alchemy Basics 6
Background and Skills 6
Availability 6
    Table 1–1: Alchemical Item Availability 6
Special Cases 6
Large Volume 6
    Table 1–2: Alchemist's Fire Damage
    Progression 6
Dilution 7
Drinking Multiple Potions 7
Alternate Item Types 7
Item Variability 7
Crafting and Researching 7
The Alchemical Laboratory 7
Research 8
Detailed Research 8
    Table 1–3:
    Spell Research and Settlement Required 8
    Table 1–4: Research DCs 9
Alchemical Item Identification 9
Potion Miscibility 9
    Table 1–5: Potion Miscibility 9
Crafting an Item 10
Addiction 10
Adding Addictive Qualities to
Alchemical and Magical Items 10
Fire and Gases 10
Fire 10
    Table 1–6: Fire Progression 10
Some Caveats 10
Gas Clouds 10
Types of Clouds 10
    Smoke 10
    Poison Gas 10
    Table 1–7: Gas Types 11
    Alchemical Gas 12
    Magical Gas 12
Gas Dispersion 12
    Table 1–8:
    Gas Types Gas Ventilation Rates 12
Chapter Two: Materials and Essences 13
Materials 13
Mineral Essences 13
Rare Earth 13
Gemstones 13
Rare Metals 13
    Table 2–1: Mineral Essences 13
Vital Essences 14
    Table 2–2: Vital Essences 14
Distilling Vital Essences 14
Vital Essence Types 15
    Table 2–3:
    Vital Essence Types by Category 15
Alternate Vital Essences 16
Not Using Essences 16
Sources of Vital Essences 16

Table 2–4: Sources of Vital Essences 16
Table 2–5: Vital Essences by Monster 18
Chapter Three: Alchemical Items 22
Reading the Formulas 22
Your Own Formulas 22
Alchemical Devices 22
    Table 3–1: Alchemical Devices 23
    Table 3–2: Elemental Energy Gloves 27
Grenades, Pellets, and Stones 32
    Table 3–3: Grenades, Pellets, and Stones .. 32
Incense 39
    Table 3–4: Incense 39
Liquids and Tonics 41
    Table 3–5: Liquids and Tonics 41
Ointments and Pastes 44
    Table 3–6: Ointments and Pastes 44
Powders 46
    Table 3–7: Powders 46
    Table 3–8: Incendiary Powder Amounts 48
Solvents 50
    Table 3–9: Solvents 50
Tinctures 52
    Table 3–10: Tinctures 52
Chapter Four: Magic Items 54
    Table 4–1: Brew Improved Potion
    Costs by Class and Level 55
Wondrous Items 55
Candles 55
    Table 4–2: Candles 55
Cusps, Eyes, and Spectacles 58
    Table 4–3: Cusps, Eyes, and Spectacles 58
Dusts 60
    Table 4–4: Dusts 60
    Table 4–5: Dust of Deprivation Effects 63
Elixirs 68
    Table 4–6: Elixir Price List 68
    Table 4–7: Elixir of Bestial Boon Physical
    Changes 70
    Table 4–8: Elixir of Animal Control 71
    Table 4–9:
    Elixir of Dragon Control Types 71
    Table 4–10:
    Elixir of Elemental Control Types 72
    Table 4–11:
    Elixir of Giant Control Types 72
    Table 4–12:
    Elixir of Human Control Types 72
    Table 4–13:
    Elixir of Undead Control Types................ 73
Table 4–14: Elixir of Defense Bonuses 73
    Table 4–15:
    Elixir of Heroic Fighting Bonuses............. 75
Table 4–16: Elixir of Super Heroic
Fighting Bonuses 76
Table 4–17: Elixir of Heroic
Larceny Bonuses 76
    Table 4–18:
    Elixir of Giant Strength Type 83
Salves 88
    Table 4–19: Salves 88
Table 4–20: Salve of Basic Blade

Enhancement Formulas 89
    Table 4–21: Salve of Expert Blade
    Enhancement Formulas 91
    Table 4–22:
    Salve of Sharpness Strength Table............. 94
Other 97
    Table 4–23: Wonderous Items 97
    Table 4–24: Production of Alchemical Jug 97
    Table 4–25:
    Carafe of Steeds Random Mounts 99
    Table 4–26: Cloak of Eyestalk's Effects .. 101
    Table 4–27:
    Energy Bolt Glove Requirements 102
Cursed 104
Chapter Five: Alchemical Magecraft 108
Mineral Alchemy 109
    Table 5–1: Mineral Alchemy Price List ... 109
    Table 5–2: Amber Fulminating Charge
    Power Increase 110
    Table 5–3: Carnelian Catagemma
    Power Increase 111
    Table 5–4: Chalcedony Fulminating Charge
    Power Increase 112
    Table 5–5: Diamond Fulminating Charge
    Power Increase 113
    Table 5–6: Fire Opal Fulminating Charge
    Power Increase 114
    Table 5–7: Onyx Fulminating Charge
    Power Increase 116
    Table 5–8:
    Ruby Catagemma Power Increase 117
Material Apotheosis 118
Sigils 122
    Table 5–9: Sigils 122
    Table 5–10: Dimensional Jaunt Essences 123
    Table 5–11:
    Sigil of Extrasensory Perception Effects... 123
Chapter Six: Alchemy in Structures 128
Alchemical Mortars 128
    Table 6–1: Alchemical Mortars 128
Chapter Seven: Spells, Spellcasting, and Alchemy
132
Alchemical Items as Spell Components 132
Using Crafted Alchemical Items to Enhance
Spells 132
Using Consumable Enchanted Items to Enhance
Spells 132
Discovery 133
Empowerment of a Spell Using Essences 133
    Table 7–1: Alchemical Enhancements 133
New Spells 134
    Table 7–2: Alchemist Spell List............... 134
    Table 7–3: Wizard/Sorcerer Spell List 134
Appendix 142
100 Alchemical Mishaps 142
    Table A–1: Alchemical Mishaps 142
100 Random Potion Effects 144
    Table A–2: Potion Mishaps 144
Alchemical Quirks 145
    Table A–3: Alchemical Quirks 145
Alchemical Ideas 146
    Table A–4: Story Ideas 146

NECROMANCER
Games™